Schumann as Critic

Da Capo Press Music Reprint Series

GENERAL EDITOR

FRANK D'ACCONE
University of California at Los Angeles

Schumann as Critic

by Leon B. Plantinga

DA CAPO PRESS • NEW YORK • 1976

Library of Congress Cataloging in Publication Data

Plantinga, Leon B
    Schumann as critic.

    (Da Capo Press music reprint series)
    Reprint of the 1967 ed. published by Yale University
Press, New Haven.
    Bibliography: p.
    1. Schumann, Robert Alexander, 1810-1856.
2. Musical criticism. I. Title.
[ML410.S4P6 1976]   780'.92'4   76-7599
ISBN 0-306-70785-3

This Da Capo Press edition of *Schumann as Critic* is an unabridged republication of
the first edition published in London and New Haven in 1967. It is reprinted with the
permission of Yale University Press.

Published by Da Capo Press, Inc.
A Subsidiary of Plenum Publishing Corporation
227 West 17th Street, New York, N. Y. 10011

Manufactured in the United States of America

YALE STUDIES IN THE HISTORY OF MUSIC, 4

William G. Waite, *Editor*

Schumann as Critic

by Leon B. Plantinga

New Haven and London   Yale University Press

1967

Preface

Were it not for the assistance of many people, this book would never have seen the light of day. I am indebted in a special way to my teacher and friend, Claude V. Palisca, who has patiently read the entire manuscript twice and has given me any number of important suggestions. I am grateful also to William G. Waite; his friendly encouragement and good advice have been invaluable. And two teachers of years past have exerted a decisive influence on my work: the late Ernst Victor Wolff, and Robert T. Laudon, who is now at the University of Minnesota. Since I have had the best of counsel, any shortcomings of this book must result from my own incorrigibility.

To Mr. Brooks Shepard, Jr., and his long-suffering staff at the Yale School of Music Library, particularly Mrs. Harriet Bishop, I must extend my thanks for seven years of kindness to an unusually difficult customer. The staffs of the music divisions of other libraries in this country and abroad have also provided indispensable assistance: especially those of the Boston Public Library, the New York Public Library, and the British Museum; it is a pleasure to acknowledge here the special helpfulness and competence of Fräulein Eveline Bartlitz of the Musik-Abteilung of the Deutsche Staatsbibliothek in East Berlin. Others have given aid of different kinds. Two philosophers, Alvin Plantinga, of Calvin College, and Ronald Jager, of Yale University, have generously read and commented upon the chapter on Schumann's aesthetics. My friend Klaus Poenicke of the *Freie Universität*, West Berlin, has helped me with some of the thornier passages in Schumann's colorful prose, and the final stages of my work have been made easier by three understanding and knowledgeable editors at Yale Press, Walter Langsam, Ronald Riddle, and Miss Jane Olson. Several grants from Yale University, notably a Sterling Fellowship and a Blanche Elizabeth MacLeish Billings award, have supported my research and the preparation of final copy.

The greatest debt of all I owe to my wife, Carol, who has cheerfully put up with the long hours, prolonged absences, and bad humor that go with the making of books. And she has sacrificed for something about which she can entertain no illusions; for in the course of typing it three times, she has come to know it well.

New Haven, Connecticut   L.B.P.
August, 1966

Contents

Introduction

At the age of twenty, Robert Schumann, thoroughly bored with his law studies at the University of Heidelberg, decided to devote himself to music. This was in the autumn of 1830, and during the next year he plunged wholeheartedly into not one, but three kinds of musical activities: piano playing, composing, and writing music criticism. In the spring of 1832 a hand injury put an end to his ambitions as a pianist; but by that time he had already published his earliest compositions as well as his first essay on music, and the pattern of his life was set for some time to come.

In one of the two musical careers left to Schumann, he seems to have achieved permanent recognition. Though his stock as a composer fluctuates mildly from time to time (less than Mendelssohn's, more than Chopin's) a good bit of his music has long been a stable part of the active repertory. But though Schumann himself once said he preferred writing music to writing about it, during much of his lifetime he was in fact better known and more influential as a critic than as a composer. That this estimate of the relative importance of his two roles has now been reversed is not hard to understand. There are, after all, more people who listen to nineteenth-century music than there are who read nineteenth-century music criticism. Moreover Schumann wrote about a full cross-section of the European musical scene in the earlier nineteenth century—not just the small part of it that is still current in the twentieth. But if this kind of comprehensiveness makes some of Schumann's writings seem a little remote from ordinary contemporary interests, it adds immeasurably to their value as a commentary on nineteenth-century European musical culture as it really was.

Schumann began writing criticism at a time when Germany's musical future looked uncertain. In the second half of the preceding century the German-speaking states had for the first time achieved a certain preeminence in music. Though opera was still borrowed from Italy, the instrumental music of the Mannheim court, of C. P. E. and J. C. Bach, and perhaps most importantly, the symphonies of Joseph Haydn, were largely indigenous—and eminently exportable—products. Beethoven added a powerful impetus to the Germans' pride in their music, but when he died in 1827 there was no one in sight to continue the tradition. Within a decade the most admired composer in the world was Meyerbeer, and the few composers like Spohr, Hummel, and Moscheles who continued to cultivate the large instrumental forms were not of sufficient influence to stem the tide of music, much of it trivial, that flowed from the salons of Paris. Once again the Germans listened, for the most part, to foreign styles of music. It was in response to this state of affairs that Schumann first sharpened his critic's pen.

A music critic in the present day, especially in the United States, is someone who makes judgments, instantaneously arrived at and promptly recorded, on musical performances. A *Rezensent* for a musical journal in Schumann's time acted quite differently: his usual duty was to evaluate not performances but scores. This practice had its beginnings in the semi-popular context of the *Kenner und Liebhaber* journals of the later eighteenth century, and when Schumann arrived on the scene such music criticism still had, usually, a gentle and tolerant tone. Schumann cut sharply from this tradition. Making the most of his pronounced gift for writing, he went about his work with caustic wit and youthful idealism, injecting into music criticism something of the professionalism and severity of standards he saw in contemporary literary criticism. The result is a unique record of the reactions of a first-rate musical mind to a whole decade of European music.

Schumann wrote almost all his criticism in the course of performing his regular duties as editor and writer for the *Neue Zeitschrift für Musik* (cited hereafter as NZfM),[1] the journal he helped establish in 1834 and edited from January 1835 until July 1844. He contributed a few scattered articles to other periodicals; his often-mentioned review of Chopin's Variations on *Là ci darem la mano* appeared in the *Allgemeine musikalische Zeitung* (hereafter AmZ) of 1831, and in 1833 two essays entitled *Der Davidsbündler* were published in a literary journal called *Der Komet*. In addition he wrote a few concert reviews for the *Allgemeine Zeitung* of Leipzig.

In 1853 Schumann himself assembled most of his published prose

---

1. Published in Leipzig by C. H. F. Hartmann (1834), J. A. Barth (1835–37), and Robert Friese (1837–51). In 1834 the journal appeared under the title *Neue Leipziger Zeitschrift für musik*, but for the sake of convenience this first *Jahrgang* will also be called "NZfM."

works, together with a few aphorisms from disparate sources, and arranged them in roughly chronological order for publication. In the spring of 1854, just after he was committed to the asylum at Endenich, they were brought out in four volumes by the Leipzig firm of Wigand under the title *Gesammelte Schriften über Musik und Musiker*.[2] Schumann remained the best editor of his own works until the fourth edition of the *Gesammelte Schriften*, prepared by the dedicated Schumann scholar F. Gustav Jansen, appeared in 1891; Jansen added a number of articles omitted by Schumann and provided some valuable commentary. Martin Kreisig, former director of the *Schumannmuseum* in Zwickau, presided over the fifth and final edition, a model of accuracy and thoroughness. But even this collection lacks several articles and a good many comments, footnotes, and the like that are unquestionably by Schumann. The form and order of the material are the same as in the 1854 edition; things Schumann omitted there are given in footnotes and in a *Nachtrag*, and the true chronological order is shown only in a somewhat abstract table.[3] Whatever the merits of Kreisig's edition, I have felt it was essential to base this study on Schumann's criticism in its original form in the NZfM.[4]

In the present day, Schumann the critic has been more used, it seems, than understood. His commentary on music has proved serviceable to countless writers on Schubert, Berlioz, and Mendelssohn; excerpts from his criticism are used in books of various kinds, but much more commonly on record jackets and in program notes. As a result, many people have a faint familiarity with Schumann's writings. Concert-goers recognize "Hats off, gentlemen—a genius!" and "these heavenly lengths," and many of them know that Schumann wrote a

2. Hereafter GS 1854.

3. Robert Schumann, *Gesammelte Schriften über Musik und Musiker,* ed. Martin Kreisig (Leipzig, 1914, hereafter cited as GSK), xxxiv–xxxv.

4. There are now three anthologies of Schumann's writings translated into English. The earliest one, Fanny Raymond Ritter's two-volume work of the late 1870s, by far the most extensive of the three, is shot through with errors. A much smaller selection prepared by Konrad Wolf and Paul Rosenfeld (Pantheon, 1946; now in a McGraw-Hill paperback), though rather dependent upon Mrs. Ritter for its translations, is more accurate. The most recent collection, that of Henry Pleasants, is so heavily edited as to be misleading. Henry Pleasants, ed., *The Musical World of Robert Schumann. A Selection from Schumann's Own Writings* (New York, 1965). See my review in *Journal of the American Musicological Society*, 17 (1965), 417–19. Quite aside from any deficiencies of these translations, they are all based on one or another edition of the *Gesammelte Schriften*, not the NZfM; for all quotations from Schumann in this book, therefore, I have made new translations. Appendix I gives the original texts for all sizable quotations.

long review of the *Symphonie fantastique* and endorsed the young Brahms. In view of this popular currency some of his work enjoys, it is remarkable how little has been written about Schumann's criticism; somehow things he said have become common knowledge without ever having been specialized knowledge.

There may be plausible enough reasons for this. In the first place, musical scholarship is still of rather a tender age, and is only now getting around to investigating the nineteenth century. Music historians have shown a lively interest, as they should, in almost all the composers of the Middle Ages and Renaissance; we know a good deal of music by the contemporaries of Machaut and Landini, and of Josquin and Palestrina. The really obscure composers in Western history are the contemporaries of Beethoven and Schumann. Important musicians like Hummel, Moscheles, Loewe, and Hiller remain obscure, and men like C.-S. Catel, F. W. Grund, and C. G. Reissiger interest almost nobody but lexicographers. Perhaps nineteenth-century music has been last to attract the attention of musical scholars because it is too much with us. Since the nineteenth century, it has—or, rather, *some* of it has —comprised the bulk of the music we hear at concerts (and now on records) and familiarity of this kind, unfortunately, sometimes breeds contempt. In the case of Schumann the field has been left for the most part to generations of simplified and derivative biographies, all based on a few books of substance written long ago.

Though specialized studies in the field are few, I have benefited from a number of publications by people who have worked with Schumann before me, especially the collections of letters edited by Clara Schumann[5] and F. Gustav Jansen.[6] Of the older secondary literature on Schumann, most helpful have been the notes in Kreisig's edition of the *Gesammelte Schriften*, Jansen's *Die Davidsbündler*,[7] and the biography of Frederick Niecks (still probably the best book in English on Schumann).[8] The most extensive research on Schumann of the last forty years is represented by the two books of Wolfgang Boetticher, *Robert Schumann, Einführung in Persönlichkeit und*

5. Clara Schumann, ed., *Jugendbriefe von Robert Schumann* (Leipzig, 1885).

6. F. Gustav Jansen, ed., *Robert Schumanns Briefe, neue Folge* (Leipzig, 1904), hereafter cited as *Briefe*.

7. F. Gustav Jansen, *Die Davidsbündler. Aus Robert Schumanns Sturm- und Drangperiode* (Leipzig, 1883).

8. Frederick Niecks, *Robert Schumann*, ed. Christina Niecks (London and Toronto, 1925).

Werk (Berlin, 1941), and *Robert Schumann in seinen Schriften und Briefen* (Berlin, 1942). These books offer a wealth of previously unpublished documentary matter (copious extracts, particularly, from Schumann's diaries), and one should, I suppose, be grateful for them. But nothing in these wartime publications can be taken on faith; calculated to make both Schumann and Boetticher acceptable to the Nazi regime, they are badly marred by distortions and suppressions. Perhaps it is just as well that murky writing makes the *Einführung*— like many books with this name, it is a gargantuan tome—almost impossible to read. Misinformation in such a form spreads slowly. More recent books on Schumann[9] show little new research, and none of them acknowledges his criticism with more than a respectful nod. The fullest discussion of Schumann's journalistic activities, strangely enough, is in a book about another composer and critic; it is Robert Pessenlehner's *Herrmann Hirschbach, der Kritiker und Künstler*.[10] There have been, from time to time, a few indifferent articles on Schumann's aesthetic views, for example those by Hermann Kretzschmar[11] and Arnold Schmitz,[12] and most recently, a very much better one by Edward A. Lippman.[13]

This book will be about Schumann's work as a critic: the content and style of his writings, and the context within which he operated. Anyone who writes about criticism is potentially two steps removed from the focal point of interest; for what he offers is essentially a commentary upon a commentary. Here I hope to avoid this pitfall by introducing prominently into evidence (especially in the later chapters) the original subject: the music Schumann was writing about. Otherwise it would be impossible in many cases to understand what Schumann is saying, and any sure assessment of his importance as a critic would be out of the question.

9. The most satisfactory of these is Karl H. Wörner's *Robert Schumann* (Zürich, 1949), a concise and accurate "life and works."

10. Düren-Rhld., 1932.

11. "Robert Schumann als Aesthetiker," *Jahrbuch der musikalischen Bibliothek Peters, 13* (1906), 50–73.

12. "Die aesthetischen Anschauungen Robert Schumanns in ihren Beziehungen zur romantischen Literatur," *Zeitschrift für Musikwissenschaft, 3* (1920), 111–18; also "Anfänge der Aesthetik Robert Schumanns," *Zeitschrift für Musikwissenschaft, 2* (1920), 535–39.

13. "Theory and Practice in Schumann's Aesthetics," *Journal of the American Musicological Society, 17* (1964), 310–45.

PART I

The *Neue Zeitschrift für Musik*

Neue Leipziger
Zeitschrift für Musik.

Herausgegeben
durch einen Verein von Künstlern und Kunstfreunden.

Erster Jahrgang. | № 1. | Den 3. April 1834.

Die allein,
Die nur ein lustig Spiel, Geräusch der Tartschen
Zu hören kommen, oder einen Mann
Im bunten Rock, mit Gold verbrämt, zu sehen,
Die irren sich. Shakspeare.

Diese Zeitschrift liefert:

Theoretische und historische Aufsätze, kunstästhetische, grammatische, pädagogische, biographische, akustische u. a. Nekrologe, Beiträge zur Bildungsgeschichte berühmter Künstler, Berichte über neue Erfindungen oder Verbesserungen, Beurtheilungen ausgezeichneter Virtuosenleistungen, Operndarstellungen; unter der Aufschrift: Zeitgenossen, Skizzen mehr oder weniger berühmter Künstler, unter der Rubrik: Journalschau, Nachrichten über das Wirken anderer kritischen Blätter, Bemerkungen über Recensionen in ihnen, Zusammenstellung verschiedener Beurtheilungen über dieselbe Sache, eigne Resultate darüber, auch Antikritiken der Künstler selbst, sodann Auszüge aus ausländischen, Interessantes aus älteren musikalischen Zeitungen.

Belletristisches, kürzere musikalische Erzählungen, Phantasiestücke, Scenen aus dem Leben, Humoristisches, Gedichte, die sich vorzugsweise zur Composition eignen.

Kritiken über Geisteserzeugnisse der Gegenwart mit vorzüglicher Berücksichtigung der Compositionen für das Pianoforte. Auf frühere schätzbare, übergangene oder vergessene Werke wird aufmerksam gemacht, wie auch auf eingesandte Manuscripte talentvoller unbekannter Componisten, die Aufmunterung verdienen. Zu derselben Gattung gehörige Compositionen werden öfter zusammengestellt, gegen einander verglichen, besonders interessante doppelt beurtheilt. Zur Beurtheilung eingesandte Werke werden durch eine vorläufige Anzeige bekannt gemacht; doch bestimmt nicht das Alter der Einsendung die frühere Besprechung, sondern die Vorzüglichkeit der Leistung.

Miscellen, kurzes Musikbezügliches, Anekdotisches, Kunstbemerkungen, literarische Notizen, Musikalisches aus Goethe, Jean Paul, Heinse, Hoffmann, Novalis, Rochlitz u. A. m.

Correspondenzartikel nur dann, wenn sie eigentliches Musikleben abschildern. Wir stehen in Verbindung mit Paris, London, Wien, Berlin, Petersburg, Neapel, Frankfurt, Hamburg, Riga, München, Dresden, Stuttgart, Cassel u. a. — Referirende Artikel fallen in die folgende Abtheilung.

Chronik, Musikaufführungen, Concertanzeigen, Reisen, Aufenthalt der Künstler, Beförderungen, Vorfälle im Leben. Es wird keine Mühe gescheuet, diese Chronik vollständig zu machen, um die Namen der Künstler so oft, wie möglich, in Erinnerung zu bringen.

Noch machen wir vorläufig bekannt, daß, wenn sich die Zeitschrift bald einer allgemeinen Theilnahme erfreuen sollte, der Verleger sich erboten hat, einen Preis auf die beste eingesandte Composition, für's erste auf die vorzüglichste Pianofortesonate, zu setzen, worüber das Nähere seiner Zeit berichtet wird.

Ueber die Stellung, die diese neue Zeitschrift unter den schon erscheinenden einzunehmen gedenkt, werden sich diese ersten Blätter thatsächlich am deutlichsten aussprechen.

Wer den Künstler erforschen will, besuche ihn in seiner Werkstatt. Es schien nothwendig, auch ihm ein Organ zu verschaffen, das ihn anrege, außer durch seinen directen Einfluß, noch durch Wort und Schrift zu wirken, einen öffentlichen Ort, in dem er das Beste von dem, was er selbst gesehen im eigenen Auge, selbst erfahren im eigenen Geist, niederlegen, eben eine Zeitschrift, in der er sich gegen einseitige oder unwahre Kritik vertheidigen könne, so weit sich das mit Gerechtigkeit und Unparteilichkeit überhaupt verträgt.

The first issue of the NZfM (orig. 20 x 26 cm.)

Wie sollten die Herausgeber die Vorzüge der bestehenden, höchst achtbaren Organe, die sich ausschließlich mit musikalischer Literatur beschäftigen, nicht anerkennen wollen. Weit entfernt, die etwaigen Mängel der Unbekanntschaft mit den Forderungen, die jetzt der Künstler an den Kritiker machen darf, oder einem abnehmenden Kunstenthusiasmus zuzuschreiben, finden sie es auf der einen Seite unmöglich, daß das Gebiet der Musik, welches quantitativ sich so ausgedehnt, von einem Einzelnen bis in's Einzelne durchdrungen werden könne, auf der andern natürlich, daß beim Zusammenwirken Mehrer, von welchen sich im Verlauf der Zeit Viele ausscheiden, an deren Stelle Andersgesinnte eintreten, der erste Plan vergessen wird, bis er endlich im Lottern und Allgemeinen vergeht.

Künstler sind wir denn und Kunstfreunde, jüngere, wie ältere, die wir durch jahrelanges Beisammenleben mit einander vertraut und im Wesentlichen derselben Ansicht zugethan, uns zur Herausgabe dieser Blätter verbunden. Ganz durchdrungen von der Bedeutung unsers Vorhabens legen wir mit Freude und Eifer Hand an das neue Werk, ja mit dem Stolz der Hoffnung, daß es als im reinen Sinn und im Interesse der Kunst von Männern begonnen, deren Lebensberuf sie ist, günstig aufgenommen werde. Alle aber, die es wohl meinen mit der schönen Kunst der Phantasie, bitten wir, das junge Unternehmen mit Rath und That wohlwollend zu fördern und zu schützen. —

Die Herausgeber.

Briefwechsel zwischen Goethe und Zelter in den Jahren 1796 bis 1832. Herausgegeben von D. F. W. Riemer. 4 Thle. Berlin 1833 u. 1834. Verlag von Duncker und Humblot. 8 Rthlr.

Uns ist keine Briefsammlung bekannt, die sich über fast alle Verhältnisse des Lebens, über alle Zweige des Wissens verbreitet, abgefaßt zugleich von zwei so bedeutenden Männern, wie der von Riemer herausgegebene Briefwechsel zwischen Goethe und Zelter, zwei der innigsten Freunde, beide verwandten Geistes, der eine der größte Dichter aller Zeiten, der andere, wenn auch ein Componist zweiten Ranges, doch ein tiefer Kenner seiner Kunst, jener im Umgange mit fast allen bedeutenden Personen der civilisirten Welt, dieser wenn auch einerseits auf einen beschränkteren Kreis hingewiesen, der jedoch nicht ohne alle Bedeutung ist, andererseits oder besser allerseits im Umgange mit dem weltüberschauenden Goethe. Beide theilen sich ihre Gedanken und Erfahrungen nicht allein über ihre conventionellen Lebensverhältnisse, die jedoch an und für sich selbst ein höchstes Interesse, sondern auch über alle Zweige der Literatur und Kunst mit; Goethe zwar mehr auf seine ruhigbeschauliche Weise, gleich einem Gott, der Opfer empfängt und seinen Dank durch beifälliges Neigen des Hauptes und Ermunterung zu neuen Mittheilungen zu erkennen giebt, Zelter dagegen in größter Freudigkeit und Ergebung zu dem großen Mann, fast ganz in Goethe lebend und mit dessen Augen schauend, das, was er durch den Freund und Gönner erworben, ihm wieder als Opfergabe zu Füßen legend. Nur in den späteren Jahren, die übrigens nicht den geringern Theil des Briefwechsels füllen, sind beide Naturen durch vieljährige Freundschaft und zum Bedürfniß gewordene Mittheilung so in einander übergegangen — Goethe sich mit ausgebreiteten Armen herabneigend zu dem ihm immermehr ähnlich werdenden Jünger und Freund, Zelter mit seligbefriedigten Blicken sich kräftig hinaufschwingend zu dem ersehnten Ziele seiner Hoffnungen und Wünsche —, daß

kein Zwischenverhältniß mehr hemmend eintritt und Goethe nicht mehr blos empfängt und zu Neuem ermuntert, sondern nun auch giebt aus den gewaltigen Schätzen, die er besitzt, nicht allein aus dem wissenschaftlichen, sondern vorzüglich aus dem Herzensschatz, ein Schatz, den nur Wenige kannten und erkennen wollten, der gleich wie der Nibelungenhort in dem Rheine, in den Tiefen des Herzens versenkt war, und den Zelter das Glück hatte zu erheben für sich und für die Nachwelt. Für den einzelnen Sterblichen war der Schatz zu groß, er konnte ihn nur zeitlich genießen und sich dessen zur Seligkeit erfreuen; er übergab ihn der ewiglebenden Welt, und immermehr und mehr nach vielen Jahren wird diese erst recht erkennen, was für ein unschätzbares Gut sie an ihm besitzt. Goethe erscheint uns als edler, als fühlender, als menschlicher Mensch, als eines Mannes Freund — eine Wahrheit, die so lange bezweifelt wurde, die aber als solche durch nichts zu theuer erkauft werden konnte.

Dagegen entwickelt sich vor uns ein Geist, der in seiner herrlichen Eigenthümlichkeit Wenigen bekannt war, der von Vielen, gleich wie ein roher Diamant, wegen seiner derben unscheinbaren Außenseite, gänzlich verkannt wurde. Mit ihm wollen wir uns nun vorzüglich, wie es unserm Zweck zukommt, beschäftigen.

Zelter lernen wir als eine eigenste Natur erkennen, tief, ja zartfühlend und dennoch kräftig, ja wohl gar starr und abstoßend. Dieser Geist fühlt sich einem der größten Geister verwandt und von nun an ist sein ganzes Streben, sich diesem gewaltigen Genius zu nähern, es gelingt ihm, und weil er sich als einen Theil desselben erkennt, giebt er sich ihm ganz als Eigenthum wieder hin. So ist Zelter in seiner eigenen Eigenthümlichkeit in Goethe übergegangen, daß er, als ein Theil desselben, ohne denselben nicht mehr leben und fortbestehen zu können glaubt und nur in steter Mittheilung mit demselben lebt. Tief empfand er, daß er sich einem gewaltigen Genius mittheilt, und darum sucht er, was er äußert, desselben würdig zu äußern, und aus den Schachten seines Geistes fördert er die edelsten Erze heraus und läutert sie erst in dem Feuer von Goethe's Genius und goß das

gewonnene reine Metall zu edlen Formen, übersandte sie
als nicht genug zu bewundernde Kunstwerke dem hohen
Freund, der sie wieder als Kunstkenner beurtheilt, wodurch
wir sie noch näher in ihren einzelnen Theilen kennen
lernen. —

(Fortsetzung folgt.)

Duo à quatre mains p. l. Pfte. comp. p. Guill. Taubert. Oeuv. 11. Pr. 20 gr. Leipzig, Hofmeister.

Nach öfterm Anhören und Durchspielen des über-
dem klaren Satze fühlte ich immer eine Lücke. Es war,
als müsse noch etwas kommen oder als wäre etwas vorweg gegangen, was das Spätere erklärte. Formell und
an sich ist es abgeschlossen, nicht der Idee nach. Ich
weiß nicht, ob eine Sonate damit angelegt war und der
Componist beim letzten Satz angefangen hat, wie das
wohl geschieht. Er muß das am besten wissen. Hält er
es für werth, so ist es ein Wunsch, daß er sich selbst in
diesen Blättern darüber ausspreche.

Die Menschen sind verdrießlich und ungebildet über-
dies, die gleich ihren Musikschrank umwenden, um Aehn-
lichkeiten oder Reminiscenzen herauszusuchen. Es kann
kein Vorwurf sein, daß der Stil des Ganzen dem der
bekannten, aber tiefer gehenden Onslow'schen Sonate in
Emoll etwas verwandt scheint, eben so wenig das, wie in
jener ein Saiteninstrumentcharakter, im vorliegenden Stücke
ein noch weiterer Instrumentalcharakter vorherrscht. Wer
sein Instrument kennt und studirt hat, wird die Linie
treffen. So wird auf den einen Seite der gezogene Ton
der menschlichen Stimme gewissen Instrumenten fremd
bleiben, während durch vielseitige Prüfung anderer, die
dem eignen Instrument mehr oder weniger verwandt sind,
neue Wirkungen sich entdecken. Wenn ich daher gleich
in den ersten Tact Pauken, in den zweiten das antwor-
tende Tutti, in die späteren kurzen Achtel Violinunisono's
legen kann, so ist der Charakter des Instruments, für
welches geschrieben werden, noch nicht verletzt, sondern der
Genuß überhaupt vielleicht erhöht. —

Nach den Proben, die Herr Taubert in den vorjährigen
Leipziger Winterconcerten von seinem Compositionstalent ab-
legte, ging ich mit etlichen Erwartungen, zu denen mich
jene berechtigten, an das Werk. Ich ging nicht ganz
fehl, Herr Taubert geht im Werke einen guten schapka-
ren Bürgerschritt, überschreitet nie*) verbotene Wege,
ohne Furcht, mit dem Paß in der Tasche. Gehen wir
alle sehr schlimm. Sitzen wir im Wagen, so beneiden
wir den Fußgänger, der langsam genießen und vor jeder
Blume so lange stehen bleiben kann, als er will. Gehen wir
zu Fuß, so werden wir's recht herzlich satt und nähmen
vorlieb mit dem Bock. Ich meine: gewisse Fehler des
Einen würden wir dem Andern für Tugenden anrechnen.
Gäbe es einen Geistertausch, so würde ich Herrn Taubert

*) Den vierten Tact auf der 14. Seite vielleicht ausgenommen.

etwas vom Blute einiger Hypergenialen, diesen etwas von
der Mäßigung und dem Anstande jenes geben. Man
mache dieser Ansicht Vorwürfe! Allerdings soll ein Kunstwerk nicht ein Alphabet aller ästhetischen Epitheten geben;
aber die Kritik soll die nothwendigen Forderungen (die
vermißten, nicht die schlenden) denen der Künstler nicht
nachgekommen ist, nicht verheimlichen. Ich glaube den
ächte poetische Schwung wäre eine. Im Werke geben
aber die Flügel nur langsam auf und nieder. Mißdeute
der Componist den Ausspruch nicht! Von welchen soll
Heil und Segen in der Kunst zu erwarten seyn, als von
denen, die außer dem edlern Trieb auch die größere Kraft
besitzen, beides in Einklang zu bringen. Gerade die Er-
wählten mögen mit ihren unbedeutenderen Sachen zurück-
bleiben! Es kann mich zornig machen, wenn ich so zu-
sammengeschriebene Souvenirs von einem Meister, wie
Moscheles, in die Hände bekomme mit componirenden Musik-
statisten hinterdrein, die rufen: „Der hat's auch nicht besser gemacht!" Das vorliegende Duo ist freilich besser,
als tausend dergleichen, aber der Anspruch an den Besseren giebt es auch tausend mehr. Gegen Talente soll man
nicht höflich seyn. Vor Herz oder Czerny ziehe ich den
Hut — höchstens mit der Bitte mich nicht ferner zu in-
commodiren.

Dies im Ganzen und für den Componisten, der
Vielen durch ein vorzügliches Pianofortecconcert, das er
der Welt bald vorlegen wolle, werth geworden ist. Wiegt
nun unser Werk bei weitem innerlich wie äußerlich leichter, so ist ihm doch Verbreitung zu wünschen. Man
kann diese sogar voraus sagen, da es ziemlich handlich,
ohne höher fliegende Passagen geschrieben, angenehm, ja
sogar schön klingen kann, wenn man es immer mit der
vortrefflichen Dilettantin, der es zugeeignet ist, spielen
konnte. —

Das Ganze geht in Amoll, obwohl es vielleicht der
einen Gmollcharakter aussprechen will. So gesanglich,
fast innig, das erste Thema ist, so arm sticht das dritte
in Emoll dagegen ab. Das Gedanken, dem ersten gezo-
genen ein zweites in abgeschlossenen Noten als Contrast
entgegenzusetzen, müsse man loben, wenn das in E minor
bedeutender im Character der Erfindung und nicht sogar harmonischer
wäre. Das Mißlungene, Unkanonische tritt bei der spä-
tern Verarbeitung um so stärker ver, die mehr gemacht,
geschrieben, wenig Genialisches hat. Gut bleibt's immer,
daß sich die Armuth hier wenigstens offenkundig, bittend
zeigt. — Wollt Ihr aber wissen, was durch Fleiß, Vor-
liebe, vor allem durch Genie aus einem einfachen, ja
an und für sich schwachen Gedanken gemacht werden kann,
so leset in unserm Beethoven und sehet zu, wie er ihn
(oft negativ, indem er die nahetliegende Schönheit zu-
rückweist) in die Höhe zieht und adelt, und wie sich das
anfangs gemeine Wort in seinem Mund endlich zum
hohen Wahrspruch gestaltet.

Ich wünschte vorhin dem Werk Verbreitung. Ich
meine so. Vor allem thut es noth, der jungen anwach-
senden Zeit etwas an die Hand zu geben, was sie ver

dem schlimmen Einfluß bewahrte, den gewisse Werke im niedrigen Interesse oder in unsittlicher Leidenschaft erzeugt auf jene ausgeübt. Je allgemeiner der Kunstsinn, je besser. Für jede Stufe der Bildung sollen Werke da seyn. Beethoven hat sicher nicht gewollt, daß man ihn meint, wenn von Musik die Rede ist. Er hätte das sogar verworfen. Darum für Alle das Rechte und Aechte! Nur für das Heuchlerische, für das Sittlichhäßliche, das sich in reizende Schleier hüllt, soll die reine Kunst kein Spielgebild haben. Wäre der Kampf nur nicht zu unwürdig! — Doch, jenen Vielschreibern, deren Werkzahl sich nach der Bezahlung richtet (es gibt berühmte Namen darunter), jenen Anmaßenden, die sich wie außer dem Gesetz stehend betrachten, endlich jenen armen oder verarmten Heuchlern, die ihre Dürftigkeit noch mit bunten Lumpen herausputzen, muß mit aller Macht und Festigkeit entgegengetreten werden. Sind diese niedergedrückt, so greift die Masse von selbst nach dem Bessern. Sonst aber wächst uns jenes Bündniß über kurz und lang über den Kopf zusammen und mit ihm eine Sündfluth von Werken, die in der tiefern Verzweigung eine allgemeine der Geistesarmuth, Geistesohnmacht werden könnte.

Correspondenz.

Paris im März.

— Unsern Tagen, in welchen die musikalische Composition durch die genialischen Werke von Beethoven, Schubert, Weber, einen so ganz idealen Schwung genommen hat, war es vielleicht vorbehalten, daß die poetische Darstellung zu einer Nothwendigkeit wurde, welche täglich mächtiger und siegender hervortritt.

Das Pianoforte, dasselbe Instrument, durch welches so viel gegen wahre Kunst gesündigt worden ist, wird auch dasjenige seyn, durch welches der Vortrag von allen Schlacken gereinigt, eine Höhe und Bedeutsamkeit erreichen wird, die man früher nicht kannte.

Jedem denkenden Musiker muß es aufgefallen seyn, daß auf dem Pianoforte etwas ganz Anderes geleistet werden kann und soll, als wir bisher zu hören gewohnt waren, vollendetes mechanisches Spiel ohne inneres Leben und Feuer, wie bei Kalkbrenner, oder, wie bei Mendelssohn und Anderen, Spiel mit Poesie und jugendlichem Kraftgefühl, doch ohne die höhere technische Bildung, die das Instrument beherrscht.

Sie kennen Liszt und Chopin. Diese sind es vorzugsweise, welche, den Beifall des großen Haufens verschmähend, muthvoll das glänzende Beispiel Paganini's im Auge, in der Darstellung dieselbe Bahn betreten, die der Genius Beethoven's in der Composition erschloß. Die Musik ist ihnen die Kunst, welche den Menschen sein höheres Princip ahnen läßt und ihn aus dem Treiben des gemeinen Lebens in den Isistempel führt, wo die

Natur in heiligen nie gehörten und doch verständlichen Lauten mit ihm spricht; daher ihr Vortrag ein großartiger, den Forderungen des gebildeten Gefühls und tiefern Gemüths entsprechender.

Chopin's Spiel ist so innig mit seinen Compositionen verschmolzen, daß Sie diese nur genau zu kennen brauchen, um einen deutlichen Begriff von seiner begeisterten, sinnig zarten Vortragsweise zu bekommen. Dagegen hat Liszt, wenn er auch bis jetzt in der Composition nichts Bedeutendes leistete, andere Eigenthümlichkeiten. Er besitzt ganz eigentlich das Genie des Vortrags. Durch sein lebendiges tiefes Eindringen in das Innere geistvoller Compositionen, welche er in der Wirklichkeit so wiederzugeben vermag, wie sie die Phantasie des Componisten im Augenblick der Begeisterung dachte, schwingt er sich selbst zur Höhe des schöpferischen Geistes. Allerdings ist Liszt nur nach jahrelangem unausgesetzten und gut geleiteten Studium dahin gekommen, daß er über die Schwierigkeit erhaben, durch seine Finger die Regungen der Seele auszudrücken vermochte. Wem anders aber als dem göttlichen Einfluß der Poesie verdankt er es, daß sein Vortrag nicht ausartete, sondern sich jene Idealität erhielt, wodurch die Kunst das Jenseits mit dem Dießseits verbindet?

Ich nehme gar keinen Anstand, fühle mich sogar gedrungen, diese Vortragsweise im Gegensatz zur Kalkbrenner= und Czerny'schen mechanischen Schule — die phantastische Schule zu nennen.

In einem andern Artikel werde ich über die Leistungen Baillot's, Rubini's, Beriot's, der Mad. Malibran und Anderer Bericht erstatten.

Chronik.

(Kirche.) Leipzig, März. Im letzten Concert des trefflichen Orgelspielers Hrn. Becker hörten wir Sätze von Bach, Händel, Krebs, Pachalbel u. a. Die Theilnahme unsers Publicums für Kirchenconcerte war von jeher eine sehr große, obwohl nicht die größte. Mit Dank erkennen wir das rege Streben des geschätzten Künstlers in dieser Hinsicht an. — Hr. Capellmeister Fr. Schneider führte am 21sten des vorigen Monats sein Oratorium: Gideon unter lebhaftem Beifall auf.

Marseille. Am Todestag Beethovens (15. Februar) wurde das Requiem von Cherubini durch 400 Musiker aufgeführt. Zweck und Mittel sind sehr zu loben.

Vermischtes.

Die Organisten HH. Becker in Leipzig und Ritter in Erfurt sind im Begriff ein Orgelarchiv bei Friese in Leipzig herauszugeben. Wir verweisen auf den Prospect.

CHAPTER 1

Ξhe Founding of the Journal

To be fully appreciated, Schumann's music criticism must be seen in its original context in the pages of the *Neue Zeitschrift für Musik*. Its most characteristic features—vigorous idealism, partisanship, and, often, irreverent impetuosity—result from Schumann's involvement in live contemporary issues in music, and it was the purpose of the NZfM to make these issues clear.

Schumann introduced the first edition of his *Gesammelte Schriften*, published in 1854, with this famous and picturesque account of the beginnings of the journal and of his own entry into the lists of music criticism:

> At the end of 1833 a few musicians in Leipzig, mostly young men, found themselves together as though by accident every evening. They met principally to enjoy each other's company; but they were also fully as interested in exchanging their ideas about the art that was for them the food and drink of life—music. The state of music in Germany was at that time hardly gratifying. Rossini still ruled the stage; Herz and Hünten,[1] almost by themselves, held the field in piano music. And yet only a few years had passed since Beethoven, C. M. von Weber, and Franz Schubert had lived among us. Mendelssohn's star, it is true, was rising, and wonderful things were heard of a Pole, Chopin. But it was only later that they began to exert a lasting effect.
>
> Then, one day, an idea occurred to these young hotheads: "Let us not look on and do nothing! Take action and improve things! Take action, so that poetic qualities may again be honored in

1. Henri Herz (1803–88), a pianist born in Vienna, was probably the most celebrated keyboard artist in Europe immediately before the ascendancy of Liszt and Thalberg. Herz made an extensive concert tour of North and South America in 1845–51. Also a composer, he produced a continuous stream of the sort of fashionable piano music Schumann regarded as superficial. Franz Hünten (1793–1878), a German pianist and composer who spent most of his time in Paris, was a close associate of Herz, and composed very much the same sort of music.

this art." In this way originated the first pages of a new musical journal (neue Zeitschrift für Musik).

But the fast ties uniting these young forces were not to be enjoyed for long. Death claimed for itself one of the most beloved of this company, Ludwig Schunke.[2] Some of the others, from time to time, left Leipzig entirely. The project stood at the point of dissolution. Then one of them, who was in fact the musical visionary of the group, and had up to this point spent more time musing at the piano than among books, decided to take charge of the editorship, and continued as editor for almost ten years, until 1844.[3]

This retrospective statement is an elliptical description of the events which in 1833–34 led to the founding of the NZfM, and in 1835 to Schumann's assumption of its editorship. But the rough edges of these events had been smoothed down in Schumann's memory; the full story of the beginnings of the NZfM casts quite a different light upon this self-portrait of the "musical visionary" reluctantly stepping forward at the last moment to save the foundering journal. Schumann assumed the posture of the visionary only when he could afford to— that is, when the work at hand was finished. The work involved in getting the journal started, and in keeping it going, was arduous, and Schumann performed it, sometimes almost single-handedly, with a decisiveness and tenacity that we too often tend to deny him. To show that this is true, let us supplement his account in some detail.

The NZfM was not born simply of a few evenings of pleasant conversation among Schumann and his friends. In their attempts to establish a journal (which began not "at the end of 1833," but at least by June of that year) these men encountered major obstacles. For months the whole project had to be abandoned, in fact, because no publisher could be found. Schumann's correspondence from the summer of 1833 recounts these events with remarkable clarity. A letter of June 28 to his mother in Zwickau contains the first reference to the proposed journal:

2. Ludwig Schunke, Schumann's closest associate in 1833–34, belonged to a prominent family of German musicians (see G. Schilling, ed., *Encyclopädie der gesammten musikalischen Wissenschaften, oder Universal-Lexikon der Tonkunst,* Stuttgart, 1840, 284–88), and was himself a promising composer and pianist. He died of consumption on December 7, 1834.

3. GS 1854, *1,* iii. See Appendix I, 1.

A group of cultivated young people, mostly music students, have drawn together a circle about me, which I have in turn drawn about the Wieck[4] house. We are preoccupied with the notion of a major new musical journal, which Hofmeister will publish. The prospectus and announcement of it will appear within the next month. . . . The journal will be under the direction of Ortlepp,[5] Wieck, myself, and two other music teachers. . . .[6] Of the other collaborators I can name for you Lühe, Privy Councillor Wendt, the deaf Lyser, Reissiger and Krägen in Dresden, and Franz Otto[7] in London.[8]

Schumann had rather fixed notions about the project, and was not particularly receptive, it seems, to the ideas of the other participants. In a letter of July 14, he tells Hofmeister that he finds in a prospectus drawn up by Ortlepp "nothing new, poetic, or striking." [9] But what he likes least is the title Ortlepp suggests for the journal:

I am inexorably opposed to the title "Tonwelt;" the expression "tone-sea" might be applied, say, to Beethoven, but "tone-world" would be fitting only for God Almighty. I interpret "tone-world" as "a world of tones" (that is, "nothing").[10]

Throughout the summer of 1833 the various participants in the project held meetings, and at one of these Schumann apparently read his own prospectus for the journal.[11]

4. Friedrich Wieck (1785–1873), Schumann's piano teacher from 1830–33, and from 1840 his father-in-law.

5. Ernst Ortlepp (1800–64) was an organist, author, and music critic. There is a biography of him by F. W. Igles, *Ernst Ortlepp. Blätter aus dem Leben eines Verschollenen* (Munich, 1901).

6. Julius Knorr and most probably either Ferdinand Stegmayer or Ernst F. Wenzel. For information about these associates of Schumann, see GSK, 2, 459–60, and Gustav Jansen, *Die Davidsbündler*, p. 217.

7. Kreisig provides a good deal of information about J. P. Lyser in GSK, 2, 458. C. G. Reissiger (1798–1859), a very famous composer during his lifetime, was active in Dresden from 1824 until his death. It appears doubtful that Reissiger knew Schumann or had agreed to contribute to the journal. C. P. Krägen (1797–1879), a pianist in Dresden, was a friend of Schumann. Franz Otto (1806–42), a singer and composer, was in Leipzig from 1831 to 1833.

8. *Jugendbriefe*, pp. 209–10.

9. *Briefe*, p. 415.

10. Ibid., p. 416.

11. In his *Die Davidsbündler*, p. 9, Gustav Jansen reports that "there were many meetings attended by E. Ortlepp, Wenzel, the physician Reuter, Stegmayer, Krägen, Wieck, Knorr, and

But by August no prospectus had been published; in a letter of August 5, Schumann explains to Ortlepp what has happened (and at the same time pointedly cuts him out of the staff of editors):

> It cannot have escaped you, sir, that Herr Hofmeister has for some time been most lukewarm toward our beloved project. And when I asked him explicitly—to be sure, he had given up the plan completely, on grounds that admittedly are always compelling—financial ones. We have turned to my brothers, book dealers in Zwickau and Schneeberg,[12] in this matter, and have promised to meet any reasonable demands for surety. It was only natural that they should have requested that I take charge of the correspondence and editing, etc., since I am so closely related to them. I should gladly entrust this task to worthier hands later, when things are in progress. Only Wieck and Knorr[13] share in the direction of the journal, though their part is a most important one.
>
> Now remains the question of whether we may yet count on your friendly collaboration, and the hope that you will not withhold this from us.[14]

In a letter of the same date to his brother Carl, Schumann suggests various practical arrangements for the journal, and pleads eloquently for him to undertake its publication:

> After all, how could such an enterprise fail—one undertaken purely for the sake of art by men for whom art is a life's-calling —one founded, moreover, on firm conviction and on experience gained in the course of many preparations—how could it ever fail?

L. Schunke. At one of these (held in Hofmeister's house) Schumann gave a paper about what the journal ought to be like. Just as everything in his hands assumed a poetic cast, so this essay was in the form of a dialogue." Jansen, as is his habit, gives no source for this information, but Kreisig (GSK, 2, 459) mentions that Jansen received it in later years directly from Ernst Wenzel. Schumann presumably refers to these meetings in his letter of July 31 to Hofmeister: "Would you be so kind to send me Ortlepp's prospectus by tomorrow so that I may look it over? I slept through the last meeting." *Briefe*, p. 416.

12. Eduard Schumann, 1799–1839 (Zwickau), and Carl Schumann, 1801–49 (Schneeberg).

13. By this time, apparently, one of the "two other music teachers"—as well as Ortlepp himself—were no longer to be included among the editors.

14. *Briefe*, p. 44.

Should the enterprise not realize enough profit, Wieck, Knorr, Ortlepp, and I shall relinquish our honoraria. My salary as editor, reckoned at 150 Thaler, I should likewise give up if worse comes to worst. The contract would be drawn up for two years.[15]

But it was not only the prospective publishers who showed signs of hesitation. In a letter of August 6 we see that one of the editors-to-be also had misgivings. The letter is to Friedrich Wieck:

> If I understood you correctly, you said, "If you attack this project energetically, I promise you my help; if you grow luke-warm, however . . ." You meant to continue, "in that case I would withdraw." What—are you not co-editor of the paper? . . . Or am I perhaps thirsty for fame? Or do you suppose I care greatly for the editorship?—if that is what you want to call taking care of the correspondence, etc.[16]

The following day, Schumann writes to Julius Mosen,[17] requesting that he make a contribution to the first number of the journal—which, he says, is to appear at the end of October. He also proposes for Mosen's approval a "publisher's notice" listing the names of prospective contributors:

> The publisher[18] of this journal takes pleasure in announcing that he has contracted for this undertaking the services of several honorable artists, poets, and scholars who are committed to a common artistic point of view. Of these, to act in a critical capacity he specifies Messrs. Ortlepp, Franz Otto, Aug. Schuster (for opera and Lied), Messrs. J. Knorr, Friedrich Wieck (for piano music), Messrs. etc.—, for "musical belles-lettres," and for artistic-aesthetic matters (in the broader sense), Messrs. W. von der Lühe,[19] Lyser, Julius Körner, Mosen, Schumann, G. Schöne, Spazier, etc.[20]

15. *Jugendbriefe*, p. 221.
16. Ibid., p. 218.
17. Julius Mosen (1803–67), a poet who made Schumann's acquaintance during a year's stay in Leipzig in 1831.
18. Schumann obviously did not yet have a publisher. Had his brothers agreed to take on the journal, Schumann would surely have left such a publisher's notice to them, or at least would have mentioned the name of the publisher to Mosen.
19. Hans E. W. von der Lühe, publisher of the *Damenkonversationslexikon*. Jansen, in a footnote to this letter, gives some biographical information about him (*Briefe*, p. 493).
20. *Briefe*, p. 45.

Schumann includes his own name here only in the alphabetical list of contributors of "musical belles-lettres" and essays dealing with "artistic-aesthetic matters." At this point he does not intend, apparently, to write formal reviews of published music; instead he plans to contribute only general musical essays with a highly literary flavor —essays, presumably, like his "Der Davidsbündler," "Charakteristik der Tonarten," and perhaps "Der Stadt- und Kommunalmusikverein zu Kyritz." Such specialization, it turned out, was never possible for Schumann because the journal was always short of contributors, and especially reviewers. The list of writers in the letter to Mosen is in general remarkable for its optimism; not all these men had by that time agreed to participate, and some of them had not even been asked. It was not until two days later (August 9), for example, that Schumann first sent a letter to Franz Otto with the request that he write for the journal.[21]

That letter to Franz Otto contains the last evidence that Schumann held out any hope for the success of these first efforts to found a journal. In a letter of September 6, Schumann writes with some bitterness to Hofmeister:

> A few weeks ago I sent you a folio half-full of writing on our journal-debates.[22] I am asking you to return this to me if you can find it without too much trouble. I doubt that my brother will undertake it now, as he is too much involved in more important publications. Are you allowing the favorable moment for this undertaking—which cannot but bring fame and honor —to slip by? Or perhaps you think there is somewhere to be found a more capable editor.[23]

In the following months, until March 1834, the journal seems to have been forgotten. During this period Schumann apparently suffered his first serious nervous disorders,[24] and underwent additional emotional strain in the death of both his brother Julius and sister-in-law, Rosalie. Nevertheless, it was during this time that he published

---

21. *Jugendbriefe*, pp. 222–23.

22. This is probably the document Schumann sent to Hofmeister with the letter of July 14. See *Briefe*, p. 415.

23. *Jugendbriefe*, p. 224.

24. See the letters to his mother in *Jugendbriefe*, pp. 226–27.

two spritely and fanciful essays under the collective title "Der Davidsbündler" in *Der Komet,* a literary journal of Leipzig.[25] Both contain topical allusions suggesting that they were written earlier in 1833. The first one, which refers in detail to Leipzig concerts of April 29 and May 11,[26] was in all likelihood intended originally for the journal that now seemed a hopeless cause.

New plans for the journal (with still further readjustments of the proposed editorial staff) appear suddenly in March of 1834. Schumann writes to his mother on March 19: "the new musical journal demands our every attention just now. Rascher[27] will bring you the plan; it is my own. Directors of the paper are Kapellmeister Stegmayer, Wieck, Schunke, Knorr, and myself." [28]

The interpretation in this quotation of the word "plan" is of some importance. May Herbert, in her translation of the *Jugendbriefe,* construes it in a very general sense as "scheme" or "idea." [29] But it is more probable that what Rascher delivered to Schumann's mother was not a "scheme," but a "gedruckter Plan," or prospectus. A prospectus had in fact been drawn up only three days earlier; if our reading of the letter is correct, Schumann claims to have written it himself. This prospectus was published, with certain variants, on three occasions: separately as a circular;[30] in a literary journal, *Der Planet* (March 21, 1834); and in the first issue of the NZfM on April 3, 1834. Gustav Wustmann first called attention to the *Planet* version

---

25. These articles appeared in *Der Komet* on December 7 and 14, 1833, and January 12, 1834. They are reprinted in GSK, 2, 260–72. I have been unable so far to find a single issue of this journal from 1833. As long ago as 1883, Jansen wrote that to his knowledge the sole remaining copy of the 1833 volume was the incomplete one in the Grossherzogliche Bibliothek at Weimar (*Die Davidsbündler,* p. 218). Kreisig reported in 1914 (GSK, 2, 457) that the Stadtbibliothek of Leipzig had a complete set of the journal. Not a trace is now to be found of either copy.

26. See GSK, 2, 461, n. 521, and Alfred Dörffel, *Geschichte der Gewandhausconcerte zu Leipzig* (Leipzig, 1844), p. 209. The second article was in all probability written shortly after September 29, the date of the dedication concert for the newly refurbished *Gewandhaus* concert hall. See *Dörffel,* p. 76. At the time that these essays were published, Schumann intended to expand the series into a novel (see *Jugendbriefe,* p. 229); their narrative form corresponds to this purpose.

27. Eduard Rascher, an old acquaintance of Schumann's from Zwickau.

28. *Jugendbriefe,* p. 233.

29. Robert Schumann, *Early Letters,* trans. May Herbert (London, 1888), p. 221.

30. This version is printed in GSK, 2, 272. The prospectus as it appeared in the first issue of the NZfM is given in Appendix I, 6.

in his article "Zur Entstehungsgeschichte der Schumannischen Zeitschrift für Musik." [31] The literary style of this prospectus, he believed,
suggested that Schumann was its author. Wustmann was certainly
right; the language of the prospectus is in fact identical at points to
that of a Schumann letter of August 5, 1833.[32]

Again in 1834 Schumann bore the brunt of the labors—which were
now rewarded, at last, with the birth of the NZfM. Boetticher lists
thirty-nine prospective contributors Schumann approached between
March 1 and September 23.[33] Despite all this industry, however, and
despite Schumann's obvious aspirations to the editorship, Schumann
was not editor-in-chief of the journal in 1834; that position went to
Julius Knorr. The publication was finally undertaken by the small
firm of C. H. F. Hartmann.[34]

Almost all writers on Schumann have assumed that he was in full
charge of the NZfM from the outset. But Schumann's own account
in the preface of 1854 suggests that this was not the case, and the
journal itself makes no mention of Schumann in the masthead until
1835. A contract[35] signed at its founding by Knorr, Schumann,
Schunke, Wieck, and Hartmann, moreover, is perfectly explicit about
the duties of the various participants. The four founders, it says, are
to hold weekly meetings—and are bound by the contract to appear
on time. "The journal, its title, and format," it specifies, belong to
these four "Herausgeber." But Knorr is named, in no uncertain terms,

31. In *Sammelbände der internationalen Musikgesellschaft, 8* (1906), 396–403.
32. See NZfM, *1* (1834), 2, and *Jugendbriefe,* p. 221.
33. Boetticher, *Einführung,* p. 137. Most of these letters have been lost; Boetticher's information is taken from Schumann's own record, i.e. his "Briefbuch."
34. It appears that Hartmann, publisher of *Der Planet,* and former publisher of *Der
Komet,* agreed to undertake the NZfM only very shortly before its first number appeared;
there is no mention of Hartmann in Schumann's letters of March, 1834, nor even in the
prospectus as drawn up on March 16. All the preparations for the journal seem to have
been hasty. Schumann requested that his mother send him volumes of the AmZ to serve
as models for the new journal as late as March 19 (*Jugendbriefe,* p. 233). Thus the prospectus for the journal was written before its format had been fully determined. And it is
astonishing to find Schumann writing to Theodore Töpken on March 27, exactly one week
before the appearance of the first issue of the NZfM, that "the other directors of the journal
are Stegmayer, Wieck, and Ludwig Schunke" (*Briefe,* p. 48). The editor-in-chief is not
even mentioned!
35. Wustmann discovered this contract in the Leipziger Ratsarchiv, and reprints it in full
(Wustmann, p. 398–99). The contract was drawn up approximately one week before the
first issue of the NZfM appeared.

editor-in-chief, and his special responsibilities are carefully spelled out.[36]

On April 3, 1834, the first number of the journal appeared under the title *Neue Leipziger Zeitschrift für Musik*. The masthead announces that it is "published by a society of artists and friends of art." A "motto" [37] appears directly below—the first of the hundreds of literary quotations that grace the front pages of individual numbers of the NZfM. There follows the prospectus, the first installment of a review of the *Briefwechsel zwischen Goethe und Zelter*, a review of a piano duet by Wilhelm Taubert, a correspondence article from Paris, and a few announcements. None of these contributions, with the exception of the prospectus, is signed.

It was not for long that the journal's affairs were conducted according to the specifications of the contract. Already as on July 2 Schumann complains that "our editor, Knorr, has now been totally incapacitated for eight weeks with ague, so that I must take care of everything—correspondence, proofreading, manuscripts," [38] and further,

> For the time being, I must devote absolutely all my energies to the journal—the others cannot be depended upon—Wieck is always traveling about, Knorr is ill, Schunke cannot manage a

36. Paragraphs nine and ten of the contract are as follows (Wustmann, p. 399):

All letters, correspondence, articles, and musical compositions sent to the journal by those residing here or elsewhere will be dispatched by Herr Hartmann to the editor, Herr Knorr, and will remain the property of the four gentlemen.

Herr Knorr will assume in a special way the editorship of the journal, that is, he will conduct the non-local correspondence, will maintain his own records of letters sent in, of correspondence, articles, and musical compositions, will determine (with the consent of the other editors) what sort of manuscripts are to be accepted and printed, will assume responsibility for the finances of the paper, and for the first proof-reading and revision.

37. These epigraphs were selected (apparently by Schumann alone) from a great variety of literary sources. The motto for Vol. 1, no. 1, identified only as "Shakespeare," is a German verse translation of some lines from the prologue of *Henry VIII*:

> Only they
> That come to hear a merry bawdy play,
> A noise of targets, or to see a fellow
> In a long motley coat guarded with yellow,
> Will be deceived.

38. *Jugendbriefe*, p. 239.

pen very well—who remains? Yet, the journal is such an extraordinary success that I work away at it with zeal and profit.[39]

If Knorr's affliction kept him from his editorial duties for eight
weeks before July 2, his career as active editor lasted altogether about
a month. Apparently this time again it was Schumann who filled the
gap; this is attested, for example, in the enormous amount of correspondence he again undertook on behalf of the NZfM.[40] In a letter
of August 18, for example, Schumann writes to Theodore Töpken in
a genuinely editorial tone: "So the review you propose of the Hünten
Klavierschule, if it does not resemble the first one too much, we find
most desirable. But perhaps you could write it in a lighter, witty
style." [41]

Schumann's testimony to Knorr's inactivity is to a certain extent
borne out by the journal itself; in the volume for 1834, only fourteen contributions, most of them very short, can be attributed with
certainty to Knorr, while Schumann's signatures appear on more than
twenty.

And at the same time, relations with the publisher began to break
down. In the letter to Töpken of August 18 Schumann complained
that Hartmann had delayed publication so long that the journal was
now two weeks behind schedule. By December things were still worse;
Schunke died on December 7, and one week later Schumann wrote to
Joseph Fischhof in Vienna about taking the journal away from its
present "slovenly" publisher.[42]

Hartmann himself issued a statement in the NZfM of December
18, announcing in elevated but ambiguous language that "part of the
former staff of editors has retired from editorial duties voluntarily,
another part at my inducement." [43] Hartmann also confidently directs
that all correspondence for the journal be sent to him, and declares
his responsibility for paying honoraria. Nevertheless, a small notice at
the end of the final number of 1834 (December 29) announces that
pursuant to a "friendly agreement" with the editorial staff, the publisher's rights for the journal have been sold to J. A. Barth of Leipzig.[44]

Since of the original four editors, one (Schunke) was dead, and

39. Ibid., p. 242.
40. See Boetticher, *Einführung*, p. 137, n. 71, and 187, n. 7.
41. *Briefe*, p. 52.
42. *Jugendbriefe*, p. 264.
43. NZfM, *1* (1834), 297. Hartmann's announcement is given in full in Appendix I, 2.
44. NZfM, *1* (1834), 312.

two "parts," according to Hartmann, had retired, there was but one editor left, and that was Schumann. Wieck was plainly the editor who withdrew voluntarily. Schumann's testimony to his desultory attitude toward the NZfM is fully corroborated by his writings in the journal; only four articles[45] in the volume for 1834 can be attributed with any confidence to Wieck. The member of the staff Hartmann induced to resign was none other than the editor-in-chief, Julius Knorr. As will become clear later, it seems that Schumann, while laying plans to rid the journal of its "slovenly" publisher, first persuaded that publisher to dismiss the editor-in-chief.

Wustmann has found in the Leipziger Ratsarchiv documents from 1835 which throw additional light on the fortunes of the NZfM at the end of its first year. On January 2, 1835, the records show, Knorr petitioned the Leipziger Bücherkommission to prohibit Barth and Schumann from publishing the journal, since the three-year contract with Hartmann named him editor-in-chief. Barth is recorded as having answered that he was only "mildly interested" in the project anyway. Schumann, however, entered a detailed reply. Knorr, he claimed, had broken the contract by consistently neglecting his editorial duties, and in December had endangered the life of the journal by withholding important copy. And because he had refused to trouble himself further with the editorship, the publisher was obliged to import help at his own expense.[46] The last three numbers of the

45. Three of these (NZfM, *1* [1834], 3, 15, and 66) are brief reviews of piano works. The fourth (NZfM, *1* [1834], 5, 9) is an article entitled "Beitrage zum Studium des Pianofortespiels."

Ascription of articles in the NZfM is often complicated, for they seldom bear authors' names. Like many German journals of the time the NZfM used a system of numbers for signatures; thus only readers with inside knowledge could recognize individual authors. Schumann explained that articles signed with numbers reflected communal opinions of the regular editors. NZfM, *2* (1835), 5. The earlier articles having number signatures in the NZfM which Schumann included in his *Gesammelte Schriften* nearly all bear a number whose last digit is "2" (2, 12, 22, etc.). In two letters of 1834 Schumann confirms that "2" is his number, and that numbers ending in "3" are Schunke's signatures. *Briefe*, p. 52, *Jugendbriefe*, p. 244. Kreisig cites a letter of 1835 by Wieck in which he identifies several of his own articles from vol. 1 of the NZfM. Two of them are signed with the number "4". This leaves only one of the original number signatures: the "1," "11," etc., that must belong to the editor-in-chief, Julius Knorr. There are a few stray numbers in vol. 1, but only one other one recurs at all frequently: the "6," "26" which Kreisig identified correctly as the signature of Carl Banck. GSK, 2, 527.

46. Wustmann (p. 402) speculates that Carl Banck, a writer for the NZfM in its first year, assisted with the editorial work. This is probable, as Banck was a regular contributor in 1834, and at the time a close friend of Schumann.

year were prepared without Knorr's participation, and Schumann had been forced to compensate the publisher's loss with a "significant sum of money." Then on December 24 Knorr had voluntarily withdrawn from the contract, ceding his rights to Schumann. Schumann produced as evidence a document signed by Hartmann, Knorr, and himself which instructed the postal authorities to send all further correspondence for the journal to Schumann. All this, Schumann asserted, proved that the journal he and Barth were about to publish had nothing whatever to do with Knorr.

On January 4 Schumann issued a statement to the subscribers:

> The consolidation of new business arrangements may delay the appearance of the first number of our journal for a few more days. We beg the indulgence of our subscribers, and hope to be able to send out the numbers 1–8, together with the portrait of Louis Spohr, at the end of the month.[47]

Knorr thereupon protested a second time to the Bücherkommission, demanding a judgment on his first petition. Schumann's predictable reply was that the notice of January 4 was directed to the subscribers of the *new* journal, not the old one Knorr had edited. "If Herr Knorr wishes," concludes Schumann, "he can still attempt with Herr Hartmann to continue the former journal; perhaps he will find satisfaction in it. For my part, I would not care to have anything to do with it." Before the Bücherkommission decided the case, Knorr withdrew his protest.

In this way, when "the project stood at the point of dissolution, the musical visionary of the group" assumed control.[48] The journal, in keeping with its legal status as a new enterprise, appeared in 1835 under a new title, the one always associated with Schumann's name, *Neue Zeitschrift für Musik*. The subhead of each number now reads, "In collaboration with many artists and friends of art, published un-

---

47. Quoted from Wustmann, p. 402.

48. In another retrospective description of these events, Schumann wrote, "But how often it happens, when a group appears ever so united and indivisible, that the sudden intervention of fate severs this bond. Death itself exacted its due: in the passing of Ludwig Schunke we lost one of our most beloved and devoted colleagues. Other circumstances loosened the bond even more. The splendid edifice trembled. Then the editorship came into the hands of a single man. This—he admits it—was quite opposed to his own plans, for he was intent alone upon the development of his own artistic potentialities. But circumstances were pressing; the existence of the journal was at stake." NZfM, *10* (1839), 1. See Appendix I, 3.

der the direction of R. Schumann." Schumann could thus write to
Töpken on February 6, 1835: "I alone am now the owner and director
of the journal . . . How do you like the first numbers? In the final
quarter of last year's volume there was little content and critical
acumen. Much of this will now be improved.[49]

Schumann's efforts toward the founding of the journal and toward
gaining for himself its editorship hardly show him as the musing
visionary loath to abandon his Parnassian reveries for the prosaic world
of copy-editing and publication deadlines. When much later at
Düsseldorf Schumann appeared at times too out of touch with reality
to lift his baton and begin a rehearsal, he scarcely resembled the man
who coaxed and cajoled and prodded the NZfM into existence, and
through persistent negotiations—some of them tinged with unscrupu-
lousness—assumed its direction.

In his work for the NZfM, Schumann always displayed a strong
practical bent, and what the Germans call *Besonnenheit*. He did not
flinch at the grinding dullness of writing hundreds of letters (without
benefit of a secretary) on behalf of the journal, or of studying for
his reviews a thousand compositions, many of which in his judgment
were at best second-rate. He was willing to exert this kind of effort
because he was convinced of the importance of what he was doing.
From the first he had in mind clear objectives for the NZfM, and in
1835 he finally felt that it was within his power to attain them.

49. *Briefe,* p. 62.

CHAPTER 2

The Goals of the Journal

Schumann had now attained what he plainly wanted all along—to be sole director of the journal. Exhilarated with his new freedom, he set about to give the journal a fresh start and to reaffirm its original aims —aims he felt had become blurred in the course of its first year. In the first issue of 1835 he used again the motto[1] from the first number of 1834, and printed as well a revised version of the prospectus.[2] Schumann's eloquent dissertation on the goals of the journal and his own goals as a critic fills virtually the rest of the issue. This is the first of his "New Year's editorials."

In his preface of 1854, quoted above at the beginning of Chapter 1, Schumann summarizes for us the objectives he had in mind upon the founding of the journal, and which he reiterated in the New Year's essay of 1835. The NZfM, he tells us, was to wage war against the degraded musical taste in his country. The most conspicuous symptom of musical degradation in Germany in the 1830s was, to Schumann's mind, the cult of the piano virtuoso.

FOR HIGHER STANDARDS IN PIANO MUSIC

Though as an adolescent Schumann like almost everybody else had been dazzled by Paganini,[3] he took a much dimmer view of the ensuing flood of virtuosi, especially piano virtuosi. In his preface of 1854 he named Herz and Hünten as representative of this group.

1. See above, p. 11.

2. One change in the prospectus is that the 1835 version explains the function of the mottos: "Every number will be prefixed with a motto having, if possible, a bearing on the subject of the lead article." NZfM 2 (1835), 2. In addition, all contributors to volume *1* and prospective contributors to volume 2 are named.

3. Schumann first heard Paganini play in Frankfurt in 1830 (See Niecks, *Robert Schumann*, pp. 85–86). His early impressions of Paganini are recorded in his diaries (see Boetticher, *Einführung*, p. 171), and Paganini is honored in the young Schumann's *Studies on Caprices of Paganini*, op. 3, of 1832 (revised in 1833 as op. 10). Paganini also makes an appearance in *Carnaval*, op. 9, in 1834–35.

Boetticher quotes from a retrospective, diary-like record of Schumann's early impressions where Herz and Czerny are cited as the founders of "insipid virtuosity"—and Paganini as a purveyor of something much more worthwhile.[4]

The early volumes of the NZfM treat the reigning virtuosi of the day with a kind of cool derision. In the very first issue (in a critique of a piano duet by Wilhelm Taubert) the reviewer remarks, "Before Herz and Czerny I doff my hat—to ask that they trouble me no more."[5] And a little later in the first volume there is a mildly insulting review of a piece whose title illustrates the predatory inclinations of the virtuosi: Friedrich Kalkbrenner's *Variations brilliantes sur une mazourka de Chopin* op. 120.[6]

Paris, the dictator of fashion for all Europe, was the place where the glittering piano virtuosi of the 1820s and the 1830s were made, and it was from there that they emanated to display their wares over all Europe (and in some cases, the new world as well). Friedrich Kalkbrenner arrived in Paris in 1799 at the age of 14, acquired his entire musical education there, and stayed for virtually the rest of his life. Henri Herz became a student at the Conservatoire in 1816, and Paris remained for him a permanent base of operations. Franz Hünten entered the Conservatoire three years later than Herz, and he too became a lifelong resident of the city. The young Liszt moved with his family to Paris in 1823 and began to scale the heights of worldwide fame with his Paris concerts of 1824. Paris was the scene, a decade later, of the bitter competition between Liszt and the only pianist who seriously threatened his popular preeminence, Sigismund Thalberg. Chopin arrived in 1831, and at about this time a host of lesser pianists also sought their fortunes in Paris, and in varying degrees found them: J. P. Pixis, Ferdinand Hiller, Theodore Döhler, Alexander Dreischock, and others. None of these pianists was born in Paris, or even in France.

In retrospect, the cultivation of the arts in Paris in the late 1820s and the 1830s appears curiously Janus-faced. On one hand the romantic artists and litterateurs formed a camp which was remarkably tight-

---

4. W. Boetticher, ed., *Schriften*, p. 13. This document, first published by Boetticher, is entitled "Materialen zu einem Lebenslauf."

5. NZfM, *1* (1834), 3. I think this unsigned article is by Wieck. According to the original arrangements, Wieck was to have been the reviewer of piano music; the rather sober style of the review, moreover, suggests an older writer.

6. NZfM, *1* (1834), 55–56. This article is probably by Schunke. The problems of signatures and attributions in the early volumes of the NZfM are discussed above, p. 13, n. 45.

knit and increasingly influential. In the City of Light musicians like Berlioz, Chopin, Liszt, and Hiller associated with Balzac, Hugo, Vigny, George Sand, Heine, and Delacroix. Some of this group founded a journal of the arts and letters, *L'Europe littéraire,* which campaigned for very much the same sort of reform in taste as Schumann championed in the NZfM. And it was at least some tribute to the effectiveness of the romantic doctrine that Shakespeare, hissed off the stage in 1822, was received with enthusiasm in 1827.

Grand opera represented quite another face of the cultural life of Paris. Under the direction of Louis Véron, with the music of Meyerbeer and Halévy, the libretti of Scribe, and the mise-en-scène of Duponchel and Cicéri, it was first of all a commercial venture—and a commercial success.[7] The venerable *Académie royale de musique,* now operated as a concession by Véron, specialized in grandiose spectacles that satisfied the taste of the newly powerful and newly moneyed bourgeoisie. This group, raised to unprecedented heights of influence during the July monarchy of Louis Philippe, virtually dictated artistic taste in Paris—especially at the opera—while the old aristocracy sulked in the background.

It was exactly this bourgeois audience for whom the virtuoso pianists played and composed; and they were rewarded for their efforts with mountains of money and acclaim. This audience is gently ridiculed in a review of a concert by Thalberg in the *Revue et gazette musicale* of March 25, 1838:

> This was the most expensive concert of the year: no one since Paganini had ventured to place so high a price on the exhibition of his talent as the young and celebrated S. Thalberg. Far be it from us to think of reproaching him for it! On the contrary, we think it honorable and significant: of all the forms of praise we choose the least banal, the least equivocal, and we report that in spite of the 20 francs it cost to hear the great pianist, the crowd pressed and jammed itself into the parlors of Erard:[8] you

---

7. See the informative book by William L. Crosten, *French Grand Opera, an Art and a Business* (New York, 1948).

8. The famous Erard family of piano makers (See the extensive article in F. J. Fétis, ed., *Biographie universelle des musiciens,* 2d ed. [Paris, 1878], *3,* 143–48), like several of the leading piano firms, maintained a concert hall where the excellence of its product could be demonstrated.

understand what sort of crowd—the fine flower, the choice aristocracy of dilettantism! It is a real pleasure to raise the tax on art for those who bear it so easily, and with such good grace! [9]

There was a strong aura of commercialism about the Parisian virtuosi, and the pianists themselves did nothing to dispel it. Kalkbrenner entered into partnership with J. B. Logier in 1818 and actively promoted the sale of the latter's invention, the "chiroplast" (a mechanical device for strengthening a pianist's fingers).[10] He later became a partner in the famous piano firm of Pleyel. Herz similarly invented and marketed a device called the "dactylion," [11] entered into partnership first with the Parisian piano factory of Klepfer, and subsequently founded his own.

There was more that bound the virtuosi to the Grand Opera than a common audience: much of the music they played consisted of their own fantasias and variations on current tunes from the opera. Between 1818 and 1871, Herz accumulated well over 100 opus numbers of this kind of music, and in the process, a sizable fortune as well. This was the proven road to success, and the leading Parisian pianists— Czerny, Kalkbrenner, Hünten and Döhler, and most of the others— followed it joyfully.

A famous episode in the chronic hostilities between Herz and the influential Parisian music publisher, Maurice Schlesinger, illustrates how the piano virtuosi coveted the newest and most popular operatic airs.[12] Meyerbeer's second Paris opera, Les Huguenots, first performed in February 1836, achieved immediate and unparalleled success, ex-

9. Revue et gazette musicale, 1838, p. 151. See Appendix I, 4.

10. Wieck belittles the value of the chiroplast in the first pages of the NZfM [1 (1834), 6] evoking a long and indignant defense from E. Weber, a proponent of the "Logier method." NZfM, 1 (1834), 237–39.

11. An illustrated advertisement of the dactylion in the Intelligenz-Blatt no. 5 of the Allgemeine musikalische Zeitung, 38 (1836), describes it as "a device equipped with springs, designed to make the fingers supple, strong, and independent, to insure proper evenness in piano playing, and promote beautiful performance." The dactylion consisted of a frame attached to the piano above the keyboard, from which there were suspended rings that fitted around the fingers, tending to hold them up away from the keys. It was very likely a device something like this that injured Schumann's finger in 1832, putting an end to his hopes of becoming a virtuoso pianist. An article in the Parisian Revue et gazette musicale (1836), pp. 165–66, maintains that the dactylion was pirated by Herz from a M. Meyer, and was in any event a useless contraption.

12. See the account by Arthur Loesser in Men, Women and Pianos (New York, 1954), pp. 359–60.

ceeding that even of *Robert-le-Diable,* first staged four and one half years earlier.[13] Berlioz describes the enthusiasm of the audience for *Les Huguenots* (an enthusiasm he apparently shared to some extent) in his review of the opera in the *Revue et gazette musicale* of March 6, 13, and 20. Schlesinger held all publisher's rights for the music; he announced that it would be released in Paris, London, and Leipzig simultaneously on May 1.[14] Exclusive rights for piano transcription had been sold to Thalberg who, it was announced, would play in a concert at the Italian theater "un grand morceau très brillant, de sa composition sur des motifs des Huguenots." [15]

But well before either the publication of the music or Thalberg's concert, Herz published in Mainz, as his opus 89, "Fantasie dramatique sur le choral protestant chanté dans l'opéra des Huguenots de Meyerbeer." [16] Schlesinger could scarcely claim exclusive rights for this protestant chorale; it was "Ein' feste Burg ist unser Gott." [17] In his announcement of the publication of the music, Schlesinger remarked, "The public will easily understand the motives which prompted M. Henry Herz to attempt this deception, in putting in the title, in large letters, the *Huguenots,* and the name of M. Meyerbeer." [18] The writers

13. A. Loewenberg records in his *Annals of Opera,* 2nd ed. (Geneva, 1955), *1,* 777, that *Les Huguenots* was given at the Paris Opéra 1,080 times until 1914. *Robert-le-Diable,* first performed on November 21, 1831, saw its 100th performance on April 20, 1834, and by 1893 had been given at the Opéra 758 times (*Annals, 1,* 736).

14. *Revue et gazette musicale,* 1836, p. 104. The music for *Les Huguenots* appeared in score, but also in a more marketable form: in twenty-one separate *morceaux.* The "Romance chantée par M. Nourrit," for instance, could be bought with obligato viola accompaniment for 5 francs, 50 centimes, or with piano accompaniment for 4f., 50c. The "Grand duo chanté par M. Nourrit et mademoiselle Falcon" cost 7f., 50c., while the cavatina extracted from it could be had for 3f., 50c. See *Revue et gazette musicale,* 1836, pp. 167–68. It was standard practice at this time throughout Europe to dissect large musical compositions and publish the fragments in a variety of arrangements. Orchestral scores were virtually unavailable; music for orchestra was regularly reduced to 4-hand piano arrangements. This was not always done with care. Schumann remarks in the course of reviewing an overture of A. Hesse that the arranger, apparently finding it impossible to transcribe the second theme, just transposed the first theme and used it over again. NZfM, *8* (1838), 15.

15. *Revue et gazette musicale,* 1836, p. 112.

16. See Adolph Hofmeister, ed., *C. F. Whistling's Handbuch der musikalischen Literatur,* 3d ed. (Leipzig, 1844) *1,* 174.

17. Schlesinger's original edition of the opera carefully grants credit where it is due. A note at the beginning of the chorale (p. 48 of the score) explains, "La partie de chant de ce Chorale (jusqu' à la coda) est de Luther."

18. *Revue et gazette musicale,* 1836, p. 104. See Appendix I, 5. Schumann reviewed Herz' composition in the NZfM of October 18, 1836. Misunderstanding the extent to which Herz

of the NZfM called this sort of chicanery "grauenhaft colossaler Materialismus." [19]

The flood of piano music turned out by the pianists of Paris and by others in imitation of their style quickly inundated the music markets of all Europe. A casual comparison of publishers' lists of piano music in the mid-1830s from France, England, Germany, and Austria reveals startling uniformity.[20] These lists repeat the names of the most famous of the pianist-composers, especially Czerny, Hünten, Herz, and Thalberg, with monotonous regularity; lesser known names vary from country to country. The categories of piano pieces in the lists follow a highly regular pattern: variations, fantasias, and rondos on operatic tunes, and etudes in a similar style—often simplified versions of what the virtuosi played in concerts—predominate overwhelmingly. This kind of music was intended partly for aspiring pianists, but more for the vast company of middle-class musical amateurs. Music in this style was supposed to be as brilliant as possible—but not too difficult.[21]

The hegemony of Parisian piano music outraged Schumann and his colleagues, and their most important reason for founding a musical journal was to combat it. Schumann's second complaint in the preface of 1854, that is, that "Rossini yet ruled the stage," surely had much less to do with it. Opera played a relatively minor role in the musical life of Leipzig in the early 1830s; the opera house there subsisted largely on performances borrowed from Magdeburg or the Hoftheater of Dresden. Its repertory, moreover, was largely German. Surely Rossini posed no serious threat to Schumann in 1834. His interest in opera, especially his passionate concern for the fortunes of German

---

appropriated Meyerbeer's music—he borrowed nothing but the chorale—Schumann compares Herz to Mozart writing down from memory the *Miserere* of Allegri.

19. In the anonymous article "Musikalischer Romantismus," NZfM, *1* (1834), 187.

20. For a random sampling, see the advertisements of "musique nouvelle" Schlesinger prints in the *Revue et gazette musicale* (e.g., 1836, p. 104); the "Weekly List of New Publications" in *The Musical World* (e.g. *1* [1836], 34); Diabelli's list in the supplement to the AmZ for 1836, between pp. 284 and 285; and Breitkopf und Härtel's own list in the same volume, between pp. 600 and 601.

21. It was always important to contemporary critics that published piano music be relatively easy to play. This is reflected in almost every page of the piano music reviews of G. W. Fink, editor of the AmZ. Chopin's compositions caused him and similar critics alarm first of all because they were so difficult. See the AmZ, *35* (1833), 357–60, and *36* (1834), 81–89. See also Ludwig Rellstab in *Iris im Gebiete der Tonkunst, 5*, 149–50 and 174–75.

opera, is not clearly detectable until about 1839; the statement about Rossini is but a retrospective assessment. The early volumes of the NZfM show little interest in opera. With but one exception,[22] there is no mention of any performance of any opera in the first volume of the NZfM (this does not take into account short reports of musical events from other cities). Two articles deal with the subject of opera in general: a rather pedantic discussion under the title "Dramaturgische Fragmente" of the propriety of Biblical opera,[23] and a short article entitled "Zur Geschichte der Oper von Rousseau." [24]

It was the contemporary state of piano music that first roused the founders of the NZfM to action, and, especially in its early years, the journal continued to specialize, sometimes almost exclusively, in this field.[25] And this is only natural, since Schumann, Knorr, Schunke, and Wieck were all pianists; Schumann and Schunke, moreover, were at this point composers of piano music alone.

The NZfM, then, was to be an instrument of propaganda, a rostrum from which Schumann and his colleagues could expose all who corrupted music and musical taste in Germany. In his restatement of the policies of the journal in 1835, Schumann specifies that it aims to combat the three archenemies of music and every other art, the "Talentlosen, Dutzendtalenten," and "talentvolle Vielschreiber." [26] In his New Year's editorial of 1839 he speaks of "erecting, in word and deed, a dam against mediocrity." This mediocrity, he believed, was not German mediocrity, but a foreign product. It was the aim of the NZfM, Schumann states in the same article, "to rip down foreign idols," and to wage a campaign against "foreign hackwork." [27] But there was a positive side to the policies of the NZfM as well: the journal pledged its support to the composers they regarded as serious artists. The prospectus states,

> It seemed necessary also to create for him [the artist] an organ which would stimulate him to effectiveness, not only through his

---

22. A review by Carl Banck of a performance of Auber's *Masked Ball* at Leipzig. NZfM, *1* (1834), 102 and 118.

23. NZfM, *1* (1834), 66, 70 and 75.

24. NZfM, *1* (1834), 305.

25. Schumann summarizes his ideas about the importance of the piano and its music in his essay "Das Clavier-Concert." NZfM, *10* (1839), 5.

26. NZfM, *2* (1835), 3.

27. NZfM, *10* (1839), 2.

direct influence, but also through the printed and spoken word, a public place for him to express what he has seen with his own eyes, and felt in his own spirit, a journal, moreover, in which he could defend himself against one-sided and false criticism.[28]

This seems to suggest that these artists, or at least some of them, were the writers of the NZfM. There is some truth to this; Schumann and his colleagues plainly thought of themselves as unjustly neglected composers and musicians, and the NZfM was to be, at least partly, a vehicle for personal and collective apologetics. But they also thought of the journal as an organ for a kind of universal brotherhood of genuine artists. Schumann and his group felt a spiritual affinity with certain composers, and to them they granted (whether or not these feelings of affinity were reciprocal) the support of the journal. The extent to which posterity has vindicated their judgment is almost uncanny. While the other musical journals in Germany sang the praises of Herz, Thalberg, Berger, Klein, Meyerbeer, and Auber, the NZfM was talking about Schubert, Chopin, Berlioz, Heller, and later, Brahms.

For Higher Standards in Music Criticism

The section of the prospectus cited above injects a new element into our discussion of the objectives of Schumann and his friends in founding a new musical journal: they wished to provide an antidote for the sorry state of German music criticism. In his preface of 1854, Schumann makes no reference to the kind of music criticism that was going on when the NZfM was begun. Only a polite, somewhat ambiguous reference to the other musical journals is included in the prospectus published both as a circular and in the first volume of the NZfM:

How could the editors fail to recognize the merits of the current highly respectable musical journals? They do not ascribe any possible faults to a lack of acquaintance with the demands which the artist may now place upon the critic, or to a declining enthusiasm for art. But they find it on the one hand impossible that the entire field of music, so extensive in quantity, could be treated in detail by any one [journal], and on the other, natural that with the participation of many, some of whom in the course of

28. NZfM, *1* (1834), 1. See Appendix I, 6.

time drop out to be replaced by others with different inclinations, the original intention should be forgotten, and degenerate into slackness and the commonplace.[29]

But there is no ambiguity whatever about the corresponding section of the prospectus published March 21, 1834 in *Der Planet*:

> What, then, are the few present musical journals? Nothing but playgrounds for ossified systems, from which, even with the best of will, hardly a drop of the sap of life can be pressed, nothing but relics of aged doctrines to which adherence is more and more openly denied, nothing but one-sidedness and rigidity to be passed over with sympathy, or indeed aggregations of individual, eccentric opinions, prejudices, fruitless personal bickering and partisanship so loathsome to the better young artists. None of this number, with the possible exception of the *Caecilia*, is capable of promoting the true interests of music; none is able to fulfill the just demands made upon it.[30]

While prudence often checked outbursts such as this, the early volumes of the NZfM leave no room for doubt about the editors' opinions of contemporary music criticism. The underlying reason for Schumann's entry into the arena of music criticism was his dissatisfaction with the level of music, especially piano music, in Germany; but it was his vexation with the laissez-faire attitude of contemporary journals and critics that finally spurred him into action.

The prospectus on the first page of the NZfM promises that the attitude of the journal toward those already in existence will soon be "clearly spelled out." This promise is fulfilled in the first volume with a series of articles in ten installments under the rubric *Journalschau*.[31] In this series the writers for the infant paper boldly—and in the view of certain rival editors, impudently—give a candid evaluation of several contemporary musical journals. Called before the tribunal are the *Allgemeine musikalische Zeitung* (hereafter AmZ),[32] *Caecilia*,[33]

---

29. NZfM, *1* (1834), 2. See Appendix I, 6. Schumann's word here for commonplace is "allgemein"—a sly dig at the AmZ.

30. Quoted in Wustmann, "Die Entstehung," p. 397.

31. NZfM, *1* (1834), 182, 186, 190, 193, 198, 210, 226, 230, 266, and 270.

32. The AmZ was founded in 1798 by Johann Friedrich Rochlitz, and continued under his editorship until 1819. From 1819–1827 it was published "under the direction of the publisher" (Breitkopf und Härtel). In 1827 Gottfried Wilhelm Fink became editor, and held this post until 1841. An invaluable source of information about this and other nine-

Iris im Gebiete der Tonkunst,[34] the *Allgemeiner musikalischer Anzeiger* of Vienna,[35] the *Allgemeiner musikalischer Anzeiger* of Frankfurt,[36] the *Revue musicale*, and the *Gazette musicale*.[37] Three of these reviews (those of *Iris* and both of the *Allgemeine musikalische Anzeiger*) clearly bear Schumann's signatures, but they are not included in Kreisig's excellent critical edition, or in any other edition of the *Gesammelte Schriften*.

In the first of these reviews, Carl Banck treats the rival Leipzig paper, the AmZ, with a certain restraint:

It is plain throughout that the criticism in this paper carefully avoids the recognition of genius or real spirit, and avoids similarly any open opposition to mediocrity and lack of talent. Its policy is one of greatest tolerance; it keeps its distance from wholehearted commendation as well as downright condemnation. Its motto: "live and let live." [38]

Only one composition reviewed in the first half of 1834, he continues, seems to have shaken the journal loose from this policy: Chopin's Etudes op. 10.[39] G. W. Fink, editor of the AmZ, in a notable

teenth-century musical journals is W. Freystätter's *Die musikalischen Zeitschriften seit ihrer Entstehung bis zur Gegenwart* (München, 1884). There is an informative monograph about the early years of the AmZ: Martha Bigenwald, *Die Anfänge der leipziger Allgemeinen musikalischen Zeitung* (Sibiu-Hermannstadt, 1938).

33. *Caecilia*, published by Schott of Mainz, was edited by the famous theorist Gottfried Weber from its beginnings in 1824 until its discontinuation in 1839. It was resumed under the editorship of S. W. Dehn from 1842–48.

34. *Iris*, the most influential Berlin musical journal of the period, was founded in 1830. During the entire twelve years of its life it was edited by the author and critic Ludwig Rellstab (the man credited with naming Beethoven's Moonlight Sonata), and published by Trautwein.

35. The *Allgemeiner musikalischer Anzeiger* of Vienna, founded in 1829, was edited by I. F. Castelli and published by Tobias Haslinger.

36. The *Allgemeiner musikalischer Anzeiger* of Frankfurt reviewed in the NZfM is a revival of the journal founded under that name in 1826. The volumes for 1834–36 were published and edited by A. Fischer.

37. F.-J. Fétis founded the *Revue musicale* in 1827, and acted as editor until 1832, when he left Paris to take up permanent residence in Brussels. The titular director of the journal in 1832–35 was his son Eduard Fétis. In 1835 the *Revue musicale* merged with Schlesinger's *Gazette musicale* to form the most durable and influential of the nineteenth-century French musical journals, the *Revue et gazette musicale*. For an account of this merger see the *Revue et gazette musicale*, 1835, pp. 353–54.

38. NZfM, *1* (1834), 183. See Appendix I, 7.

39. Reviewed in the AmZ, *36* (1834), 81–89.

departure from his usual pleasant policies wrote a long and rather sour review of this collection in February of 1834.

Caecilia is described in a brief article by Julius Knorr. Its reviews of music, he reports, "are not likely to offend anybody, as they usually pass over in silence whatever is worthy of blame, or even seek to excuse it."[40] In his article on Fétis' *Revue musicale*, Ludwig Schunke complains about its historical emphasis, and poses a rhetorical question to M. Fétis:

> Now perhaps Herr Fétis will allow us to ask a question. Is French music really on so high a level that criticism of its recent products, good or bad, is entirely unnecessary? The ill-informed would be led to believe this when he finds in the *Revue* for an entire half-year but four things reviewed.[41]

Schlesinger's *Gazette musicale,* which in 1835 absorbed Fétis' journal, is in a final anonymous article given the somewhat bland approval of the NZfM. The reviewer is impressed, he says, with the number of musicians among its writers, and he approves of the "confession of faith" in which the *Gazette musicale* determines "to oppose with extensive and impartial criticism the prevailing poor taste in France."[42]

Schumann's critique of Rellstab's *Iris* is the lead article in the NZfM of September 18. It appears under a motto extracted from Schumann's own "Davidsbündler" articles in *Der Komet* of 1833 where he lashes out impetuously at contemporary music criticism:

> What? Rellstab is too severe? Must this damnable German politeness last for centuries? While literary factions draw up battle lines and attack each other openly, in art criticism there is nothing but diffident shoulder-shrugging. This is incredible, and we cannot go too far in denouncing it. Why can't we simply reject the talentless? Why not throw out the shallow and sickly along with the arrogant pretenders? Why not warning notices before works for which a critique would be futile? Why don't

40. NZfM, *1* (1834), 191.
41. NZfM, *1* (1834), 231. See Appendix I, 8.
42. Quoted in NZfM, *1* (1834), 266.

the composers write their own journal against the critics, and demand harsher judgments on their works? [43]

This tirade is aimed at contemporary music criticism as a whole, and not, as the motto itself suggests, at Rellstab and the journal he writes almost single-handedly, the *Iris im Gebiete der Tonkunst*. Schumann begins his review with a few droll observations about the title of the journal and then quotes almost without comment examples of the music criticism in *Iris*. Rellstab's attitude toward contemporary music, it soon becomes clear, is not one of benign indifference such as Schumann deprecated in his motto, but one of active partisanship. Yet this is a partisanship Schumann could hardly be expected to applaud, for Rellstab writes (and Schumann quotes),

> We have often lamented that young composers of recent times have no real composition teachers, not to mention teachers of thorough-bass; without guidance or study, wild and heedless, they just compose. We considered this already an unhealthy situation. But something quite different was still to come. Now, not only do they fail to learn what is good, but they even have systematic instruction in what is bad—they make a study of perversity. For this young talent [J. C. Kessler], Chopin's most recent compositions have obviously served as a model, as a bad example. . . .
>
> Thus there is a tendency to strive for effects never heard before on the instrument, be the musical ideas ever so trivial and hackneyed. Unfortunately we are witnessing the formation of a whole school for error; we could see it first in Chopin, then in Schumann and others, and now also in this young composer.[44]

Rellstab's harshest words, Schumann observes, are reserved for the founder of the "school for error," Chopin: "But so long as he hacks out such abortive things as these Etudes[45] (they caused a good deal of merriment when I showed them to all my friends, especially the pi-

43. NZfM, *1* (1834), 193. See Appendix I, 9.
44. *Iris im Gebiete der Tonkunst, 5* (1834), 91; NZfM, *1* (1834), 194, 198. See Appendix I, 10.
45. Op. 10.

anists) we will continue to laugh at both them and his letter."[46] The most glaring error Rellstab finds in the piano compositions of both Chopin and Kessler is their difficulty. Schumann remarks politely, "We hope and believe that Rellstab's abilities as a virtuoso are not a determining factor in his judgment."[47]

Despite all this, Schumann embarks on an extended and remarkably appreciative assessment of Rellstab and his paper. Rellstab was the first, he says, to check a German inclination to follow blindly the cultural fashions of France and Italy, and to launch an offensive against that noncommittal brand of music criticism that conceals characterlessness under a cloak of impartiality. Praise and blame in Rellstab's criticism, in fact, occur in a ratio of about one to five. But the younger generation of composers are not in Rellstab's estimation the agents for improving music and musical taste in Germany. He looks for the salvation of German music in the work of certain older contemporaries, especially Ludwig Berger and Bernhard Klein.[48] Yet Rellstab has had a salutary effect on the younger artists, Schumann concludes, if for no other reason than that he incites them to action. At this level, he admits, allowances must be made for differences of opinion.[49]

There was an uneasy peace between the NZfM and *Iris* throughout the period when the two journals existed concurrently (1834–41). Rellstab campaigned valiantly for the cultivation of indigenous German musical style, and for a serious German music criticism—both principles dear to Schumann's heart. Schumann even printed Rellstab's long article on Wilhelmine Schröder-Devrient in the NZfM of 1834;[50] with a gentle touch of irony, he filled numbers 49 and 50 almost entirely with Rellstab's article on the famous singer and his own article on Rellstab. But Rellstab remained an outspoken opponent of the

46. *Iris*, 5 (1834), 20; quoted in NZfM, *1* (1834), 198. In this review of Chopin's Etudes, Rellstab prints an outrageously abusive letter he claims to have received from Chopin. Its colorful language defies translation: "Verstehen Sie mich, Sie kleiner Mensch, Sie liebloser und partheiischer Recensentenhund, Sie musikalischer Schnurrbart, Sie Berliner Witzemacher." Schumann reports in a footnote to his review Chopin's claim "that he has had no occasion to write to him [Rellstab]."

47. NZfM, *1* (1834), 198.

48. Ludwig Berger (1777–1839), Rellstab's composition teacher at Berlin, composed piano music, and is especially remembered for his lieder. Bernhard Klein (1793–1832) also taught composition in Berlin, and composed lieder, church music, and two operas.

49. NZfM, *1* (1834), 198–99.

50. NZfM, *1* (1834), 185, 189, 194, 197, 201, 205, 209, 213, 225, and 229.

favorite composers of the NZfM, and of the music by its composer-authors as well. His acidulous comments on Chopin's music in the early 1830s, when it first began to attain a wide currency, evoked repeated protests from the NZfM.[51] And it was not only against the younger composers themselves, Chopin, Schumann, Hiller, and Kessler, that Rellstab directed his invective; he even denounced Franz Schubert, whom Schumann and the NZfM canonized as their spiritual ancestor.[52]

In 1837 Rellstab wrote a series of articles on "the present state of music in Germany" for the *Revue et gazette musicale*. In the installment on Leipzig, he answered the *Journalschau* with his own evaluation of the NZfM; he found fault with the "esprit de coterie" in which its writers liked to "s'encenser eux-mêmes." [53] Schumann sent off an indignant reply to the *Revue*,[54] and printed an extensive defense in the NZfM denying that its criticism was ever intended to promote the special interests of the composers on its staff.[55] Despite occasional skirmishes of this sort, Schumann and his journal remained respectful toward Rellstab. When Rellstab retired from his post as editor at the end of 1841, the NZfM printed a notice which ended, "We genuinely regret the retirement of this man; he was often stubborn, but he was honest and honorable." [56]

In his second *Journalschau* review, Schumann disposes of the Viennese *Allgemeiner musikalischer Anzeiger* with more dispatch and less charity. It is well named, he suggests, for it is indeed "commonplace."

51. August Gathy, writing in the NZfM of 1837, points to Rellstab's rejection of Chopin as a continuation of the tradition of criticism in which the AmZ of 1799 rejected Beethoven. NZfM, 7 (1837), 53–54. The AmZ's censure of Beethoven certainly does look similar; he is charged with extravagance of expression, lack of pleasing melody, and above all, "a piling up of difficulty upon difficulty." AmZ, *1* (1799), 570–71.

52. *Iris, 4* (1833), 130.

53. *Revue et gazette musicale*, 1837, p. 536.

54. Ibid., p. 577.

55. NZfM, *8* (1838), 28. This heated and theatrical answer to Rellstab has not been reprinted in any of the editions of the *Gesammelte Schriften*. See Appendix II, 12. In it Schumann lists (with a substantial number of omissions) the reviews in the NZfM of compositions by its staff; then he continues, "And on this Herr Rellstab bases so injurious an accusation. This accusation is directed against an institution which is sustained through sacrifice, and which stakes its honor precisely upon its demonstrated impartiality and cherished artistic convictions. And it is directed against artists who, in their love for the cause and in renunciation of their own interests, were wlling to forgo even the satisfaction of seeing their own accomplishments mentioned. Now let the public judge!" See Appendix I, 11.

56. NZfM, *16* (1842), 8.

He says of this leading musical periodical of Vienna, the most sophisti-
cated and cosmopolitan of German-speaking cities, "It is throughout
naive and unassuming, something like a village newspaper." [57] In recent years, he continues, this journal has devoted itself more and more
to advertising the musical releases of its publisher, Haslinger. But
the Vienna journal was still preferable in Schumann's opinion to its
namesake in Frankfurt. In his review of the latter, Schumann cites a
series of its opinions he considers plainly wrong. He concludes, "And
so we in no way recommend this *Anzeiger,* from which, incidentally,
nothing has been heard since May. If it has expired, mourn not, ye
graces; it is no Adonis that has left us." [58]

While the *Journalschau* articles are perfectly explicit in their
censure of most of these periodicals, they do not indulge in the kind
of intemperate invective we saw first in the *Planet* version of the
prospectus for the NZfM, and then in the motto from Schumann's
"Davidsbündler" article. A reason for this is that the dissatisfaction
of the writers of the NZfM with music criticism in general had its
focal point in Schumann's supreme contempt for G. W. Fink, editor
of the AmZ; but Schumann did not write the *Journalschau* article on
the rival Leipzig paper.

When he called contemporary musical journals "playgrounds for
ossified systems," "relics of aged doctrines," and "aggregations of
eccentric opinions" in the prospectus in the *Planet,* Schumann had in
mind Rellstab and his *Iris.* For Rellstab, as we have seen, there was
forgiveness; though his opinions may have been eccentric, he at least
had opinions. But the "shoulder-shrugging" and "damnable German
politeness" he excoriated in "Der Davidsbündler" was quite another
matter. And more than anyone else it was Fink and the AmZ who
committed this unforgivable sin of being neither hot nor cold. This is
the journal with which Schumann had most contact in the years
immediately preceding the founding of the NZfM, and it served to
fix his impressions of current music criticism. For Schumann the AmZ

---

57. NZfM, *1* (1834), 210. It is not hard to understand that the NZfM made enemies in
Vienna. Schumann's friend in that city, Joseph Fischhof, testified that this was the case (Cf.
Boetticher, ed., *Schriften,* p. 97). The Vienna *Allgemeiner musikalischer Anzeiger* gave
more favorable reviews than any other journal to Schumann's music in 1832–35; Schumann's
letter of December 1834 to Fischhof suggests that this rather sweetened his impressions of
the paper. See *Jugendbriefe,* p. 265.

58. NZfM, *1* (1834), 227. See Appendix II, 3. But the journal was not yet dead; it lived
on until the end of 1836.

became a symbol for everything that was wrong with German music, and the most salient features of his journal and his own criticism are a reaction against it.

Almost all of the musical journals in existence when the NZfM was founded were issued by music publishers. The ones subjected to the scrutiny of the *Journalschau* were without exception products of the foremost music houses in their respective cities of publication: the AmZ of Breitkopf und Härtel in Leipzig, *Caecilia* of Schott in Mainz, *Iris im Gebiete der Tonkunst* of Trautwein in Berlin, the two *Allgemeine musikalische Anzeiger* of Haslinger in Vienna and Fischer in Frankfurt, and the *Revue et gazette musicale* of Schlesinger in Paris. And they all showed the effects of these connections. The journals were the accepted place for publishers to print lists of their recent releases, and since they printed their lists and advertisements in each other's as well as their own papers, the advertising of music took up a good deal of the space in these periodicals.[59] In many cases, unfortunately, the spirit of advertising carried over unmistakably into the journals' criticism. The journals seemed to exist first of all to promote the sale of mass-produced music to a receptive, middle-class public; their music reviews simply fell into line.

This explains the "shoulder-shrugging" and "Honigpinselei" [60] Schumann complained about; and that he was aware of this explanation is clear from his *Journalschau* review of the Viennese *Allgemeiner musikalischer Anzeiger*.[61] Rellstab's criticism was free from this blight; hence Schumann's long-suffering charity toward his most outspoken opponent. It is significant that the NZfM was published first by C. H. F. Hartmann, and later by Johann A. Barth and Robert Friese—none of them primarily music publishers. Schumann's first attempts to found a journal in 1833 foundered when Hofmeister, the prospective publisher, decided that the kind of journal Schumann had in mind would not promote the financial interests of his music publishing house. In a letter to Wieck of January, 1833, Schumann quoted Hofmeister as saying, "As a businessman, I must count the favor of the public as everything, that of the critic as nothing." [62] Schumann

59. The AmZ also issued periodical supplements consisting entirely of advertising.
60. See *Briefe*, p. 52.
61. Cf. above, p. 30.
62. *Jugendbriefe*, p. 201.

declared his own position with a flourish: "We don't write to make businessmen rich, but to honor artists." [63]

Of all the musical journals in Germany, the AmZ gave itself over most joyfully to commercial interests. Its founder, J. F. Rochlitz, had directed the journal's criticism with independence and distinction for twenty years.[64] But Fink, from the time he became editor in 1827, carefully catered to popular taste and the music market; the criticism he published was bland and characterless—the epitome of the "Honigpinselei" that enraged Schumann.

Fink ordinarily introduced each *Jahrgang* of the AmZ with an assurance to his readers that the paper's innocuous policies and his own sanguine views about things remained unchanged. In 1832 he writes,

> Among composers there are two opposing camps. In the first are men of fashion who are heard to inquire, "Do you like this little polonaise?" The others stand there like soldiers; they want to be "solid." The first are many, the others few. The first travel a broad highway; the others are looking for a narrow gate. The first give the crowd a friendly clap on the back; the others ignore you. But both tendencies are natural, cannot be, and never have been otherwise . . . There is not the slightest fault to be found with either type of artist.[65]

His New Year's editorial for 1833 is a seven-column defense of "der Dilettantismus der Teutschen in der Musik." [66] But in 1835, his editorials begin to shed some of their rosy benignancy as Fink returns the barbs hurled at him by the NZfM. The introductory article for that year, entitled "Was wir sollen, wollen, und nicht wollen," declares the journal's benevolent attitude toward everything in music except "the drivel of shrieking ignorance which despises every rule because it hasn't learned it." [67] Fink had in mind Schumann and the NZfM.

63. NZfM, *10* (1839), 2.

64. There is a good discussion of Rochlitz's policies in Bigenwald, *Die Anfänge der leipziger AmZ*, pp. 72–74.

65. AmZ, *34* (1832), 1–3. See Appendix I, 12.

66. AmZ, *35* (1833), 7–13. He writes, for example, "But is dilettantism in Germany really so injurious to art as some of the professionals and alarmists would have us believe? We don't think so; in fact we are inclined to expect far more good than evil from it."

67. AmZ, *37* (1835), 1–2.

Music reviews in Fink's paper, especially those written by the editor, are consistent with the easy tolerance espoused in his earlier editorials. They are essentially of two kinds: full-length reviews (usually by Fink himself), and short "Anzeigen." These two classes differ little in content: the principal distinction is that the longer reviews are decked out in a more expansive prose style—Fink had unusual proclivities along these lines. The usual longer review[68] begins with allusions to the composer's excellent reputation, references to favorable reviews of his works in back issues of the AmZ, and assurances that all those who were pleased with his earlier compositions will also like this one. The author thereupon describes each movement, noting the performance directions, time signature, and key, and finally recommends the work to the accomplished musician, or the downright novice, or both. The shorter review may omit one or more of these component parts— it does not usually include the superficial analysis of individual movements—but its style is the same in miniature. A very brief but typically vacuous example may be quoted in full; this is Fink's review of Friedrich Kalkbrenner's Rondeau fantastique op. 106:

> When mentioning truly beautiful piano compositions, we cannot help but call attention also to this rondo, published in so lovely an edition. It is short, only nine pages long, but it is beautiful. There is something extremely neat and highly piquant about it. It looks easy to play; it is indeed not difficult. But the staccato! The shadings! They demand something of the player. But the piece is surely worthwhile, and it will be especially welcome in sociable company.[69]

In the first part of "Der Davidsbündler," published in the Komet in 1833, Schumann parodies the kind of pseudo-analysis in the longer reviews in the AmZ.[70] In his own review of a series of rondos in 1836, he mimics the shorter type:

> About the first rondo, one might, in the humdrum style of music criticism, say something like this: "The rondo—not an easy one—is in A-flat major, and is an elaboration of a theme by the popular and prolific Auber. As one cannot deny that the

---

68. For an example, see Fink's review of the Trio, op. 95, by J. P. Pixis in the AmZ, _33_ (1831), 233–35.

69. AmZ, _34_ (1832), 580. See Appendix I, 13.

70. See GSK, 2, 264.

(presumably still young) composer has a knowledge of modern, brilliant passage work, so . . . etc. There are no significant printing errors." Though I admit to having seen some bad reviews, never before in a piece of music have I run into such talentless impotence, such unredeemable nothingness and unspeakable wretchedness. Before it everything withers—the normal observations of a short review, any witty insinuations about saws, carpentry,[71] and the like. Jammed between two planks, one stands at the edge of the world, unable to go forward or back. Out the window with it![72]

Fink's music reviews, like his editorials, began to change color in the middle 1830s under the pressure applied by Schumann and the NZfM. His reviews of Chopin's music became increasingly long, ambiguous, and sometimes unfavorable; those of Herz's and Thalberg's music became more and more defensive. The AmZ was gradually forced from its position as caterer to public taste; it became more and more an organ for veiled but bitter polemics.

Now it would be agreeable if we could say that the protracted hostilities between the two editors were all Fink's fault; for here, surely, is a clear case of high standards versus no standards, of artistic sensibility set over against undiluted philistinism—and besides, in the perspective of history Schumann has turned out to be important and Fink a nonentity. But it was not that simple. Schumann's antipathy for Fink and the AmZ—an antipathy that loomed large in the shaping of the policies of the NZfM and of his own criticism—included a generous admixture of personal pique, and Schumann was not nearly always above reproach in his dealings with the rival editor.

The roots of this quarrel go back to Schumann's attempts to get his review of Chopin's *Là ci darem* variations published in the AmZ in 1831. He sent this unsolicited article to Fink on September 27, enclosing with it a letter about which the respectable, middle-aged editor might understandably be irritated. The twenty-one-year-old Schumann brashly proposed to lighten Fink's labors by contributing his own services as a "Mitarbeiter" for the AmZ. This article, he explained, was only the first of a series which, when completed, he speculated, might appear under the title "Cäciliana," "Odeon," "Kritische Phan-

---

71. The composer's name is S. A. Zimmermann.
72. NZfM, 4 (1836), 208–09. See Appendix I, 14.

tasien," or "Synoptische Blätter." He asked Fink to let him know soon when the articles would be published.[73] On November 10, having received no answer, Schumann wrote again, asking Fink, in effect, either to print the review or return it, since he now had an opportunity to publish it in the *Allgemeiner musikalischer Anzeiger* of Vienna.[74]

On December 7, 1831, Fink finally printed Schumann's famous essay, and the shadowy characters Florestan, Eusebius, and Raro first capered about in the real world. But the context in which it appeared was less than propitious. Fink placed immediately after it a review of the same piece written in the typical fashion of the AmZ; and he prefaced them both with this announcement:

> We are giving two opinions of the same work together here; the first is by a young man who has called himself a representative of modernity; the other is by a recognized and distinguished representative of the older school. He has not called himself this, but we hardly need give assurances that he is thoroughly qualified, experienced, and widely informed.[75]

Now it appears that what Fink published was in fact only half of Schumann's review; he had sent the second half back to Schumann and regarded the matter as closed. In a letter of April, 1832, Schumann asks Ignaz Castelli, editor of the Viennese *Allgemeiner musikalischer Anzeiger* to publish the remainder—which he never did.[76] And it is perfectly clear from the language of the letter that the question of publishing this article in Castelli's paper had not come up before; Schumann's claim in his letter to Fink of November 10 that his essay had been accepted by the Vienna journal was obviously groundless.

Schumann did not publish another word in Fink's journal, though, it appears, he tried to; in 1832 someone, at least, was forcing an altera-

73. *Jugendbriefe*, pp. 154–55.

74. *Briefe*, pp. 33–34.

75. AmZ, *33* (1831), 805. See Appendix I, 15. Schumann's cause is not helped by a misprint which identifies him as "K. Schumann." Fink appended a postscript to the second review promising later to print a review of the same piece by Wieck. This never materialized.

76. *Briefe*, p. 36. Thus only half of Schumann's best-known prose work is available to us. This has escaped even the most recent biographers of Schumann; Paula and Walter Rehberg write in their recent bulky work, *Robert Schumann, sein Leben und Werk* (Zürich, 1954), p. 88, "To Schumann's astonishment, the editor-in-chief, G. W. Fink, printed his Chopin article word-for-word." The second half of this review is apparently lost; neither Jansen nor Kreisig mentions its existence.

tion of the traditionally relaxed policies of the journal[77] by sending in unwelcome copy. On May 16, 1832, Fink prints this notice:

Because of something absurd that has happened (out of consideration for the responsible party we will not explain it), we are obliged to recall once again: no review can be accepted which is not assigned to the author in advance by the editor. Otherwise unnecessary irregularities and misunderstandings will multiply. The experienced will know this; the reasonably thoughtful will gladly take this into consideration; the others will not wish to trouble themselves and us in vain.[78]

Only Schumann could be so successful in arousing Fink's ire.

The quarrel with Fink did more than close an important outlet for Schumann's incipient efforts as a critic; it delayed appreciably the spread of his reputation as a composer. It was in 1831 to 1833 that Schumann's earliest compositions were published.[79] As was customary, Schumann sent review copies to the AmZ, apparently even before the music was released to the public. His opus 1 accompanied the letter he sent to Fink on November 10, 1831.[80] In no hurry whatever to review the compositions of his very temporary "Mitarbeiter," Fink did not mention Schumann's music until September 11, 1833—almost two years later.[81] At that time he printed his own review of almost all Schumann's music published to date: op. 1, and op. 3-5.[82] This

77. Rochlitz had explained, "We will gladly accept articles that are sent in if they would be of interest to our readers." AmZ, *1* (1798), *Intelligenz-Blatt* no. 1, p. 1.

78. AmZ, *34* (1832), 339. See Appendix I, 16.

79. The *Abegg* variations, op. 1, and *Papillons,* op. 2, were printed by Kistner in 1831. The *Etudes on Caprices of Paganini,* op. 3, Intermezzi, op. 4, and *Impromptus on a Theme of Clara Wieck,* op. 5, were published by Hofmeister in 1832–33.

80. *Briefe,* p. 33.

81. In August 1833, while busily laying plans to establish a rival journal, and launching blistering attacks upon the established ones, including the AmZ, Schumann sent Fink his Impromptus and, with tongue-in-cheek, wrote:

Your silence about several compositions I sent you years ago is very surprising and painful for me, especially since I do not know why I should deserve this slighting treatment. Nevertheless I shall try once more to prevail upon you for a critical notice of the accompanying impromptus. I ask you, sir, not to count me among those who would aggravate the difficulties an editor already faces; and I assure you that I should never have taken this step—perhaps an immodest one—if it were not for my aged, troubled mother, who in every letter inquires anxiously, "But why is there nothing about you in the Leipzig paper?" And every time I must answer, "Mother, I just don't know." In this perhaps you, sir, may find an excuse for this letter. *Jugendbriefe,* pp. 225–26.

82. AmZ, *35* (1833), 613–17.

critique is on the surface blandly neutral, but it has overtones of condescension and bitterness that Fink usually reserved for Chopin reviews. While Schumann is "obviously talented," he says, the idea of transcribing Paganini's pieces in his opus 3 wasn't original—it was borrowed from Kalkbrenner's *Pianoforte-Schule*. He takes issue with the suggestion in Schumann's Introduction that one prepare for playing these pieces by improvising "fantasias," and in the Impromptus, op. 5, he finds excessive "excrescences."

Schumann felt he had been damned with faint praise, and this review added fuel to the flame of his controversy with Fink. Schumann was probably the writer of an attack on Fink that appeared in *Der Komet* very shortly thereafter; the grievances it airs are exactly Schumann's: Fink's judgments of music are neither hot nor cold.[83] Fink strikes back in the November 13 issue of his paper. Without hazarding a guess as to its author, he labels the attack in *Der Komet* "retched-out gall from beginning to end . . . It is admittedly true," he says, "that this journal indulges in neither slovenly praise nor crude insult; we gladly leave these virtues to all who feel themselves called to such high things." [84] And a month later Fink finds it necessary once more to defend himself against the "little man of gall" who writes in *Der Komet*—doubtless Schumann.[85]

Fink's next outburst is unmistakably directed toward Schumann. In an irrelevant (and somewhat unintelligible) appendix to a long article defending his paper against a slighting remark in the Berlin *Freimütige Zeitung für gebildete, unbefangene Leser,* Fink complains of the vexations an editor has to put up with:

> Bündler left, Bündler right, Figaro here, Figaro there! We have, if you will permit, a proposition which we would like to print presently, for the sake of all those souls who unfortunately have not been sufficiently acclaimed in these pages—i.e. according to their own lofty estimation of their own extraordinary merit. This cannot easily even be intimated properly by means of just any

83. Since this article has remained unavailable to me, my information about it is derived entirely from Fink's response to it. He reports that it is entitled "Curiosum," appears in no. 44 of the *Beilage* to *Der Komet,* and is dated Nov. 1 (1833). At this time Schumann was a regular associate of Carl Herlesssohn, editor of *Der Komet* (see *Jugendbriefe*, pp. 176 and 229); on December 14, it will be recalled, Herlesssohn published the first of Schumann's *Davidsbündler* articles in his journal.

84. AmZ, 35 (1833), 772.

85. AmZ, 35 (1833), 873-74.

language, much less actually expressed. At the right time, a little place and a fitting word will be found for this.[86]

Kreisig knew of this notice, but mistakenly took it for an answer to a favorable review in the *Freimütige* of the prospectus for the NZfM.[87] But that review appeared on April 10; Fink's notice is in the AmZ of March 12, and the prospectus for the NZfM is dated March 16. It is safe to presume that the "Bündler" bothering Fink were the ones in Schumann's *Davidsbündler* articles—they had appeared in *Der Komet* about two months previously. The characters Florestan, Eusebius, and Raro had participated in the Chopin review of 1831; but the name and notion "Davidsbund" first became public in these later essays.

By 1834, when Schumann had his own journal, the rift with Fink was complete, and reciprocal animosity was built into the editorial policy of both papers. It was only for the AmZ, however, that this hostility became an obsession, almost a raison d'être. Fink's strategy was to launch continuous assaults at Schumann and the NZfM, without ever mentioning either by name—which sometimes makes the AmZ strange reading for anyone who doesn't know about this. Almost all of Fink's editorials, beginning in 1834, are veiled attacks on the NZfM, its criticism, the music it favors, and the music its editor composes. The same is true of many of his reviews, whatever their ostensible subject.[88]

The strife between the two journals continued to be a hindrance to Schumann in his struggle for recognition as a piano composer. He was not able to introduce his works himself through performance— the usual way of presenting them to the public—and now his compositions were denied any mention in the oldest and most widely-disseminated of the German musical journals. Even in his occasional

86. AmZ, *36* (1834), 180. See Appendix I, 17.

87. GSK, *2*, 372. Kreisig quotes the end of this review: "During the course of this year it should become clear whether or not the older journal [the AmZ], formerly so worthwhile, will take on new vigor, or doze on in senility, no longer able to cope with contemporary issues."

88. A review of the fifteenth volume of *Caecilia*, for example, is nothing but an attack on the *Journalschau* in the NZfM. AmZ, *36* (1834), 458–60. And in another review, while he allows that Chopin shows some promise, Fink warns him to beware of his "friends." AmZ, *36* (1834), 539. In a Chopin review of 1835 (*37*, 337–38), he parodies the rapturous style of Schumann's earlier reviews, closing with a plea that the musical world be spared the excesses of Chopin's imitators. Several of Fink's reviews, such as that of Hummel's Etudes, op. 125 (AmZ, *37* [1835], 164–65) can be understood only as rejoinders to reviews in the NZfM of the same music.

THE GOALS OF THE JOURNAL

"Uebersichten" of recent piano music, which amount to nothing more than lists of publications, Fink for years omitted Schumann's name altogether.[89] But Schumann's claim[90] in 1842 that none of his piano compositions had been discussed in the AmZ for ten years was not strictly accurate. While there had been no formal review of Schumann's works since September of 1833, Fink could hardly avoid mentioning the *Carnaval* when Liszt played selections from it in Leipzig on March 30, 1840. He wrote,

> The *Carnaval*-scenes of R. Schumann, despite the excellent playing of Herr Liszt, did not have the effect expected of them. This resulted especially from excessive length; it would surely have been better to choose a more limited selection of these scenes, instead of performing so many of them (ten) all at once, and in immediate succession.[91]

Schumann's disgust with the policies of the AmZ—together with his personal animosity toward Fink—provided perhaps the strongest and most immediate impetus toward the founding of the NZfM. While the ensuing polemics threw the AmZ entirely off its normal course, they seemed to have almost a stabilizing effect on the NZfM. Its writers behaved in this wrangle with the self-possession and humor —Schumann was fond of calling the AmZ "die allgemeinste musikalische Zeitung"—of men who knew right was on their side. Again and again, pressure from the rival journal with its diametrically opposed policies and tastes forced the writers of the NZfM to clarify their position and sharpen their opinions. In this way the sour visage of Fink, always present in the background, served as a continuous reminder of what the NZfM was all about,[92] and as time passed it helped preserve some of the vigor and exuberance of the journal's first years.

89. A composition of Schumann appears in such a list for the first time in 1840 (AmZ, *42*, 12).
90. *Briefe*, p. 218.
91. AmZ, *42* (1840), 298. See Appendix I, 18.
92. The strife between the two musical journals in Leipzig continued unabated until Fink retired at the end of 1841, and his post was taken by C. F. Becker, a friend of Schumann and regular contributor to the NZfM. Commenting on Fink's rather theatrical announcement of his own retirement (AmZ, *43* [1841], 1135-36), the NZfM had this to say: "Herr Dr. Fink, who otherwise treads about very lightly, is taking rather a noisy leave of the editorship of the AmZ. Just read him. He even speaks of enemies he has acquired—referring, clearly, to this journal. He errs. We have never troubled ourselves much about him, and we don't plan to do so in the future." NZfM, *16* (1842), 8. See Appendix I, 19.

CHAPTER 3

Ṫꞕe Ꞑature of tꞕe Ꞧournal

For all Schumann's opposition to the policies and practices of the AmZ, his journal came out looking, outwardly at least, remarkably like the venerable organ of Breitkopf und Härtel; its format, the general kinds of articles it included, and its method of arranging its contents under various headings all depended strongly upon the AmZ. During the final preparations for launching the NZfM, it will be remembered, Schumann sent home to Zwickau for back issues of the AmZ,[1] and he seems to have studied them closely.

Schumann's journal, like the AmZ, is made up of general articles, or "freie Aufsätze" on various subjects, reviews of recently published music (and occasionally books), reports of musical performances, correspondence articles (usually concert reports) from other cities, and miscellaneous announcements of things having to do with music.[2] General articles, unlike most of the other contents, do not appear under a rubric in either journal.[3] Both papers publish reports from other cities under the rubric "Correspondenz," while other reports and announcements appear in the NZfM under the somewhat fluid headings, "Chronik," "Vermischtes," and "Tagesbegebenheiten," and in the AmZ, under "Nachrichten."

1. *Jugendbriefe*, p. 233 (see above, p. 10, n. 34). The prospectus for the NZfM shows certain similarities to the one Rochlitz printed in the *Intelligenz-Blatt* of the first issue of the AmZ. But Schumann probably did not have Rochlitz' prospectus before him when he drew up his own, since the letter requesting the early volumes of the AmZ is dated three days later than the prospectus of the NZfM.

2. Bigenwald, pp. 34–35, provides a good description of the format of the AmZ.

3. They are described somewhat flamboyantly in the prospectus of the NZfM as "theoretical and historical essays, articles dealing with aesthetics, grammar, pedagogy, biography, acoustics, etc." NZfM, *1* (1834), 1. In the prospectus for the AmZ they are called "short discussions of philosophical or historical subjects in the field of music—but presented in such a way that not only the aesthetician, but every alert musician and music lover will find them interesting, understandable, and enjoyable." AmZ, *1* (1798), *Intelligenz-Blatt* no. 1, p. 1. The NZfM in its prospectus also promises to include certain things not to be found in the AmZ: "belletristic pieces, short musical tales, fantasies, scenes from life, humorous items, poems that are particularly good for setting to music." See Appendix I, 6. The mottos in every issue of the NZfM are another feature entirely independent of the AmZ.

The initial number of each volume of the AmZ was decorated with a portrait of some famous musician—J. S. Bach, J. A. P. Schulze, C. P. E. Bach, and many others. Even this detail the NZfM at first imitated. Schumann had intended originally to include a portrait of Spohr with the first issue of the journal;[4] but he did not fulfill this intention until 1835, when he became editor-in-chief.

From its earliest issues, the AmZ provided its readers (at no extra cost) periodic musical supplements; they contained musical examples too extensive to be included in the text of its reviews, and sometimes even entire compositions.[5] Since the NZfM had no connection with a music publisher, it was not easy for Schumann to follow suit. When the NZfM was published by Hartmann and Barth, the only music in it was a few brief examples. Its third publisher, Robert Friese, was better equipped to print music,[6] and immediately after he took charge in July 1837, plans for musical supplements were set in motion. Schumann requested contributions for them as early as August 17, and outlined elaborate plans for them in a letter to Moscheles of August 23;[7] two announcements of his plans appeared in the NZfM of 1837, in October and December.[8]

These musical supplements were very important to Schumann; he intended that they should play a role close to the central aims of the journal. The music in the supplements, he explained, was to be reviewed in the journal, so that the subscriber could read the review

---

4. See *Jugendbriefe*, p. 221.

5. There was an immediate precedent for this practice in J. A. Hiller's *Wöchentliche Nachrichten und Anmerkungen die Musik betreffend* (Leipzig, 1766–70). The weekly issues of this journal often ended with short compositions. Longer ones were continued from issue to issue, for instance, the duet "Dal tuo soglio" from Hasse's oratorio *Sant' Elena al Calvario* in *1* (1766), 349–52 and 360–62. This duet (as well as the beginning of the chorus "Di quanta pena," *1*, 328–30) are given in connection with an extended discussion of the oratorio. The printing of complete musical compositions was characteristic of the late eighteenth-century journals, like Hiller's, addressed to the "Kenner und Liebhaber." *Der musikalische Dilettante*, another such journal, was modeled after the *Wöchentliche Nachrichten*, and regularly devoted the second half of each issue to music. See *Freystätter, Die musikalischen Zeitschriften*, p. 19, and Kurt Dolinski, *Die Anfänge der musikalischen Fachpresse in Deutschland* (Berlin, n.d.), pp. 145–46. Ferdinand Krome, the pioneer of research in musical journalism, distinguishes a special type of periodical called "Musikjournal" which consisted almost entirely of music. The earliest of these was Telemann's *Getreuer Musikmeister* (1728). Hiller's similar *Wöchentlicher musikalischer Zeitvertreib* appeared in 1759–60. F. Krome, *Die Anfänge des musikalischen Journalismus* (Leipzig, 1896), p. 6.

6. Friese printed the first edition of Schumann's *Davidsbündlertänze* op. 6, in 1837.

7. *Briefe*, pp. 90 and 92–93.

8. NZfM, 7 (1837), 120 and 196.

while looking at the music. The purpose of such a review, then, would not be simply to recommend that the reader buy or not buy this music. It would instead have a kind of didactic aim; it would present, plainly documented, the editors' ideas about what constitutes good music.[9] This aim was in harmony with the professed designs of the NZfM. Its criticism was supposed to be didactic; it was meant to enlighten the reader and win him over to a certain point of view, not merely to amuse him—and certainly not to sell him anything.

Besides serving as grist for the mills of the journal's criticism, Schumann said, the musical supplements would provide an outlet for the music of talented young composers who found the road to public recognition difficult[10]—i.e. composers like Schumann. The supplements served this purpose in printing music by men such as Adolph Henselt, Stephen Heller, Oswald Lorenz, K. Kossmaly, Ferdinand Hiller, Wilhelm Taubert, J. J. H. Verhulst, and Schumann himself.[11] Though the idea of printing music in conjunction with the journal was probably borrowed from the AmZ, Schumann's supplements, here again, served the peculiar interests of the NZfM.

The articles that together with the "freie Aufsätze" accounted for most of the space in both journals were the reviews of new music. It

9. The musical supplements appeared quarterly from 1838 to 1841, and Schumann himself reviewed its volumes *1*, *2*, and *3* (though not so extensively as the original announcement might have led one to expect). NZfM, *8* (1838), 164; 9 (1838), 106 and 174.

10. NZfM, 7 (1837), 120.

11. Eight compositions of Schumann are printed in the supplements:

1) "Intermezzo" (Suppl. *2*, 12). This piece was taken from the *Novelletten*, op. 21, published by Breitkopf und Härtel two months earlier (March, 1838).

2) "Gigue" (Suppl., *5*, 16). Taken from the *Scherzo, Romanze und Fughetta*, op. 32, published the preceding year by Schuberth.

3) "Fragment aus Nachtstücke" (Suppl. *8*, 11). This piece was not included in the *Nachtstücke* op. 23; instead Schumann incorporated it into his *Faschingsschwank aus Wien* op. 26, under the title "Intermezzo." The supplement edition of it thus constitutes a "pre-first edition." That this piece was not originally intended for the *Faschingsschwank* seems to have eluded all of the writers on Schumann's works. See e.g. P. and W. Rehberg, *Schumann*, p. 483.

4) Two songs of Robert Burns, "Hauptmanns Weib" and "Weit, Weit!" (Suppl., *9*, 13 and 15), published the same year (1840) by Breitkopf und Härtel in the four volumes of *Lieder* op. 25.

5) "Fughetta" (Suppl., *10*, 14). See no. 2 above.

6) "Nur ein lächelnder Blick" (Suppl., *12*, 14), published in the same year by Whistling as op. 27, no. 5.

7) "Stille Thränen" (Suppl., *13*, 13), from the *Lieder* op. 35 published the previous year (1840) by Klemm.

8) "Mondnacht" (Suppl., *14*, 9), from the *Lieder* op. 35 published in 1840 by Heinze.

was in its music criticism more than anything else that the AmZ had offended Schumann, and the criticism in the NZfM showed a vivid contrast to it. All the same, the reviews in Schumann's journal are cast in the same forms as those in the AmZ: extensive critiques appearing, often, under the rubric "Kritik" (equivalent to the "Recension" of the AmZ), and brief notices under the heading "Anzeiger" ("kurze Anzeigen" in the AmZ).

Reviews of printed music had always been a prominent feature of the AmZ. When it was founded in 1798, this feature was relatively new to musical journalism—enough so, at least, that several articles in the early AmZ were devoted to an explanation of it.[12] The practice had grown up in the last four decades of the eighteenth century in the musical journals intended for the *Kenner und Liebhaber*, the earliest and most important of which was J. A. Hiller's *Wöchentliche Nachrichten und Anmerkungen die Musik betreffend*.[13] Reviews of music are a regular feature of this periodical; they are usually of considerable length, and, though gentle in tone, honestly critical.[14] The

12. AmZ, *1* (1798), *Intelligenz-Blatt* no. 1, p. 3, and *5* (1802), 445–52. See Bigenwald, *Die Anfänge der leipziger AmZ*, pp. 72–74.

13. The distinction between the *Künstler, Kenner* and *Liebhaber* is explained at length in the article "Kenner" in J. G. Sulzer's *Allgemeine Theorie der schönen Künste* (Biel, 1777), Theil 2, Bd. *1*, pp. 5–14. J. A. Hiller recognized three classes of Kenner. See *Wöchentliche Nachrichten, 3* (1768), 327. See also Arnold Schering's "Künstler, Kenner, und Liebhaber der Musik im Zeitalter Haydns und Goethes" in *Jahrbuch der Musikbibliothek Peters, 38* (1931), 9–23. There was an earlier class of musical journals intended for an amateur, middle-class audience: those modeled after the literary "moral weeklies." One of the first German literary moral weeklies was directed by a musician: Mattheson's *Vernünftler* (1713–14), which consisted mostly of translated selections from the *Tatler* and *Spectator* papers. Mattheson was also responsible for the earliest musical moral weekly, *Der musikalische Patriot* (1728). Dolinski (*Die Anfänge der musikalischen Fachpresse,* pp. 32ff.) discusses at length the impact of the moral weeklies upon German musical journalism. The primary distinction between the musical moral weeklies and the later "Kenner und Liebhaber" journals was this: the former consisted mostly of discussions of abstract questions in music; the latter avowedly dealt with current musical events. In the first issue of his periodical Hiller declared, "We will devote our attention to that which, so to speak, takes place before our eyes."

14. See, for instance, the reviews in the first volume, pp. 19, 28, 35, 36, 45, 52, etc. Hiller's journal is the earliest, so far as I know, to include reviews of music with anything approaching this kind of regularity. The earliest German musical journals, beginning with Mattheson's *Critica musica* (1722–25), Mizler's *Musikalische Bibliothek* (irregularly from 1735–54), and Scheibe's *Critischer Musicus* (1737–40), reviewed books more than music. But in his *Critica musica*, Mattheson includes a most extensive and detailed critique of Handel's early St. John's Passion (without mentioning the composer's name), a critique really amounting to an insidious comparison of Handel's work to his own setting of the text. *Critica musica, 2*, 1–56. This isolated critique can hardly be counted as a forerunner of

music criticism of the early AmZ stood in this tradition, and Rochlitz' policies closely resembled Hiller's: attention was focused on good music; bad music was to be ignored rather than castigated.[15] In the early years of Fink's administration this policy degenerated to the point where the possibility of bad music was no longer acknowledged.

There was nothing new, then, about the preoccupation of the NZfM with criticism of published music, or even with the format of its reviews; in both it followed the example of the AmZ. But here the resemblance ended. Schumann and his colleagues set up formidable standards for musical composition, and on the basis of these standards meted out praise and blame with equal relish. As a result the gentleness and cordiality traditional in music criticism were missing, and in their place there was a new professionalism and a new seriousness. This seriousness was nothing at all like Rellstab's hand-wringing despair about the passing of the older style; the criticism in the NZfM had an almost enlightenment-like progressiveness and optimism, together with— and this would have been anathema to the enlightenment sensibility, or at least to Voltaire—a tone of ardent enthusiasm.

Musical journals toward the end of the eighteenth century were directed toward an ever-expanding circle of readers—which corresponded to an ever-expanding musical audience.[16] A symptom of this change was the gradual disappearance in the titles of musical journals of the word "kritisch"—a word ubiquitous in German periodical and

---

Hiller's or Rochlitz' criticism, especially since neither of the works under consideration was at the time published. The earliest example I have been able to locate in a German periodical of a sustained series of reviews of published music is in the second volume of F. W. Marpurg's *Kritische Briefe über die Tonkunst*, 1761, in the *Briefe* 82–89 (pp. 141–95).

15. The distinction between two classes of reviews (the long and short types imitated by the NZfM) was originally a part of this policy. Rochlitz explained it this way in the *Intelligenz-Blatt* accompanying the first issue of the AmZ (see Appendix I, 20):

> a. Only the best and most important musical publications will be treated extensively, and it will be indicated not only that they are outstanding, but also what it is that makes them so.
>
> b. Compositions which are not bad, but also not really distinguished will be treated in a short notice. Their special characteristics will be pointed out, and it will be indicated for whom they would be appropriate; this would spare amateur musicians from buying music, as they so often do, which is all right in itself, but simply not for them.
>
> c. Inconsiderable and downright bad music will be noted—simply as existing—in the *Intelligenz-Blatt*.

16. Eberhard Preussner's *Die bürgerliche Musikkultur, ein Beitrag zur deutschen Musikgeschichte des 18. Jahrhunderts* (Hamburg, 1935 and Kassel, 1954) gives a well documented chronicle of the changing and expanding musical audience of the eighteenth century.

book titles since Gottsched's *Versuch einer kritischen Dichtkunst* (1730).[17] A term that took its place in the early nineteenth century was "allgemein." [18] More and more journals in literature and the arts now were meant not primarily for professional scholars or artists, or even for serious amateurs, but for the educated general public. Of the musical journals, the AmZ shows this most clearly; it was designed for a larger and more diverse circle of readers than any of the earlier musical journals.[19]

If "allgemein" points to one characteristic of the AmZ, namely its broad appeal, "Zeitung" indicates another. Bigenwald cites a letter of Rochlitz from 1805 in which he complains, "Against my will, the journal is becoming almost nothing but a 'Zeitung'—but what can be done about it?" Bigenwald continues,

> The AmZ is not, in fact, a *Zeitschrift* written for a small group of professionals and treating profound scholarly problems, but a *Zeitung*, addressed to every layman interested in music who wishes to inform himself about the most recent musical events. Not only the various kinds of reports, but also the articles dealing with the most recent state of affairs in diverse musical areas are coördinated to this end.[20]

Joachim Kirchner, author of several authoritative works on the history of German journals and journalism, provides a careful distinction between "Zeitschrift" and "Zeitung"—one which, he says, was in force since the end of the seventeenth century: the Zeitung is supposed to treat current matters, and inform its readers about them promptly. To describe this essential attribute of the Zeitung, Kirchner uses the very handy French word—often a snare for the unvigilant first-year student of French—"actualité." Actualité was not expected

---

17. Arnold Schering, in his article "Aus der Geschichte der musikalischen Kritik in Deutschland," *Peters Jahrbuch, 35* (1928), 13, says that the term "kritisch" implied not only "evaluation," but also "investigation."

18. The AmZ of Leipzig was the first musical journal to make use of this term in its name. Freystätter (pp. 33–55) lists ten other musical journals founded between 1798 and 1834 with this word in their titles.

19. Bigenwald (pp. 60–63) indicates that, though intended first of all for the casual amateur, the AmZ made efforts to offer something even for the professional musician. Its circulation, vastly larger than that of any previous musical journal, amounted for many years to about 1000—an unusually large number at this time for any kind of "Fachzeitung."

20. Bigenwald, p. 60. "Zeitschrift" is the approximate equivalent of the English "journal." "Zeitung" is more like "news magazine" or "newspaper."

of the Zeitschrift; its contents tended to be more general, more abstract, and more critical.[21] Among the musical journals, Hiller's *Wöchentliche Nachrichten*, the AmZ, and the vast majority of the other nineteenth-century musical periodicals fall easily into the category of the Zeitung.

Schumann was very eager that his journal should be neither "general" nor a "news magazine." He intended it, in the first place, for a much more select circle of readers than that of the AmZ. It was established by professional musicians who had special interests to promote. It was addressed primarily to people who might be expected to share its point of view, and who might have some influence in implementing its aims: musicians first of all (composers, teachers, performers), and anyone else seriously concerned about the state of German music. The NZfM was not at all intended for the typical readers of the AmZ: people who were interested in music only as a pleasant diversion. And the NZfM was far less committed to reporting the facts of the current musical scene than would be expected of a Zeitung. It had far fewer concert reviews than did, for instance, the AmZ, and often took up whole series of concerts in a single review— Schumann, an inveterate concert-goer, was in the habit of writing about a whole season of them in the spring.[22] Concert reviews in the *Neue Zeitschrift*, moreover, tended to focus upon music, not performances.

But if the seriousness and professional standards of the NZfM tended to restrict its circle of readers, its range of subject matter had exactly the opposite effect: the journal always showed a keen interest in the sister arts, and it clearly reflects, particularly, Schumann's own preoccupation with literature. The longest article in the first volume of the NZfM is August Bürck's review of the published correspondence between Goethe and Zelter, and in the issue completing this review, Schumann explains, "We do not mean to share with our fellow art lovers only that having to do immediately with music. We wish also to provide them enjoyment and spiritual nourishment with things that would interest them as connoisseurs of the arts in general." [23]

21. Joachim Kirchner, *Die Grundlagen des deutschen Zeitschriftwesens* (Leipzig, 1928), *I*, 23–25.
22. See NZfM, *8* (1838), 107, 111, 115, and *12* (1840), 139, 143, 151, 154, 159.
23. NZfM, *1* (1834), 36. Schumann loved to collect statements about music from literary

Some of the most important movements in German intellectual history during the century before Schumann owed their success at least partly to that marvelous seventeenth-century invention, the periodical. It allowed for immediate dissemination of new ideas and theories, and made possible public discussion, clarification, and, if necessary, retraction of them. Thus the writings of the Berlin circle of Lessing, Mendelssohn, and Nicolai appeared in the *Bibliothek der schönen Wissenschaften und freien Künste* and *Briefe, die neuste Literatur betreffend*. Schiller's most influential treatise, *Ueber naïve und sentimentalische Dichtung* was first published as a series of essays in *Die Horen*, and the single most important document in early romanticism was the *Athenaeum*—again a periodical publication.

In the eighteenth century, significant developments in music theory and music criticism as well took place in the pages of journals, notably those of Mattheson, Scheibe, and Hiller. But the great rash of musical periodicals in the earlier nineteenth century was something quite different; most of them only catered to popular taste instead of attempting to guide it. And the exceptions, such as the journals of Rellstab and Fétis, were the work of men whose sensibilities belonged to the preceding generation.

Among musical journals of its time, the NZfM was unique; partisan, but progressive, seeking to enlighten rather than to entertain, it had, in a certain sense, more in common with contemporary literary journals than with the musical ones. Nor was this an accident; Schumann, musician and littérateur, consciously adopted for his journal the seriousness and rigor he saw in literary criticism and found utterly wanting in contemporary musical periodicals.

Like several of the best-known literary journals, the NZfM quickly established itself in Germany as the organ for a special movement or school of opinion. Thus some older German writers have been tempted to seek out specific counterparts in the literary world for Schumann's circle and its journal. Two of them, quite independently and, I believe, quite mistakenly, have seen Schumann's group and the NZfM as a musical counterpart of the exactly contemporaneous *Junges Deutsch-*

---

sources, and occasionally he printed them in the NZfM. In explanation of a dozen quotations from Novalis in the NZfM, 5 (1836), 189, he wrote "It should be of interest to get to know the views about our art held by important people, even though they are not professional musicians."

land movement.[24] It is true that the protagonists of *Das junge Deutschland*, Wienbarg, Gutzkow, and Mundt, assaulted conventional bourgeois values with the same enthusiasm as Schumann attacked his Philistines, but this is only a superficial resemblance. For *Das junge Deutschland* was really less of a literary or artistic movement than a political one; it was political enough, at least, so that the writings of its principal members were suppressed in 1835 by the German *Bundestag*. Schumann and his group witnessed the most turbulent days of the German struggle for unification and the radical uprisings against restoration powers of which Metternich was the figurehead. Their corner of Germany, in fact, was the center for political radicalism led by *Das junge Deutschland*. Neither Schumann nor the NZfM has anything whatever to say about all of this. Only once did Schumann show any concern about the Metternich system: he feared for a time that the severity of censorship laws in Vienna might prevent him from moving the NZfM there. But he hopefully asked Fischhof if the Viennese government could possibly object to a journal so single-mindedly devoted to the arts as his was.[25]

Even as a literary movement *Das junge Deutschland* showed a kind of nihilistic radicalism thoroughly at odds with the tenets of Schumann and his journal. Rejecting late romantic writers for suspected royalist and Catholic leanings, and Goethe and Schiller for their scant interest in politics, the writers for this movement consciously cut themselves off from virtually their entire heritage in German literature. Nothing in Schumann's ideas bears any resemblance to this. Intent upon reviving central traditions in music temporarily obscured, Schumann worshipped at the shrines of Bach, Beethoven, and Schubert—as well as those of Goethe and Shakespeare—with a piety unknown to the *Junges Deutschland* circle.

If there were literary counterparts to the NZfM and its artistic principles, they were not among the contemporaneous political-literary feuilletons. To find a literary journal showing similar idealism and progressiveness coupled with a similar regard for tradition, we must

24. Freystätter, *Die musikalischen Zeitschriften*, p. 57, and A. Schering, "Aus den Jugendjahren der musikalischen Neuromantik," *Peters Jahrbuch*, 24 (1917), 49ff. In his recent article "Romantik" in *Die Musik in Geschichte und Gegenwart*, 11, 799, Friedrich Blume restates this idea.

25. *Briefe*, pp. 127–28.

go back to the journals of early literary romanticism—perhaps to the *Athenaeum* itself. During its first decade the NZfM was stamped with the personality of Schumann. If it looked like a product of early romanticism, this was because of his convictions and inclinations. And it was with the early romantics that Schumann's strongest affinities lay.

PART II

Schumann as Editor and Critic
for the
Neue Zeitschrift für Musik

CHAPTER 4

Schumann's Role as Editor and Writer

It was largely because of Schumann's efforts, as we have seen, that the NZfM existed at all, and Schumann was never comfortable until he had full control of it. When in 1835 he became owner, business manager, and editor of the journal, he was determined to maintain a firm grip on its policies. And a firm grip it was, for a considerable degree of personal control was necessary to assure any uniformity and continuity in the journal when the original staff was replaced, after 1834, with a constantly changing procession of writers.

One way in which Schumann sought to maintain a united front for the journal was to seek out writers whose views he thought would coincide with his own. With tireless zeal he wrote letters again and again to valuable prospective writers, pleading, cajoling, even threatening them into contributing. He showed less interest in established critics or scholars than in practicing musicians, particularly composers. In February 1835, for example, he wrote persuasively to Moscheles in London, asking him to recommend someone to serve as the London correspondent (preferably a German), since he hardly dared hope that Moscheles himself would care for the job.[1] Some of the other composers Schumann approached from time to time were Carl Loewe, Heinrich Marschner, Wenzel J. Tomascheck, Otto Nicolai, William Sterndale Bennett, Wilhelm Taubert, and Heinrich Dorn.[2] But these efforts were not very successful; none of these men ever contributed substantially to the journal. The only composers of stature other than Schumann whose writings appeared in the NZfM in any quantity were Stephen Heller and Berlioz; beginning in 1840 Schumann printed a long series of Berlioz' reviews from the *Journal des debats*,[3]

1. *Briefe,* pp. 62–63. Moscheles did not accept, but he did contribute in 1836 a favorable review of Schumann's Sonata in F♯ Minor, op. 11. NZfM, *5,* 135–37.
2. See Boetticher's lists of musicians from whom Schumann requested contributions in *Einführung,* p. 137, n. 71, and 187, n. 7.
3. See NZfM, *12* (1840), 59ff.

and Heller (usually under the name "Jeanquirit") contributed a good many correspondence articles from Paris.

Once he had his contributors in tow, Schumann bombarded them with instructions and advice. He did this to Töpken, as we have seen, even before he became editor. Some of these instructions were about practical matters; for example he, like every other editor, encouraged his contributors to write short articles and to use no more musical examples than absolutely necessary.[4] But other instructions were meant to ensure an evenness of style and tone in the NZfM. Anton von Zuccamaglio and Karl Weitzmann were urged to emulate in their writing the fanciful tone of the *Davidsbündlerbriefe* by Heller and others[5]— which Zuccamaglio did with conspicuous success under the pseudonyms "Gottschalk Wedel" and "Waldbrühl."

Schumann sometimes simply refused to print articles even from "approved" writers. The essay on Franz Lachner's Prize Symphony by Zuccamaglio—which became well known because Schumann later printed it in the *Gesammelte Schriften* in conjunction with his own review of the symphony—was at first rejected.[6] In 1838 Schumann returned an article to his friend J. Fischhof in Vienna for rewriting, and subsequently refused also to publish the revised version.[7]

Another way Schumann exercised control over his journal was to subject contributions to vigorous editorial revision. A review,[8] for example, of Heinrich Dorn's opera *Schöffe von Paris*, Schumann reports in a letter to the composer, he found it necessary to revise because it was too "Fink-like." [9] In this way, by a careful consideration of writers for the journal, and a rigid process of selection, screening, and revision of copy, Schumann preserved the special character of the journal. He often did not hesitate to publish articles with which at

4. See e.g. *Briefe*, p. 113.

5. *Briefe*, pp. 70–71, and 79.

6. See *Briefe*, p. 80. Zuccamaglio's review, which was finally printed in the NZfM, 5 (1836), 147–48, really amounts to a veiled but pointed attack on Berlioz. Schumann was hesitant about printing it because the NZfM usually looked with favor upon Berlioz. His solution was to follow Zuccamaglio's article with his own (pp. 151–52), thus setting matters straight. The following year there was a sharp controversy in the NZfM—again about Berlioz—between Zuccamaglio and the theorist Johann Christian Lobe. This time the dispute was over the worth of Berlioz' *Francs-Juges* overture, and Schumann was inclined to agree with Zuccamaglio's low estimation of it. See *Briefe*, pp. 91–92.

7. See *Briefe*, pp. 117 and 123–24.

8. This review by Carl Alt appeared, presumably with Schumann's revisions, in the NZfM, *10* (1839), 155–56, 157–58, and 162–63.

9. *Briefe*, p. 153.

certain points he disagreed, but in the footnotes he always specified the stand of "die Redaction," that is, Schumann.[10]

Schumann supervised the contents of the NZfM down to the last detail. He was a compulsive proofreader, of his journal no less than of his musical compositions. And careful planning went into the arrangement of each issue. Long articles were divided neatly into installments—one of these was almost always in progress—and shorter pieces on a great variety of subjects (and by a great variety of authors) filled the remainder of the issues.

In the choice of music for review, too, the journal benefited from Schumann's firm control. It was customary for composers and music publishers to send copies of their new music to the journals for review; thus the editor would not normally exercise much control over the amount and kind of music on hand. Schumann was not satisfied with this arrangement. He explained,

> We do not subscribe to the policy of others who review only publications that are sent to them. Instead we take note of the most interesting music listed in the Hofmeister monthly report and try to procure it. Under this arrangement music that is more worthwhile is given a more prominent place, and a larger proportion of space is devoted to it than to less valuable things— which is as it should be.[11]

While everything about the journal did not always turn out exactly as hoped, the NZfM, largely as a result of Schumann's care and industry, makes uncommonly interesting and instructive reading.

When Schumann became editor of the NZfM in 1835, he began to review personally almost all new instrumental music other than organ music (which was assigned to C. F. Becker). Reviews of vocal music were usually undertaken by Banck, and later Oswald Lorenz. A great majority of the compositions criticized by Schumann in the earlier years of his editorship were for piano. He reviewed literally hundreds of etudes, rondos, variations, capriccios, and similar pieces, not only because they were there to be reviewed, but also because he was convinced that success in the lesser genres was important for composers

10. The bottoms of the pages of the NZfM are liberally sprinkled with Schumann's comments on other peoples' articles. See NZfM, 2 (1835), 135; 3 (1835), 55, 175; 4 (1836), 9; 5 (1836), 83; 8 (1838), 205; 9 (1838), 4, 9, 20, 27, etc.

11. NZfM, 6 (1837), 6. See Appendix I, 21.

and for musical culture as a whole. The enormous volume of piano music confronting Schumann in the 1830s led him to write composite reviews in which a large number of compositions of a single genre by various composers are discussed together. Three columns sufficed on one occasion to dispose of the rondos of twenty-one different composers.[12] Schumann usually adjusted these reviews in such a way as to feature the best pieces most prominently: articles were arranged in "ascending" order with the best saved until last.[13] That is why one must often wait until the end of Schumann's reviews to read about Schubert, Mendelssohn, or Chopin. The list of compositions for review usually had been edited in advance, moreover, so as to include only the "best" or "most interesting" pieces[14]—apparently Schumann sometimes found also very bad compositions interesting.

While the bulk of Schumann's writing for the NZfM before 1840 consisted of reviews of instrumental music, he also contributed articles in almost every other category: "freie Aufsätze" on a variety of subjects, concert reports, reviews of vocal music, even occasional reviews of books, and during his half-year's stay in Vienna, correspondence reports. Several writers on Schumann have perpetuated the fiction that Schumann never wrote reviews of vocal music until later in his career as a critic.[15] It is quite true that Schumann did not write reviews of vocal music as a matter of course until after 1839. In 1838, for example, he wrote to J. Vesque von Püttlingen, who had sent him his lieder for review, "Since the category of lieder is not my department, you will find a different cipher under the review of your songs." [16] Yet Schumann occasionally wrote critiques of vocal music, especially lieder, beginning with the earliest issues. In 1834, he reviewed a song by the famous singer Mme. Malibran and a "Mono-

12. NZfM, 6 (1837), 163–65.
13. Schumann explained, "The reader knows that we like to build up his interest, in such survey articles, by arranging the compositions in a definite order, so that he always has the best presented to him last." NZfM, 7 (1837), 131.
14. Schumann explains this in footnote to a composite review in NZfM, 4 (1836), 150.
15. Hermann Kretzschmar, for example, states categorically that Schumann's review of a performance of St. Paul in 1837 was the first notice Schumann took of contemporary vocal music. H. Kretzschmar, "Robert Schumann als Aesthetiker," Peters Jahrbuch, 13 (1906), 69. Kretzschmar apparently refers to Schumann's article "Fest in Zwickau," NZfM, 7 (1837), 31–32. Schumann's review of another oratorio performance (of Beethoven's Christus am Oelberg) appears as early as the second issue of the journal in 1834.
16. Briefe, p. 120.

drama" by J. Brandl,[17] and in 1835, two volumes of lieder by F. Oel-schläger.[18] In 1836 he undertook a whole series of reviews of lieder by Carl Loewe, Bernhard Klein, Heinrich Marschner, Ferdinand Steg-mayer, Joseph Klein, Heinrich Wilhelm Triest, Ferdinand Ries, and Wenzel Johann Tomaschek.[19]

When Schumann left Leipzig in September 1838 for a half-year's stay in Vienna, the volume of material he contributed to the NZfM was sharply cut, and from 1840 it dwindled progressively until his retirement from the journal in mid-1844. But from 1840—the year he suddenly turned to the composition of lieder—the proportion of his reviews dealing with vocal music increased markedly. Although Oswald Lorenz, the usual reviewer of lieder, remained an active member of the staff, from this time on Schumann wrote gradually increasing numbers of lieder reviews.[20] It was about this time, too, that Schumann's interest in dramatic music was quickened. It was in 1840 that he first began to write extended and serious critiques of operas and oratorios in score. Eschewing the fashionable French and Italian productions, he reviewed things like *Ravnen*, a Danish opera by J. P. E. Hartmann, C. G. Reissiger's *Adéle de Foix*, and Heinrich Esser's *Thomas Riquiqui*.[21] Among the oratorios that attracted Schumann's attention were *Die Zerstörung Jerusalems* by Ferdinand Hiller, *Der Erlöser* by Eduard Sobolewsky, and Carl Loewe's *Johann Huss*.[22]

Schumann's activities as writer and editor, conducted in the 1830s with such astonishing vigor and success, were enormously time-consuming. In about 1839 he began to begrudge the time given to the NZfM—time he would then have preferred to spend composing.[23] Schumann's burst of creative energy in 1840 produced a prodigious number of lieder, but left little time for the journal. And then Schumann's interest in dramatic music had also been awakened, as his critical writings testify. But the realization of the goal which most fascinated him, the writing of an opera, he confessed in a letter of

17. NZfM, *1* (1834), 15 and 19.
18. NZfM, *3* (1835), 175.
19. NZfM, *5* (1836), 143–44, 167–68, 175, 200–01.
20. Only one of the composers represented in these reviews, Robert Franz, has proved to be at all durable. Some of the others were Norbert Burgmüller, Ludwig Berger, Henry Hugh Pearson, Theodore Kirchner, and Karl Kossmaly.
21. NZfM, *13* (1840), 49–51; *17* (1842), 79–81; and *19* (1843), 41–42.
22. NZfM, *12* (1840), 120 and *14* (1841), 2–4; *15* (1841), 1–2; and *17* (1842), 119–22.
23. See *Briefe*, p. 153.

February 1840 to Keferstein, depended upon his being rid of the editorship of the NZfM.[24] In 1844 he finally retired from the journal, and four years later his opera *Genoveva* was finished.

Schumann's wish to free his time for composition was obviously an important factor in his declining interest and activity for the NZfM after 1840. But there is another factor which must not be overlooked. By the early 1840s many of the original reasons for the journal's existence had vanished. By Schumann's own testimony, the most vacuous of the virtuoso piano composers had either retired or lost public favor.[25] Chopin, Berlioz, and Schumann himself, on the other hand, had now attained a considerable measure of recognition in Germany. The controversy with Fink, and Schumann's disgust with his kind of music criticism were no longer issues, for Fink had been replaced in 1841 by C. F. Becker, long a friend of Schumann and a contributor to the NZfM. The same year saw the retirement of Ludwig Rellstab, the most dedicated enemy of Schumann and romantic music. If Schumann had wished to continue his career as editor and music critic, he would have been forced to find new reasons for doing so. The NZfM was an instrument of revolution, and when Schumann stepped down from its editorship in 1844, the revolution it had been designed to precipitate was all but over.

24. *Briefe,* p. 184.
25. NZfM, *17* (1842), 167.

CHAPTER 5

Schumann's Style of Criticism

Until 1830 the young Schumann's interests were about equally divided between literature and music. When in that year he decided to devote himself fully to music, his formal training in the field appears to have been slight—if anything, inferior to his literary education. It consisted almost solely of about eight years' piano study under Johann Gottfried Kuntsch (1775–1855), organist and choir director of the Zwickau Marienkirche, himself an amateur in music, and a man branded by most of the Schumann biographers as decidedly mediocre.[1] Schumann's knowledge of music was otherwise acquired in the homes of amateur musicians where he took part in musical soirées, accompanying vocal music and participating in chamber ensembles. Carl E. Carus (1774–1842),[2] merchant and manufacturer in Bautzen, and later in Zwickau, was the first and perhaps most important patron of the young Schumann's musical career. Upon his death in 1843, Schumann wrote an extended eulogy in the NZfM:

> And it was in his house that the names Mozart, Haydn, and Beethoven were spoken of daily with enthusiasm. It was in his house that I first became acquainted with the rarer works of these masters, otherwise never to be heard in a small town, especially their quartets; I was often even permitted to participate at the piano.[3]

In the spring of 1828, Schumann, like many great German musicians before him, enrolled at the University of Leipzig to study law.

1. See W. J. von Wasielewski, *Robert Schumann,* trans. A. L. Alger (Boston, 1871), p. 17, where Kuntsch is described as provincial and amateurish; also K. Wörner, *Schumann,* p. 27, and Rehberg, *Schumann,* pp. 19–20. Jansen, in the footnotes to the *Briefe,* p. 528, offers some defense of Kuntsch's competence. Schumann was always respectful toward Kuntsch (See *Jugendbriefe,* p. 186), and Clara reported in later years to Frederick Niecks that "my husband thought a great deal of him. He certainly was not distinguished enough to be my husband's teacher." Frederick Niecks, *Robert Schumann* (London, 1925), p. 32.
2. See Niecks, pp. 35–36.
3. NZfM, *18* (1843), 27. See Appendix I, 22.

In his first year there, though law appears to have taken up little of his time, he had no formal studies in music except for a few sporadic piano lessons with Wieck. During this year he submitted some of his compositions to the composer Gottlob Wiedebein (1779–1854), and in a later letter confessed to him, "I have no knowledge of harmony, thorough bass, etc., or counterpoint; I am but a pure, simple disciple of guiding nature, and I merely followed a blind, vain impulse which wanted to shake off all fetters.[4]

This pristine innocence Schumann claimed for himself was surely something of a pose; he was strongly attracted at this time to a naive adulation of nature such as that in Edward Young's "Some are pupils of nature only, nor go further to school." And though during this year in Leipzig, as well as the following one in Heidelberg, his principal contacts with music were through amateur musical circles,[5] in 1830 Schumann was a good enough pianist for Wieck to promise him that, if he applied himself, in three years he would rival Moscheles and Hummel.[6] Schumann's attempts at composing before his return to Leipzig in 1830 were limited for the most part to the improvisation of free fantasias and variations. Yet a few of his early attempts were written down, and some incorporated into later compositions.[7] Between Schumann's return to Leipzig in 1830 and the founding of the NZfM in 1834, he studied piano with Wieck, and counterpoint (from July 1831 to April 1832) with Heinrich Dorn—his first sustained

4. *Briefe*, p. 7.

5. In Heidelberg, Schumann was exposed to many performances of Baroque music at the home of A. F. J. Thibaut, jurist, amateur musician and author of *Ueber Reinheit der Tonkunst* (Heidelberg, 1825; 2d ed., 1826). This work was furiously attacked for its amateurish reactionism by Hans Georg Nägeli in his *Der Streit zwischen der alten und der neuen Musik* (Breslau, 1826). Mendelssohn as a youth of 18 years describes his favorable impressions of Thibaut (and especially of his library) in a letter from Heidelberg in 1827. Yet he remarks, "It is strange; the man does not know much about music, even his historical knowledge of it is limited, his judgments are mostly purely instinctive." Felix Mendelssohn, *Letters*, ed. Seldon Goth (New York, 1945), *1*, 34. Schumann always remembered Thibaut with respect. *Ueber Reinheit der Tonkunst* provided a large number of the mottos heading individual issues of the NZfM, and one of Schumann's "Musikalische Haus- und Lebensregeln," written about 1848, reads, "Thibaut's *Ueber Reinheit der Tonkunst* is a fine book. Read it often when you are older." GSK, 2, 167.

6. See Niecks, pp. 93–94.

7. Many passages of the four-hand polonaises (1828) published by Geiringer (Universal edition, 1933), for example, reappear in the *Papillons*, op. 2. See Geiringer's explanation of the relationship of the compositions in "Ein unbekanntes Klavierwerk von Robert Schumann," *Die Musik, 25, Bd. 2* (1932), 725–26.

professional musical training. Yet by 1834 Schumann had demonstrated his musical proficiency. Some of his best-known compositions date from this period: the *Papillons* op. 2, the Etudes on Caprices of Paganini op. 3 and 10, the Toccata op. 7, and parts of the *Carnaval* op. 9.

Schumann showed marked literary proclivities from the time of his boyhood in Zwickau. The son of a book dealer and publisher who had literary inclinations himself,[8] Schumann was early immersed in literature ranging from the Greek classics to the writings of Byron and Scott. His school friend, Emil Flechsig, reminisces in his *Erinnerungen* (c. 1875), that "there was abundant opportunity to become acquainted with literature; the entire Schumann house was full of classics."[9] Schumann's linguistic and literary training at the Gymnasium in Zwickau must have been excellent, for if we believe his own report in his "Materialen zu einem Lebenslauf," at the age of fifteen he was making translations from Anacreon, and later from Bion, Theocrites, Homer, Sophocles, Tibullus, Horace and the Latin poetry of the seventeenth-century Polish writer, Matthias Kasmir Sarbiewski. At this time, the report continues, his studies of German literature included the works of Klopstock, Schiller, and Hölderlin, and, especially in 1827, Shakespeare and the novelist who was to exert a formidable influence on his prose style, Jean Paul.[10] Schumann's study of Goethe, as Wörner indicates, did not really begin until about 1830.[11]

In 1825 Schumann and several of his friends, with adolescent exuberance, formed a "German Literary Society" where they discussed literature of various kinds and presented their own poetry for criticism; this society continued to meet until 1828.[12] As a Gymnasium student Schumann was forever composing poetry, essays, aphorisms, and fragments for novels (none of which was ever completed). Jansen

8. August Schumann was well known as the translator of the works of Sir Walter Scott. Wörner, pp. 12 ff.

9. Quoted in Boetticher, ed., *Schriften*, p. 8.

10. Cited in Boetticher, *Einführung*, p. 225. Boetticher's transcription of Schumann's entries appears to be in error at some points. I have taken "Anacova" to mean Anacreon, "Titull" I interpret as Tibull, and "Sarbiesky" as Sarbiewsky. Schumann's report of his own linguistic prowess seems almost too good to be true. Even the best Gymnasium education would hardly equip him to unscramble the Doric dialect of Bion.

11. Wörner, p. 11.

12. See the description in Niecks, pp. 41–42.

pointed out Schumann's remarkable literary precocity in an article in
Die Musik in 1906.[13] He described there a small manuscript volume
from 1823 entitled "Blätter und Blümchen aus der goldenen Aue," in
which Schumann had assembled extracts that appealed to him from a
great variety of literary sources. He gave a list of Schumann's writings
from the years 1826–27, and printed some of them. There are essays
entitled "Ueber die Zufälligkeit und Nichtigkeit des Nachruhms," [14]
"Das Leben des Dichters," and a few poems. Kreisig adds to the list
of youthful essays now in print one on a theme that always interested
Schumann, "Ueber die innige Verwandschaft der Poesie und Tonkunst," and one entitled "Einfluss der Einsamkeit auf die Bildung des
Geistes und die Veredelung des Herzens." [15] Boetticher's two books on
Schumann add considerably to our information about his early literary
activities; Boetticher cites fragments of projected novels entitled
"Selene" and "Juniusabende und Julitage," and prints extracts from
an attempt at musical aesthetics called "Die Tonwelt," all from
1826–28.[16]

During his years in Zwickau, Schumann's familiarity with books
was further nurtured in his family's publishing house. In March 1828,
Schumann wrote to Flechsig,

> I am hard at work with Forcellini, correcting, selecting, look-
> ing things up, reading through the Grüter inscriptions. The work
> is interesting; one learns much from it . . . besides, all the dis-
> tinguished philologists are working on it . . . I have had to
> ransack the whole library, and have found many unprinted *col-
> lectanea* of Gronow, Gräv, Scalliger, Heinsius, Barth, Daum,
> etc.[17]

13. F. Gustav Jansen, "Aus Robert Schumanns Schulzeit." *Die Musik,* 5 (1906), *Bd.* 4,
pp. 83–99.

14. Kreisig (GSK, 2, 449) points out a similarity of part of this essay to some of the
commentary in an encyclopedic series called *Bildnisse berühmter Männer aller Zeit,* a publication of August Schumann with which Robert had recently assisted.

15. GSK, 2, 173–75, and 186–90.

16. Boetticher, ed., *Schriften,* pp. 9–10, 24–28, and *Einführung,* pp. 114–15 and 623.
Perhaps it was an indication of Schumann's maturing tastes that in 1833 he ridiculed the
idea of naming his musical journal "Tonwelt."

17. *Jugendbriefe,* pp. 16–17. The work with whose publication Schumann assisted was
correctly identified by Niecks (p. 42) as Forcellini's *Totius Latinitatis Lexikon* (first edition,
Padua, 1771). More precisely, it was the four-volume German version of the third edition
of this work that Schumann's brother published (the original third edition appeared in
Padua in 1827).

The first half of this letter is an extreme example of Schumann's most rapturous, ornate prose—a striking contrast to his exacting, sober work on a major Latin lexicon, and even his description of that work. Schumann was by this time an unabashed admirer of Jean Paul, and often imitated his diffuse, extravagant prose. He did this for a time very consciously—he could turn this kind of writing off and on like a water tap—but his fascination with the rapturous late romantic prose style was a passing phase. Schumann continued to appreciate Jean Paul for the rest of his life; but he stopped imitating him as maturity set in.

Wörner says that Schumann's interests in music and literature interfered with each other, and that his literary activities, in fact, long held him to an amateur level in music.[18] Schumann was painfully aware of this; in December, 1830, after his decision to become a professional musician, Schumann wrote, "If only my talent for music and poetry would converge into a single point, the light would not be so scattered, and I could attempt a great deal." [19] In his career as a music critic, especially the earlier part of it, Schumann was able to reconcile, in more than a superficial sense, his talents for music and literature.

Schumann's earliest journal articles are fantasies in ornate prose that are only incidentally about music. His famous Chopin review in the AmZ of 1831 and his *Davidsbündler* articles in *Der Komet* of 1833 are cast as narratives, complete with description of characters, dialogue, and even some action. They look exactly like fragments of novels; the first of the *Davidsbündler* articles (with the subtitle "Leipziger Musikleben") begins:

> A window above me was suddenly thrown open, and behind it, in the half-shadows, I recognized a pointed, angular-nosed Swedish head. And as I was still looking up, something like fragrant falling leaves floated and played about my temples: it was scraps of paper thrown down from above. But at home, as though rooted to the spot, I read (in a paper that held together better) the following:
>
> Our Italian nights go on. The heaven-storming Florestan has for a time been quieter than usual, and seems to have something

18. Wörner, p. 26.
19. *Jugendbriefe*, p. 136.

on his mind. But then recently Eusebius let fall a few words that reawakened the demon in him. After reading a number of *Iris*, he said, namely, "He is just too severe." "What? What did you say, Eusebius?" said Florestan, rising up, "Rellstab is too severe? Is then this damnable German politeness to last for centuries? . . . But the time is coming when we must stand up against this unholy alliance of patronage and perversity, before it engulfs us and makes for no end of trouble. But what do you think, Master Raro?

You know Raro's methodical way of speaking—made even stranger because of his Italian accent—how he, fugue-like, sets phrase upon phrase, makes various distinctions, narrows down his material, limits it yet more, finally brings everything together again and seems to say, I agree.[20]

Schumann had no intention that the Chopin review and the *Davidsbündler* articles should remain as isolated essays; both were to have been merely the first installments of extended series, and the *Davidsbündler* articles Schumann specifically intended to expand into a novel. These pieces are clearly examples of the "musical belles-lettres" Schumann mentioned to Mosen in 1833. Schumann apparently intended to give essays like this a prominent place in his journal; he asked Mosen to write a musical *Novelle* for the first issues, and to Franz Otto he suggested "English letters" addressed to an "imaginary person (a sweetheart, a Vult Harnisch or Peter Schoppe)."[21]

As 1834 wore on, the duties of editor and reviewer of instrumental music fell more and more to Schumann. It was already clear from his Chopin review that his novelistic style seemed to him perfectly serviceable for writing music reviews, and he used variations of this style—usually with an element of moderation lacking in 1831—in a good many of his early critiques of piano music in the NZfM. The results varied: a review of Hummel's Etudes op. 125 is divided into three parts, each stating a slightly different point of view, and each signed by one of Schumann's imaginary Jean-Paulian characters, Florestan, Eusebius, and Raro (the entire review appears under the heading, "Die Davidsbündler").[22] The gentle Eusebius says,

20. GSK, 2, 260–61.
21. *Briefe*, p. 45 and *Jugendbriefe*, p. 223.
22. NZfM, *1* (1834), 73–75. In GS 1854 and succeeding editions of the *Gesammelte Schriften*, this heading was changed to "Aus den kritischen Büchern der Davidsbündler." In

The experienced, reflective master writes etudes differently from the young fantast. The former knows intimately the forces with which he must deal, their beginning and end, their means and goals; he lays out his circle of activity about him and never steps over that line. The latter, on the other hand, lays piece on piece, piles up rocks one atop the other, until finally he himself can surmount the herculean structure only at the peril of his life. . . .

In view of the lightning-fast development of music to the heights of poetic freedom—of this no other art can offer a parallel example—it is inevitable that even the better things can remain current for only about a decade. It is an act of intolerance that many of the younger spirits are ungrateful, forgetting that they are building a superstructure upon a foundation they have not laid. Every younger generation has committed this act of intolerance, and every future one will too.

Florestan answers:

Good, kindly Eusebius, you make me laugh. And when you have all turned back your clocks, the sun will still rise as before. However highly I value your tendency to assign everything to its proper place, I think you are really a repressed romantic—but with a certain diffidence about famous names, which time will cure.

Really, my friend, if some had their way, we would soon be back to those golden days when you got your ears boxed for putting your thumb on the black keys. But I won't even go into

---

a footnote to this review in the NZfM, Schumann promises a later explanation of the *Davids-bund*. A "clarification" in a later issue (NZfM, *1* [1834], 152. See Appendix I, 23) merely says:

> "There are many rumors afoot about the fraternity whose name appears below. Since, unfortunately, we must still withhold the reasons for concealing our identity, we will ask Herr Schumann (should he be known to any of the editors) to represent us, should the occasion arise, under his own name.
>
> —THE DAVIDSBÜNDLER
>
> "I shall do so with pleasure.
>
> —ROBERT SCHUMANN"

The most lucid and concise discussion of the nature of the *Davidsbund* and its members, Florestan, Eusebius, and Raro, is in Kreisig's footnotes to his edition of the *Gesammelte Schriften* (GSK, 2, 367–69).

the falsities of some of your effusions, but instead get to the work itself.

Methods and schools make for rapid progress, to be sure, but such progress is one-sided and trivial. O pedants, what sinners you are! With your Logier-natures you pull the bud forcibly out of its covering. Like falconers you clip the feathers of your students lest they fly too high. You ought to be guides who show the way—without always coming along yourselves! (I'm too embroiled in these ideas to come to the point.) . . .

Who could deny that most of these etudes show an exemplary plan and execution, that each has a distinctive, pure character, and that they were produced with that masterly ease which results from years of application? But that which is necessary to enchant the youth and to make him forget all the difficulties of the work because of its beauties is utterly lacking—imaginative originality . . . I speak of fantasy, the prophetess with covered eyes from whom nothing is hidden, and who in her errors is often most charming of all. But what do you say to this, master?

Master Raro says:

My young friends, you are both wrong—but especially you Eusebius. A famous name has made one of you captive and the other rebellious. But what does it say in the *Westöstlicher Divan?*

> Als wenn das auf Namen ruhte,
> Was sich schweigend nur entfaltet
> Lieb' ich doch das schöne Gute,
> Wie es sich aus Gott gestaltet.[23]

The second article under the rubric *Die Davidsbündler* is a review of the "Bouquet musical" op. 10, by Schumann's former counterpoint teacher, Heinrich Dorn.[24] This conspicuously disjointed essay begins with a section (signed by Eusebius) in which the various flowers in the bouquet converse, the violet even telling a short story. This device is dropped in the next section where Florestan complains about the French titles. In the final section (unsigned), Schumann gives a short analysis of the music. This style is more consistent and clearly more successful in Schumann's discussion of a series of sonatas by Delphine

23. NZfM, *1* (1834), 73–75. See Appendix I, 24.
24. NZfM, *1* (1834), 97–99.

Hill Handley, Carl Loewe, Wilhelm Taubert, and Ludwig Schunke in the NZfM of 1835.[25] Here Schumann writes a review in which the large sections are again represented as speeches by Eusebius, Florestan, and Raro. But within each section there is dialogue and a bit of action. In the course of all this, Schumann actually manages to describe and evaluate the compositions—complete with musical examples.

The more general articles Schumann contributed (in accordance with his original plans) to the early volumes of the NZfM were obviously more amenable to his narrative style than were the reviews. In such essays as the "Fastnachtsrede von Florestan," the "Schwärmbriefe," and the "Monument für Beethoven," [26] Schumann writes about the German musical scene in narrative prose that is diffuse, but facile and imaginative. The third of the "Schwärmbriefe" includes this remarkable discussion of Beethoven's Seventh Symphony:

> I had to laugh—Florestan began, as he launched into the A-major Symphony—I had to laugh at a dry old actuary who found in it a battle of giants, and in the last movement their final destruction—though he had to pass lightly over the Allegretto because it didn't fit into his plan . . . But most of all my fingers itch to get at those who insist that Beethoven always presented in his symphonies the most exalted sentiments: lofty ideas about God, immortality, and the courses of the stars. While the floral crown of the genius, to be sure, points to the heavens, ' his roots are planted in his beloved earth.
>
> Now about the symphony itself; this idea is not my own, but taken from an old volume of *Cäcilia* (though there the setting is changed to the parlor of a count, perhaps out of too great a diffidence for Beethoven—which was misguided) . . . it is a most merry wedding. The bride is an angelic child with a rose in her hair, but only one. Unless I am greatly mistaken, in the Introduction the guests gather together, greeting each other with inverted commas, and, unless I am wrong, merry flutes recall that in the entire village, full of maypoles with many-colored ribbons, -there reigns joy for the bride Rosa. And unless I am mistaken, the pale mother looks at her with a trembling glance that seems to

25. NZfM, 2 (1835), 125–27, 133–34, and 145–46.
26. NZfM, 2 (1835), 116–17; 3 (1835), 126–27, 147, 151–52, 182–83; and 4 (1836), 211–13.

ask, "Do you know that now we must part?" And Rosa, overcome, throws herself into her arms, drawing after her, with the
other hand, that of the bridegroom . . . Now it becomes very
still in the village outside (here Florestan came to the Allegretto,
taking passages from it here and there); only a butterfly flits
past or a cherry blossom falls . . . The organ begins; the sun is
high in the sky, and single long, oblique rays play upon the parti-
cles of dust throughout the church. The bells ring vigorously—
parishioners arrive a few at a time—pews are clapped open and
shut—some peasants peer into hymnbooks, others gaze up at
the superstructure—the procession draws closer—first choirboys
with lighted candles and censers, then friends who often look
back at the couple accompanied by the priest—then the parents,
friends of the bride, and finally all the young people of the village. And now all is in order and the priest approaches the altar,
and speaks first to the bride, and then to the happiest of men.
And he admonishes them about the sacred responsibilities and
purposes of this union, and bids them find their happiness in profound harmony and love; then he asks for the "I do" that is to
last forever; and the bride pronounces it firmly and deliberately
—I don't want to continue this picture, and you can do it your
own way in the finale. Florestan thus broke off abruptly and
tore into the close of the Allegretto; the sound was as if the
sacristan was slamming the doors so that the noise reverberated
through the whole church.[27]

Schumann's love of aphorism stands in almost paradoxical contrast
to his fascination with this kind of discursive prose. During his ten-
years' occupation with the NZfM, Schuman was continually busy col-
lecting pithy and pertinent quotations from literary sources to be
used as mottos. His own aphorisms as well appeared from time to time
in the early volumes of the journal.[28] In 1848 he assembled his "Musikalische Haus- und Lebensregeln," [29] and in 1853–54 he gathered to-

27. NZfM, 3 (1835), 152. See Appendix I, 25.
28. See, for example, the series under the heading "Grobes und Feines" in NZfM, 1
(1834), 147–48, and 150–51.
29. The "Musikalische Haus- und Lebensregeln," according to Kreisig (GSK, 2, 448),
were originally to have been inserted between individual numbers of the Jugendalbum, op. 68,
composed in 1848. Instead they were first published in an "Extrabeilage" of the NZfM in
1850, and they appeared together as an appendix to the second edition of the Jugendalbum
in 1851.

gether from various of his earlier writings the sets of aphorisms in the *Gesammelte Schriften*. In the first volume of the NZfM Schumann printed—in one of the collections of aphorisms—a paragraph in defense of aphorism. This selection is really an extract, only slightly altered, from the second of Schumann's *Davidsbündler* articles, and it shows the undisciplined vehemence of some of Schumann's early writing:

> Why do you turn up your noses with such a superior air at aphorism, you tall Philistines? [30] By God, is the world all a level surface? Doesn't it have Alps, rivers, and all different kinds of people? And is life to be reduced to a system? Isn't it a book put together from single, half torn-up pages, full of children's scrawlings, youthful ideas, overturned epitaphs, and blank, ungovernable fate? I think it is. In fact it might not be uninteresting to portray life with all its concomitants in art,[31] just as Platner and Jacobi[32] have given whole philosophical systems.[33]

Schumann's most fanciful prose stands directly in the tradition of the German literary–musical figures of the early nineteenth century, Jean Paul, E. T. A. Hoffmann, and W. H. Wackenroder. Abert has said that most of the style and content of Schumann's early writing can be attributed to the influence of Jean Paul. The importance of his novels as a model for Schumann's early style is hardly to be doubted; virtually all of Schumann's biographers agree on this point.[34] Boetticher has shown from a diary of 1831 that Schumann also admired and consciously imitated Hoffmann at this time; he was even thinking about writing a "poetic biography" of Hoffmann.[35]

Another important forerunner for Schumann's earlier style, this one from the eighteenth century, is usually overlooked: Christian Daniel Schubart (1739–91). Schubart, who acted out the excesses of the *Sturm und Drang* for most of his adult life, had much in common with the young Schumann: untutored enthusiasm for poetic qualities in music, and a love of rapturous improvisation both in music

30. An allusion, apparently, to Goliath.

31. The original version of this passage in the *Davidsbündler* article (GSK, 2, 268) makes more sense: it has "Aphorismen" instead of "der Kunst."

32. Schumann refers to the German philosophers Ernst Platner (1744–1818), and Friedrich Heinrich Jacobi (1743–1819).

33. NZfM, *1* (1834), 151. See Appendix I, 26.

34. Except Niecks (pp. 122–23) who tends to dismiss Jean Paul's influence as negligible. He is undoubtedly right in limiting it almost exclusively to Schumann's earlier years.

35. Boetticher, *Einführung*, p. 144, n. 90, and p. 319.

and prose. Schumann as a boy of thirteen already knew Schubart's *Ideen zu einer Aesthetik der Tonkunst;* Schumann's "Blätter und Blümchen aus der goldenen Aue," compiled in 1823, contains excerpts from this book.[36] Among the articles Schumann wrote for the *Damenkonversationslexikon* in 1834 is one called "Charakteristik der Tonleitern und Tonarten." [37] His model for this essay, he tells us, was Schubart; though he disagrees at several points with Schubart's characterization of keys, he finds in it much that is "graceful and poetic." [38] Toward the end of 1838, when Schumann was in Vienna, he borrowed a copy of Schubart's book from Fischhof and read it again.[39] And in March of 1839, mottos from Schubart's *Ideen* began again to appear in the NZfM.[40]

It would strike us as peculiar behavior if a present-day critic should write little stories instead of telling us in a straightforward fashion about the things he is reviewing, and Schumann's behavior as a critic certainly seemed peculiar to some of his contemporaries. Fink, for example, sneered in the AmZ about the "insufferable followers of Chopin who pursue dreams they aren't dreaming." [41] The special forms of Schumann's fancy—the half-imaginary characters, and the personification of several sides to his own personality—might suggest the aberrations of incipient schizophrenia.[42] But to attribute any substantial part of Schumann's style of music criticism to mental disturbance would be a real error. There is little reason to think that Schumann failed to distinguish between the real world and the

36. Jansen, "Aus Robert Schumanns Schulzeit," *Die Musik, 5* (1906), *Bd.* 4, p. 85.

37. *Damenkonversationslexikon, 2,* 332–33. Schumann incorporated this essay, with certain changes, into the NZfM in 1835 (NZfM, *2,* 43–44), and Kreisig has reprinted both versions (GSK, *1,* 105–06, and *2,* 207–08).

38. Schubart's essay on the keys is in his *Ideen zu einer Aesthetik der Tonkunst* (Vienna, 1806), pp. 377–82.

39. See *Briefe,* p. 145, and Erich Schenk, "Halbjahr der Erwartung," in H. J. Moser and E. Rebling, eds., *Robert Schumann, aus Anlass seines 100. Todestages* (Leipzig, 1956), p. 21. The page reference to the *Briefe* in Schenk's citation is in error.

40. NZfM, *10* (1839), 77, 157, and 185.

41. AmZ, *40* (1838), 668.

42. There is little reasonably scientific information on Schumann's illness. P. J. Möbius considered the problem in an entire book, *Ueber Robert Schumann's Krankheit* (Halle, 1906). A more recent study is Gerhard Granzow's "Florestan und Eusebius, zur Psychologie Robert Schumanns," *Die Musik, 20* (1928) *Bd.* 2, pp. 660–63. Despite Boetticher's infatuation with a movement in German psychology called Charakterologie (a study of personality which became contaminated with strong implications of racism), his discussion of Schumann's illness (*Einführung,* pp. 161 ff., and 167 ff.), appears to be sensible. There is general agreement that Schumann's affliction would now be diagnosed as schizophrenia.

imaginary one he peopled with the members of the *Davidsbund*. It was with consciousness and even purposefulness that he indulged his love of anagrams, pseudonyms, and Jean Paulian mystification. He explained all this with perfect lucidity to Zuccamaglio:

> If by any chance you approve of the tone of the *Davidsbünd-lerbriefe* from Augsburg, Berlin, Dresden, and Munich, I suggest that you adopt it for your own correspondence articles. Indifferent material can thus be presented in an interesting way; the journal gains solidity and colorfulness this way, and the readers will be shown a kindness. Think of the *Davidsbund* merely as a spiritual brotherhood which is now expanding to fairly sizable proportions, also externally, and will, I hope, bear much good fruit. The mystification of this, after all, has an unusual charm for many people; moreover, like everything mysterious, it has a special power.[43]

G. Noren-Herzberg has suggested that Schumann adopted a highly "poetic" style for his journal because literature of all kinds was in great vogue in Germany.[44] Post office clerks read Goethe and accountants tried their hand at sonnets and essays. In such a milieu Schumann's early style of criticism would find a friendly reception. Schumann did not write extravagant and fanciful criticism because he was detached from reality, nor because of any other personal idiosyncrasy. In his work for the journal, as we have seen, he showed a never-failing presence of mind, and his writing for it was no exception. Schumann wrote this way deliberately because he thought this kind of criticism would be effective.

Schumann's early style of music criticism is a highly personal variation of a type that goes back to the music reviews of E. T. A. Hoffmann. Hoffmann's reviews of Beethoven's Fifth Symphony and his Trios op. 70 in the AmZ of 1810 and 1813[45] mark the beginning of a new kind of music criticism. Here, language rich in images and figures strains to communicate in words the qualities of music; the result is really the use of one artistic medium to explicate another. In

43. *Briefe*, p. 70.

44. G. Noren-Herzberg, "Robert Schumann als Musikschriftsteller," *Die Musik*, 5 (1906), *Bd*. 4, p. 104.

45. AmZ, *12* (1810), 630–42, and 652–59; *15* (1813), 141–54. See the later condensed version of these reviews in Strunk, ed., *Source Readings*, pp. 775–81.

the introduction to his review of Hiller's Etudes op. 15, Schumann offers an eloquent apology for this kind of procedure:

The editors of this paper have been reproached for emphasizing and extending the poetic side of music at the expense of its scientific side. They have been called young fantasts who have not always been informed that basically not much is known about Ethiopian[46] and other such music, etc. This accusation contains exactly that element by means of which we would hope to distinguish our paper from others. We do not wish to pursue the question of to what degree the cause of art is advanced faster by one manner or the other. We certainly confess, however, that we hold as the highest kind of criticism that which itself leaves an impression similar to the one created by the subject that stimulated it.

A footnote to this passage contains the famous statement,

In this sense, Jean Paul could possibly contribute more to the understanding of a Beethoven symphony or fantasia through a poetic counterpart (even without talking about the symphony or fantasia alone) than a dozen critics who lean their ladders against the colossus to take his exact measurements.[47]

The style of Hoffmann's reviews and Schumann's early criticism is a natural concomitant of the changing standards for music in the romantic milieu of which both men were so much a part. A critic whose foremost demands have to do with subjective elements—emotion, imagination (in the modern sense), "the characteristic," or Schumann's elusive "poetic" [48]—cuts himself off from established ra-

46. In the *Gesammelte Schriften,* Schumann changed this to "griechischer . . . Musik." GSK, *1,* 44.

47. NZfM, 2 (1835), 42. See Appendix I, 27.

48. In his *Einführung,* p. 106, n. 5, Boetticher has assembled a series of early statements to show what Schumann meant by "poetic." Schumann almost always used this word in an analogical sense, that is, not to distinguish poetry from prose, but to distinguish works of art which were original and imaginative from those which were not. The term "poetry," in German literary criticism as well, no longer referred only to a general category of literary composition; it described any literary creation rich in imagery and emotional connotations. Thus Novalis said, "The novel must be poetry through and through." See R. Wellek, *A History of Modern Criticism* (New Haven, 1955), 2, 85. Schumann referred in a similar vein to his journal as "the defender of the rights of poetry." *Jugendbriefe,* p. 222.

tionalistic ways of talking about his subject. For the romantic music critic it is precisely those qualities he most cherishes that are least susceptible of any kind of conventional discussion. He must find new ways to intimate that which—by his own admission—is inexpressible; it is hardly surprising that the result is something original, subjective, and, in Schumann's sense, poetic. And for Schumann, convinced of a basic similarity of all the arts, but particularly of literature and music,[49] a poetic literary style must have seemed a perfectly appropriate vehicle for conveying his ideas.

In literary criticism there were striking parallels—or more precisely, precedents—for the subjective music criticism Schumann wrote in the early 1830s. They too followed in the train of important changes in standards for the arts in the later eighteenth and earlier nineteenth centuries. The dissolution of the literary principles of the Enlightenment, and their gradual replacement with views of literature associated with romanticism began in Germany in the late 1760s. Lessing, who preferred Shakespeare to Corneille, began to counteract the French neoclassicism so wholeheartedly embraced by the Germans since Gottsched. In the high tide of the *Sturm und Drang*, shortly afterward, all the old rules about the integrity of genre, the unities, the view of art as a product of judgment, the theory of mimesis—all of this was denied. The most important (though hardly the most readable) spokesman for the literary *Sturm und Drang*, this precursor of romanticism more violent in its rejection of established traditions than romanticism itself, was Johann Gottfried Herder.[50] The values he substituted for the neoclassical complex of rules were those we associate with romanticism: an appreciation for history, a "high estimation of the unique, the original, and the irrational . . . [a] conviction of the value of individuality and personality." [51]

René Wellek describes Herder's style of criticism in this way:

49. A typical statement is this: "We believe that the painter can learn from a Beethoven symphony, just as the musician, for his part, can learn from a work of art by Goethe." NZfM, *1* (1834), 36.

50. Wellek (*1*, 176–81) considers none of the other writers associated with the *Sturm und Drang*, Lenz, Bürger, Stolberg, Gerstenberg, or even Hamann an important critic. Herder played a vital role as a forerunner of the literary theories of both the German classicists and romantics. The romantics themselves tended not to recognize this in Herder, but to extract from Goethe and Schiller ideas they could have gotten firsthand from Herder.

51. Walter Silz, *Early German Romanticism. Its Founders and Heinrich von Kleist* (Cambridge, Mass., 1929), p. 6.

Herder differs from all other critics of the century not only in his radicalism, but also in his method of presentation and argument. In his writings there is a new fervid, shrill, enthusiastic tone, an emotional heightening, a style which uses rhetorical questions, exclamations, passages marked by dashes in wearisome profusion, a style full of metaphors and similes, a composition which often abandons any pretense at argument and chain of reasoning. It is that of a lyrical address, of constant questions, cumulative intensifying adjectives, verbs of motion, of metaphors drawn from the movement of water, light, flame, and the growth of plants and animals.[52]

Wellek also sees in Herder's work:

the germs of much that is bad in criticism since Herder's time: mere impressionism, the idea of "creative" criticism with its pretensions to duplicating a work of art by another work of art.[53]

"Creative" criticism—criticism which seeks to elucidate a work of art by means of evocative, figurative, impressionistic language— was renewed with the romantic writers. Friedrich Schlegel's attitude toward this kind of criticism, Wellek points out, was favorable but cautious. Schlegel says on one occasion:

Poetry can only be criticized by poetry. A judgment on art which is not itself a work of art, either in its matter, as presentation of a necessary impression in its genesis, or in its beautiful form and a liberal tone in the spirit of old Roman satire, has no citizens' right in the realm of art.[54]

But on another occasion he is skeptical of any criticism which has no other aim but reproduction of an impression:

If many mystical lovers of art who consider all criticism dissection and every dissection a destruction of enjoyment were to think consistently, "I'll be damned!" would be the best judgment on

52. Wellek, *1*, 182.
53. Wellek, *1*, 184.
54. Wellek, *2*, 10.

the greatest work. There are critics who do not say more, though at much greater length.[55]

Although Schlegel agreed, at least partly, with Herder in his estimation of creative criticism, he differed fundamentally from his predecessor in his love of polemic, and his faith in the possibility and importance of censure. It was out of the acknowledged subjectivity of Herder's judgments that his own tolerant, liberal tone was born. Schlegel, though he absorbed (if indirectly) something of the theory and style of Herder's criticism, was convinced that a critic's judgments can have an objective validity. The possibility of censure in criticism cut loose from the rationalistic moorings of the earlier eighteenth century depends upon such a conviction, and in a very real sense, the justification for it was provided by Kant in his *Critique of Judgment*. In this connection it is easy to appreciate Walter Silz's statement, "One might say that the difference between 'Sturm und Drang' and Romanticism is due chiefly to the appearance of Kant's writings in the interval." [56]

Schumann's impressionistic style of music criticism arose out of the difficulties inherent in talking about anything intangible; in his solution to these difficulties he was by no means alone. In his outlook as a critic Schumann had a good deal more in common with Schlegel than with Herder. Criticism was for him not mere description and appreciation; it entailed serious evaluation. Schumann always had a special talent, in fact, for polemics and censure. He saw the critic's role as a didactic one; he must act not only as an interpreter, but also as a guide.

Like Friedrich Schlegel, Schumann was keenly aware that creative criticism is not by itself sufficient for the fulfillment of the critic's responsibility. From the earliest issues of the NZfM Schumann's writings include, too, a radically different type of criticism: an analytic dissection of the composer's craft.[57] Creative criticism was a way of get-

---

55. Ibid. Though Schlegel shows vacillation on this point, his earlier writings are as a whole conspicuously coherent and perceptive. It is inconceivable that an impartial reader of his works should, like Irving Babbitt, repeat Nietzsche's senseless aspersion that "no one had a more intimate knowledge of all the bypaths to chaos." *Rousseau and Romanticism* (Cleveland, 1962), p. 85.

56. Silz, *Early German Romanticism*, pp. 6–7.

57. Almost all writers on Schumann have ignored this side to Schumann's criticism. See, for example, the description by H. Kretzschmar in "Robert Schumann als Aesthetiker," *Peters Jahrbuch, 13* (1906), 47–73.

ting at what Schumann would call the poetic qualities of a work of art. But he readily acknowledged his duty as a critic to deal with other aspects of a composition as well—and in any event much of the music he reviewed did not have, in his opinion, anything poetic about it. In his review of Hiller's Etudes, adopting a favorite romantic organic metaphor, Schumann proposes to discuss the "flower, root, and fruit, that is, the poetic, harmonic-melodic, and mechanical "elements" of the music.[58] Vivid contrasts in style within Schumann's criticism result from this variety of elements in music he wanted to talk about: in the NZfM of 1834–35 we have conversations between flowers, an account of a dream about a fair, and a painstaking analysis, complete with diagrams, of the form and harmony of the first of Hiller's etudes—an analysis intended to show a "looseness, which even degenerates into a lack of clarity and balance." [59]

The vivid extremes of Schumann's early style are combined in his famous review of Berlioz' *Symphonie fantastique* in the NZfM of 1835. This review is generally known only in its reduced (but nevertheless enormous) form in the various editions of the *Gesammelte Schriften*. A large section of the review deleted in the *Gesammelte Schriften* is the introductory installment,[60] an extravagant tribute to Berlioz finishing off with a poem by Franz von Sonnenberg—a "poetic counterpart" to Berlioz' symphony.[61] Here Schumann engages in the most outright kind of creative criticism: he offers to his readers a poem by way of explication of a symphony. In the following analysis of the first movement, he employs diagrams and musical examples, indulging in an almost painful degree of detail. Thus in a single review

58. NZfM, 2 (1835), 43.
59. NZfM, 2 (1835), 56.
60. NZfM, 3 (1835), 1–2. Schumann also deleted in his *Gesammelte Schriften* the first two paragraphs of the second installment (3, 33). The first installment is signed "Florestan." The opening paragraphs of the second offer the pretense of having been written by a different author and question the adequacy of the "psychological method" of the first installment.
61. NZfM, 3 (1835), 2. The opening lines of the poem are:

Du bist!—und bist das glühend ersehnte Herz,
Durch stumme Mitternächte so heiss ersehnt

   * * *

Du bist's, die einst süsschauernd am Busen mir
In langem Tiefverstummen, in bebenden
Gebrochnen Ach's, verwirrt, mit holdem
Jungfraunerröthen in's Herz mir lispelt:
"Ich bin das Ach, das ewig die Brust dir eng
Zusammenkrampft' und wieder zum Weltraum hob."

Schumann touches both extremes of his style as a critic—subjective, metaphorical suggestion, and meticulous, technical dissection.

During his earlier years as a critic Schumann's writings showed signs that he struggled to reconcile the divergent ways in which he wanted to talk about music. Dissatisfied with both the evocative and technical types of reviews by themselves,[62] he adopted something of a middle course and wrote a great many in a mixed style. His review of Mendelssohn's *Melusina* overture, for example, treats the "subject" of the music in richly figurative prose, finishing with an admission that the description falls short of duplicating the evocative qualities of the music. With an abrupt shift in language Schumann then begins to talk about such technical elements as form and orchestration.[63] Schumann still felt confronted with these two possible styles of criticism when he reviewed Berlioz' *Waverly* overture in 1839:

> It would be easy for me to depict the overture either in a poetic fashion by reproducing the various images it evokes in me, or in a dissection of the mechanics of the work. Each method of explaining music has something to recommend it. The first at least escapes the danger of dryness, into which the second, for better or worse, often falls.[64]

The shift in style long remained characteristic of Schumann's more important reviews. But it was often modified to a form in which general observations about the composer and his composition would be couched in a literary style, and specific points about the music dealt with in technical language.[65] It must be remembered that the shift in

62. Schumann's comment in the Berlioz review about the inadequacy of "psychological criticism" is one of his few explicit statements to this effect. His doubts about the efficacy of "technical" criticism, however, he reiterated frequently. A most explicit discussion of this subject also appears in the review of Berlioz' symphony (NZfM, *3* [1835], 37). A review that analyzes the form and harmony of a piece of music, Schumann maintains (quite sensibly), is of no use whatever to those completely unfamiliar with the music. An analysis, when addressed to readers who do know the music, can be useful if the reviewer has some special point to make about the form or harmony of the piece (as in the case of the Berlioz symphony to demonstrate that the first movement has a clear and rather traditional form). Schumann had no use for the aimless, matter-of-course analysis that was habitual in the longer reviews of the AmZ.

63. NZfM, *4* (1836), 6–7.

64. NZfM, *10* (1839), 187. See Appendix I, 28. C. M. von Weber discusses the possibilities open to the critic in a similar fashion in his review of E. T. A. Hoffmann's opera *Undine*. See Strunk, ed., *Source Readings*, p. 802.

65. A good example of this style in Schumann's later writing is his review of the *Marienlieder* of his erstwhile *Mitarbeiter*, Carl Banck. NZfM, *17* (1842), 10–12.

style, in fact the use of any poetic language at all, was always limited
to reviews of music in which Schumann detected poetic qualities. It
would have been impossible and pointless for Schumann to lavish his
poetic style on every piece of music that crossed his desk. He was in
fact very good at adapting his tone and style to the task at hand. If
necessary, as we have seen, Schumann could deal with a great stack of
mediocre music in a very short space; and in such a situation there is
little reason for poetizing.

Schumann's most extravagant literary style disappeared rather
quickly from the pages of the NZfM. The novelistic type of review
was really confined to the years 1834–35, and the *Davidsbündler*
names appeared only infrequently after 1836.[66] In his soberer style of
the later 1830s and the 1840s Schumann began to use more of the
technical language of music theorists. Terms such as "Anlage" and
"Ausführung," common in music theory since Sulzer and Koch, begin
to appear frequently in his writings of the early 1840s.[67] But the
stimulus of a talented new composer such as Hirschbach, Gade, or
much later, Brahms, or of a new, exciting composition from Mendelssohn, Chopin, or William Sterndale Bennett never failed to resurrect
in Schumann some of his original flair for poetic description.

66. Of the principal names representing Schumann, "Raro" was the first to be dropped,
in 1836. "Eusebius" appeared sporadically until 1839, and "Florestan" made one final appearance in 1842. A Paris correspondent (Stephen Heller?) persisted in signing his contributions "Dblr" until 1843. See NZfM, *18* (1843), 146. In 1837 Schumann was disinclined to protract the half-imaginary existence of the *Davidsbund,* and wished to form in its
place a real musical society. See *Briefe*, p. 87.

67. See NZfM, *18* (1843), 14, 31; *21* (1844), 58.

PART III

Schumann on the History and Aesthetics of Music

CHAPTER 6

Schumann's View of the History of Music

Even so literate a musician as Schumann could hardly be expected, in the 1830s, to have any extensive knowledge of the history of music, for musical historiography had at that time hardly begun. The wave of historical interest that swept over the literary world in the early nineteenth century left music largely untouched until much later. Dante and Shakespeare were household names when even the most well-informed musicians had scarcely heard of Machaut or Monteverdi. To be sure, in the second half of the preceding century there had appeared a rash of histories by Marpurg, G. B. Martini, de Blainville, Hawkins, Burney, and Forkel. Yet in the first four decades of the nineteenth century not a great deal of note was added to this repertory. W. C. Müller's *Aesthetisch-historische Einleitungen in die Wissenschaft der Tonkunst* (Leipzig, 1830), Kiesewetter's *Geschichte der europäisch-abendländischen oder unsrer heutigen Musik* (Leipzig, 1834), and the *Musikalisches Handwörterbuch* of Gustav Schilling[1] were perhaps the most influential in Germany. But the value of all these works lies mostly in the information they provide on contemporary topics, or merely in their importance as landmarks in the "history of historiography." The earliest large-scale work to treat older music (especially the music of the Renaissance) with impartiality and scholarly thoroughness is August Wilhelm Ambros' five-volume *Geschichte der Musik* (1862–78).[2]

1. This dictionary, published in 1830, was the first of a series of historical and aesthetical works by Schilling, founder and director of the *Deutscher National-Verein für Musik und ihre Wissenschaft*. Schilling's publications, most of which appeared in the 1830s and 1840s, were often greeted by a storm of accusations of plagiarism (See Appendix II, 21). Schilling later came to the United States, and died on a farm in Nebraska.

2. Ambros' contribution is somewhat slighted, I feel, in Professor Harrison's valuable account of European musical historiography. See F. Ll. Harrison, M. Hood, and C. V. Palisca, *American Musicology and the European Tradition* (Englewood Cliffs, N.J., 1963), pp. 10–33. Though Ambros labored under a strongly Hegelian view of history, his work shows rare scholarly detachment from contemporary criteria and tastes; it does not seem to belong under Harrison's heading "romantic re-creation."

Though Schumann was well acquainted with Ambros ln the 1840s, his contacts with musical historiography were always very limited, and before 1840 almost nonexistent. Having acquired his musical education under a provincial schoolmaster and organist, in the fashionable homes of patrons and musical amateurs, and briefly under a professional piano pedagogue and a mediocre opera composer, Schumann had no one to interest him in the history of music or to guide him to the few reliable books in the field.

Of the books about music Schumann is known to have read before 1834, two that particularly absorbed him deal with historical subjects. From his early years in Zwickau, as we have observed, he was impressed with Christian Friedrich Daniel Schubart's *Ideen zu einer Aesthetik der Tonkunst.* The first section of this work is a "Skizzirte Geschichte der Musik." In the first part of this sketch, Schubart devotes seven pages to an amusingly naive discussion of the music of pre-Christian Judaism, and then abruptly remarks that there are still some admirable Jewish musicians about, especially in Prague, though he doubts that they continue the traditions of ancient Israel.[3] After a short section on the music of ancient Greece, Schubart takes up Roman and medieval music, which occupies his attention for four pages. Then after a passing reference to Zarlino, he speaks of the first opera performance, which, he notes, took place in Venice in 1624. But the Venetians' most important contribution, he states, was the invention of the modern system of musical notation. German organ tablature, woefully inadequate, was replaced by Guido of Arezzo with the modern system, complete with measure lines, rests, and key signatures.[4]

The other book in which, before 1834, Schumann read about the history of music is only a little more reliable: A. F. J. Thibaut's *Ueber Reinheit der Tonkunst.* This book, in its emotional strictures against all "modern" music, and its exaltation of "the old masters," whether they be the composers of Gregorian chant, Palestrina and Lassus, or Handel and Bach, shows no appreciation of even the most elementary distinctions between styles.[5] Schumann certainly could not have ac-

3. Schubart, p. 15.
4. Ibid., p. 38. Schubart seems to confuse Arezzo with Venice. We ought to keep in mind that Schubart wrote his *Ideen* during his ten-year imprisonment in the Asperg fortress.
5. The second edition of Thibaut's book, which appeared in 1826, is very much expanded and altered. While the basic premise of the two editions is the same, the second edition includes a great deal more factual material, and is in general more accurate historically.

quired any sure knowledge of the history of music from Schubart or Thibaut; but from Thibaut—through his book and through personal contact—Schumann learned to love Baroque music, particularly the music of Handel.[6]

A review of Schumann's education and reading before 1834 would hardly lead one to expect of him much in the way of historical knowledge. And his writings, especially before 1840, show that he had little more familiarity with the history of music than the average practical musician of his time. Of the numerous contributions Schumann made in 1833–34 to Herlesssohn's *Damenkonversationslexikon*, one is a marvelously uncomprehending definition of the Allemande:

> Allemande, originally a happy dance which had its origins in Swabia. It has now practically disappeared. In earlier times this name was applied to a special category of short musical compositions. Now, its place, like that of the Gigue, Sarabande, and others, has been taken by Scherzos, Capriccios, Bagatelles, etc.[7]

And in a review of a series of keyboard variations in 1836, Schumann remarks innocently, "The inventor of the first variations (it was, after all, Bach) was surely no slouch." [8] This statement is symptomatic of the limitations of Schumann's historical knowledge: especially before 1840, it extended back no further than Bach. Schumann's position—which would be, for us, like ignoring everything before Wagner—was the usual one; it was common for Germans in his day (and sometimes it still is in ours) to regard Bach as the founder of "real" music.

Musical culture in Western civilization has always had a short memory. With the advent of each new style the older one is usually promptly forgotten;[9] and in many cases even the musical notation

---

There is some discussion of Thibaut's knowledge of the history of music in Wilhelm Ehmann's "Der Thibaut-Behaghel-Kreis. Ein Beitrag zur Geschichte der musikalischen Restauration im 19. Jahrhundert." *Archiv für Musikforschung, 4* (1939), 21–67.

6. During his stay in Heidelberg Schumann often participated in performances of Handel's music at Thibaut's home. See Boetticher, ed., *Schriften*, p. 45.

7. *Damenkonversationslexikon, 1,* 149. (This entry, so far as I know, has never been reprinted.) See Appendix I, 29.

8. NZfM, 5 (1836), 63.

9. Except under special circumstances, as when the church attempted to codify and preserve its liturgical chant, and later, the polyphonic style of the sixteenth century. These efforts to retain the old and proscribe the new were only partly successful; there resulted in one case a multitude of additions to the prescribed music and a proliferation of para-liturgical forms, and, in the other, the simultaneous existence within the church of both old and new styles.

of one century is unintelligible to the next. In the later middle ages, especially in England, musical manuscripts were snipped up to make book bindings and lampshades a generation after they were written. Tinctoris said in his *Liber de arte contrapuncti* in 1477 that nothing composed more than forty years ago (that is, before Dunstable and Dufay) was worth hearing. And through the eighteenth century, composers produced music for immediate consumption, giving scarcely a thought to posterity because posterity was expected to make its own music. In Schumann's generation all this was just beginning to change. The active musical repertory now extended back about eighty years instead of Tinctoris' forty, and with the Bach revival—in which Schumann was an active participant—this span was increased to more than a century. It was the music from this period that interested Schumann, and he knew it exceedingly well.

Under Schumann's regime the NZfM paid a good deal of attention to historical publications, though Schumann seldom reviewed them himself.[10] They were normally assigned to C. F. Becker, a permanent and prolific member of the staff, and a competent historian. Becker also published his well-known *Zur Geschichte der Hausmusik in früheren Jahrhunderten* for the first time as a series of articles in the NZfM. An article in this series written in 1840 must have proven instructive for Schumann: a history of variation forms beginning with examples from the fifteenth century.[11] At about this time Schumann, doubtless under the influence of Becker, made moves to improve his historical knowledge. He made for himself a twenty-page chart tracing the course of the history of music from ancient times. As Boetticher observes, Schumann's sketch is based largely on Wilhelm Christian Müller's *Aesthetisch-historische Einleitungen* published ten

10. In 1837 Schumann wrote a brief review of Becker's collection *Ausgewählte Tonstücke . . . aus dem 17. und 18. Jahrhundert* (NZfM, 6, 40), and in 1839 he reviewed the first four volumes of Czerny's edition of Scarlatti sonatas (NZfM, 10, 153–54). This is the only pre-nineteenth-century music Schumann reviewed other than that of Bach. Historical books were frequently reviewed in the NZfM; there is a notice (apparently by Carl Banck) of Winterfeld's *Johannes Gabrieli und sein Zeitalter*, for example, in the NZfM, 1 (1834), 75–76. Schumann occasionally reviewed books, but included no book reviews in his *Gesammelte Schriften*. Kreisig has added to his edition four of Schumann's book reviews from 1836 (GSK, 2, 314–18). But two others, both reviews of historical books, apparently escaped his notice. The books are *Geschichte der Musik aller Nationen* of Staffert and Fétis (Weimar, 1835), reviewed in the NZfM, 3 (1835), 119–20; and F. G. Wegeler and Ferdinand Ries, *Biographische Notizen über Ludwig von Beethoven* (Coblenz, n.d.), reviewed in the NZfM, 8 (1838), 187–88. See Appendix II, 14.

11. NZfM, 12 (1840), 22 ff.

years earlier. Boetticher also found some evidence that in the years
after his retirement from the NZfM Schumann studied the writings
of Kiesewetter, the biography of Palestrina by Baini, and several other
historical books.[12]

Schumann's early ideas about historical studies in music emerge
from the second of his *Davidsbündler* articles, of January 1834:

> And, Raro continued, I am no devoté of antiquarianism; in
> fact I tend to think of this antediluvian research as so much his-
> torical dilettantism. In my opinion it has little influence on our
> artistic culture. You also know, however, how emphatically I
> have encouraged you to study the ancients. The master painter
> sends his students to Herculaneum, not to sketch every torso, but
> to gain strength from the bearing and dignity of it as a whole,
> and to observe, enjoy and imitate art works in their natural sur-
> roundings. In the same way, I have encouraged in you that atti-
> tude, not that you might muster erudite astonishment at every
> minute detail, but that you might learn to trace the expanded
> artistic means of today back to their sources, and to discover how
> they can be intelligently employed.[13]

This is Schumann the practical musician speaking. For him historical
study is useful primarily because it can enrich contemporary procedures in musical composition and stimulate contemporary artists.
Schumann himself returned time and again to the study of Bach's
music, and as a critic he recommended the same course to many young
composers. This is not to deny music of previous eras any intrinsic
value. For though Schumann's criteria were clearly "zeitgebunden,"
and he tended to judge older music by the standards of his own time,
he sometimes felt that Bach, for example, was fully as successful in
fulfilling these standards as contemporary composers.

For Schumann, Bach was the first of a series of great composers
whose personal contributions comprised the locus of an inevitable
line of progress leading to his own time. This line extended from
Bach through Beethoven and Schubert to the romantics of Schumann's
day, with an important spur, just off the principal line, occupied by
Mozart. This was the tradition in German music, now stifled by a

---

12. W. Boetticher, *Einführung*, pp. 291–92. Boetticher provides rather extensive quotes
from the ten *Zeiträume* into which Schumann divided musical history.

13. GSK, 2, 269–70.

flood of inferior imported stuff, that Schumann wanted to reinstate, and the NZfM was to provide the means. With this general characterization in mind let us examine Schumann's "historical progression" a little more closely.

THE HISTORICAL PROGRESSION: BACH

For Schumann, Bach was not the last and best composer of an epoch, but the inaugurator of a new one—the creator (to borrow a phrase) of modern music.[14] Schumann always objected to the association of Bach's name with other composers of his period. His review of Becker's collection of seventeenth- and eighteenth-century keyboard music begins:

> In a time when all eyes are fastened with redoubled intensity on one of the greatest creators of all times, Johann Sebastian Bach, it might also be fitting to call attention to his contemporaries. In respect to composition for organ and piano, no one of his century, to be sure, can compare with him. To me, in fact, everything else appears in comparison to the development of this giant figure as something conceived in childhood. Nevertheless, certain isolated voices of that time have something to offer which is charming and too interesting to be entirely ignored.[15]

And in his review of Scarlatti sonatas in an edition by Czerny, Schumann writes in 1839:

> There is much that is excellent in Scarlatti—which distinguishes him from his contemporaries. The iron-clad orderliness, so to speak, of Bach's progression of ideas is not to be found here. He is far emptier, flightier, and more rhapsodic. One has all he can do to follow him completely, so quickly are the strands woven and loosed. His style, in comparison with that of his time, is brief, pleasant, and piquant . . . We must confess that much of this can no longer satisfy us, nor should satisfy us. How could such a composition be compared with the music of one of our

---

14. Schumann thought of Bach as an isolated genius, not as a representative of a certain period or style. The term "baroque" was not yet used in Schumann's day as a period designation; it occurs several times in Schumann's writings, but always with its earlier pejorative meaning. See Boetticher, *Einführung*, p. 202; NZfM, 5 (1836), 48; and *10* (1839), 206.

15. NZfM, 6 (1837), 40. See Appendix I, 30.

better composers . . . Think of comparing this to Bach! It is, as a spirited composer[16] once said in a comparison between Emanuel and Sebastian Bach, "as if a dwarf appeared among giants."[17]

In Schumann's scheme of things, Bach's importance was many-sided. He made the first important contribution Schumann knew of to keyboard music, raising it to a position of equality with vocal music.[18] But far more importantly, Bach was the first to endow his music with the intangible spiritual and poetic qualities Schumann associated with the best composers of his own day. In Bach's luxuriant secondary dominants and dense polyphonic textures Schumann saw a real similarity to the expressive harmonies of romantic music. In a review of Czerny's edition of the *Well-Tempered Clavier,* he writes,

> Czerny's contribution consists, thus, of a foreword, the fingerings, indications of tempos according to Mälzel's metronome, and suggestions about the character and performance of the pieces. The first is cut somewhat short and was written in haste.[19] Rich ideas should certainly accompany this work of all works for piano . . . Most of Bach's fugues are character pieces of the highest sort, at times genuinely poetic creations, of which each demands its own expression, its peculiar lights and shadows.[20]

There are many more indications that Schumann saw a real kinship between Bach and the romantic composers. In his *Damenkonversationslexikon* article on Bach Schumann writes,

> How great and rich was the contrast between his inner being and his exterior! It was not only industry that allowed him to triumph over all the difficulties of musical combination, but an innate acumen. When we who come after him think we have discovered some marvelous configuration of tones, we find he has already used it or even developed it further. Besides this consummate mastery of the craft, his work has ideas and spirit;

16. Mendelssohn. See Schumann's *Briefe,* p. 218.

17. NZfM, *10* (1839), 153. See Appendix I, 31.

18. Schumans attributed to Bach the first significant keyboard variations (see above, p. 83), and the first "exercises" with real musical value. NZfM, *1* (1834), 45. Elsewhere (NZfM, *4* [1836], 45) he makes it clear that the exercises he has in mind are the *Clavierübung.*

19. Czerny's introduction discusses only fingering, tempo, and similar "mechanical" matters.

20. NZfM, *8* (1838), 22. See Appendix I, 32.

he was a real man; he did nothing by halves; his work is always complete, written for all eternity.[21]

As this selection shows, Schumann admired Bach's music for both its expressiveness and its craftsmanship. As a source for these two kinds of excellence, Bach was the founder, in Schumann's view, of nearly all that mattered in music.[22] The trouble with many of Bach's contemporaries (and most of his predecessors), Schumann thought, was that they exalted mechanical skills in composition to the exclusion of everything else. He writes in his review of Becker's collection of early keyboard music,

> The recent champions of old music err especially in this: they always seek out that in which our forefathers were strong, to be sure, but which often should be called by almost any name other than music, that is, all the categories of composition associated with the fugue and canon. They do themselves and their good cause an injustice when they fail to recognize the deeper, more fanciful, and more musical products of that time.[23]

THE BACH REVIVAL

A salient feature of the romantic period was a new interest in history, and the development of a historical perspective—one that sometimes tended, however, to be a bit biased and self-centered. The first and most powerful sign of historicism during this period in music was the Bach revival. In 1840 Schumann pointed to Mendelssohn as its prime mover, as the man who "first renewed Germany's awareness of Bach."[24] Schumann himself never contributed anything so dramatic as Mendelssohn's performance of the *St. Matthew's Passion*. Yet through the NZfM he made persistent and effective propaganda for the music of Bach, and he advocated the preparation of a *Gesamtaus-*

21. *Damenkonversationslexikon, 1,* 400. See Appendix I, 33.

22. See Georg von Dadelsen's "Schumann und die Musik Bachs," *Archiv für Musikwissenschaft, 14* (1957), 49–51.

23. NZfM, *6* (1837), 40. See Appendix I, 34. There is an engaging discussion of the fugue, both in Bach's time and his own, in Schumann's review of Mendelssohn's Preludes and Fugues, op. 35. NZfM, *7* (1837), 135–36. The best fugue, he says, is one in which the mechanics are so successfully concealed that it might be mistaken for a Strauss waltz.

24. NZfM, *13* (1840), 56.

gabe as a sort of national project thirteen years before the *Bach-Gesellschaft* was founded.[25]

But Schumann's most tangible contribution to the Bach revival has hardly been noticed. In his initial announcement of the musical supplements to the NZfM he wrote: "But we shall also be mindful of earlier times. More specifically, there are many unprinted works of J. S. Bach awaiting publication, and some of the finest of these are already in our possession." [26]

Schumann made good his promise by publishing seven keyboard compositions of Bach in the various musical supplements. They are:

1) Fugue in C-minor, BWV 575.
   NZfM Suppl., 5 (1839), 3.
2) Fugue in E-minor, BWV 945.
   NZfM Suppl., 7 (1839), 12.
3) *Ich ruf zu dir, Herr Jesu Christ* (from the *Orgel-Büchlein*), BWV 639.
   NZfM Suppl., 8 (1839), 3.
4) *Das alte Jahr vergangen ist* (from the *Orgel-Büchlein*), BWV 614.
   NZfM Suppl., 8 (1839), 15.
5) *Durch Adams Fall ist ganz verderbt* (from the *Orgel-Büchlein*), BWV 637.
   NZfM Suppl., 10 (1840), 3.
6) Fantasia for Organ, BWV 562.
   NZfM Suppl., 13 (1841), 3.
7) *O Mensch, bewein' dein' Sünde gross* (from the *Orgel-Büchlein*), BWV 622.
   NZfM Suppl., 16 (1841), 3.

Schumann undoubtedly thought his publication of these pieces constituted in each case a first edition (numbers 1 and 2 are specifically labeled "bisher ungedruckt" and "bis jetzt ungedruckt"), and, except in the case *Das alte Jahr vergangen ist*, he was apparently right.[27] These first editions have not attracted the attention of Bach

25. NZfM, 6 (1837), 146.

26. NZfM, 7 (1837), 120. See Appendix I, 35.

27. The earliest printing of any of this music mentioned in W. Schmieder's *Thematisch-systematisches Verzeichnis der musikalischen Werke von Johann Sebastian Bach* (Leipzig, 1950), pp. 432, 530, 447, and 427, is the original Peters *Orgelwerke* edited by Forkel's

scholars. The editors of the *Bach-Gesellschaft* edition were in possession of a later copy of the two fugues and the fantasia made from the Supplements by A. Schuberth, and all seven of Schumann's editions are entered in Max Schneider's catalog of early publications of Bach (here they are attributed only to Friese, publisher of the NZfM).²⁸ I have seen no other reference to these printings; even the Bach specialist Georg von Dadelsen, in an article that would seem to be a fine place to discuss Schumann's editions, "Robert Schumann und die Musik Bachs," ²⁹ does not mention them.

In the Supplement edition of *Das alte Jahr vergangen ist,* a footnote reports provocatively that this piece is "printed from the original manuscript." Now two manuscripts would be likely candidates for Schumann's source. They are the only ones, so far as I know, that contain this composition and have been usually regarded as autographs— that is what Schumann meant, apparently, when he called his manuscript "original." The first of these is the "Cöthen autograph" in the Berlin Staatsbibliothek, the most nearly complete source for the *Orgel-Büchlein.* A comparison with the Supplement edition of *Das alte Jahr* rather conclusively rules it out as a source. The minor deviations from it in the Supplement edition are not at all of the kind an editor would make.

Schumann's other possible source is the so-called Mendelssohn autograph which disappeared from the Berlin library sometime before the Second World War.³⁰ This manuscript, Spitta tells us, was in Leipzig in Mendelssohn's possession in 1836—i.e. shortly before the publication of the Supplements. Mendelssohn subsequently gave two leaves from it to his fiancée and a third to Clara Schumann. But in its origi-

---

students, Griepenkerl and Roitsch. The preface to the first volume of this edition bears the date 1844; all of the NZfM supplements appeared between 1838 and 1841. But an edition in four volumes of Bach's chorale preludes, including *Das alte Jahr vergangen ist,* had been published in Leipzig in 1803–06. I have not yet seen this collection; my information is from the remarkably thorough volumes of commentary to the *Neue Bach-Ausgabe* (Ser. *4, Bd. 2*).

28. Max Schneider, "Verzeichnis der bis zum Jahre 1851 gedruckten (und geschrieben in Handel gewesenen) Werke von Johann Sebastian Bach," *Bach-Jahrbuch,* 1906, pp. 92, 94–95.

29. *Archiv für Musikwissenschaft, 14* (1957), 46–59.

30. Spitta was convinced that this manuscript was an autograph and of earlier provenance than the one from Cöthen. *Johann Sebastian Bach,* trans. C. Bell and J. A. Fuller-Maitland (London and New York, 1951), *1, 647* ff. I am indebted to Dr. Alfred Dürr of the Bach-Institut at Göttingen for informing me (letter, April 1, 1965) that the one leaf of the manuscript he has seen is not, in his opinion, an autograph after all, but the work of the man he calls Hauptkopist B. This leaf was written, he says, "not before 1725, and possibly much later."

nal form, though it included only a few more than half of the chorale preludes from the *Orgel-Büchlein*, it contained all four of those published in the Supplements. This increases markedly the probability that the Supplement editions preserve the readings of the lost "Mendelssohn autograph," not only for *Das alte Jahr*, but for the other three chorale preludes as well.[31]

There can be little doubt that Schumann personally supervised the editions of Bach in the Supplement. His correspondence and his comments in the NZfM show his powerful concern for the Supplements, and, in any event, he personally took charge of almost all the journal's affairs. His attitude toward Bach and toward older music in general is clearly reflected in these editions. They are, from all available indications, very scrupulous and clean. There are no added expression marks or performance indications (in this respect the Supplement editions concur almost exactly with the Cöthen autograph and the *Bach-Gesellschaft* edition), and their publisher, Robert Friese—undoubtedly at Schumann's inducement—took pains to reproduce Bach's ornaments exactly. These editions are nothing at all like Robert Franz' doctored-up versions of Bach; Schumann never believed in "modernizing" older music—least of all Bach's. And the care for textual accuracy so strikingly demonstrated when he ferreted out errors in standard editions of Bach, Mozart, and Beethoven[32] is also plainly evident in these editions.

Schumann's choice of Bach pieces for the Supplements seems to follow a pattern. The fugues are, as Bach fugues go, very free in construction, and all of these compositions make use of an elaborate harmonic vocabulary. This is particularly true of the chorale preludes— and if Schumann was in fact using the Mendelssohn manuscript, he would have had a considerable selection of them from which to choose. The anguished chromaticism of a piece like *Das alte Jahr vergangen ist*

31. The three leaves Mendelssohn removed from the manuscript are yet extant. One of them, now in private hands at Oxford, contains a piece published in the supplements, *Durch Adams Fall ist ganz verderbt.* This leaf has not been available to me, as yet, for comparison with the Supplement edition. I am grateful to Mr. Walter Emery of London for a letter (January 7, 1965) informing me about the location of the extant leaves, and about the fate of the manuscript as a whole.

42. In his article "Ueber einige muthmasslich corrumpirte Stellen in Bach'schen, Mozart'schen, und Beethoven'schen Werken." NZfM, *15* (1841), 149–51. In a letter of 1845 to Härtel, Schumann laments that there is yet no thoroughly reliable edition of the *Well-Tempered Clavier,* and urges a new one "based on the original manuscript and the earliest prints," complete with a *Revisionsbericht. Briefe,* p. 441.

represented for Schumann the pinnacle of musical expressiveness, and he saw nothing incongruous about introducing this composition into a context of romantic music by Schubert, Hiller, and himself.

Mozart

Schumann's most significant statements of his views about the history of music occur in the little historical sketches with which he often prefaced his reviews. The review of Hummel's Etudes even has two such sketches, one showing the traditions in which Hummel operated, and the other outlining the history of the keyboard etude. These sketches show Schumann's evolutionary view of history: a linear progression from hero to hero with only occasional disturbances and occasional subsidiary branches along the way.

Schumann was never quite sure how Mozart fitted into his scheme. In at least one of his sketches he shows Mozart as an immediate heir of Bach.[33] Nevertheless, the qualities he sees in Mozart are radically different from those he values in Bach, and in Beethoven. The review of Hummel's Etudes begins:

> Tranquillity, grace, ideality, and objectivity—these are the marks of ancient works of art, and of Mozart's school as well. Just as the humane Greek pictures his thundering Jupiter with a serene countenance, so Mozart withholds his bolts of lightning.[34]

This notion of Greek art had been popular from the time of Winckelmann's *Gedanken über die Nachahmung der griechischen Werke* (1755) and *Geschichte der Kunst des Altertums* (1764). And this was a favorite illustration of the Greek artist's regard for decorum: he pictured Zeus, the "mighty thunderer," in an attitude of serenity and repose. Despite Lessing's prompt and persuasive refutation, in the first part of his *Laokoon*, of Winckelmann's doctrines of "noble simplicity and quiet grandeur," they remained a cornerstone for theories of art and art history far into the nineteenth century.

It was in Schumann's generation for the first time that the charac-

---

33. In a review of nocturnes by John Field. NZfM, 2 (1835), 30. This sketch is most unusual; in it Schumann couples Handel with Bach and Haydn with Mozart. The influence of Thibaut is probably still a factor in this early formulation.

34. NZfM, 1 (1834), 73. See Appendix I, 36.

teristics of classicism (exactly in Winckelmann's sense) were imputed to Mozart. Twenty years earlier E. T. A. Hoffmann wrote thus of the effect of Mozart's music:

> Love and melancholy call to us with lovely spirit voices; night comes on with a bright purple luster, and with inexpressible longing we follow these figures which, waving us familiarly in their train, soar through the clouds in eternal dances of the spheres.[35]

For Schumann, Mozart was "that playful, blessed wonder-child" who remained somewhat aloof to the emerging movement in which composers were to explore the heights and depths of musical expressiveness.

In a letter of 1840 to his friend Keferstein, Schumann explicitly denies Mozart a place in his central line of development from Bach to the romantic era, and offers this explanation:

> Mozart and Haydn had but a partial and one-sided knowledge of Bach. No one can guess how Bach would have influenced their productivity, had they known him in all his greatness. The profound powers of combination, the poetry and humor of recent music have their origin largely in Bach. Mendelssohn, Bennett, Chopin, Hiller, all the so-called romantics (I mean the Germans, of course) are in their music much closer to Bach than Mozart was; all of them have a most thorough knowledge of Bach.[36]

No one, of course, romantic or otherwise, could have had a "thorough knowledge of Bach" in 1840. Only a scattered selection of keyboard works had been published, and the great bulk of Bach's vocal compositions, particularly the cantatas, were hardly known at all. But Schumann was surely right when he said that the romantics paid a good deal more attention to Bach, and knew his music much better than Mozart did. Nor should we be too condescending toward Schumann's

---

35. Strunk, *Source Readings*, p. 777.

36. *Briefe*, pp. 177–78. The end of this passage in Schumann's letter ("die sogenannten Romantiker . . . stehen in ihrer Musik weit näher als Mozart") is a bit ambiguous. In Professor Blume's article in the *Musical Quarterly, 50* (1964), 298, it is translated "are musically much closer to Bach than to Mozart." But if this is what he wanted to say, Schumann would probably have made a parallel construction and written "Bach'en weit näher als Mozart'en."

views about the German romantic composers'[37] closeness to Bach. Quite aside from conscious imitations like Schumann's or Mendelssohn's fugues, the rich palette of harmonies and rapid harmonic rhythm cultivated in Schumann's time—and not in Mozart's—may well have had something to do with the new interest in Bach. Schumann thought so, and he was in a position to know.

Whatever Mozart's position in Schumann's historical scheme, there was never any doubt about Schumann's admiration for his music. The same cannot really be said for Haydn; especially in his later statements, Schumann is not particularly appreciative of Haydn's works. In a concert review of 1840, he finds the "Janitscharenmusik" of a Haydn symphony in G major "somewhat childish and tasteless."[38] And in a review of a series of *Gewandhaus* concerts of the following year, Schumann declares that Mozart's music becomes ever fresher with repeated hearings, while "nothing new is to be found in the music of Haydn."[39]

Some of the minor composers active at the turn of the nineteenth century, Schumann acknowledges, made certain contributions to the unfolding of the new era in music. In a concert review of 1838 he remarks that Abbé Vogler's music is not enough appreciated. Clementi and Cramer, he says, contributed significantly to the development of keyboard technique, and Tomaschek was a pioneer in the composition of short lyrical piano pieces—an important vehicle for the poetic music of his own day.[40] But the real founder of romantic music, in Schumann's opinion, was Beethoven.

BEETHOVEN

While Schumann detected in Bach's music a strong admixture of the expressiveness he most valued, it was in Beethoven's music, he maintained, that this first achieved a complete victory; Beethoven emerges from Schumann's writings as the familiar revolutionary and

37. Schumann's inclusion of a Pole and an Englishman in his list of German romantic composers is an amusing slip. What he meant, undoubtedly, was to exclude certain French and Italian composers who were sometimes called "romantic," but were clearly outside the pale of the Bach influence.

38. NZfM, *13* (1840), 160. The symphony was probably no. 100, the "Military Symphony."

39. NZfM, *14* (1841), 89.

40. NZfM, *8* (1838), 111; *4* (1836), 45; and *10* (1839), 174.

iconoclast who sweeps away all artificial conventions, providing for the free expression of subjective musical values. In Beethoven Schumann and his colleagues saw the beginning of a new era in music, namely their own.[41] August Gathy wrote with no little piety thus about Beethoven: "He, a romantic by the grace of God, is the founder of the romantic school." [42]

There was nothing very remarkable about the reverence of Schumann and his colleagues for Beethoven. Beethoven's music, especially the symphonies, were played by every German orchestra, and his mighty crescendos fanned the spark of chauvinism in every patriotic German heart. Fink, in an acidulous editorial of 1838, protested, quite rightly, that Schumann and his group could hardly lay any special claim to Beethoven, since his music was a model for every composer in Germany.[43] But Schumann and his journal were almost alone in championing Beethoven's little-appreciated late works. The late quartets and sonatas and the Ninth Symphony were in Schumann's opinion Beethoven's highest achievements, and the ideal models for contemporary composers.

This adulation of late Beethoven is particularly apparent in Schumann's dealings with Hermann Hirschbach, a promising composer and a contributor to the NZfM in the later years of Schumann's editorship. In a letter to Hirschbach of June 1838, Schumann calls the Ninth Symphony "the most important work in instrumental music of recent times," [44] and in a review of Hirschbach's quartets in 1842, Schumann congratulates the composer for seeing in Beethoven's late quartets "the beginning of a new poetic era," and for adopting them as his models.[45] When Hirschbach criticized some elements of Beethoven's late style in the NZfM, Schumann repeatedly sprang to Beethoven's defense in the footnotes. Schumann objected, for example, to Hirschbach's contention that in the late piano sonatas Beethoven was never able to reconcile his heightened expressiveness with his proclivities for counterpoint.[46] And elsewhere Schumann refers to the

41. See the historical sketches in the NZfM, 2 (1835), 5, 30, 153; and the much later review of Hirschbach's quartet in NZfM, 16 (1842), 159.

42. NZfM, 7 (1837), 55.

43. AmZ, 40 (1838), 665.

44. Briefe, p. 121. Schumann's admiration for the Ninth Symphony—and his sensitivity about German audiences' reactions to it—gave rise earlier to his whimsical essay "Fastnachtsrede von Florestan." NZfM, 2 (1835), 116–17.

45. NZfM, 16 (1842), 159.

46. NZfM, 8 (1838), 205.

Hammerklavier Sonata, fugue and all, apparently, as "uniquely great." [47]

SCHUBERT AND OTHER ROMANTICS

If Schumann celebrated Beethoven, at least early Beethoven, with all Germany, the next composer in his historical progression was almost unknown: Franz Schubert. Schumann's decisive role in the revival of Schubert's music in 1839 and the years following is well known. But Schumann's visit to Vienna in 1838–39, and his presentation of the C-major symphony and other of Schubert's instrumental compositions to the world by no means mark the beginning of his admiration for Schubert's music. Schumann's earliest diaries are full of enthusiastic references to Schubert,[48] and the NZfM stressed Schubert's importance from the first. In one of the earliest of his historical sketches in the NZfM, Schumann writes:

> Franz Schubert, in his most individual way, developed a strain of Beethovenian romanticism (which one could call provençal) to the point of virtuosity. Upon this foundation there has arisen, whether consciously or unconsciously, a new school, not yet fully developed and recognized.[49]

Schumann often coupled Schubert's name with Beethoven's; in his review of Field's Nocturnes, for example, Schumann speaks of the "starry night" first portrayed in music by Beethoven and Schubert.[50]

In the early 1830s only a few of Schubert's songs and fewer still of his instrumental works were known. A footnote to the first review in the NZfM of 1834 of a piece by Schubert promises "to acquaint our readers, little by little, with all the works of this rich spirit." [51] If the editors were at that time unaware of the extent of Schubert's works, they learned more about it the following year; in the second volume of the NZfM there is a report about the manuscripts of Schubert's large works held by his brother, Ferdinand. This report lists nine dramatic works, seven symphonies, and five masses.[52] It is usually

47. NZfM, _11_ (1839), 186.
48. See Boetticher, ed., _Schriften_, pp. 10–13.
49. NZfM, 2 (1835), 5. See Appendix I, 37.
50. NZfM, 2 (1835), 30.
51. NZfM, _1_ (1834), 78. This review is apparently by Ludwig Schunke.
52. NZfM, 2 (1835), 110.

assumed that Schumann knew nothing of Ferdinand Schubert's cache of music by his brother until he visited him in Vienna in January of 1839.[53] The report in the NZfM shows that as early as 1835 Schumann was quite aware of the extent of Schubert's unprinted music.

Schumann published first editions of three pieces by Schubert, only one of them a complete composition, in the Supplements to the NZfM: *Chor der Engel*, the andante movement from a piano sonata, and an aria and chorus from *Fierabras*.[54] In addition, he published for the first time in the NZfM of 1839 several letters, poems, and the famous literary effusion, "Mein Traum," all attributed to Schubert.[55] And in the same volume there is an extended description of 'Schubert's life and works by his brother Ferdinand.

Schumann's most spectacular and best known contribution to the Schubert revival was his work on behalf of the Great C-major Symphony. He singled out this composition from Ferdinand's many manuscripts, arranged for its performance and publication in Leipzig, and eulogized it in one of his most impressive reviews.[56] Schumann had an unerring eye for really important music. If he was the first to recognize the stature of Chopin and Brahms, he was also the first to raise Schubert from near oblivion.

Three other composers from the early nineteenth century are occasionally mentioned in Schumann's writings as contributors to the romantic movement in music: Prince Louis Ferdinand of Prussia (1772–1806), Carl Maria von Weber, and John Field. In a review of the opus 1 Variations of Adolph Henselt, Schumann writes: "If the characterization of music as romantic and classic is accepted, Prince Louis was the romantic of the classic period while Henselt is the classicist of a romantic period." [57]

53. Even Otto Erich Deutsch, in his exemplary *Schubert, a Documentary Biography*, trans. Eric Blom (London, 1946), pp. 910–11, mentions Schumann's "astonishment and admiration" upon seeing Ferdinand's store of manuscripts. But by this time Ferdinand's holdings had been considerably diminished, for some of the music had been sold to Diabelli. Schumann reports in a letter to Breitkopf und Härtel that he found there "a few operas, four great masses, four or five symphonies, and many other things." *Briefe*, p. 425. Ferdinand lists in detail the musical output of his brother in an article in the NZfM, *10* (1839), 129–30, 133–34, 138–40, and 142–43.

54. Supplement, *6*, 4; *8*, 4; and *16*, 7. The sonata is the one in C called "Reliquie" (Deutsch no. 840). Deutsch confirms that these Supplement printings are first editions. *Schubert, Thematic Catalog of all his Works* (London, 1951), pp. 197, 408, and 380.

55. NZfM, *10*, 37–39, 41–44.

56. NZfM, *12* (1840), 81–83.

57. NZfM, *7* (1837), 70. See Appendix I, 38.

Prince Louis Ferdinand, nephew of Frederick the Great, was famous as a warrior, composer, pianist, and libertine—Fétis remarks disapprovingly in his *Biographie universelle* that he "was not able to
control his passions, and his indiscretions were often a national scan-
dal." Schumann came to know Louis Ferdinand's chamber music
when as a youth he participated in musical soirées in Zwickau. And
in 1839 he still maintained in a letter to Simonin de Sire that "Of the
older composers who exerted a powerful influence on the new music,
I should mention first of all Franz Schubert and Prince Louis Ferdinand of Prussia." [58]

In Schumann's preface to his *Gesammelte Schriften* of 1854, it
will be remembered, Weber is mentioned with Beethoven and Schubert as a participant in the musical traditions Schumann and his
journal wished to promote.[59] Weber had a reputation in Schumann's
time as a champion of German opera, and, especially during his years
in Dresden, he was an influential opponent of the hegemony of Italian
style. The "Harmonischer Verein" he organized earlier in Mannheim
was even similar in many ways to Schumann's own circle of participants in the NZfM. But Weber's piano music was too glossy for Schumann's taste, and most of his statements on Weber place him clearly
outside the "central tradition." In a review of a sonata by one Franz,
Count of Pocci, Schumann says that were he the composer's teacher,
he would give him a great deal of Bach and Beethoven to study, but
"of Weber, whom you so love, nothing at all." [60]

A figure more important than Weber, in Schumann's judgment,
was John Field. Field's nocturnes, then as now, were his best known
works, and Schumann regarded them as a valuable and unique contribution to the literature of the piano. But the compositions of Field
he liked best were the concertos; the Seventh Concerto in C, published
a year before the composer's death, prompted Schumann to write one
of his most rapturous reviews.[61] Schumann considered Field's music
important as a forerunner, not only of Chopin's style, but of romantic piano style in general. Field's brand of ornamentation, and, more
particularly, his pedaling effects,[62] were in Schumann's opinion endur-

58. *Briefe*, p. 149.
59. See above, p. 3.
60. NZfM, *3* (1835), 161.
61. NZfM, *4* (1836), 122.
62. NZfM, *2* (1835), 127.

ing contributions, and Field's name often figures prominently in Schumann's explanations of the origins of romantic music.[63]

For Schumann the period from 1820 to the early 1830s—that is, the period of his own adolescence—was one of transition and ambiguity; the musical ideals of Beethoven and Schubert were almost buried in these years under a deluge of superficial piano music. In his review of a sonata by Dorn, Schumann refers to "that period of sleep, 1820–30, when one half of the musical world was still occupied with Beethoven, while the other followed the fashions of the day." [64] And when his career as a critic was drawing to a close, Schumann, in his review of Franz' lieder, wrote about a rebellion against those "fashions of the day":

> It is known that in the years 1830–34 there arose a reaction against the prevailing taste. The battle was really not a difficult one; it was mounted against that flowery banality, which, except in the works of Weber, Loewe, and a few others, could be seen in all music, but especially in music for piano.[65]

The revolution Schumann was talking about was the one he had organized himself and carried on in the pages of the NZfM. This revolution was meant to be, in one sense, a conservative one, for Schumann and his colleagues never proposed to replace prevailing tastes and standards with something totally new. This was a revolution directed toward the preservation and cultivation of the best that tradition had to offer. This was what Schumann meant when he wrote in his policy statement of 1835:

> Our intentions have been firm from the beginning, and they are quite simple: to be mindful of former times and their contributions, and to point them out as the only pure source at which present artistic endeavor can find renewed strength. Further, we propose to attack the inartistic tendencies of the immediate past, which has nothing to offer by way of compensation except for great strides in mechanical technique. Finally, we wish to prepare the way for a youthful, poetic future, and to speed its realization.[66]

63. See NZfM, 2 (1835), 30, and 154.
64. NZfM, 10 (1839), 139.
65. NZfM, 19 (1843), 34–35. See Appendix I, 39.
66. NZfM, 2 (1835), 3. See Appendix I, 40.

Schumann's critical writings are thoroughly permeated with his view of musical history; everything of significance that happened in the music of his time had to be fitted into his historical scheme. Because the romantic composers were the lawful heirs of a tradition extending back to Bach, he was forever referring them to that tradition for their models and inspiration. Just what a composer is supposed to get from a historical model is not always clear. Certainly Schumann never advised anybody simply to write in an earlier style; he always urged composers to make use of the "greater richness of means of recent times." [67] And "the sonata style of 1790 is not that of 1840," he wrote in a review of a sonata by F. A. Lecerf, "the demands in respect to form and content are in every way much higher now." [68] Schumann even disapproved somewhat of Spohr's conscious attempt to write in several earlier styles in his *Historische Symphonie*.[69]

In his aphorism "Das Anlehnen" in the first volume of the NZfM, Schumann shows that he believes there is no basic contradiction between dependence upon models and artistic freedom.[70] But never are historical models to be imitated literally; they serve instead as a fund of ideas and techniques usable for the enrichment of contemporary style—but it must always remain contemporary style. Thus elements of Bach's powerful harmonic vocabulary, Beethoven's technique of achieving climax, and Schubert's abrupt and delicate modulations are all fair game for the contemporary composer if he knows how to use them. There are also lessons of a more general nature that a composer can learn from historical models: by studying the best music of his forebears, he comes to understand better the enriched means of expression of his own time, avoids the pitfalls of mannerism, and learns genuine individuality by observing the work of great individuals.[71]

"ROMANTIC"

In this chapter I have made use—though not without some misgivings—of a term that seems almost unavoidable in any discussion of the arts in the earlier nineteenth century: "romantic." In his recent book on Mendelssohn, Eric Werner takes a strong stand against the use of

67. NZfM, 7 (1837), 61.
68. NZfM, *14* (1841), 27.
69. NZfM, *14* (1841), 53–54.
70. NZfM, *1* (1834), 148.
71. See above, p. 85, and NZfM, *10* (1839), 74.

this word, because "it is derived from another art. There it is well defined; in music history it is vague and debatable, and, worse yet, is used to describe diametrically opposed manifestations." [72] But surely the origins of the words we use as style and period designations are not a determining factor. It makes little difference whether "baroque"— perhaps the most bizarre of these—was originally an imperfect pearl or the fourth mood of the second figure of the categorical syllogism.[73] Most of these words, if their original meanings were retained, would make little sense when applied to musical styles or periods: "medieval," for example, or "renaissance," or romantic in the sense of romance-like—though this is probably what Weber meant when he called his *Freischütz* a romantic opera.

What counts, as the last part of Werner's statement implies, is that if we are to use these words we should agree to some extent as to what they mean. In the field of literature, where the word "romantic" originated, things are not nearly so untroubled as Werner thinks. So numerous and disparate have been the apparent meanings of this term that some literary historians have thrown up their hands in despair and advocated that it be dropped; the best-known statement of this position is Arthur O. Lovejoy's essay "On the Discrimination of Romanticisms," [74] first published in 1924. In an impressive article written in 1949, "The Concept of 'Romanticism' in Literary History," [75] Wellek defended the usefulness of the word by showing an

---

72. E. Werner, *Mendelssohn* (New York, 1963), ix.

73. The mnemonic syllables designating the valid forms of the syllogism have been used in teaching logic since the thirteenth century. The first two figures are:

> barbara, celarent, darii, ferioque prioris
> cesare, camestres, festino, baroco secundae.

The baroco syllogism has the form:

> All crows are black
> Some birds are not black
> ∴ Some birds are not crows.

This kind of argument fell into disrepute as early as the sixteenth century, and the name baroco subsequently became a general term of opprobrium. In his article "The Concept of Baroque in Literary Scholarship," *Journal of Aesthetics and Art Criticism*, 5 (1946), 77–109, Wellek wrote that this was the origin of our term *baroque;* but in 1962 he defended a confluence of this etymology with the traditional derivation from the Portuguese *barroco*. *Concepts of Criticism* (New Haven, 1963), pp. 115–16.

74. Reprinted in *Essays in the History of Ideas* (Baltimore, 1948), pp. 228–53.

75. *Comparative Literature*, 1 (1949), 1–23, 147–72. Reprinted with additions in *Concepts of Criticism*, pp. 128–221.

underlying unity of "dominant norms" among the various literary romanticisms.

In music as well as in literature the word "romantic" is too firmly entrenched in our vocabularies to be rooted out; what we ought to do instead is to clarify what we mean by it. Literary historians have made exhaustive studies showing what the word has meant, and particularly, what it meant to the romantics themselves.[76] Historians of music have not looked into this matter with comparable thoroughness, even though the word was in regular use in a musical context almost as early as it was in literature. Now there is no reason to think that we should accept on faith the romantics' notion of "romantic," once we find out what it is. But their testimony surely ought to be taken into consideration in any attempts we make to clarify our understanding of the word and the artistic phenomena it designates.

Schumann and the NZfM have something to say about this. The word "romantic" had been current in German musical circles at least from the time of E. T. A. Hoffmann's famous reviews of Beethoven's Fifth Symphony and Trios op. 70, published in the AmZ of 1810 and 1813,[77] and Schumann was very conscious, both as composer and critic, of representing a "romantic" movement. Romanticism was a popular subject for discussion in the musical journals of Schumann's time, and the NZfM devoted a good deal of effort to explaining it and defending it. In an article in the first volume entitled "Musikalischer Romantismus," the anonymous author described the romantics as musicians who rose in rebellion against low standards and "materialism" in music.[78] Carl Banck, a regular contributor to the early volumes of the journal, declared in an 1836 review of Schubert lieder that this composer, like Beethoven, was a romantic, and in an article in the NZfM of 1837, August Gathy speaks of the "romantic school" founded by Beethoven.[79]

As had been true when it was first applied to literature, the word "romantic" was vastly more popular among the opponents of romanticism than among its adherents. Fink often referred contemptuously

---

76. See especially Fernand Baldensperger, "Romantique et ses analogues et ses équivalents: tableau synoptique de 1650 à 1810," *Harvard Studies and Notes in Philology and Literature,* *19* (1937), 13–105; and R. Ullmann and H. Gotthard, *Geschichte des Begriffes "Romantisch" in Deutschland* (Berlin, 1927).

77. AmZ, *12* (1810), 630–42 and 652–59; *15* (1813), 141–54.

78. NZfM, *1* (1834), 187.

79. NZfM, *4* (1836), 2–3, and 7 (1837), 55.

to a romantic movement in piano music represented by Chopin, Liszt, Hiller, "and a few others"—Schumann's name, of course, could not be mentioned in the AmZ.[80] In a review of Hummel's Etudes, op. 125 (this essay is unintelligible except as an answer to Schumann's earlier review of the same collection) Fink wrote that the expression "romantic school" was a contradiction in terms; the chaotic ideas, one-sidedness, and blind enthusiasm characteristic of the romantics could never comprise a school.[81] Schumann's answers to attacks such as these were usually only half serious. In 1839 Fink printed a report from Breslau by J. T. Mosewius which extolls the music of Alexander Dreischock, one of the most vacuous of the Parisian virtuosi, and ridicules a group of unnamed composers Mosewius calls "Teufelsromantiker." Schumann rose to the bait and wrote this notice in his own journal:

> Where are these "Teufelsromantiker?" The good old Mosewius in Breslau suddenly declares himself their determined enemy, and the AmZ, too, is always catching their scent. But where are they? Are they perhaps Mendelssohn, Chopin, Bennett, Hiller, Henselt, and Taubert? What do the old gentlemen have against these? Or do they mean people like Vanhal and Pleyel, or Herz and Hünten? But if they mean some of these and not others they ought to be more specific . . . Let us stop mixing everything together and making the younger German composers suffer for what may seem to be faults in the German–French school, as with Berlioz, Liszt, etc. But if you don't like this either, then give us your own works, you old gentlemen, works, works! [82]

Schumann was of course not nearly this uncertain about who the romantic composers were. He was purely facetious in suggesting the names of Vanhal, Pleyel, Herz, and Hünten. His first list is substantially accurate, except that Fink and Mosewius would never think of including Mendelssohn in their attack; and the name of their prime target—Schumann himself—was missing altogether.

In established musical circles in Germany the word "romantic" was often used in one of its earliest senses, namely as a synonym for bizarre, extravagant, or baroque. This is usually the case in the music criticism of the AmZ; Schumann alluded to this in a remark of 1842: "The

80. AmZ, 37 (1835), 33.
81. AmZ, 37 (1835), 164–65.
82. NZfM, 10 (1839), 131–32. See Appendix I, 41.

Philistine, to be sure, mixes everything together, and what he doesn't understand he calls romantic." [83] This use of the word made Schumann very wary of it, and in 1837 he exclaimed, "I am heartily sick of the term romantic, though I have not spoken it ten times in my entire life." [84]

The name "romantic" was sometimes applied to music and composers quite at odds with Schumann's tastes. This note appears in the AmZ of 1835:

> The so-called romantic, or fantastic school, as it is also called by its adherents, has acquired a sister. Italian papers now call the school of Rossini "romantic" as opposed to the classic, or old-Italian. Will the most recent romantics of Germany and France acknowledge their Italian namesake? [85]

Schumann had a very low opinion of Rossini's music, and any equation of musical romanticism with the "school of Rossini" was surely distasteful to him; this kind of application of the term must have contributed to Schumann's caution about using it. [86]

Despite his misgivings about the word "romantic," Schumann continued to use it on occasion—though usually with a qualifying adjective or phrase of some sort—to describe the music and the composers of whom he and the NZfM approved. In his New Year's editorial of 1839, for example, he said the NZfM "meant to promote those younger talents, the best of whom are called romantics." [87] Several years earlier, Schumann had explained succinctly how he meant to use the word. In his *Journalschau* article on the *Iris*, he cited Rellstab's rejection of the "so-called romantic school," and added, "we approve of this name merely as designative, not descriptive." [88] Schumann felt that the adjective "romantic" did not have a clear and unequivocal meaning—and he was obviously right, for he and Fink, for example, would give quite unlike definitions of it. But he was nevertheless willing to accept it as an arbitrary designation or "conventional symbol" for a certain group of composers and their music. Schumann was per-

83. NZfM, *16* (1842), 143.
84. NZfM, *7* (1837), 70.
85. AmZ, *37* (1835), 100. See Appendix I, 42.
86. In his preface of 1854 Schumann named Rossini along with Herz and Hünten as a corruptor of music.
87. NZfM, *10* (1839), 1.
88. NZfM, *1* (1834), 199.

haps loath to discard this word entirely because it emphasized the affinities he felt so strongly between music and literature. And by this time—despite Goethe's famous dictum "classic means that which is sound, and romantic, that which is sick"—the word as used in literary criticism had lost most of its early pejorative connotation.

Schumann obviously thought there was a movement in music in his time that could legitimately be called romantic. Composers who in his estimation contributed to it in the 1830s and '40s were Chopin, Berlioz, Stephen Heller, Ferdinand Hiller, Mendelssohn, William Sterndale Bennett, Schumann himself, as well as various lesser known composers such as the cofounder of the NZfM, Ludwig Schunke, and possibly Norbert Burgmüller. But if Schumann was willing to accept, with some reservations, the designation "romantic" from the field of literature, he was much less inclined to borrow from it the pair of antipodal terms just then becoming fashionable, "classic-romantic." The romantics were in a sense revolutionaries, but their revolution was never mounted against anything which Schumann called (or we call) classic. Schumann did not think of a progression from a classic to a romantic period in the late eighteenth and early nineteenth centuries. In fact he did not normally recognize a classic period in music. The only time he so designated the late eighteenth century, so far as I know, is in his statement about Louis Ferdinand and Henselt: "If the characterization of music as romantic and classic is accepted, Prince Louis was the romantic of a classic period." [89] But the "classic period" in which Louis Ferdinand lived doesn't even coincide very well with that of Mozart and Haydn; he was born later than Beethoven, the founder, by common consent in Schumann's day, of the romantic era.

As we have observed, Schumann, like many in his time, saw in Mozart's music the embodiment of Winckelmannian classicism: "tranquillity, grace, ideality, objectivity." But he saw these qualities more as the achievements of a single individual than the standards of an era; he never ascribed them, for example, to the music of Haydn. Even if he saw Mozart as a proponent of a classic art, Schumann and his fellow romantics certainly never proposed a rebellion against it; Schumann was always a sincere admirer of Mozart's music.

While there was at least a modicum of agreement in Schumann's time about the identity of the romantic composers and the character-

89. NZfM, *1* (1837), 70.

istics of romantic music, attempts to borrow from literature the words and ideas of the current classic–romantic debate led to utter confusion. F. A. Gelbcke's long article "Classisch und Romantisch" in the NZfM of 1841 is a good example of this confusion. Classic art, he says, is typically representational; it always depicts objects. The primary effect of romantic art, on the other hand, is the communication of pure feeling. Music is by nature a romantic art, and when it does something other than express feelings, it becomes "defective and insupportable." [90] This is often the case, he continues, with the so-called romantic school; their programmatic titles and attempts at musical representation deny the essence of both romanticism and music. The true function of music—and by extension, romanticism in music—was lost with the passing of Mozart and Haydn; the contemporary "romantic school" has no claim to that title, for it violates the romantic nature of music by introducing into it inimical principles of classicism.[91]

Schumann did not let this unique interpretation of musical history —which in effect reverses the present-day view of a progression from a classic to a romantic period—pass without comment. He observed in a footnote that Gelbcke's article, circulated in manuscript, had already elicited several conflicting opinions.[92] This article represents a somewhat eccentric position;[93] but it shows that the application of the classic-romantic antithesis to music was considered novel and debatable in Schumann's circle. Any construction, such as Gelbcke's, which used the antithesis classic–romantic obscured the real nature of the romantic movement of Schumann's day. It was not directed against anything Schumann would consider classic, but against styles of a more recent vintage—and Schumann would never think of dignifying them with that name. Nor could he be expected to appreciate

90. NZfM, *14* (1841), 188.
91. NZfM, p. 189.
92. NZfM, p. 187.
93. Gelbcke's notion that music was essentially a romantic art was, of course, a popular one. Hegel included music along with painting and poetry as a characteristically romantic art in his *Vorlesungen über die Aesthetik*. See the preface to this work in the edition by J. Loewenberg (New York, 1957), pp. 333–35. German musical litterateurs such as E. T. A. Hoffmann and Jean Paul supported this idea enthusiastically. Hoffmann wrote, "It [instrumental music] is the most romantic of all the arts—one might say, the only genuinely romantic one—for its sole subject is the infinite." Strunk, ed., *Source Readings*, p. 775. And Schumann himself wrote, "It is difficult to conceive that there should be a special romantic school in music, which is in itself romantic." GSK, *1*, 26.

Gelbcke's attempts to deny the romantic composers' interest in communicating feeling. This kind of communication, not programmatic or pictorial effects, was for Schumann the essential ingredient of romantic music.

Schumann and the German composers favored by the NZfM were often called by a name which underscores their position as restorers rather than innovators: "neoromantic." While this term occurs in musical–literary sources in Germany as early as 1833,[94] it was not a common designation for Schumann and the favorites of the NZfM until the appearance in 1839 of Der Neuromantiker, a "musical novel" by Constantin Julius Becker. Waldau, the hero of this Jean Paul-like novel, is a wandering composer who in the course of his travels associates with Kinschky, a sentimental old violinist, Hedwig, his Mignon-like daughter who plays the harp, and Kathinka, a Polish countess in exile. Waldau periodically lapses into long monologues in which he reveals the author's opinions about contemporary music. The leading composer among the neoromantics in his opinion is clearly Schumann; Waldau's raptures over Schumann's piano music last for about fifteen pages.[95] Speaking for himself in the preface, Becker explains his title: "Beethoven was the founder of a new epoch in music; our colleagues call it the 'neoromantic school.'" [96]

By the later 1830s Schumann was widely recognized as a leader of the romantic composers and his journal as an organ for a romantic (or neoromantic) movement in music. When Schumann set out for Vienna in 1838, J. P. Lyser prepared the way for him with an article

94. AmZ, 35 (1833), 357. This word was not, apparently, borrowed from literary criticism. In her dissertation Kritische Auseinandersetzungen mit dem Begriff "Neuromantik" in der Literaturgeschichtsschreibung (Tübingen, 1936), Anne Kimmich does not mention any use of the word before the late nineteenth century in France where in the form "néoromantisme" it was applied to symbolist poetry.

95. C. J. Becker, Der Neuromantiker (Leipzig, 1840), pp. 90–104. Constantin Julius Becker was a lieder composer and an acquaintance of Schumann. He was always called simply "Julius Becker," and his book was published under that name. The only surviving copy I know of is the one at the British Museum; even this was hard to find in the columns of Beckers in the B. M. catalogues, because some industrious cataloguer in 1840 happened to know the gentleman's real first name.

96. Der Neuromantiker, p. iii. This statement ("Beethoven ward der Begründer einer neuen Epoche der Musik. Unser Mitgenossen bezeichnen sie mit dem Namen 'neuromantische Schule'") doesn't explain what the "neo" means. From other sources, such as the review of Becker's book in the NZfM, 11 (1839), 190, and Fink's acidulous editorial "Die neuromantische Schule," AmZ, 40 (1838), 665–67, it is clear that the neoromantics were so called because they wished to continue the "romanticism" of Beethoven. Schumann approved of Becker's ideas but called the composition of the novel "terribly weak." Briefe, p. 187.

in Saphir's *Humorist* entitled "Robert Schumann und die romantische Schule in Leipzig." [97] As we have seen, Schumann himself was very sensitive about the use of the word "romantic," but he was willing to accept it as a more-or-less arbitrary designation for a certain group of composers whom he admired and for their music. Yet he had very definite notions about the characteristics of this music he was willing to call romantic, and so, in a sense, willy-nilly he made his own definition of the term.

Schumann saw the romantic composers, first of all, as artists who subscribed to the now familiar tenets of nineteenth-century aesthetics: an emphasis on originality rather than the normative, an interest in the unique effect and the individual emotion, or, to use Schumann's own language, in fantasy, the characteristic, and the poetic. Schumann would surely not care to give a precise definition of these qualities, but, he says on several occasions, they are made possible by the "expanded artistic means" of his time. Original effects are made possible by an enriched harmonic vocabulary, a new rhythmic freedom, and—perhaps most important of all in Schumann's thinking—a powerful new piano with seemingly endless possibilities for unusual sonorities and novel pedaling effects.

Yet novelty and originality were not enough. The romantic composers must contribute to the development of a central musical language. The established canons of musical craftsmanship inherited from the eighteenth century were always important to Schumann; when he wished to defend Berlioz' *Symphonie fantastique* against its detractors, he did so by demonstrating its similarity to the traditional symphonic pattern. For Schumann, the romantic was a bold progressive who operated within a tradition; his whole purpose was to enrich that tradition, not to supplant it.

At least a couple of suggestions which may be important for us emerge from Schumann's interpretation of "romantic." In the first place, his testimony lends added support to Friedrich Blume's contention that we must discard the popular notion of a classic period in music followed by a romantic rebellion against it. The romantics viewed Beethoven as a champion of subjective musical expression, but not as "the man who set music free" from the shackles of Mozartean classicism. Schumann thought of Beethoven, instead, as the most important continuer of a movement which in its origins was a rebellion

97. Most of this article is reprinted in GSK, 2, 421–23.

against the stiff rationalism of the baroque. And the neoromantics of Schumann's generation were still rebelling, this time against a detestable interloper: the shallow, mass-produced music imported for the amusement of the bourgeoisie.

We ought to take careful note, further, that the musical romantics in the 1830s were a dissenting minority. When Schumann on a few occasions called his own time a romantic era, he did not mean that all, or even most contemporaneous music, would qualify as romantic. He meant instead to single out the romantic movement as the *most important* development in music in his time. When we call Schumann's period romantic, we ought to be aware of this distinction. Otherwise we would tend to drain the term of any specific meaning, and hence destroy its usefulness; it would thus become approximately synonymous with "nineteenth-century," or "early nineteenth-century," or whatever. Now an observance of this distinction does not preclude the use of the word as a period designation. A period designation is the name for a set of norms that are dominant at a particular time in history, and, as Wellek points out, " 'domination' must not be conceived of statistically: it is entirely possible to envisage a situation in which older norms still prevailed numerically while the new conventions were created or used by writers of greatest artistic importance." [98] To apply a period designation on the strength of a "more important minority" involves an act of judgment—as the writing of history always must. In the case of music in Schumann's time, succeeding generations have made this judgment unequivocally and convincingly.

Such an understanding of the period designation will help guard against the temptation to which many—not only the Germans—have succumbed: of trying to reconcile every last phenomenon with the dominant spirit of its times. If there is such a thing as a *Zeitgeist*, it must always be arrived at inductively; we may never treat it as an axiom which will yield reliable conclusions. Arnold Schering followed such a procedure in an article written in 1917, "Aus den Jugendjahren der musikalischen Neuromantik," [99] and the errors begotten as a result have found their way into the most recent literature on romanticism in music. In his excellent article "Romantik," Blume follows Schering's example in singling out *Neuromantik* as a kind of sub-

98. *Concepts of Criticism*, p. 129. See also Wellek's stimulating article "Periods and Movements in Literary History," *English Institute Annual*, 1940, pp. 73–93.
99. *Peters Jahrbuch*, 24 (1917), 45–63.

period in nineteenth-century German music. And (still following Schering) he includes as one of the elements of neoromanticism the cult of the brilliant piano virtuoso—precisely that element against which the neoromantics in Germany took their strongest stand.[100] When we extract a single term from the crosscurrents of variegated styles and ideas of a period and then apply it indiscriminately to everything in that period, we do violence to both.

100. *Die Musik in Geschichte und Gegenwart, 11,* 801.

CHAPTER 7

Schumann's Aesthetics of Music

Philosophers in Schumann's time were very fond of talking about art. The notion of a system of fine arts—distinct from all the other kinds of activities in which people engage—become gradually more articulate in the preceding century in the writings of Abbé Dubos (*Réflexions critiques sur la poésie et la peinture*, 1719), Charles Batteux (*Les Beaux Arts réduits à un même principe*, 1746), and Alexander Baumgarten (*Aesthetica*, 1750).[1] Kant wrote about art somewhat as an afterthought; he felt that his philosophical system, though largely complete after the *Critique of Practical Reason* (1788), still contained a lacuna. This lacuna, he thought, could be filled by developing his ideas about the mental faculty he called "judgment." In his *Critique of Judgment* (1790), Kant characteristically divides this faculty into "determinant" and "reflective" judgment, and then separates the latter into "teleological" and "aesthetical" judgment. Here, finally, in this rather obscure corner of the splendid edifice of Kant's system, he discusses the arts.

The German idealists who followed Kant devoted an ever increasing share of their attention to the arts; the wave of enthusiasm for romantic (i.e. postclassical) art stimulated by Schiller's *Ueber naive und sentimentalische Dichtung* (1795) and the subsequent writings of the Schlegels undoubtedly contributed to this preoccupation with the branch of philosophy now called aesthetics. Schelling, in his *System of Transcendental Idealism* (1800), declared, "the universal organon of philosophy, and the keystone of its entire arch, is the philosophy of art."[2] Schelling and the other idealists usually thought of the arts as reflections, in one way or another, of things which are very important

---

1. For Baumgarten, "aesthetics" was a science of sensation or perception in general (from αἰσθητικός, capable of perceiving). He discusses, among other things, telescopes and thermometers as aids to perception. It was only somewhat later, especially after Hegel's *Vorlesungen über die Aesthetik,* that the word came to mean specifically "the science of the perception of the beautiful in art."

2. Quoted in B. Bosanquet, *A History of Aesthetic* (New York, 1957), p. 321.

to idealist philosophers—things they call by such names as "idea," "the absolute," "absolute ego," and "Urselbst."

The German philosophers who discussed art in this period often indulged in classifications of the individual arts and evaluations of their relative importance. In these ratings music came out better and better. Kant's classification divides the field into the arts of speech, the formative arts, and the arts of the "play of sensations"—music belonging to the last of these.[3] In his "Comparison of the respective aesthetical worth of the beautiful arts," Kant places music (with some reservations) second to poetry. One defect music suffers, he says, is "a certain want of urbanity"—it often bothers the neighbors.[4] Less than thirty years later Schopenhauer assigned to music a place of unique importance among the arts. While all the other arts, he tells us, are only indirect portrayals—like the figures on the wall in Plato's cave—of the "Will" (something like an *id* of the universe), music is the *immediate representation* of it.[5]

Such explanations of music attained a wide currency in Schumann's time. Dozens of formidable and sometimes murky books on musical aesthetics appeared in Germany in the 1830s and '40s, most of them strongly influenced by idealistic philosophy and produced by minor writers whose specialties lay somewhere between history, philosophy, and music: for example, Gustav Nauenburg, Gustav Schilling, Ferdinand Hand, Eduard Krüger, August Kahlert, and Amadeus Wendt. Articles on aesthetics appeared in the musical journals (rarely in the NZfM), and these journals were occasionally the arenas for lively philosophical debates about music.

In the 1830s Schuman was largely ignorant of what was going on in philosophy. In the dozens of pages in Boetticher's two books devoted to extracts from Schumann's diaries—always rich in records of his reading—there is little evidence that he read philosophy or aesthetics.[6] It is characteristic of Schumann that he read and reread Jean

3. I. Kant, *Critique of Judgment*, trans. Bernard (New York, 1951), pp. 164–69.

4. *Critique of Judgment*, pp. 172–74. Kant adds in a footnote, "Those who recommend the singing of spiritual songs at family prayers do not consider that they inflict a great hardship upon the public by such noisy (and therefore in general pharisaical) devotions, for they force the neighbors either to sing with them or to abandon their meditations."

5. A. Schopenhauer, *Die Welt als Wille und Vorstellung*, ed. Deussen (Munich, 1924), *I*, pp. 303 ff.

6. Boetticher was very much bent upon showing that "Schumann is to be included among the philosophers of art of his time" (*Einführung*, p. 340) and musters all the evidence he can to prove that Schumann was abreast of current events in philosophy. His evidence is

Paul's novels, but apparently ignored his *Vorschule der Aesthetik*. Schumann showed his naiveté about philosophy and philosophers in an interesting way in the extract from his second *Davidsbündler* article reprinted in the NZfM under the title "Das Aphoristische." [7] Here, when he wants to give an example of some philosophers who have made "complete philosophical systems," he doesn't mention Kant or Hegel, but Ernst Platner and F. H. Jacobi, two distinctly provincial writers, neither of whom left anything that could conceivably be called a complete philosophical system.

Like most practitioners of the arts (but unlike Wagner), Schumann was wary of philosophical explanations of his occupation. In his "motto-book" he cited as the height of the ridiculous a perfectly normal-sounding definition by Christian Weisse: "The idea of beauty is the form of all true being perceived under the pattern of necessity." [8] While his distaste for formal aesthetics was somewhat tempered later on, Schumann always remained aloof from any disputes of a philosophical nature about music;[9] and though he reviewed almost anything else, he never wrote a review of a book on aesthetics.[10]

Several writers have noted that Schumann once began to write an

---

thoroughly unconvincing; he is reduced, for example, to making a great deal of Schumann's casual acquaintance with the "psycho-physicist" and amateur philosopher Gustav Theodore Fechner (Friedrich Wieck's brother-in-law). Ibid., pp. 337–38.

7. NZfM, *1* (1834), 151. Quoted above, p. 69.

8. Quoted in Boetticher, ed., *Schriften*, p. 58.

9. Schumann's closest brush with such a controversy was in his article known as "Das Komische in der Musik." NZfM, *1* (1834), 10. This is the title appearing over the article in all the editions of the *Gesammelte Schriften*; consequently almost all writers on Schumann have taken it to be an autonomous essay. The title of the article in the NZfM is "Ueber den Aufsatz: das Komische in der Musik von C. Stein im 60. Hft. der Cäcilia." In this article in the *Caecilia* (*60* [1833], 221–66), Gustav Keferstein (who wrote in several of the musical journals under the pseudonym K. Stein, or C. Stein) refutes an article in an earlier volume of the *Caecilia* (*51*) by one Stephan Schütze, who claimed that music cannot be comic. Keferstein gives a lengthy, systematic exposition of his position and provides a number of musical examples to show that music often is comic. Schumann's article, which consists almost entirely of musical examples, was meant only as a supplement to the examples given by Keferstein.

The fight about "the comic" went on and on—in the *Caecilia,* the *Iris,* and the AmZ (See the description of the controversy in Julius Knorr's *Journalschau* article on the *Caecilia,* NZfM, *1* (1834), 190–91). Schumann never paid any more attention to it in print.

10. Schumann once wrote to Ferdinand Hand that he had been reading the review copy of his *Aesthetik der Tonkunst. Briefe,* p. 230. Nevertheless, Schumann would not undertake the review of the book himself, but, after it had been on his desk "for a year and a day," asked August Kahlert to take care of it. *Briefe,* p. 216. Kahlert's review appears in the NZfM, *17* (1842), 75–77 and 85–86.

aesthetics of music, but never completed it.[11] They seem to imply that had this work been finished and preserved we should have a systematic exposition of his philosophical views about music. But the evidence these writers rely upon is the nineteen-year-old Schumann's letter to Wieck of November 1829, claiming that he had begun "years ago" to write an aesthetics of music;[12] from what is known about Schumann's adolescent writings one could hardly expect this to be aesthetics in any usual sense of the term. There is in fact a fragmentary document by Schumann, written in 1827 or 1828, that is probably the "aesthetics of music" he mentioned to Wieck. It is called "Die Tonwelt," and it makes some show of describing the effects of music and how they operate. But it really amounts only to a rhapsodic literary effusion similar to many of Schumann's other writings from this period; it may be described as something like the "In praise of music" section from an early medieval treatise as it might have been written by Jean Paul.[13]

The fact is that Schumann paid little attention to aesthetics divorced from artistic practice. Yet some of the ideas of the philosophers reached him indirectly by way of the literary men who absorbed their influence. E. T. A. Hoffmann, for example, one of Schumann's favorite authors, sounded like almost any one of the idealist philosophers when he said of instrumental music that "its sole subject is the infinite." [14] Thus Schumann, quite unintentionally, became interested in some of the questions that occupied the philosophers, and he shared some of their vaguely Platonic views about art. One of the subjects both the philosophers and Schumann discussed, but from quite differing vantage points, was the problem of musical reference.

PROGRAMS AND MUSICAL REFERENCE

Aestheticians of music have for a long time concerned themselves with: (1) whether music refers to anything outside itself (or, simply, whether it *means* anything); and (2) whether it depends for its effect upon association, either by the composer or the listener, with

11. See H. Kretzschmar, "Robert Schumann als Aesthetiker" *Peters Jahrbuch, 13* (1906), p. 50, and the recent article by Edward A. Lippman, "Theory and Practice in Schumann's Aesthetics," *Journal of the American Musicological Society, 17* (1964), 310.
12. *Jugendbriefe*, p. 83.
13. Parts of it are printed in Boetticher, *Einführung*, pp. 114–15.
14. Strunk, ed., *Source Readings*, p. 775.

extraneous events, experiences, feelings, and the like.[15] It is often assumed that in the nineteenth century, especially the earlier part of it, most composers and others who thought about these questions believed in musical reference, and that most twentieth-century composers and writers have put away childish things and embraced the "autonomist" position.[16] In other words, most romantics would, roughly speaking, answer "yes" to the questions posed above, and most modern composers and critics would answer "no." But things aren't nearly that simple; for as these answers have changed, the questions, none too clear at the outset, have changed as well.

Onomatopoeic effects, presumably, ought not to be the issue here; not even the most confirmed autonomist would deny that Respighi is able to make his listeners think of the cuckoo bird when he introduces into his music a phonograph recording of its call. Nor would he deny that Strauss can remind his audience of a flock of sheep by a skillful orchestral imitation of their bleating. What he does deny is that the composer *ought* to do these things. So far as onomatopoeic effects are concerned, at least, the question is not "Can a piece of music refer to anything outside itself?" It has become "*Should* a piece of music refer to anything outside itself?" And in answering "no," the twentieth-century critic agrees with most of the major writers on music beginning at least with Vicenzo Galilei.

The real battles between autonomists and referentialists have raged over questions about the relationship between music and the emotions. From the beginning of the seventeenth century, when people began to see in music more similarities to rhetoric than to mathematics, theories about music have allotted a prominent place to the emotions or passions. The most usual and durable explanation of the relationship between music and the emotions has two parts: (1) music expresses or portrays emotions, and (2) its most important effect is to arouse the emotions of the listener. When Hanslick, perhaps the first and certainly the most articulate of the modern autonomists, wrote his famous book in 1854—the same year that Schumann published his *Gesammelte Schriften*—it was still precisely these two propositions, he felt, that had to be refuted. He wrote:

15. I shall use the term "musical reference" somewhat broadly, admittedly, to cover the subjects of both these questions.

16. See Leonard B. Meyer's review of Donald M. Ferguson, *Music as Metaphor* in *Journal of the American Musicological Society, 15* (1962), 234.

On one hand it is said that the aim and object of music is to excite emotions, i.e., pleasurable emotions; on the other hand, the emotions are said to be the subject matter which musical works are intended to illustrate.

Both propositions are alike in this, that one is as false as the other.[17]

The first of these statements that Hanslick so vigorously denies—that "the aim and object of music is to excite emotions"—is on the surface a bit puzzling. For can music really have any aim? Aims, objectives, and intentions are the sort of thing, so far as we know, that only people (and perhaps some animals) have. Certainly Hanslick was speaking figuratively—as we did above in calling one chapter of this study "the goals of the journal." What he meant was undoubtedly something like this: "The aim and object a composer has in writing music (or a performer has in performing it) is to excite emotions." But in this case his categorical denial of the proposition is puzzling. Does he really mean to say that no composer or performer aims to excite the emotions of his listeners? Wagner, for one, claimed that he did; and Hanslick was his bitter opponent, not because he thought Wagner was lying (in this instance, at least), but because he thought Wagner's objective (that is, to excite the emotions) was a bad one.

Hanslick's book as a whole reinforces our suspicions that his formulations are more prescriptive than descriptive. He does not deny that music sometimes excites emotions; he admits this on the very next page, and in a later section he gives the improviser permission to do all the things he denied the composer.[18] In any event, as Hanslick would doubtless admit, the way to find out whether or not music excites emotions is to ask those who listen to music; and Hanslick's world was full of people who reported that it did. His point was simply this: that arousing the emotions of the listener ought not to be the primary objective of the composer, and that the kind and intensity of emotion the listener feels is not a stable criterion for judging a musical composition.[19] So again the original question has

17. E. Hanslick, *The Beautiful in Music,* trans. G. Cohen (New York, 1957), p. 9.

18. Ibid., pp. 76 ff.

19. In his enthusiasm for making this point Hanslick tends to overstate his opponents' views. "Beauty in music," he says, "is still as much as ever viewed only in connection with its subjective impressions, and books, critiques, and conversations continually remind us that the emotions are the only aesthetic foundations of music, and that they alone are warranted in defining its scope" (*The Beautiful in Music,* p. 9). Which critics could these be who view

changed; it is not now "*Is* it the goal of music (or its composer) to excite the emotions?," but more like "*Should* it be the goal of the composer to excite the emotions?" [20]

If an examination of the statements of an arch-autonomist like Hanslick begins to break down the popular notion of a sharp dichotomy between a "romantic" and "modern" view of music, a careful reading of the romantics does so even more. Schumann, like Hanslick, thought a great deal about problems of musical reference, and his thinking was remarkably critical and consistent. He doubted, with Hanslick, that music can portray, as a painting would, a nude reclining on a couch or a group of peasants gathering grain. And he thought that it probably cannot, like a novel, tell a story about a countess who marries an aging duke in order to be near her current lover who is a police official at court. Schumann even agreed with Hanslick that the psychological reactions of people listening to music are not entirely predictable. But he differed with him in the importance he assigned to these psychological reactions and in his interest in discovering their causes and controlling them.

Schumann did not leave us a treatise on the relationship between music and the emotions or on any kind of musical reference because, nonphilosopher that he was, he could never muster up much enthusiasm for these subjects in the abstract. But in the course of performing his duties as a critic he nevertheless discussed them a good deal. Questions about whether or not music refers to events or objects come up most often, as we might expect, in his reviews of program music— that is, instrumental music which the composer provides with specific

---

music "only in connection with its subjective impression," and who regard the emotions as the "only aesthetic foundations of music"? Schumann, clearly, was not one of them. The late baroque music theorists probably believed more implicitly than anybody else in a connection between music and the emotions (although their term "passion," deriving largely from Descartes' *Les Passions de l'âme,* was a somewhat broader one than our "emotion"). Yet these theorists were also concerned, as their composition books show, with a host of other considerations: correct harmony, facile melody, and the like. When Heinichen shows how to extract the proper passions from an "unfruitful" text and illustrate them in music, it is assumed that the illustrations will take all these other considerations into account. See J. D. Heinichen, *Der General-Bass in der Composition* (Dresden, 1728), pp. 31 ff.

20. Stravinsky, the most determined autonomist of all (in his writing, that is—many of his compositions are of types that presuppose close association with stories, events, and scenes), also gives us more preferences than postulates. For if his dicta about the independence of music are taken as descriptions of fact (see his *Autobiography,* New York, 1936, p. 53), he would seem to be condemning the romantics (and Berlioz in particular) for doing what he claims is impossible. See also his *Poetics of Music* (New York, 1936), pp. 74 and 130.

narratives or evocative titles (like E. Haberbier's piano etude, "Coeur insensé sois calme ou brise-toi"), and which may make use of onomatopoeic effects (like the sound of the head bouncing from the guillotine in Berlioz' *Symphonie fantastique*). Schumann's ideas about programs and musical reference have been subject to such a variety of interpretations that a reexamination of his statements on these subjects seems to be in order.

Aside from musical imitations of the sounds of bouncing heads and the like (which he hardly ever deigned to discuss), Schumann, as I have said, was very skeptical about the ability of music to refer to events, people, or objects in the way that language and pictures do. He never posited a program of any kind as the single possible referent or meaning of a piece of music. In his review of Berlioz' *Waverly Overture* in 1839, in fact, he specifically denied that this was possible, even for the composer:

> Berlioz has now written music to it [Scott's novel]. Some will ask, "to which chapter?, which scene?, for what purpose?, to what end?" For critics always want to know what the composers themselves could not tell them, and critics often hardly understand a tenth part of what they talk about.[21]

Even in 1835, when Schumann was writing his programmatic piano music, he worried about the risks a composer took that the composer's intentions in using programs might be misinterpreted:

> Beethoven was very well aware of the dangers involved with his *Pastoral Symphony*. In the few words with which he prefaced it, "more the expression of emotion than tone-painting," there lies an entire aesthetics for composers. It is ridiculous that a painter should represent him in portraits sitting at a brook, his head resting on his hand, listening to the splashing.[22]

Schumann denied that composers of programmatic music usually have any intention of portraying events, scenes, or characters. In his best-known discussion of programs, that in the review of Berlioz' *Symphonie fantastique*, he wrote: "He surely deceives himself who believes that the composer simply takes up his pen and paper with the

21. NZfM, *10* (1839), 187. See Appendix I, 43.
22. NZfM, *2* (1835), 65. See Appendix I, 44.

sickly intention of expressing, depicting, or painting something or other." [23]

And in his later review of Spohr's programmatic symphony, *Irdisches und Göttliches im Menschenleben,* he declared,

> They [the philosophers] are clearly wrong when they think that a composer working with an idea sits down like a preacher on Saturday afternoon, schematizes his theme according to the usual three points, and works it out in the accepted way—to be sure, they are wrong.[24]

It is clear from Schumann's writings that he seriously doubted that music can denote objects or events or state propositions.[25] A musical composition, in Schumann's opinion, does not *mean* the same thing as its program. If it did, there would seem to be little reason for having both. Yet Schumann thought that the connection between a literary program and the music it accompanies can be an intimate one, and on occasion he found programs and programmatic titles useful. In a review of Julius Schaeffer's *Lieder ohne Worte* he explained, "There are certain mysterious moods of the soul which can be more readily understood by means of these verbal indications from the composer, and we must be thankful for them." [26] And, he said, they can prevent a misinterpretation of the composer's intent; Schumann wrote about Henselt's etude, *Ave Maria,* "Here is an example of how a well-chosen heading can enhance the effect of the music. Without this

---

23. NZfM *3* (1835), 50. See Appendix I, 45.

24. NZfM, *18* (1843), 140. See Appendix I, 46.

25. In saying this I believe (though I cannot be sure) that I am contradicting Boetticher. He repeats throughout his *Einführung* that genuine German romantic music is always referential; the kind of reference involved is "symbolism" (See pp. 66–83). And because Schumann was a genuine German romantic, he used symbolism in his music and insisted that everyone else do so. Boetticher tries to show this, typically, by stating what he claims is Schumann's position, and then by way of demonstration, quoting something irrelevant from Schumann's writings (see especially p. 323). Though it is very difficult to discern what Boetticher means by "symbols," it is clear that he considers their significance to be universally valid; the connection between a musical symbol (he gives a schematic list of them on pp. 84–86) and its referent, he states, is a "necessary" one. But why this should be true he explains in language I cannot understand (and shall not attempt to translate): "Der äussere und innere Teilsinn erreicht niemals den Hochgrad der Verschmelzung, die Erkenntnisnotwendigkeit muss aus einer Spannung zwischen Symbolträger und -gehalt hervorgehen." *Einführung,* p. 68.

26. NZfM, *15* (1841), 33.

title most players would rattle it off like a Cramer etude." [27] But a composition should be able, ideally, to achieve its effect independently: "I always say, 'first of all let me hear that you have made beautiful music; after that I will like your program too.' " [28]

The quotation above from the Schaeffer review provides a key to Schumann's ideas about the workings of programs and about the nature of the connection between music and its program. This connection involves a third participant, namely Schumann's "mysterious moods of the soul," which, he tells us, the program can help us to understand. Now it was these moods of the soul (*Seelenzustände*) that Schumann associated with all the best music of his time, not just programmatic music. The program, he felt, could serve as an aid to their clearer apprehension and hence toward a clearer apprehension of an essential part of the music. A program or suggestive title, according to Schumann's notion, acts very much like the poetic descriptions of creative criticism. The Jean Paulian "poetic counterpart" could serve equally well as a descriptive assessment of a composition, or as a program for it; in Schumann's work as a composer and critic, it did both. Thus the music does not denote or portray the program; something like the reverse is true: the program suggests and clarifies certain qualities of the music.

Music and its program are related to each other because both are related to something else, namely certain psychological states, or emotions, or, as Schumann sometimes said, *Stimmungen*. Schumann was never very explicit about the nature of this relationship between the program and the emotions, or—and this is of more immediate concern to us—between music and the emotions. Is it simply that music elicits the emotions of the listener? Or does it express emotion the composer was feeling at the time of composition, or the one the performer feels during performance? Or does it, as language could, communicate the *idea* of an emotion, quite aside from whether or not any of these people experienced it at any particular time?

---

27. NZfM, *10* (1839), 74. And in his review of Moscheles' Etudes op. 95 (which bear titles such as "Das Bacchanal" and "Volksfestscenen"), Schumann wrote, "The use of such headings for musical compositions, which have become common again recently, is now and then criticized. It is said 'a good piece of music has no need of such indications.' Certainly not, but neither does it become less valuable because of them, and they are the surest means by which a composer can guard against gross misunderstandings of the character of a composition." NZfM, *8* (1838), 201. See Appendix I, 47.

28. NZfM, *18* (1843), 140.

Schumann seemed to admit more than one of these possibilities. There can be no doubt that he thought music elicits emotion; his descriptions of his own reactions to music show this plainly enough. But he believed that the listener does more, ideally, than merely react; a full appreciation of music involves receiving and understanding a kind of communication. One of the clearest statements to this effect is in Schumann's article "The Comic in Music":

> less well informed people usually tend to hear in music without text only sorrow or only joy, or that which lies halfway between, melancholy. They are not able to perceive the finer shades of passion, as in one composition, anger and penitence, in another, feelings of satisfaction, comfort, and the like. Because of this it is very hard for them to understand masters like Beethoven and Schubert, who could translate every circumstance of life into the language of tone.[29]

We can gather from this passage (and from a number of others as well) that Schumann thought music is able to *communicate* feelings or psychological states, and in this he was apparently at odds with Hanslick. Schumann surely did not think this would always work— that the reference of music to the emotions was universally valid or necessary, as Boetticher claims. In order to understand it you need to be "well informed"; the whole apparatus of programs, programmatic titles, and poetic critiques in which Schumann indulged, moreover, would have been useless were there no possibility of misunderstanding the emotional message of music.

But we still have not determined whether the communication of which Schumann speaks belongs to the second or to the third of the possibilities suggested above, that is, does music communicate the *idea* of an emotion, or does it express directly the emotions the composer is feeling? The difference between these two possible functions of music amounts to the distinction Susanne Langer draws between a sign and a symbol.[30] A sign, as she uses the word, announces that

---

29. NZfM, *1* (1834), 10. See Appendix I, 48.

30. Susanne Langer, *Philosophy in a New Key* (New York, 1951), pp. 54 ff. Philosophers and literary critics often do not mean the same thing by "symbol." Philosophers speak of "conventional symbols." The symbols of logic provide examples; there is nothing about the figure ⊃ which makes it more suitable than any other to denote negation. But in literary criticism (this has been true at least since the time of Goethe) symbols are thought to have some kind of intrinsic affinity with their referents. The bull, for example, has long been

something is present or that it is occurring. Smoke is a *sign* of fire; a train whistle is a sign that the train is approaching. A symbol conveys the *idea* of something (whether it is present or not); a symbol for fire is simply the word "fire." A symbol for what one feels in a stubbed toe is "pain," while a sign of it might be "ouch." [31]

When Schumann, then, says that a composition communicates anger or penitence, is this the particular anger or penitence of the composer (or of the performer)—i.e. is it a *sign* of someone's psychological state? Or is the music a *symbol* for an abstract anger or penitence? Schumann does not really say. His never-failing interest in such things as form and development of musical materials seems to preclude a view of music as an immediate, exclamatory expression of anyone's feelings. But the composer's ability to communicate any feeling depended, it seems, upon his having experienced it at some time or other; the "circumstances of life" Beethoven and Schubert translated into music were the ones they knew at first hand. The inevitable influence of a composer's experiences, impressions, and temperament upon his music is a dominant theme in Schumann's writings. He explains in a letter to Clara how this works in his own case: "Everything that happens in the world affects me, politics, literature, people; I reflect on all of this in my own way, and then whatever can find release in music seeks its outlet." [32] And in his review of Schubert's Symphony in C, Schumann reflects on the beauties of Vienna, concluding, "it becomes perfectly clear to me how such works could be born precisely in these surroundings." [33]

If music cannot, in Schumann's opinion, induce with any certainty into the mind of the listener a vision of a radiant sunset or thoughts about a heroic woman risking her life to save her husband, it *can* communicate the kind of feelings which attend such things—provided

a symbol for passion and virility, and most people would agree that it is more appropriate for this than would be, say, a butterfly.

31. In the preface to the second edition of her book Miss Langer suggests the substitution of "signal" for "sign." Whichever term is used, there remain, I believe, certain loose ends to this distinction as she presents it. The utterances: "The train is approaching," and "I am in pain" would function, apparently, just as the train-whistle and the exclamation "ouch." But these statements certainly do not appear to be signs (or signals) as she thinks of them; both, for one thing, make use of symbols ("train" and "pain").

32. *Jugendbriefe*, p. 282.

33. NZfM, *12* (1840), 82. Schumann was convinced that a composer's geographical location had an important effect on his music. On several occasions he printed his audacious aphorism, "Tell me where you live, and I will tell you how you compose." NZfM, *4* (1836), 198, and *5* (1836), 128.

that the listener is properly perceptive and properly conditioned. Feeling in a broad sense (or "conditions of the soul" or *Stimmungen*), then, lies at the center of Schumann's theories about musical significance. They become part of the composer's experience simply as a result of his own environment and his own impressions. They are communicated in music to the receptive listener, who, the composer hopes, will understand them and at least to some extent experience them himself. The literary program is meant to reinforce this communication by suggesting to the listener ideas, events, or narratives with which he might associate such feelings. It is an alternate route to the same goal.

Perhaps this interpretation of Schumann's ideas will help to explain his seemingly inconsistent statements about program music. For sometimes he favors programs and at other times not; sometimes he wants to substitute different programs and titles for the ones composers have given their music, or he provides more than one program for the same piece; sometimes, as in the case of the *Papillons*, he associates a single program with pieces composed independently and at various times, and always stoutly insists that the programs and titles, even of his most programmatic music, are applied ex post facto.

Schumann's apparent inconsistency about the value he sets upon programs is now easier to understand. If the music itself is communicative, a program, ideally, should not be necessary. Several times Schumann said that it would be "a good test of the composer's success" if his listeners knew nothing of his programs or titles.[34] And he reproved Berlioz and Spohr for habitually providing their music with programs or programmatic titles, though he never had any serious quarrel with either their music or their programs per se.[35] In Schumann's opinion, attaching a program to a piece of music was something like telling a joke and then explaining the punchline.

If the music itself were not communicative, Schumann insists, attaching a program or evocative title to it would be as futile as writing a poetic critique of it. This is true of the etude by Haberbier mentioned above, "Coeur insensé sois calme ou brise-toi." Such a heartbreaking title, he says, can do nothing for this pedestrian music.[36]

34. NZfM, 2 (1835), 65, 202.
35. NZfM, 2 (1835), 65; *18* (1843), 140; and *20* (1844), 11.
36. NZfM, *16* (1842), 103.

Schumann was sometimes willing to accept more than one program for the same composition; in his review of the Schubert C-major Symphony he implies that the suitability of a program or poetic counterpart may depend upon the sensibilities of the listener:

> I will not attempt to provide the symphony with a foil, for the different generations choose very different words and pictures to apply to music. And the youth of eighteen often hears in a piece of music an event of worldwide importance, while the grown man sees only a local happening, and the musician thought of neither the one nor the other.[37]

The possibility of fitting more than one program to a composition with satisfactory results is consistent with Schumann's view of the program as a supplement or accessory. Just as a single piece of music could be subject to various poetic descriptions—and often was by the contrasting personalities of Florestan and Eusebius in Schumann's early criticism—so its message could be suggested by more than one program.

But in many cases, Schumann seems to say, the composer describes in his program the very events, experiences, or impressions that aroused in him the feelings he wishes to communicate in his composition. Schumann apparently thought Berlioz did this in his *Symphonie fantastique*.[38] But even such a program has no special claims to authenticity. Schumann, in fact, wanted to forget Berlioz' program and make his own: "In the beginning the program spoiled all my enjoyment and all my freedom of outlook. But as this receded more and more into the background and my own imagination became creative, I found all this and much more. . . ."[39] But this is not to say that program-making was an arbitrary and entirely subjective matter. Not just any one would do; Schumann often quarreled with the names composers gave their music (Johann Kittl was a habitual offender in this respect) and the programs they associated with it.

37. NZfM, *12* (1840), 82. See Appendix I, 49.

38. He says, "In any case, the five principal headings would have sufficed; oral tradition would have passed on the other details of these events quickly enough. The interest stimulated in the person of the composer, who himself lived through this symphony, would assure that." NZfM, *3* (1835), 50. See Appendix I, 50.

Barzun has shown convincingly enough that Berlioz' program for the *Symphonie fantastique* is not autobiographical; it was synthesized from various literary sources. Jacques Barzun, *Berlioz and the Romantic Century* (Boston, 1950), *1*, 157 ff.

39. NZfM, *3* (1835), p. 50.

Though more than one poetic counterpart to a piece of music was possible, finding a really appropriate one, Schumann thought, was a difficult and exacting task.

The ideas about musical reference emerging from Schumann's writings also cast some light on the seemingly erratic treatment of programmatic elements in his own music.[40] The individual movements of the *Phantasie* op. 17, for example, were originally to have borne the names *Ruinen, Trophaeen,* and *Palmen;* Schumann later changed these to *Ruine, Siegesbogen und Sternbild,* and *Dichtungen,*[41] and finally eliminated them altogether. The Intermezzo from the *Faschingschwank aus Wien,* as we have seen, was to have been included in a set of pieces with quite different programmatic connotations, the *Nachtstücke*—which itself Schumann first intended to call *Leichenphantasie.*[42] This kind of indecision bolsters Schumann's claim that he did not compose to illustrate preexistent literary schemes, but that, as he said, programs and titles occurred to him only after he had composed the music.[43] This is perfectly consistent with Schumann's view of the program as a supplement to a composition, not a subject of it.

In the case of one of Schumann's compositions, the *Papillons,* he certainly seems to say that he composed the music with a preexistent literary scheme in mind, namely the last chapter of Jean Paul's *Flegeljahre.* When copies of the *Papillons* were sent to various journals for review in 1832, Schumann, fearful that the reviewers would not know what to make of it, sent a few words of explanation to each of four editors, Rellstab, Fink, Castelli, and Gottfried Weber. These explanations are substantially similar; this one is from his letter to Rellstab:

> Less for the editor of *Iris* than for the poet and spiritual kin of Jean Paul, I shall allow myself a few words about the origins of

40. Mr. Lippman's article on this subject (*Journal of the American Musicological Society,* 17 [1964], 310–45) is thorough and thoughtful. But it does not take sufficient note, I think, of Schumann's profound skepticism about the ability of music to depict events, objects, or people.

41. *Jugendbriefe,* p. 281.

42. Ibid., p. 301.

43. In 1837 Schumann wrote to Moscheles about the *Carnaval,* "I hardly need assure you that the arrangement of the individual numbers as well as the headings came about only after the composition of the music." *Briefe,* p. 92. And later he wrote to his admirer Simonin de Sire, "The titles of all my compositions occur to me only after I have finished composing the music." Ibid., p. 148. Boetticher (*Einführung,* p. 332) collects a series of Schumann's statements to this effect, but chooses not to believe them.

the *Papillons*; for the thread that binds them together is barely visible. You will remember the last scene of the *Flegeljahre*— masked ball—Walt—Vult—masks—Wina—Vult's dancing— the exchange of masks—confessions—anger—disclosures—hurrying away—closing scene and then the departing brother.—I turned the last page over again and again; for the end seemed to me but a new beginning—and almost without knowing it I was at the piano, and thus arose one *Papillon* after another. May you find in these origins an apology for the whole, which in its particulars often needs one! [44]

And in a letter to his family in Zwickau he says,

and tell them all to read, as soon as possible, the final scene of Jean Paul's *Flegeljahre*, and that the *Papillons* are in fact meant as a translation into tone of this masked ball. And then ask them if the *Papillons* accurately reflect, perhaps, something of Wina's angelic love, Walt's poetic nature, and Vult's lightning-sharp spirit.[45]

Boetticher has found some marginal notes in Schumann's own copy of the *Flegeljahre* (now in the Robert Schumann-Haus, Zwickau) which seem to make the connection between the *Papillons* and Jean Paul's novel even more explicit. Schumann marked specific passages in the last chapter of the *Flegeljahre* with numbers designating the individual *Papillons*.[46] Thus the *Papillon* no. 1, for example, is linked with this passage:

As he stepped out of the little room, he asked God that he might be happy when he returned to it; he felt like a hero who, thirsty for fame, goes forth into his first battle.[47]

So Schumann's own testimony apparently indicates that in this case a literary program (though one unmentioned in the published music) preceded and in some sense gave rise to the composition. Schumann

44. *Jugendbriefe*, pp. 167–68.

45. Ibid., p. 166.

46. *Einführung*, pp. 331–32, and 611–13. Boetticher provides for each of the *Papillons*, in parallel columns, the passage Schumann marked in Jean Paul, his own description of the music (this is in some places seriously inaccurate; the *Papillon* no. 5, for example, is in B-flat major, not G minor), and the later explanations of the *Papillons* given by Julius Knorr.

47. From Boetticher, *Einführung*, p. 611. The remainder of these passages are given in accurate translation in Lippman, pp. 315–16.

seems to be afraid, furthermore, that the music will not be intelligible without this program, and he even speaks of his music as a "translation into tone." Boetticher's discovery, moreover, shows very detailed connections between program and music; these would tend to strengthen his position that Schumann was trying in his *Papillons* to communicate directly the events of Jean Paul's story. All of this apparently contradicts Schumann's statements that he always made connections with programs after the music was finished, and his professed belief that programs are but extrinsic aids—that music communicates states of the soul, not events.

Now when Schumann insisted that he always chose his titles, mottos, and programs ex post facto, he surely did not mean to say that a single piece of literature could never serve both as the impetus for a composition and as its program. The factors which influenced a composer in the making of a piece of music often became part of its program, as in the case, Schumann said, of Berlioz' *Symphonie fantastique*. His point is simply that the whole question of programs and titles had to be settled after the music was finished, and, as in the case of the *Symphonie fantastique* again, even things which influenced the composer have no inviolable claim to validity as programmatic aids for his music.

Thus if Schumann in fact composed the *Papillons* under the spell of the *Flegeljahre* and then recommended that novel to various people as a program for it, this was not inconsistent with his assertions that he applied programs ex post facto. But it is very doubtful that this is even what happened. For whatever Schumann told the editors, he wrote thus to Henrietta Voigt about the *Papillons*:

> I must also mention that I added the text to the music, not the reverse—for that would seem to me a silly beginning. Only the last, which by strange coincidence formed an answer to the first,[48] was aroused by Jean Paul.[49]

If we must make a choice as to which we are to believe, Schumann's statement to the editors, or to Henrietta Voigt, surely it has to be the latter. Schumann felt that the editors would require a plausible explanation for the novel form of the *Papillons*, while he could be much more frank with an intimate friend. The history of the *Papillons*

48. Lippman, p. 320, has a good explanation for this passage.
49. *Briefe*, p. 54.

throws even more suspicion on Schumann's report to Rellstab and the others that he read Jean Paul and then immediately composed these pieces. For they existed previously as independent waltzes and polonaises, and were composed intermittently over a long period of time.[50]

Boetticher treats the marginal notes in the *Flegeljahre* as final authority on what Schumann meant to communicate in composing the *Papillons*.[51] But we do not know what Schumann intended by these markings, nor even when they were made. It is perfectly plausible that he wrote these notations (his letter to Henrietta Voigt clearly suggests this) after the *Papillons* were complete, just as he suddenly discovered in his *In der Nacht* from the *Fantasiestücke*, long after it was finished, a certain kinship with the legend of Hero and Leander.[52] The notes in the *Flegeljahre* certainly do not justify Boetticher's opinion that Schumann intended in his *Papillons* to depict the specific events and characters of Jean Paul's novel.

Schumann's literary style is often highly figurative and sometimes it is more notable for its grace than for its precision. Yet it will pay us to read his statements about the *Papillons* and their program attentively. The letter to his family cited above comes closest, seemingly, to positing an immediate connection between the *Papillons* and events in the *Flegeljahre*. But even here Schumann does not say that

50. See Wolfgang Gertler, *Robert Schumann in seinen frühen Klavierwerken* (Leipzig, 1931), pp. 4 ff. Some of the polonaises incorporated into the *Papillons* have been published by Geiringer in a Universal edition; Geiringer discusses them in "Ein unbekanntes Klavierwerk von Robert Schumann," *Die Musik*, 25 (1932), Bd. 2, pp. 725–26.

51. Several of these passages seem disturbingly unconvincing as counterparts to the music. The scherzando, leaping, harmonically spicy middle section to the *Papillon* no. 4 (see Ex. 1)

Example 1. R. Schumann, *Papillons* op. 2, no. 4

refers, Boetticher tells us, to "a simple nun with a half mask and a fragrant bunch of auriculas." Boetticher attempts to mitigate this incongruity by describing the music as "stepwise and pianissimo"—neither of which it is. *Einführung*, p. 611.

52. *Jugendbriefe*, pp. 286–87

the *Papillons* portrays Wina, Walt, or Vult, or anything they did, but "something of Wina's angelic love, Walt's poetic nature, and Vult's lightning-sharp spirit"—in short, it communicates states of the soul. And when Schumann speaks of his music as "a translation into tone," he specifies what it is that is translated: the masked ball. A ball is precisely the sort of thing that music can imitate through onomatopoeia, for the most noticeable sound at a ball is, of course, music. And the *Papillons*, like the music for a ball, consists simply of a series of dances.[53]

For Schumann the literary program was an aid to comprehension, a means for getting at an elusive and fragile content which is already present in the music—a content that any number of conventional performance directions or any straightforward, literal description would be helpless to communicate. Schumann's programmatic piano compositions, like his essays in creative criticism, were largely confined to the 1830s. As time passed, Schumann apparently became convinced that if the music itself is really communicative, there is no need for either of them.

INSPIRATION AND CRAFTSMANSHIP

If music communicates feeling, as Schumann says it does, it would seem perfectly reasonable to ask *"How?"* We know that language employs symbols with fairly well fixed referents, so that a person speaking or writing these symbols can communicate information of many kinds (including information about feelings). Whatever the claims of Schering, Boetticher, and others, music lacks a repertory of defined symbols; thus if music communicates anything, it must do so in some other way. The question, then, is "How?" This problem has been written about a good deal, especially by philosophers. Susanne Langer, for example, whose ideas about musical significance are in some respects very much like Schumann's, argues that music can symbolize and communicate "general forms of feeling," or "the morphology of feeling." [54] It can do this, she says, because music fulfills various requirements (which she enumerates) for a nonverbal

53. A number of these pieces (e.g. nos. 1, 2, 6, 10) even have the introductory section which announces the next dance of the ball. This collection of dances reflects the importance in Schumann's early musical experience of amateur music-making; many of them clearly show the influence of the style of four-hand piano music in vogue at the time.

54. Langer, p. 202.

language. Among these is that it shows a "logical form" similar to that of its referent; the motions of waxing and waning and of tension and relaxation, which serve to define its "logical form," are characteristic of both music and our feelings. In fact, Langer continues, "Because the forms of human feeling are much more congruent with musical forms than with the forms of language, music can *reveal* the nature of feelings with a detail and truth that language cannot approach."[55]

The principal clause of this last sentence might have been uttered by Schumann or almost any of the romantics. But Schumann would not have been interested in the explanatory dependent clause. Schumann's "mysterious states of the soul" are mysterious because they are inaccessible to any ordinary linguistic description. The workings by which music conveys them, too, are mysterious, and Schumann was not particularly eager to explore these mysteries. Music that is genuinely expressive, Schumann believed, is at least partly a gift of inspiration, and he sometimes showed a real reticence about inquiring too closely into the nature of that gift.

There was of course nothing new in Schumann's belief that inspiration—nonrational and inexplicable—plays a role in musical invention. Even the most formal descriptions of the process of musical composition in the late eighteenth century emphasized the importance of inspiration. In his book on composition, Heinrich Christoph Koch, for example, makes use of J. G. Sulzer's term *Anlage* ("laying out," or initial conception) and explains to his readers "the manner in which such an *Anlage* arises in the soul of the composer." Before this can happen at all, he says, the composer must be in "a special state of inspiration."[56] This special state of inspiration—sometimes indistinguishable from a kind of feverish emotional excitement—is further emphasized as a factor in musical creation by the earlier romantic writers on music, Wackenroder, Tieck, and Jean Paul.

Schumann too was convinced of its importance, and at times he seems to embrace the peculiarly romantic doctrine of the infallibility of initial inspiration. In a review of Cherubini's second string quartet,

55. Langer, p. 199. In Miss Langer's opinion, then, music is a symbol for the emotions, but not a "conventional symbol"; for its significance is not based on either general agreement or a stated definition, but on a natural similarity to its referent. But why this similarity—i.e. that both music and the emotions wax and wane, etc.—should be called a similarity of *logical form* is not clear.

56. Heinrich Christoph Koch, *Versuch einer Anleitung zur Composition* (Leipzig, 1787), 2, 70.

he says he suspects that the composition is really a reworking of an unsuccessful symphony. "I am averse to all such transformations," he writes, "for they seem to me like a sin against the divine first inspiration." [57] And in his review of F. W. Grund's sonata for piano, op. 27, Schumann speculates that the second of the two movements was written much later than the first, and that the composer was unable to recapture the original mood of the piece:

> For the stimulation of the composer's imagination is such a delicate matter, that once the track is lost, or time intervenes, it is only by a happy coincidence that in a later rare moment it can be recovered. For this reason, a work discontinued and laid aside is seldom completed; it would be preferable for the composer to begin a new one, and give himself over completely to its *Stimmung*.[58]

Schumann included in his *Gesammelte Schriften* an aphorism to the same effect—one which shows that Schumann, like many of his predecessors, tended to identify inspiration with the strong emotions accompanying artistic creation: "The first conception is always the most natural and the best. Reason errs, but never feeling." [59]

During his ten-year stint as critic, Schumann's descriptions of the process of composition changed somewhat in emphasis. He became more and more impressed with the importance of the rational processes of the craft—of systematic development of themes, of revision and refining. In the 1840s Schumann began to find *Ausführung* ("working out") fully as necessary as *Erfindung* ("invention").[60] Expressions foreign to his early vocabulary, such as *Reinheit des Satzes* ("purity of phrasing") and *Geschicklichkeit der Anordnung* ("skill in ordering"),[61] began to show up in his reviews, and in 1843 he even recommended to his readers one of the most rationalistic of all books on composition, Mattheson's *Kern melodischer Wissenschaft*.[62]

57. NZfM, 9 (1838), 79.
58. NZfM, 11 (1840), 186. See Appendix I, 51.
59. GSK, 1, 25.
60. See the review of C. G. Likl's *Elegies*. NZfM, 19 (1843), 121.
61. See NZfM, 19 (1843), 158.
62. NZfM, 19 (1843), 124. Schumann prints some short excerpts from the book with this comment: "This book (which appeared 107 years ago and is now out of print) contains a good deal that is practical, substantial, and still valid today."

But this change was one only of emphasis. For Schumann had a healthy respect—as any active composer must—for the ordinary operations of musical craftsmanship from the time he first became a critic. In one of his early critical essays, a review of sonata by Wilhelm Taubert, Schumann (in the person of Raro) praises Taubert's *Fortführung* and *Ausbauung* (approximately "carrying out" and "finishing off") as well as his *Anlagung*.[63] A major proportion of Schumann's attention in both the Hiller and Berlioz reviews of 1835 is addressed to technical matters such as form, harmony, and phrase structure—the sort of things that are hardly the free gift of inspiration. And even when inspiration is dispensing her bounties, a good deal is left to the discretion of the composer; in another review from 1835, Schumann speculates rather accurately about Beethoven's method of composition:

> In his *Pastoral Symphony* Beethoven sings simple themes such as any child-like mind could invent. Yet surely he did not merely write down everything presented by the initial inspiration, but made his choices from among many possibilities.[64]

In their explanations of how art is made, the early romantics in Germany, as heirs of both Herder and Kant, wavered in their allegiances between the inexplicable visitations of *furor poeticus* and the controlled operations of reason and craftsmanship. Both as theorists and practitioners, they often longed for an ideal balance between craftsmanship and inspiration, between reason and feeling. Wackenroder writes in his *Wesen der Tonkunst:*

> But when beneficent nature brings together the unlike artistic sensibilities, when the feelings of the listener burn more brightly in the heart of the learned master artist, and he forges his profound science in these flames, there will result a work of indescribable value. In it feeling and science will be bound together inseparably, like the stone and coloring of an enamel.[65]

Schumann offers some explanation of how both inspiration and craftsmanship can affect the outcome of a composition in his review of a concerto by E. H. Schornstein:

63. NZfM, 2 (1835), 133.
64. NZfM, 3 (1835), 158. See Appendix I, 52.
65. W. H. Wackenroder, *Werke und Briefe* (Jena, 1910), *1*, 185–86.

But in general we might wish for more sifting, selection, and refinement. The first plan for the whole, to be sure, is always the most successful. Yet details must often be molded and polished; in this way talent gains for itself recognition, and for its product, permanence. And in this way, too, interest is maintained —an interest not inherent in the first conception of the whole. In this we include elegance of passagework, the charm of accompaniments to cantabile melodies, color in the middle voices, the elaboration and fashioning of the themes, the juxtaposition and combination of various ideas.[66]

Here Schumann describes the learned procedures of musical crafts-manship as a second stage in the process of composition. Inspiration provides not a finished product, but only an outline. The detail—figuration, accompaniments, and even developmental procedures—must all be worked out later. So the two kinds of processes Schumann says are involved in composing music turn out to be not contradictory, but complementary. Schumann explains the origins of music much as Wordsworth explains the origins of poetry; it results from a powerful emotion (or inspiration) recollected—and improved upon—in tranquillity. But there always remained a duality in the qualities Schumann appreciated in music and the ways in which he thought these qualities came about. In 1841 (in a review of a set of piano pieces by A. H. Sponholtz) Schumann mused about the difficulty of enjoying the "freedom of genius," and still constructing pieces with a good form,[67] and in one of his last reviews for the NZfM, he asserted that a composition must have two quite different kinds of excellence: purity of form, orderliness, and, on the other hand, "richness of invention, freshness, originality." [68]

In the quotations above from the Schornstein and Sponholtz reviews, Schumann seems to associate the two kinds of operations involved in composing music, the rational and nonrational ones, with "talent" and "genius" respectively. This association is rather consistent in his writings as a whole. Kant had defined genius as the "innate mental disposition (*ingenium*) through which nature gives the rule to art," and he explained its operation this way:

66. NZfM, *4* (1834), 71–72. See Appendix I, 53.
67. NZfM, *15* (1841), 17.
68. NZfM, *19* (1843), 158.

It cannot describe or indicate scientifically how it brings about its products, but it gives the rule just as nature does. Hence the author of a product for which he is indebted to his genius does not know himself how he has come by his ideas; and he has not the power to devise the like at pleasure or in accordance with a plan, and to communicate it to others in precepts that will enable them to produce similar products.[69]

In Schumann's time genius was still regarded as a quality—like inspiration—whose operation could be neither understood nor explained; genius was a kind of direct pipeline from a higher reality, and the value and authority of its products were unassailable. Schumann himself usually understood the term in this way.[70] Talent, the faculty responsible for the details and final form of the art work, deals with procedures that can be learned, and is itself susceptible to training and development. As Schumann said, "Talent labors, but genius creates."[71]

Schumann did not explore very far the implications of his ideas about inspiration and craftsmanship and their correlation to genius and talent. He never said, for example, whether inspiration entailed genius, or genius entailed either inspiration or talent. His statements about these matters are not systematic, but sketchy and suggestive. They are like the first *Entwurf* given by inspiration; they have not been submitted to the rational processes of development and working out of detail. This is because Schumann's expressions of his aesthetic views were always to some extent by-products of his criticism. He was always interested, first of all, in discussing music, and in particular, specific musical compositions. In the following chapters we shall see what he had to say about them.

69. *Critique of Judgment*, p. 151.

70. In some of his early letters and diaries Schumann used the word in its earlier sense, to mean a kind of personal attendant spirit.

71. GSK, *1*, 25. See also the comparison between genius and talent in GSK, *1*, 21.

PART IV

Schumann on Contemporary Music
and Musicians

CHAPTER 8

Some Older Contemporaries

For the casual reader of the NZfM or the *Gesammelte Schriften,* what is immediately striking about Schumann's criticism is simply how much of it there is. While Schumann's memorable essays on the *Symphonie fantastique* and Schubert's C-major Symphony are often admired and quoted, the bulk of his criticism has been largely ignored. During his ten years as a critic he reviewed more than eight hundred musical publications. This music ranges from inconsequential piano pieces made for the recreation of amateurs to extended works for orchestra and choruses; its composers range from minor and forgotten musicians like Louis Anger, Adele Bratchi, Johann F. Diethe, and Friedrich Glanz to the foremost composers of Schumann's era, Schubert, Mendelssohn, Spohr, Berlioz, Chopin, and Liszt. This great body of reviews makes it perfectly clear that for Schumann criticism was no mere hobby. His writings in the NZfM are a serious and detailed commentary by a thoroughly competent critic—who also happened to be a leading composer—on the musical culture of his time. In this chapter and those that follow we shall examine some of this commentary in the hope, first of all, of illuminating Schumann's own criteria and procedures as a critic. But this discussion is also intended to yield an important by-product: a greater familiarity with some of the vast repertory of music Schumann reviewed.

By far the greater part of the music Schumann criticized is today totally forgotten. We hardly remember the names of composers like J. W. Kalliwoda, Julius Rietz, Heinrich Dorn, and W. H. Veit, much less perform their music. And in most cases this is all for the best; from a period when music was produced in such staggering volume, posterity can afford to be highly selective. But the historian of nineteenth-century music must investigate a full cross-section of the repertory. This is not simply so that he can unearth occasional jewels neglected by the caprice of time, or exhume unsung geniuses lying forgotten in country churchyards. To the historian, ordinary products

of undistinguished artists are not unworthy of scrutiny; the commonplace is often of special value in determining the prevailing norms
and procedures of an era. And a knowledge of these norms and
procedures is essential to anyone who wishes to assess and understand
the really important—and hence in some ways, atypical—works of
the time.

In this discussion of Schumann's criticism, too, we cannot entirely
ignore Schumann's somewhat ordinary reviews of somewhat ordinary
music. What most interested Schumann was the best achievements
of his romantic contemporaries; but he always saw their work against
the backdrop of contemporary musical culture as a whole. They drew
their craft from it and most of their artistic criteria as well. Schumann
explained this in 1839:

> Ought the artist then to attempt to accomplish everything on his
> own? Cannot he arrive at his goal far more quickly by studying
> all the best things that are available, modeling his own work on
> them and assimilating their form and spirit? But he must also be
> familiar with the masters of the present day, from the first
> to the last; he must know, for example, even Johann Strauss, who
> in his own way is a real representative of his times.[1]

Schumann the critic paid a good deal of attention to the "real represen-
tatives of their times," and if we are to understand his criticism, we
cannot ignore this part of it.

HUMMEL, GRUND, ENCKHAUSEN, AND SPOHR

Schumann's first extended review in the NZfM discusses the music
of a composer whom Schumann did not rank among the foremost of
his era: J. N. Hummel. Hummel enjoyed immense prestige as a pianist
and composer, and Schumann had been impressed with at least a few
of his compositions. In 1829, when Schumann planned to return to
Leipzig from Heidelberg to take up serious piano study with Wieck,
he wrote this to his prospective teacher: "I am busy studying the last
movement of Hummel's F-sharp minor Sonata. It is truly a great
epic, titanic work; it is a portrait of a heroic spirit, struggling but re-
signed." [2] By 1834, when Schumann wrote his review of Hummel's

1. NZfM, *10* (1839), 74. See Appendix I, 54.
2. *Jugendbriefe*, p. 80.

Etudes op. 125, his ardor for the famous pianist's music had cooled somewhat. In this review, as we have seen,[3] Eusebius describes Hummel as a clearheaded, deliberate craftsman—a true heir to Mozart—while Florestan seems to regard him as a superannuated pedant; these etudes, he insists, are totally devoid of imagination and originality.

Florestan's statement is perhaps less an indictment of Hummel's abilities as a composer than a sign of certain disagreements about what a piano etude ought to be. During the seventeenth and eighteenth centuries a good deal of important keyboard music was published with titles or prefaces which indicated the composer's didactic intent: Purcell's and Handel's "Lessons," Scarlatti's *Essercizi*, Bach's *Clavier-Büchlein*, *Well-Tempered Clavier*, and *Clavierübung*. During the earlier part of the nineteenth century, as the piano became an indispensable item of furniture in every well-appointed parlor, music publishers began to turn out a deluge of instruction books and etudes. These etudes were for the most part "exercises" pure and simple; any musical attractiveness in pieces of this kind often seemed quite incidental. Though there were certain exceptions to this rule—some numbers of Clementi's *Gradus ad parnassum* are musically very worthwhile—Chopin was the first composer to make a conspicuous improvement in the artistic level of the piano etude. His Etudes op. 10, published in 1833, were certainly "exercises" in a sense (they incorporated almost unprecedented technical difficulties), but they were meant to be serious musical compositions as well. How novel they were can be seen from the critical response to them. Conservative critics like Rellstab ridiculed them, first of all because of their difficulty, but also because they simply did not conform to the usual norms for etudes.[4]

Other pianists of Chopin's generation soon joined him in writing etudes with some claims to artistic importance. Schumann's Etudes on Caprices of Paganini appeared in 1833, and Hiller's Etudes op. 15 in 1834; Liszt reworked an early set of etudes for publication in 1838, and Henselt's Etudes op. 2 were published in the same year. The older generation of pianists, among them Czerny, Cramer, and Hummel, however, continued to write etudes that were purely exercises. Hummel's Etudes op. 125 are very much of this kind. Each of them has a certain obvious technical aim; they concentrate, in turn, exclusively upon standard patterns of scales, arpeggios, double thirds, octaves, re-

3. See the quotations from this review above, pp. 65–66.
4. See above, pp. 27–28.

peated notes, and the like. Their harmony is very bland, and almost all of them fall into a standard formal pattern: a single theme or figure proceeds to the harmony of the dominant, and in the second half of the piece, back to the tonic.[5] When Schumann wrote his review of this collection, Chopin's op. 10 had already appeared; by comparison with the novel figurations and strong harmonies of these pieces, Hummel's etudes seemed to him extraordinarily pale and anachronistic.

Schumann was always fascinated with the piano etude, and a good deal of space in the NZfM was devoted to reviews of etude collections and discussions of this category of music. In the first pages of the NZfM Ludwig Schunke wrote:

> Exercises and studies for the piano, of which countless have appeared since those of the great master Bach, exert a far greater influence on the writing for this instrument than all the other kinds of musical composition . . . We take pleasure in announcing that an eminent writer for this journal is now gathering materials for a "reasonable survey and criticism of all clavier and piano etudes since J. S. Bach." [6]

The "eminent writer" Schunke mentions is obviously Schumann; his "reasonable survey" of etudes finally appeared almost two years later under the title, "Die Pianoforte-Etuden, ihren Zwecken nach geordnet." [7] In this article Schumann arranges an enormous number of etude collections according to the element of piano technique in which they specialize: speed and lightness, speed and power, legato playing, staccato playing, playing of melody and harmony in the same hand, scales in octaves, and many more. The detail and care Schumann lavished on this review show a kind of professional interest in the technical side of piano playing, at least as a means to an end, even when Schumann himself had long since given up all hope of a virtuoso's career. Like Schunke, Schumann thought the etude was an important vehicle for the development of technique, not only for players, but for composers as well.

It is plain from this article that the etude, in Schumann's opinion,

5. The sixth etude, in D minor, has an exceptional construction. It is a "fughetta" (in which several voices must often be played by the same hand), and does not follow the normal tonic-dominant-tonic harmony.

6. NZfM, _1_ (1834), 22. See Appendix I, 55.

7. NZfM, _4_ (1836), 45–46.

was still supposed to function as a technical exercise; "etude" was not merely another possible name for any of the various kinds of short piano pieces whose categorization always seemed such a flexible matter.[8] In his review of a set of etudes by J. P. Pixis, in 1836, Schumann explained,

> In the broadest sense, every piece of music is an etude—and the easiest is often really the most difficult. In a narrower sense, however, we must demand of an etude that it have some particular purpose, that it develop some special facility, and lead to the mastery of some single difficulty, whether this lie in technique, rhythm, expression, execution, or whatever. If several technical problems are combined in a piece, then it belongs more to the category of the capriccio.[9]

And two years later he emphasized that what is expected of an etude is both a distinct technical aim and a clear form:

> What is remarkable about them [C. E. F. Weyse's Etudes] is their rebellion against strict form; they often lose themselves in the realm of the more fanciful capriccio, and only begrudgingly get back onto the track. We noted something similar in his earlier volume.[10] Yet there he did not sacrifice the beautiful form we require of an etude, nor neglect the clearly articulated mechanical aim that is also expected of this category of composition.[11]

8. In 1836, Schumann reviewed a set of pieces called *Divertissements ou Exercises en forme d'Ecossaises,* by J. Pohl. He informs us that these are the same pieces that appeared earlier under the title *Caprices en forme d'Anglaises.* NZfM, *4* (1836), 17.

9. NZfM, *4* (1836), 16. See Appendix I, 56. Apparently Schumann was not thinking here of the capriccio as a composition based on a preexistent theme, but only of the general style of that category. Many capriccios from this period, moreover, were entirely original.

10. An earlier collection of etudes by the noted Danish composer was reviewed in the NZfM, *4* (1836), 33. It is interesting to see Schumann again making comparisons between the etude and the capriccio; he seems to say that a capriccio is like an etude that lacks a single technical purpose or a strict form. In 1843, in a review of a set of capriccios by Emil Hornemann, Schumann broaches the subject again: "To begin with, the form of these pieces, a compromise between the etude and the capriccio, seems to us a fortunate one. Reminiscent of the etude is the well-defined shape and the frequent use of a single continuous figuration. But they avoid—and in this they resemble the capriccio—the uneasy preoccupation with mechanics to which composers are often misled by the etude." NZfM, *18* (1843), 14.

11. NZfM, *8* (1838), 170. See Appendix I, 57.

Hummel's Etudes op. 125 certainly appear to fulfill Schumann's basic requirements for etudes, namely that they have a clear form and a single technical aim. But these prescriptions were meant simply to indicate what an etude is, not necessarily what a *good* etude is. Hummel's work did not satisfy Schumann because it was devoid of the expressiveness and originality he expected of all music, whatever its category. The etude, Schumann said, had its beginnings in the *Clavierübung* of Bach, and all who made unmusical exercises out of it degraded it. In the preface to his survey of etudes, Schumann described its progress thus:

No one can deny the indebtedness of Clementi and Cramer to him [Bach]. From them to Moscheles there is a hiatus; perhaps it is due to the influence of Beethoven, who was an enemy of anything mechanical, and incited composers more to purely poetic creation. In Moscheles, and yet to a higher degree in Chopin, therefore, imagination reigns along with technique. Behind these five, who stand out as the most important figures, the most original are L. Berger and C. Weyse. Ries and Hummel have demonstrated their individual styles more clearly in free composition than in etudes. Kessler and Grund [12] must be mentioned as solid and able, as well as A. Schmitt [13] whose admirable clarity must appeal to the young at heart. Kalkbrenner, Czerny, and Herz have provided nothing of stature, but their works are worthwhile for their treatment of the instrument. Potter[14] and Hiller, on account of their romantic spirit, cannot be passed over, nor can the gentle Szymanowska,[15] or the admirable C. Mayer.[16] Bertini is disappointing—but in a graceful way. Whoever is interested in the most difficult will find it in the Paganini-Etudes of the undersigned.[17]

For each of the composers mentioned in this preface, Schumann indi-

---

12. Friedrich Wilhelm Grund (1791–1874), a prolific composer, and conductor of the Hamburg Philharmonic concerts from 1828–63.
13. Aloys Schmitt (1788–1866), German composer and piano pedagogue.
14. Philipp Cipriani Hambly Potter (1792–1871), English composer and pianist.
15. Marie Szymanowska (1789–1831), Polish pianist and composer.
16. Charles Mayer (1799–1862), a student of John Field, pianist and composer.
17. NZfM, 4 (1836), 45. See Appendix I, 58.

cates in a footnote the specific works he has in mind, as well as references to reviews of them in the NZfM. Together with the schematic listing of etudes which follows, this constitutes a remarkably comprehensive catalogue of the best of the countless collections of etudes written in the earlier nineteenth century.

It is surprising to find in Schumann's survey that the contributions of F. W. Grund are listed as merely "solid and able," for only a few pages earlier in the same volume of the NZfM there is a thoroughly enthusiastic review of Grund's Etudes op. 21 by Schumann himself.[18] Grund, one of the few etude composers who was not a professional pianist, was among the first of the older generation to write etudes in the new style. In his op. 21 Schumann found both useful technical exercises and expressive music: "What in our opinion makes these etudes especially worthwhile is that they are *characteristic* as well as valuable for technical development. They offer nourishment for both hand and spirit." [19]

Schumann then comments upon each of the individual etudes in order. Of the first he writes:

> The first one makes use throughout of a figure designed to strengthen the fingers of the right hand, especially the weaker ones. A tendency which for this composer has become almost a mannerism shows up in this etude as well as almost all the others; namely, toward the end of the piece he regularly introduces a new melodic idea. In this way the exercise itself appears somewhat relegated to the background, though without being entirely stilled. This certainly meets with our approval.[20]

In the right hand part of this etude there is a figure in sixteenth notes, while the left hand plays a motive with a strong dotted rhythm something like that in Chopin's "Revolutionary Etude" (see Ex. 2).

18. NZfM, 4 (1836), 25–26. Since the survey of etudes was long in preparation, it may well have been written before Schumann's review of Grund's Etudes, op. 21.

A misprint in GS 1854 has been perpetuated in all the succeeding editions of the *Gesammelte Schriften,* and even in Kreisig's catalog of the compositions discussed by Schumann (GSK 2, 490). This collection of etudes is incorrectly listed in all these places as op. 24.

19. NZfM, 4 (1836), 25.

20. Ibid. See Appendix I, 59. In a footnote to this passage Schumann gives the page and measure numbers where new themes are introduced in seven of the twelve etudes. This footnote has not been retained in any of the editions of the *Gesammelte Schriften.*

Example 2. F. W. Grund, Etudes op. 21, no. 1

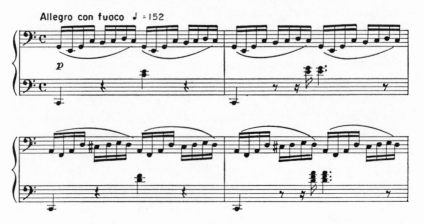

In measure 27, the new melodic idea appears in octaves in the bass while the original figuration is retained in the right hand (see Ex. 3).

Example 3. F. W. Grund, Etudes op. 21, no. 1

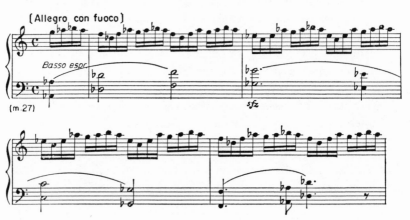

Schumann calls the second of these etudes "an exercise in octaves, and more than that: a poetic image sketched by the sensitive hand of an artist." This etude shows something quite different from the usual passagework in octaves of the contemporary piano style. Its dynamics are predominately in the soft range, and its octaves seldom follow the normal chromatic or diatonic scale patterns, but instead often trace an intricate course dictated by a complex harmony. Almost throughout, the octaves appear in a syncopated pattern (see Ex. 4).

Example 4. F. W. Grund, Etudes op. 21, no. 2

The "new melody" in this piece is again introduced in the bass (see Ex. 5).

Example 5. F. W. Grund, Etudes op. 21, no. 2

Of the third etude, Schumann says:

> It is placid and even, without a particularly distinctive character. We would not lift the pedal until the end of the measure, for the many tones of the principal harmony immediately silence the others. There is a very similar etude in Bach's Exercises, volume 1, number 2.[21]

This piece makes use of a continuous figuration in broken triads. The pedaling Schumann wished to correct is indicated in the original edition (see Ex. 6).

21. Ibid. See Appendix I, 60.

Example 6. F. W. Grund, Etudes op. 21, no. 3

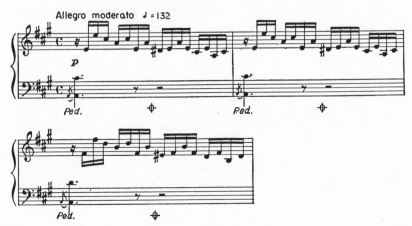

Schumann's casual remark about the similarity of this etude to an "etude" or "exercise" of Bach is somewhat startling. As we have previously seen, when he spoke of Bach's "etudes," Schumann had in mind the *Clavierübung*, the great collection of keyboard compositions published in 1731 ff. by Bach himself, containing such diverse items as the Partitas, the Italian Concerto, and the Goldberg Variations. Peters later published the *Clavierübung* under the title "Exercises," and this is the edition Schumann cites in his survey of etudes. The first volume of the *Clavierübung* consists of the six Partitas. Schumann's "number 2" obviously refers, not to the second Partita, but to the second movement, or Allemande, of the first Partita in B-flat major. The figuration of this Allemande is in fact similar to that of Grund's etude (see Ex. 7).

Example 7. J. S. Bach, Partita no. 1, Allemande

Apparently Schumann and his contemporaries thought of the *Clavierübung* as simply a series of etudes. The Partitas were, for Schumann, not a collection of six suites of dances, but a series of thirty-eight short exercises which also bore names such as Allemande,

Courante, etc.[22] This might seem to us like a naive misapprehension; yet it is justified to some extent by Bach's original publication. The title page of the first volume begins: "Clavir Ubung/bestehend in/ Praeludien, Allemanden, Couranten, Sarabanden, Giguen,/Menuetten, und andern Galanterien."

Of all the etudes in this collection by Grund, Schumann's favorite is the one that seems least etude-like. He calls the tenth etude "the most spirited and individual throughout, from the first measure to the last." [23] This piece, one of the shortest of the set, has but minimal value as a technical exercise; it consists of a single-line melody above, accompanied by a staccato figure in the bass somewhat reminiscent of a *Moment musical* of Schubert[24] (see Ex. 8).

Example 8. F. W. Grund, Etudes op. 21, no. 10

The parts are exchanged later in the composition, and it becomes clear that the intended pianistic exercise consists of the leaps in the accompaniment. But at the tempo indicated these seldom offer much difficulty. In this etude, the technical aim has been suppressed in favor of purely musical considerations, and Schumann, despite his prescription of a clear, single technical purpose for the etude, obviously approves wholeheartedly.

Schumann reviewed compositions by Grund on two other occasions:

22. In his survey of etudes Schumann says of Bach's contribution to the category, "And as he conceived of everything on a gigantic scale, so he did not compose, say, 24 etudes in the various keys, but more like a whole volume for each of them." NZfM, *4* (1836), 45.

This statement is certainly not easy to understand. Perhaps Schumann thought that in addition to the six Partitas (or, for him, "series of etudes"), the French Overture, the Goldberg Variations, etc., there were other collections, belonging to the *Clavierübung,* in all the remaining keys. The Peters edition, which Schumann knew, does not distinguish between the various contents of the *Clavierübung,* but presents it all simply under the title "Exercises."

23. NZfM, *4* (1836), 26.

24. Deutsch no. 780 (no. 3).

in 1837 he contributed a short notice of Grund's Rondo op. 25, and
two years later, a substantial critique of his Sonata op. 27. The latter
review again shows Schumann's enthusiasm for Grund's music:

> Hats off to the first movement! For me it makes the entire
> sonata; here there is dedication, verve, and imagination. The
> others are less successful. There is a sonata of Beethoven with a
> similar construction[25]—one of his most wonderful—where the
> bold, passionate first movement (E minor) is followed by a
> closing movement (E major) in a simple arioso style.[26]

The first movement of Grund's sonata which strikes Schumann as so
successful is a vigorous sonata-allegro form in G minor. It presents
very little material in the exposition, but concentrates on persistent
working-out of short motives. A good deal of the section consists of
a sharp, detached, syncopated fabric like that shown in Example 9.

Example 9. F. W. Grund, Sonata op. 27, 1st movement

Snatches of cantabile melody are introduced but intermittently; there
is no real second theme. The development section makes use throughout of a new motive with a sharp dotted rhythm. In measure 28 of
this section, a real cantabile melody, the first in the movement, is
added to this motive (see Ex. 10).

Example 10. F. W. Grund, Sonata op. 27, 1st movement

Characteristic of this movement is an almost tiring use of violent

25. Beethoven's Sonata, op. 109.
26. NZfM, *11* (1839), 186. See Appendix I, 61.

syncopation. In measure 52 of the exposition, the syncopated motive shown in Example 9 is combined with a middle voice and compressed into a 2/4 measure, as is seen in Example 11.

Example 11. F. W. Grund, Sonata op. 27, 1st movement

Schumann wished to make a correction in this passage in order to begin the chain of suspensions one beat earlier:

> Were I to make any carping criticisms, they would be directed against the melody of the 2/4 measures; this section in other respects has great vitality. In the third measure, instead of the B flat of the syncopated melody, I would prefer the transitory A. Though this might seem but a minute alteration, I like my A much better.[27]

Grund's refreshingly vigorous and original sonata was particularly welcome to Schumann in a time when the sonata, the most "exalted" category of piano music, in Schumann's opinion, seemed about to expire. Earlier in 1839, in an extended preface to a review of three new sonatas by minor composers, Schumann wrote:

> For a long time now we have been silent about any achievements in the category of the sonata, and we really have nothing extraordinary to tell about today. Yet it is always a pleasure, amidst the wild array of fashionable portraits and caricatures, to see again one of these sober faces. For once they were the order of the day, but we see them now only by way of exception. It is strange that sonatas are written mostly by unknown composers; the older living composers who grew up in the heyday of the sonata (the most significant of these are Cramer and then Moscheles) cultivate this category the least. What prompts the

27. NZfM, 11 (1839), 186–87. See Appendix I, 62.

former (principally young artists) to compose is easy to guess; there is no more distinguished form with which they could make themselves known and respected by higher criticism. Most of the sonatas of this kind are therefore to be regarded merely as examples, or studies in form; they were hardly born out of strong inner necessity. If the older composers don't compose any sonatas now, they must have their reasons. We will leave it to them to decide what these are.

It was Hummel who vigorously continued the Mozartean manner; his F-sharp minor sonata alone would perpetuate his memory. But Beethoven's example was followed especially by Franz Schubert, who sought after new terrain and won it. Ries worked too quickly. Berger contributed individual things that are excellent, without penetrating deeply; the same with Onslow. C. M. von Weber quickly achieved a telling effect with the individual style he developed. More than any other, it is his example that the younger composers have followed. Thus the sonata stood ten years ago, and thus it stands now. Single beautiful examples in this category will surely show up here and there, and already have, but in general it appears that the form has run its course.[28]

One "unknown composer" (largely unknown in Schumann's time, and totally unknown in ours) who wrote sonatas was Heinrich Enckhausen (1799–1885), a student of Aloys Schmitt, and for many years court organist at Hannover.[29] His Sonata op. 32 which Schumann reviewed in 1837 is a good illustration of the prevailing style of sonatas in Germany at that time. The first two movements of this work, Schumann says, "cannot escape from a certain 'old-Frankish' seriousness."[30] This is a play on the subtitle of the sonata, "altfrankische"; but Schumann also refers, apparently, to the obviously old-fashioned style of the first two movements. The first movement is a textbook sonata-allegro form with balanced periods and consistent arrangement of phrases into antecedent (proceeding to the dominant) and consequent functions (proceeding back to the tonic); it begins as shown in Example 12.

28. NZfM, 10 (1839), 134. See Appendix I, 63.
29. See the article in G. Schilling, Encyclopädie der gesammten musikalischen Wissenschaften, 2, 587–88.
30. NZfM, 6 (1837), 7.

Example 12. H. Enckhausen, Sonata op. 32, 1st movement

There follows an Adagio of the ornamented-aria type, in a style again belonging very much to the eighteenth century.

The third movement of this sonata, in Schumann's opinion, is "more animated, more original, and borders more on the domain of Beethoven." [31] This movement (Allegro di molto) is conspicuously more modern in style than the others. It begins, like the op. 31, no. 2 sonata of Beethoven, with an alternation of very slow and very fast sections (see Ex. 13).

Example 13. H. Enckhausen, Sonata op. 32, 3d movement

In this example the Adagio chords, like many other parts of the move-

31. Ibid.

ment, exploit low-lying sonorities (the entire first phrase of the second theme remains below middle C); this appears to be a conscious imitation of Beethoven. And the main theme, introduced in measure 16, is strongly reminiscent of the last movement of Beethoven's op. 31, no. 2 sonata (see Ex. 14).

Example 14. H. Enckhausen, Sonata op. 32, 3d movement

Enckhausen's stylistic backwardness in this sonata was not exceptional. Schumann often observed ruefully that composers of larger forms such as the sonata consistently reverted to an earlier style—that of early Beethoven, or even of Mozart and Haydn. Later in 1837, cheered by the appearance of seven new sonatas to be reviewed, Schumann nevertheless remarked, "One can see that there is no dearth of new sonatas; but in another sense there certainly is—again, almost every one of the sonatas listed above, except for the last two, must be regarded as a straggler from former times." [32] Schumann, like most romantic composers, was zealous for the continued development of the large instrumental forms: the sonata, quartet, and symphony. For many composers (and sometimes for Schumann) this seemed, after the gigantic achievements of Beethoven, to be wishing for the impossible. A dominant theme in Schumann's criticism is his disappointment that the enriched musical language of the romantic composers was not very often—and not very successfully—used to cultivate these inherited categories of instrumental music.

One older composer who consistently wrote large instrumental forms was Louis Spohr (1784–1859). One of Germany's most admired composers during his lifetime, he turned out nine symphonies, fifteen

---

32. NZfM, 7 (1837), 127. The last two sonatas in the list are by H. Triest (op. 4), and William Sterndale Bennett (op. 15).

concertos, and a substantial amount of chamber music (of which the Nonett op. 31 is still occasionally performed)—in addition to ten operas and more than one hundred lieder. Schumann mentioned Spohr frequently in his criticism, and wrote full-length reviews of five works: the Quartet op. 93, the Trio op. 119, and the fourth, sixth, and seventh symphonies.

All of these reviews are appreciative, or at least respectful. Schumann notes approvingly that Spohr has his own unmistakable, characteristic style; in the Quartet op. 93, Schumann says, "the well-known master is recognizable from the very first measures." [33] And even in the Sixth Symphony, the "Historical," where Spohr imitates in successive movements "the period of Bach-Handel, of Haydn-Mozart, of Beethoven, and of the present," Schumann declares,

> He remains the master as we have always known him and loved him. In fact these forms to which he is not accustomed bring out his individuality even more strongly, just as one with a particularly characteristic bearing reveals himself most clearly when he assumes a disguise. Once Napoleon went to a masked ball; and he had been there hardly a moment before he—clasped his arms together. Like a brush fire the cry spread through the hall: "the emperor!" Similarly, when this symphony was played, one could hear from every corner of the hall the sound "Spohr," and again, "Spohr." [34]

Spohr's fourth and seventh symphonies, entitled respectively *Die Weihe der Töne*,[35] and *Irdisches und gottliches im Menschenleben*, are both programmatic. In his discussion of these symphonies Schumann is most interested in their programs and the relation of the music to them. The poem which serves as a program for the fourth

33. NZfM, *8* (1838), 181–82.
34. NZfM, *14* (1841), 53. See Appendix I, 64.
35. The program for this symphony is a poem of that name by Carl Pfeiffer. This note by Spohr is printed in the first edition:
"For a full understanding of the present symphony the listener will require, in addition to the indications of the contents of individual movements (which are to be printed on the concert program), a familiarity with the poem itself; for it is the content of this poem that the composer has attempted to reproduce. The directors of the concert are asked, therefore, to distribute copies of the poem in the concert hall, or to have it read aloud before the symphony is performed."

symphony is only a feeble "eulogy of music," he feels, and there is no sense trying to reflect the pale spirit of this poem in music itself.[36]

Spohr's seventh symphony, *Irdisches und gottliches im Menschenleben*, whose movements are entitled *Kinderwelt, Zeit der Leidenschaften*, and *Endlicher Sieg des Gottlichen*, is meant as a musical portrayal of the "ages of man." Again, Schumann has serious reservations:

> We admit to holding a predisposition against this kind of creation, and share this with perhaps a hundred men of learning. They, to be sure, often have peculiar notions about composition, and they always appeal to Mozart, who didn't want you to think about anything in connection with his music. As we have said, though, many unlearned people have this prejudice as well, and if a composer presents us with a program *before* his music, I say, "first of all let me hear that you have made beautiful music; after that I will like your program too." [37]

In his Seventh Symphony Spohr apparently passes the test—though hardly with flying colors—that Schumann proposes; he has "made beautiful music" quite aside from the program:

> We cannot say that we find here great new ideas different from what we already know of Spohr. But this purity and radiance of sound will not easily be found elsewhere . . . The industry evident in every line of the score is genuinely touching. May he, along with all our greatest Germans, be a shining example for us.[38]

Schumann was impressed with Spohr's original instrumental effects,[39] with his experiments with double orchestras and double quartets, and with his overall mastery of the craft of composition. Nevertheless, his praise of Spohr always comes out sounding lame. He never seems to care particularly for Spohr's themes; the best he can think of to say about the first theme of the last movement of the Quartet op. 93 (see Ex. 15) is that it is "very pleasant."

36. NZfM, 2 (1835), 66.

37. NZfM, *18* (1843), 140.

38. NZfM, *18* (1843), 140–41.

39. One of Spohr's favorite effects was produced by doubling a low-lying violin melody with a bass instrument, such as the bassoon, playing in its high register. Schumann alludes to C. G. Reissiger's imitation of this device in his Symphony no. 1 (op. 120). NZfM, *11* (1839), 17.

Example 15. L. Spohr, Quartet op. 93, 4th movement

This theme is rather typical for Spohr; it is smooth, regular, gently undulating—and featureless. Schumann repeatedly credits Spohr with a "mastery born of industry and study," and that is about all. Spohr was a German composer who was doing exactly what Schumann thought a German composer ought to do, and what he himself always aspired to do: compose symphonies, quartets, and operas. But he lacked genuine musical inventiveness, and Schumann, in the face of Spohr's enormous fame, was quite aware of it.

MOSCHELES AND FIELD

Another musician of the older generation who cultivated large instrumental forms was the famous composer, pianist, and pedagogue, Ignaz Moscheles. Schumann reviewed a good many extended works by this composer—one sonata, a trio, a sextet, a septet, three piano concertos, and a concert overture. In his survey of etudes, it will be remembered, Schumann mentions Moscheles' etudes in the same breath as those of Chopin; they are imaginative music, he says, as well as technical exercises.[40] He was equally enthusiastic about Moscheles' large works. He begins his glowing review of Moscheles' Concert Overture to Schiller's *Jungfrau von Orleans*—a piece that alternates melodious andantes and sharply rhythmical marches—with this declaration: "One becomes most conscious of the inadequacy of verbal description when faced with the compositions he values most

40. In 1838 (NZfM, *8*, 201–02) Schumann wrote a most appreciative review of Moscheles' *Characteristische Studien*, op. 95. These etudes are modern and original; their style as well as their titles ("Bacchanal," "Volksfestszenen," "Mondnacht am Seegestade," etc.) show that the composer intended them as more than technical exercises.

highly; for me this overture is one of those compositions—and not only among the works of Moscheles." [41]

At a time when the piano concerto was strongly dominated by the stereotyped and somewhat garish products of the Parisian virtuosi, Schumann welcomed Moscheles' craftsmanlike contributions to the category. In the "magical dark luminosity which hovers over them [the fifth and sixth concertos]," [42] Schumann detected a kinship with the music of the younger romantic composers. "It is difficult to seize upon individual passages where the romantic half-light glows most strongly," he writes, "but one feels throughout that it is there, especially in the rare E-minor Adagio of the Fifth Concerto, with its almost church-like character." [43] This impressive movement is dominated by the somber colors of the lower strings; its beginning is shown in Example 16.

Example 16. I. Moscheles, Piano Concerto no. 5, op. 87, 2d movement

Moscheles' Sixth Concerto, the *Concert fantastique,* consists of four

41. NZfM, 4 (1836), 102.
42. NZfM, 4 (1836), 123.
43. Ibid.

movements of varying characters played without pause; the material for the third movement is entirely derived from the first theme of the first movement. Though he approved of the concerto in general, Schumann did not care for the form: "Though it may be possible to construct a successful, unified composition in this way, the aesthetic danger is too great in relation to what could be achieved." [44] Schumann's objection surely does not reflect a conservative interest in retaining the traditional concerto form with its three separate movements. In the same review, in fact, he proposes that someone ought to attempt a single-movement concerto; in such a composition "the opening section would take the place of the Allegro, the melodic second theme substitute for the Adagio, and a brilliant close for the final Rondo."

In January 1839 Schumann wrote a final review of a piano concerto by Moscheles: his *Concert pathetique* op. 93. This, again, is a very favorable review; Schumann notes with satisfaction that in this concerto the orchestra engages in real dialogue with the piano—a rare virtue at a time when the orchestra was relegated increasingly to the background. Schumann gives a few more suggestions for concertos in this review:

We owe a special vote of thanks to recent concerto composers for no longer boring us with concluding trills and, especially, leaping octave passages. The old cadenza, in which virtuosi used to include all possible forms of bravura playing, was really much more reasonable, and perhaps it could still be used successfully. And the Scherzo—common to the symphony and sonata—would it not be an effective addition to the concerto? It could add a spritely exchange with individual instruments of the orchestra without altering to any degree the overall form. Mendelssohn could probably do this better than anyone else. [45]

Moscheles played a leading role in the development of piano technique and of the piano itself in the earlier part of the century. [46] A

44. Ibid.
45. NZfM, *10* (1839), 6. See Appendix I, 65.
46. It was probably the hope of obtaining Moscheles' endorsement that prompted Erard to develop the double escapement action in the 1820s.

brilliant performer, he sometimes seemed to cultivate glittering virtuosity to the exclusion of anything else. Schumann was quite aware of this but saw it as characteristic only of Moscheles' earlier career, especially the years 1814–20, when "the word 'brilliant' was all the rage, and legions of young ladies were in love with Czerny." [47] But in his review of the Seventh Concerto in 1839, Schumann wrote,

> In Moscheles we have a rare example of a musician who, though always an avid student of the old masters, yet has observed the most recent developments and made use of them. Because he has now mastered both these influences together with his own natural propensities, there has resulted from the mingling of these elements—the old, the new, and the individual—a work like this new concerto, formally clear and sharp, almost romantic in character, and thoroughly original. [48]

According to Schumann's judgment, it seems that we have made a mistake in banishing all of Moscheles' music from the concert repertory.

Moscheles was, in Schumann's scheme of things, a transitional figure who made certain important contributions to the development of musical style, especially piano style, in the "in-between" generation after Beethoven. As we have seen, an even more significant composer in this transitional period, Schumann thought, was the Irish pianist John Field. The young man of awkward appearance, protégé of Clementi who long made a living by demonstrating his master's pianos, later became famous as the originator of the nocturne (though he himself named only twelve of his twenty pieces published under that title). Schumann wrote a brief but enthusiastic review of three Field nocturnes in 1836. [49] But it was the composer's concertos that impressed him most profoundly; in the same series of articles where he reviewed Moscheles' fifth and sixth concertos, Schumann wrote an encomium to Field's Seventh Concerto that is for modern taste almost embarrassing in its ardor:

The best review, and, to be sure, an expensive one, would be to

47. NZfM, 4 (1836), 123.
48. NZfM, 10 (1839), 6. See Appendix I, 66.
49. NZfM, 4 (1836), 168.

distribute 10,000 copies[50] for the journal's readers. For I am
completely taken by it, and I cannot think of anything intelli-
gent to say about it except to praise it endlessly. And when
Goethe says, "A man reveals himself by whom he praises," he
was right, as always. And I would happily have that artist
[Field] bind my eyes and hands, and say nothing but that I
am his prisoner, and I follow him blindly. . . .

   All of it is beautiful and fit to kiss, and especially thou, final
movement, in thy divine tedium, thy loving enchantment, thy
awkwardness, thy beauty of spirit—fit to kiss from beginning
to end.[51]

This is an example of the sort of "exclamatory criticism" Schlegel
derided. It is unfortunate that the more Schumann likes a composition,
sometimes, the less he really says about it. His reviews of Moscheles'
concertos in this series include a great many satisfying details—comments about form, about the role of the orchestra, and astute observations about Moscheles' style of writing in general. But when a composition impresses Schumann enough so that he shifts into poetic criticism, all this disappears. From this review, were it not for the heading
the reader would not be able to determine the key of the piece, how
many movements it has, or even that it is a piano concerto rather than,
say, a violin concerto. In his poetic criticism the danger of vagueness
was ever near at hand for Schumann, but in many of his reviews he
avoided it more successfully than in this one.

   Though Schumann does not really tell us, it is easy to see what appealed to him about this concerto. The first movement, in C minor,
begins with a substantial orchestral exposition—no longer fashionable
in the 1830s—consisting of several themes, potently harmonized, later
developed in intricate patterns by the piano. The ornamental writing
in the solo instrument strikingly prefigures, in some places, Chopin's
style. And the first theme taken by the piano is like a Field nocturne:
a single-line, ornamented cantilena with a rich, arpeggiated accompaniment (see Ex. 17). Here and in the second (and final) movement,
there is scarcely a sign of the usual bravura figurations of the then-
current virtuoso concertos.

50. This number was changed to a more modest "1000" in the *Gesammelte Schriften*.
51. NZfM, 4 (1836), 122. See Appendix I, 67.

Example 17. J. Field, Piano Concerto no. 7, 1st movement

MEYERBEER

The largest letters on the title page of the original Haslinger edition of Moscheles' Seventh Concerto are enframed in a sort of sunset pattern, and they spell the name of Giacomo Meyerbeer. Meyerbeer's connection with Moscheles' concerto is simply that it was dedicated to him. It is difficult now to appreciate fully the uniqueness of Meyerbeer's position in the later 1830s. After *Les Huguenots* he was not merely the most famous of all living composers. He was almost a deity to both the French and German bourgeoisie, and the mere mention of his name on a musical publication or program was often enough to assure its success. As we have already seen, publishers and performers alike went to any lengths to reap the benefits of this magic.

For Schumann, Meyerbeer came to be a symbol for everything that was wrong with contemporary music. He had little to say about Meyerbeer before 1837, and there is no reason to think that he was very familiar with his music except in the "decompositions," as he once called them, of the Parisian variation-composers. But in the spring of that year there began a whole series of performances of *Les Huguenots* in Leipzig, and at several of them an attentive member of the audience was Schumann. He held his peace until he had seen the opera a number of times; then, finally, in September of 1837, he burst forth with his famous essay on *Les Huguenots* and another current Leipzig production, Mendelssohn's *St. Paul.* It begins,

> Today I feel like a brave young warrior drawing his sword for the first time in a great cause! Just as certain issues of worldwide significance have been settled in our little Leipzig, so it seems that this should be the case in music as well. It was appropriate that in this place, apparently for the first time in the whole world, the two most important compositions of our day have been performed concurrently—Meyerbeer's *Huguenots* and Mendelssohn's *St. Paul.*
>
> Where to begin and where to end? There is no question here of rivalry, or of a simple preference of one over the other. The reader knows only too well what sort of principles this journal upholds, so that when Mendelssohn is under discussion, there can be no talk of Meyerbeer—for their paths proceed in opposite directions. He knows only too well that to arrive at a description of these two he needs only to attribute to each the characteristics the other doesn't have—except for talent, which they have in common. Sometimes one feels like taking his head in his hands to see if everything is still in place up there when he sees the great following Meyerbeer has in the sound musical life of Germany, and when he sees otherwise honorable people, even musicians who also rejoice in the quieter victories of Mendelssohn saying that Meyerbeer's music is worth something.[52]

From what follows it becomes clear that the drama fully as much as the music of *Les Huguenots* made Schumann "weary and faint with anger." It is revolting to a good Protestant, he declares with righteous indignation,

> to hear his most treasured hymn screamed from the stage, to see the bloodiest drama in the history of his religion reduced to the level of a farce at a county fair, all for the sake of money and applause; he is shocked by this opera from the ridiculously vul-

52. NZfM, 7 (1837), 73. See Appendix I, 68.

gar sanctity of the overture to the finale, after which, apparently, we are all to be burned alive immediately.[53] After *Les Huguenots*, what remains to be done on the stage but the actual beheading of criminals and the exhibition of loose women? [54]

Yet the scene of the dedication of the sword in the fourth act, Schumann begrudgingly admits, is very effective—particularly so is the chorus. But from a purely musical standpoint, what is this melody, he demands, but a "slicked-up Marseillaise?" This remark is but one evidence of Schumann's hypersensitivity to thematic resemblances. He retained a prodigious number of themes in his memory, and as a result his enjoyment of music was frequently disturbed by strong feelings of *déjà entendu*. In the case of Meyerbeer's chorus, the resemblance that disturbed him is rather plain (see Ex. 18).

Example 18. G. Meyerbeer, *Les Huguenots*, 4th act

gloi - - - re, oui gloire au Dieu ven - geur

From here to the end of his review, Schumann concentrates on the music of this opera, and on Meyerbeer's style in general. He charges him with superficiality and undiscriminating eclecticism:

> It is well known that Meyerbeer tends to be utterly superficial, unoriginal, and without style. Equally well known are his talent for easy embellishment, brilliance, dramatic effects and instrumentation, and his variety of formal structures. With little effort one can point out things belonging to Rossini, Mozart, Hérold, Weber, Bellini, and even Spohr—in short, the entire musical repertory. What he adds all by himself, though, is that famous, deadly, bleating, unbecoming rhythm that runs through practically all the themes of the opera. I had begun to write down the

53. In a footnote Schumann quotes the closing lines of the opera:

> Par le fer et l'incendie
> Exterminons la race impie
> Frappons, poursuivons l'hérétique!
> Dieu le veut, Dieu veut le sang,
> Oui, Dieu veut le sang!

54. NZfM, 7 (1837), 73–74. See Appendix I, 69.

pages where it appears (pp. 6, 17, 59, 68, 77, 100, 117), but finally got tired of it.[55]

Meyerbeer's stylistic eclecticism made a powerful impression on Schumann. This can be seen in the many subsequent remarks about Meyerbeer (the *Huguenots* essay is his only formal review of Meyerbeer's music) scattered throughout his criticism. In a review of a quintet by Léon de St.-Lubin, for example, Schumann wrote, "His quintet is a mixture of French and German strains, not unlike the music of Meyerbeer, who obviously borrows from all the European nations for his art." [56]

While in this review Schumann ostensibly evaluates *Les Huguenots* on the strength of performances of it he attended, it is clear from the last part of the section quoted above that he also had a score for the work. The only score available in 1837, as far as I know, was Schlesinger's piano–vocal score, released in May of that year. A rhythm that recurs on all the pages Schumann mentioned in this score is a figure based on a three-note anacrusis. It appears in either the vocal parts or in the accompaniment, and takes either of these forms: ♪♪♪♩ | ♩ or ↱ ♪♪♪ | ♩. Schumann was forever finding this rhythm (which reminded him no less than us of the beginning of Beethoven's Fifth Symphony) in the music he reviewed, and he was always offended by it. He wrote, for example, of Lachner's Prize Symphony:

> The first and second movements proceed throughout in that well-known rhythm beginning with an upbeat of three eighth notes, to which (as one may recall from a remark in the series of trio reviews in this volume) many composers have fallen prey.[57]

Schumann saw in Meyerbeer's opera a glorification of the contrived effect: a plot calculated to shock, sensational staging, and musical forces designed to overpower the listener with mere quantity of sound. But perhaps Schumann was not altogether fair to Meyerbeer. Such moral indignation at the abuse of the chorale and at the "blasphemy" of the text (he quotes the line, "Je ris du Dieu de l'universe,") does not quite ring true; for Schumann was never particularly religious. Despite his protestations to the contrary, there can be little doubt

55. NZfM, 7 (1837), 74. See Appendix I, 70.
56. NZfM, 9 (1838), 79.
57. NZfM, 5 (1836), 151. See Appendix I, 71.

that Schumann approached this opera with a powerful predisposition against it. Meyerbeer and his *Huguenots* were a figurehead for Parisian opera and all its accessories—the prime source of the artistic ills of his time. Schumann was not simply judging a certain opera by a certain composer; in his comparison of *Les Huguenots* and *St. Paul* he was giving an object lesson in musical taste, and campaigning heatedly in behalf of the German romantic composers.

LOEWE AND KLEIN

Les Huguenots is one of but a very few operas that Schumann reviewed. His rising interest in opera during the 1840s coincided with his declining activity for the NZfM. As a result he wrote very little about opera; aside from *Les Huguenots,* the only operas he reviewed are minor works by minor German composers, for example C. G. Reissiger, J. P. E. Hartmann, and Heinrich Esser. From the reviews of these works it is impossible to extract any reasonably complete notion of his views about either opera or vocal music as a whole. Although the same circumstances apply, to a degree, to Schumann's criticism of lieder— he began to review them regularly only when his career as a critic was drawing to a close—this branch of his criticism is extensive and detailed enough to show rather clearly what he thought about lieder and about the special problems of vocal composition.

For Schumann, the problem of writing music for voice was the awesomely difficult task of fitting one art form with another. Both text and music have a "physical form" (long and short, accented and unaccented syllables, line lengths, and rhyme schemes in the text, and in music, rhythm, meter, melody, and harmony) and in addition, ideally, a cargo of emotional connotations and what he called *Stimmung.* All these things, Schumann said, had to be combined to produce a harmonious result. The task of providing for proper declamation of the text, and of producing a pleasing musical form and a good vocal line (the satisfactory treatment of the "physical characteristics" of text and music) were only elementary considerations. Only infrequently did Schumann pay much attention to these technical elements of vocal composition—usually when he was particularly displeased with the music he was reviewing. A good example of this is his vitriolic review of the *Marienlieder* of his former colleague on the staff of NZfM, Carl Banck.[58] Here Schumann criticizes in turn the harmony, melody, musical form, and declamation of the text. All these, he decides, are deficient; about more important things, he says, "character, poetic interpretation, higher declamatory expression, and the like, in this case one should not even waste his breath." [59]

Schumann's principal requirement of vocal music, most simply put, was that it should interpret the text. In a review of a set of lieder by J. P. F. Hartmann, he comments approvingly that the composer successfully reflects "down to the individual words, the sense of the text." [60] Few composers, he complains, understand this art:

The mere ability of an artist to comprehend and master the sense of a poem is remarkable now when the field of the lied is afflicted with so much utter mediocrity. Even many of the best-known composers apparently have not so much as read through their poems, so absurd often is the relationship of the poetry to the music—which itself isn't usually much good either.[61]

In a review of Norbert Burgmüller's lieder, Schumann is interested in the same thing: "To reproduce with subtle musical means the effect of the poem in its finest nuances is his principal concern—as it should be with everyone." [62]

Schumann's exacting prescriptions for relating music to text were satisfied by few lieder composers of the older generation. Schubert was one of the few—and even his settings, Schumann thought, were not wholly above criticism. One other composer born in the eighteenth century whose lieder in Schumann's opinion showed sensitive and detailed coordination of music and text was Karl Loewe. Schumann's

58. NZfM, *17* (1843), 10–12. On the face of it, this review would seem not to be by Schumann. It is signed "W. Z.," and does not appear in GS 1854. Both Jansen and Kreisig include it without comment in their editions, however, and, I believe, with good reason. Since there was no known writer for the NZfM at the time with the initials "W. Z.," this signature must have been used in an attempt to conceal the identity of the author. The article, moreover, occurs in a series of lieder reviews by Schumann, one other of which bears the same signature. The latter review, a critique of the Lieder op. 7 of Henry Hugh Pearson is included in GS 1854. The bitter tone of the Banck review undoubtedly reflects the deteriorating personal relationship between Schumann and Banck. Cf. GSK II, 406–07.

59. NZfM, *17* (1842), 10.

60. NZfM, *17* (1842), 9.

61. Ibid. See Appendix I, 72.

62. NZfM, *13* (1840), 118.

first major discussion of lieder in the NZfM is his review, written in 1836, of Loewe's *Esther*, a "song cycle in ballad form" set to the poetry of Ludwig Giesebrecht.

Serving as a moto are these lines from Wolfgang Menzel:

Fruchtbar werden in dir die verborgensten Keime der Dichtung, Dass sich der Dichter in dir neu sieht und doch nur sich selbst.[63]

Like so many of the mottos in the NZfM, this one could almost be a part of the review immediately following; it is obvious that what Schumann is looking for—and finds—in these lieder is a faithful reflection in music of the emotions implied by the poetry. He begins his review simply by recounting the narrative of the text, a story of a medieval Polish king and a beautiful Jewish heroine, Esther, who, like her Old-Testament namesake, courageously represents her people. Schumann continues,

Anyone can see how many musical elements are implied in the action: an insolent master and an oppressed folk, a proud king and a beautiful Jewess, the suffering of a mother and the sacrifice for her people—contrasts that music is well equipped to reflect, and whose impressions no one would be better able to unite into a single picture than Loewe.[64]

Each of these lieder, Schumann says, has its own "special tone." The subject of the first one is a "fiery declaration of love, and the parrying reply of the Jewess." "Almost all the music is in A minor," he observes, "except for a little in C major. The closing question could have been more poetically expressed, perhaps, through a modulation to the dominant." Loewe deliberately juxtaposed A minor with its relative major to emphasize the contrasted moods of the text. Where the king intimidates Esther with threats of banishment, the music is all A minor; when he turns to gentle persuasion ("komm, meine Esther, nimm die Taufe, nimm meinen Ring"), it modulates to C major. Esther's spirited rejoinder which follows is again in A minor; this includes the closing question ("Von Israel sollt' ich mich trennen, das Gott erwählt, das Gott verwarf?") set with a conclusive cadence that Schumann thought somewhat inappropriate (see Ex. 19).

63. NZfM, 5 (1836), 143. "In thee the most hidden seeds of the poetry come to fruition, so that in thee the poet sees anew, but yet sees himself alone."
64. Ibid. See Appendix I, 73.

Example 19. K. Loewe, *Esther* op. 52, no. 1

das Gott er - wählt, —— das Gott ver - warf

Schumann describes the remaining lieder of the series in a similar fashion: he tells what happens in the text, mixing in without warning references to the music. He says, for example,

> In the fourth lied, Esther's joy in her twin daughters who have been left to her; a very original accompaniment. The news of the death of her son ("Gott Abrahams, du hast gegeben, was du genommen hast, ist dein"). Splendid chords which dissolve into a tolling of bells. The marshal announces the death of the king, and she is directed to leave ("Kommt Kinder, kommt zu unsern Volke, die Judengasse nimmt uns auf"). The backward glance at the beginning of the whole is emphasized in a graceful way in the music.[65]

Such mingling of textual and musical exegesis is typical of Schumann's criticism of vocal music, or at least of vocal music where text and music are suitably unified. In this lied, the "original accompaniment" at the beginning (an irregular running figuration in sixteenth notes); the "splendid chords dissolving into the tolling of bells" (measures 54 ff.), and the restatement, finally, of the first theme of the entire collection, are for Schumann simply constituent parts of an integral dramatic scene. The text and music cooperate to produce a certain effect, and it makes little sense to talk about either in isolation. Schumann's method of describing all this is a little like his early essays in creative criticism. He seeks to communicate the effect of the work in words, not by inventing poetic counterparts for it—for the poetic counterpart is already there—but by recounting the combined impressions of text and music. In a slightly later review of Marschner's setting of Stieglitz' *Bilder des Orients*, Schumann declared,

65. Ibid. See Appendix I, 74.

"Everyone should be stimulated by the effect of such a work—of this double existence in language and music." [66]

In the same series as the Loewe review Schumann discussed the works of another very well-known lieder composer of the older generation, Bernhard Klein (1793–1832). Upon his death in 1832, Klein left a sizable musical *Nachlass* whose publication was soon undertaken by Mompour of Bonn and Betzhold of Elberfeld. Schumann reviewed the first six volumes of lieder from this *Nachlass* in the NZfM of 1836. In his review he explicitly compares Klein's habits of text setting with Loewe's:

> If Loewe characteristically portrays almost every word of the poem in the music, Bernhard Klein sketches his subject, whatever it may be, only in the most essential outlines—with a simplicity that can be unbelievably effective, but which can also be severely limiting and annoying. Simplicity does not after all constitute art, and under certain circumstances it can be as undesirable as its opposite, profuse adornment. The sound master always uses all means with discretion, and at the right time. [67]

Schumann objects to this "simplicity" and lack of intimate rapport between text and music, for example, in Klein's setting of Goethe's *Der Gott und die Bajadere*:

> In the restful, sublime passages, the spirit of *Der Gott und die Bajadere*, this most grandly humanistic of all poems, could hardly have been more successfully captured than in this setting of B. Klein. But where the poetry becomes more sensuous, more figurative, and more "Indian," the music, unhappily, remains behind . . . In many places, if one should take away the meaningful words little would remain but ordinary harmonies and commonplace rhythms and melodies. [68]

Yet at the end of this lied, Schumann feels, Klein does much better; Schumann exclaims with a rhetorical flourish, "at the close of the Mahadöh, [69] particularly, he rises to the occasion like the God with

66. NZfM, 5 (1836), 167.
67. NZfM, 5 (1836), 144. See Appendix I, 75.
68. Ibid. See Appendix I, 76.
69. The name Mahadöh, the Christ-like Indian god of Goethe's poem, is used as a subtitle to Klein's lied.

the Bajadere, so that one is gripped by this mysterious spectacle, and continues to gaze upward long after it has vanished into the ether."

Schumann is certainly right that Klein makes very much less of textual interpretation than Loewe does. In the latter's *Esther*, the textures and keys of the music change easily with the quickly shifting moods of the text. In Klein's settings any internal changes of tempo, rhythm, and dynamics usually occur only between large sections. But the most obvious difference between Klein's lieder and those of Loewe is in the piano accompaniments. Klein's accompaniments are for the most part very plain; they consist often of nothing but the barest harmonic outlines presented in simple chords or in some kind of thin-textured triadic figure. Example 20 shows a typical accompanimental pattern from *Der Gott und die Bajadere*.

Example 20. B. Klein, *Der Gott und die Bajadere*

What is different about the end of the lied—which won Schumann's approval—is principally a difference in the accompaniment. Here the piano takes a rather more active role, and it continues for eight measures after the voice part has ended, thus leaving the listener "gazing into the sky" after the ascended God and Bajadere (see Ex. 21).

One very specific complaint Schumann makes about Klein's settings is that they never make use of what he calls the "material" means— that is, onomatopoeic or illustrative devices, like Schubert's well-known imitations of spinning wheels and brooks. While both Schubert and Loewe, as well as many more recent composers, tend to overdo this sort of thing, Schumann says, Klein's stubborn avoidance of such effects deprives him of one means of relating text and music. Yet this amounts to a minor criticism. Though Schumann thought Klein was wrong in eschewing altogether the devices of *Tonmalerei*, the use of such devices was never an important part of his theories about setting of texts. Schumann was always rather wary of graphic

Example 21. B. Klein, *Der Gott und die Bajedere*

feu - ri - gen   Ar - men zum   Him - mel   em -

por

or onomatopoeic text interpretation, in fact, as his criticism of Loewe, Schubert, and many others shows.

An ideal relationship between music and its text, Schumann believed, was something much subtler than that provided by *Tonmalerei*. Music and text in vocal music ought to be related, he felt, much as an instrumental composition is related to an appropriate literary program or a poetic critique. In each case an impression or *Stimmung* is approached in two ways: through music and through words. In the case of an instrumental composition the music is the point of departure; it provides the inspiration for any "poetic counterpart." But in vocal music the situation is reversed. Here the text is given, and appropriate music must be found to reinforce and enhance its *Stimmung*. This reversal of roles in vocal music may explain, at least partly, Schumann's long abstention from the field as a composer. As we have seen, he preferred never to think of the program as causal, or a necessary part of any music. Nor did he think that the impression of a single composition could be approximated by one particular program or literary counterpart alone—the listener must be free, in some degree, to choose his own. In vocal composition, a single poem and a single piece of music are inseparably bound together; perhaps the very explicitness of this connection between music and literature kept Schumann at a distance for a long time.

Of all the forms of music cultivated in his time, the one showing the clearest signs of artistic improvement, in Schumann's opinion, was the lied. In 1843 he even said, "the lied is perhaps the single category in which there has been really significant progress since Beethoven." [70] Klein's lieder clearly belong to an earlier type, and even "the epoch of Franz Schubert," Schumann claimed, "has been followed by a new one." [71] It was Schumann's own generation—and to a considerable extent Schumann himself—that was responsible for this progress.

70. NZfM, *19* (1843), 35.
71. NZfM, *18* (1843), 120.

CHAPTER 9

Some Younger Contemporaries

KIRCHNER, BURGMÜLLER, AND FRANZ

Schumann's statement, "the epoch of Franz Schubert has been followed by a new one" occurs in a review of the Lieder op. 1 by the young German composer Theodore Kirchner (1823–1903)—a pupil of Mendelssohn, and the first student of the Leipzig Conservatory. The review continues,

[This new period in lied composition] has availed itself as well of the continuing cultivation of the accompanying instrument, the piano. The composer names his songs "Lieder with Piano," and this is important. For the singing voice certainly is not sufficient in itself; it cannot carry out the task of interpretation unaided. In addition to the overall expression of the poem, its finer shadings must be represented as well—provided that the voice part does not suffer in the process. And this young composer, to be sure, has to be careful about this. His songs seem, often, like independent instrumental pieces that hardly need the voice to achieve their effect . . . The voice part, thus, often only sings along quietly—most of the expression lies in the accompaniment.[1]

The real distinction Schumann wanted to make between the old and new styles of lieder lay in the type of accompaniment. Klein's rather threadbare figurations are replaced, in Kirchner's lieder, with active, harmonically luxuriant, and sometimes thick-textured piano music; long introductions and epilogues are attached to short songs, and the accompaniments frequently play well above the voice part. All this emphasis on the accompaniment was characteristic of the newest style, and Schumann approved of it in principle, though Kirchner, he felt, tended to overdo it. Perhaps the delicate coordination of

1. NZfM, *18* (1843), 120. See Appendix I, 77.

piano and voice in Schumann's own "Der Nussbaum" is an example of the balance of parts he favored.

In the Kirchner review Schumann prescribes a kind of division of labor in the interpretation of the text of the lied: the broad outlines of the text's *Stimmung* are reflected in the voice part, while the accompaniment, making use of recent advances in expressive piano style, suggest the finer nuances. Elsewhere Schumann reveals in more detail his prescriptions for the piano accompaniment. His extended article on Norbert Burgmüller (1810–36)[2] includes this discussion of the composer's lieder:

> We have everything here that could be asked of a lied: poetic interpretation, lively detail, a happy relationship between the voice and accompanying instrument . . . On this score I am least satisfied with the Goethe setting. This figure, though it can be explained as a reference to the harp player,[3] strikes me as too external and arbitrary; it tends to obscure the organic sensitivity of the poem. With Franz Schubert, the use of a single continuous figure from the beginning of a lied to the end was something new. But young lieder composers need to be cautioned lest this become a mannerism.[4]

The Goethe song in question, *Wer nie sein Brot*, has a peculiar, strumming accompanimental figure throughout (see Ex. 22).

It is easy to see why Schumann should frown on this "single-figure" technique. While the figure may be immediately related to some element in the text, it tends to unify the entire piece around a single idea. Schumann favored much more flexibility in the texture of the accompaniment so that it could reflect finer nuances of feeling.

In 1842, in his review of the Lieder op. 3 of H. F. Kufferath, Schu-

2. Burgmüller, an epileptic, a friend of Mendelssohn, and for a time a student of Spohr, managed in his short lifetime to produce two symphonies (one incomplete), one piano concerto, a piano sonata, three string quartets, various other chamber works, and four collections of lieder. Schumann considered Burgmüller an extraordinarily promising composer. He begins his essay on him thus: "After Franz Schubert's premature death, none is so painful as Burgmüller's. Instead of striking into the regiments of mediocrity, fate carries away our most talented generals."

3. The poem is "Wer nie sein Brot mit Thränen ass," one of the three sung by the Harp-player in Goethe's *Wilhelm Meister*. This song is printed in the collection *Ausgewählte Lieder* (Munich, 1928) edited by Willi Kahl.

4. NZfM, *11* (1839), 71. See Appendix I, 78.

Example 22. N. Burgmüller, *Wer nie sein Brot*

mann expressed dissatisfaction with another accompanimental technique:

> Almost throughout, these lieder show the peculiarity that the piano accompaniment doubles the melody, so that it could even stand by itself without the vocal part. This is certainly nothing to be admired in lied composition; it is especially limiting for the singer. But we always see this in the lieder of the younger composers who have formerly been preoccupied with instrumental composition.[5]

It was not, of course, only the younger composers of Schumann's time who doubled the vocal part in the accompaniment. This had been common practice in eighteenth-century lied composition—when lieder

---

5. NZfM, *16* (1842), 207. See Appendix I, 79. Only shortly after writing this review, interestingly enough, Schumann was lavish in his praise of a lied in which almost every note of the vocal line is doubled in the accompaniment; this is a setting of Franz Dingelstedt's poem "Unterwegs" by Louis Spohr, published in a collection of music called *Mozartalbum* (ed. L. Pott). In his review of this collection Schumann called Spohr's lied "perhaps the most beautiful in the album" (NZfM, *17* [1842], 141)—despite the fact that he himself contributed a lied to it (the *Volksliedchen* op. 51, no. 2 republished in the same year by Whistling).

were normally printed on two staves—and it was done precisely so the piano part could be played as a solo. The simpler, old-fashioned accompaniments of Kufferath, in which the piano doubles the vocal line, and the powerful accompaniments of Kirchner both result in a piano part that achieves a kind of independence. In both cases this apparently violated Schumann's notions about the role the accompaniment ought to play in interpreting the poem.

Of the older, established composers, Schumann would have counted only Loewe, perhaps, as a participant in the "new school of the lied" he discerned in the early 1840s. And even among the younger composers, Schumann indicated, there were but a handful who were really successful in combining expressive poetry with expressive music. In his article "Drei gute Liederhefte," written in 1840, he claimed that it was necessary to examine "about fifty" volumes of lieder before he found three he liked. The article begins,

> Even the most hard-hearted critic sometimes feels an urge to *praise*. "What good is it," I said to myself, "to give lukewarm encouragement to passable beginners in song composition, or to try to stop the throats of the mediocre screamers? Instead I will set before me a whole stack of new lieder, and not rest until I have found a few good ones—so that for once I will be able to praise something to my heart's desire." [6]

The three volumes of lieder that Schumann decided upon were by W. H. Veit (1806–64), Heinrich Esser (1818–72), and Norbert Burgmüller; the best of them, he said, was Burgmüller's op. 10 collection. These songs prompted this statement about Burgmüller: "His foremost concern is—as it should be with everyone—to recreate in a subtle musical realization the most delicate effects of the poem. Seldom does any connotation escape him; nor, if he has grasped it, does his interpretation of it miscarry.[7]

Schumann's enthusiasm for Burgmüller's songs was not at all a momentary fancy or a sentimental attachment to a paradigmatically tragic-romantic figure—talented, emotional, consumed by disease, and early-deceased. He saw in Burgmüller's music, in both his lieder and his piano works,[8] a genuine excellence: whatever their category, his

6. NZfM, *13* (1840), 118. See Appendix I, 80.
7. Ibid. See Appendix I, 81.
8. One piano composition Schumann mentions in his article on Burgmüller is the Sonata op. 8. Its first movement particularly impressed him: "Throughout the movement there is

compositions were progressive in style, harmonically adventurous, and genuinely expressive. Hardly known in Schumann's time, Burgmüller has now been entirely forgotten. Willi Kahl published a little collection of eight Burgmüller songs in 1827; the remainder of his work surely deserves investigation.

The critique of Robert Franz' opus 1, published by Whistling in 1843, was Schumann's last review of lieder. He considered this collection thoroughly representative of the newer and better type of lied, and it prompted him to reflect expansively on the recent fortunes of European music as a whole:

> There is much that one could say about the songs of Robert Franz; no isolated phenomenon, they are intimately connected with the whole development of our art in the last decade. It is known that in the years 1830–34 there arose a reaction against the prevailing taste. The battle was really not a difficult one; it was mounted against that flowery banality which, except in the works of Weber, Loewe, and a few others, could be seen in all music for piano. The first attack, too, was in the field of piano music; passage-work pieces gave way to more thoughtful structures in which one could detect the influence of two masters in particular: Beethoven and Bach. The younger composers increased in number, and the new life penetrated into other categories. Franz Schubert had laid the groundwork for the lied, but principally after the manner of Beethoven; the work of the north Germans, on the other hand, showed more of the effect of Bach's spirit.
>
> The emergence of a new school of German poetry also speeded this development. Rückert and Eichendorff, though they had flourished earlier, became better known to musicians; but more than any others, the verses of Heine and Uhland were set to music. Thus there arose a more artistic and more profound kind

---

a beautiful, powerful passion; and the poet, despite his agitation, has the mastery both to excite and to calm." NZfM, *11* (1839), 71. This composition is quite out of the ordinary for sonatas written in Germany in this period. Harmonically very resourceful, it has in its first theme an obstinate pedal point on F that for 11 measures withstands every intimidation of the upper parts—even of chords built upon E-natural and F-sharp. Chordal passages in this piece show similarities to Schumann's own style in their emphasis of the subdominant and occasional ambiguity of tonal center—as in the beginning of Schumann's *Carnaval* and of *Grillen* from the *Fantasiestücke*.

of lied of which the earlier composers could have no inkling—
for it was but a reflection in music of the new poetic spirit.

Robert Franz' lieder belong throughout to this distinguished
new type . . . Just compare, for example, the painstaking interpretation of the present lieder, where an attempt is made to
reflect the ideas of the text almost to the very word, with the
negligence of the older type of setting, where the poem merely
ran along beside [the music]. Or compare the entire structure of
harmony here with the wobbly accompanimental formulae that
earlier styles could not seem to shake off. Only the ignorant can
disagree. We have already described here the characteristic quality of Robert Franz' lieder: he is interested in something other
than music that merely sounds good or bad; he strives to recreate
for us the real essence of the poem.[9]

Schumann declines to point out details, or even individual lieder in
this collection that please him most; those who are really musical, he
says, will quickly find the best things for themselves. Instead he
talks about places he does *not* like. "Certain details," he says, "offend
my ear, as the beginning of the seventh and twelfth lieder—in the
latter, the often-repeated E." This criticism again shows Schumann's
preoccupation with the piano accompaniment. The beginning of the
seventh lied, *Sonntag,* is shown in Example 23.

Example 23. R. Franz, Lieder op. 1, no. 7

If he had an opportunity to delete a single lied from the collection,
Schumann indicates, it would be this one; "in melody and harmony,"
he says, "it looks too contrived to me." This is one of the few numbers of the volume in which the accompaniment is little more than a

9. NZfM, *19* (1843), 34–35. See Appendix I, 82.

four-part harmonization. Significantly, too, the vocal line is doubled almost throughout in the accompaniment. The "repeated E" that disturbed Schumann in the last number of the set is a very persistent tone in the opening of the vocal lines, as shown in Example 24. This opening, stated three times during the course of a song only two pages in length, is decidedly cloying.

Example 24. R. Franz, Lieder op. 1, no. 12

Of all the lieder in this collection, one of the most successful, Schumann says, is the *Schlummerlied* of Tieck (no. 10); he would wish, though, for a "richer, more musical ending." This lied is surely one of the most impressive of the set, and what makes it impressive, again, is largely the accompaniment; it is very active, flexible in texture, and rich in suggestions of polyphonic inner voices. Schumann was disappointed with its ending, and it is easy to see why; it trails off with a figure in the piano that leaves the sound of the tonic sixth chord—already hackneyed in 1843—ringing in the listener's ears (see Ex. 25).

Example 25. R. Franz, Lieder op. 1, no. 10

Schumann's judgment of Franz is of course only a preliminary one based on a single book of lieder. Twelve years later, with a good deal more evidence available, Liszt concurred emphatically with Schumann's high estimate of Franz' importance as a lieder composer.[10] This may be surprising to the modern observer for whom Franz' name conjures up only memories of slight, saccharine tunes like *Widmung* (op. 14, no. 1). That Franz is thus remembered probably results from the later popularization of exactly such songs, especially in Victorian England. The lieder with simple, chordal accompaniments and uncomplicated vocal parts, performable by any amateur, were the ones most often reprinted; and this has somewhat distorted our view of Franz' music.

SCHUMANN'S CONVERSION TO VOCAL MUSIC

Though Schumann never said so, he must have included himself among the younger set of composers who cultivated the new, potently expressive style of lied. Three years before he wrote the Franz review Schumann took a step that has always puzzled and intrigued students of nineteenth-century music. In 1840, after compiling twenty-three opus numbers of piano music alone,[11] Schumann abruptly shifted to lieder composition; in that year and the following one he turned out a prodigious number of them—the Heine cycle, *Myrthen*, the *Frauenliebe und -leben*, the *Dichterliebe*, and many others. Of his entire output of lieder, in fact, more than half were composed in 1840 alone. And, as we have seen, it was precisely at this time that Schumann the critic, too, began to show a really lively interest in lieder.

Instead of looking for the causes of this sudden change of direction, it might seem more appropriate to inquire why it did not happen earlier. Schumann's love of poetry, the easy blending of his musical and literary talents in his early writings, as well as his unshakable belief in the closeness of literature and music—stated and elaborated upon as early as 1828—would surely lead one to expect from him an earlier interest in the lied.

To find satisfactory answers to the question about Schumann's *Liederjahr*, to understand, in fact, the whole course of Schumann's musical development, it is essential to understand first his profound

---

10. F. Liszt, *Gesammelte Schriften* (Leipzig, 1882), 4, 211 ff.

11. Schumann had privately tried his hand at lieder, we have seen, as early as 1828 when he set some verses of Kerner and sent them to the composer Gottlob Wiedebein for criticism. See *Briefe*, pp. 6–7.

attachment to that romantic musical instrument par excellence, the piano. All his early musical experiences had been at the keyboard. The music that elicited the immoderate Jean-Paulian effusions of the early diaries and letters was almost always piano music, and his own musical response to the stimulus of romantic literature took the form of improvisations at the piano. Schumann returned to Leipzig from Heidelberg in 1831 with but one purpose: to fulfill a burning ambition to become a piano virtuoso. The musicians with whom he associated in Leipzig were almost all pianists, including the three with whom he collaborated to found the NZfM—a journal devoted to improving conditions in piano music. So strong an attachment to his instrument was not easily broken; Schumann's musical thinking was so solidly rooted in the piano that any rapprochement in his composition between music and literature was almost bound to take the form, not of vocal composition, but, as it did, of programmatic music for piano.

Many reasons have been suggested for Schumann's sudden plunge, finally in 1840, into vocal music: emotional stresses attendant to his difficulties with Wieck and impending marriage to Clara, a decline in his imagination, a wish for more "definite expression," and others.[12] While some of these explanations are plausible enough, Schumann's own writings, read attentively, provide more compelling ones. His turn to vocal music in the early 1840s is part of a larger pattern—it is a symptom of his shifting ideas about the progress of romantic music and the future of German musical traditions. That Schumann thought about such expansive questions specifically in connection with lieder is quite clear from the Franz review.

During his earlier years as a critic, too, Schumann was always preoccupied with piano music; all problems of musical style were reduced in his mind to problems about piano music and piano playing. Composers were heroes or villains depending upon what they did or did not do at the piano. Most of the contemporary composers whose music interested Schumann, especially before 1840, concentrated on short pieces for piano—as did, of course, Schumann himself. While Schumann showed a lively interest in this music, reviewing in the 1830s literally hundreds of etudes, capriccios, rondos, and the like, he viewed these pieces only as a kind of preparatory study for the more important business of writing sonatas, concertos, and sym-

12. See F. Feldmann, "Zur Frage des 'Liederjahres' bei Robert Schumann," *Archiv für Musikwissenschaft*, 9 (1952), 246.

phonies. A familiar refrain in Schumann's criticism is his warning against a prolonged preoccupation with these small forms. In a review of assorted short pieces for piano by J. C. Kessler in the first volume of the NZfM, Schumann says he hopes this young composer will soon stop "dissipating" his talents in such music.[13] In 1837 Schumann frets that Chopin always writes short genre pieces instead of the larger forms (part of the trouble, Schumann speculates, is that Chopin is living in Paris).[14] Not long after, he advises Henselt, in a review of his Etudes op. 5, to discontinue his efforts along these lines and write in the "higher forms: the sonata or concerto."[15] Schumann repeatedly gave the same advice to Heller[16] and Bennett.[17]

Schumann long took for granted that the real future for the romantic movement, founded by Beethoven, lay in the cultivation of Beethoven's kind of music: the large instrumental forms. But writing sonatas and symphonies, as he well knew, often simply was not possible early in a composer's career. An enriched harmonic idiom, original rhythms and textures—all the elements of the heightened expressiveness he valued—could best be explored by a young composer, he conceded, in short piano pieces. But he expected the most promising composers of his generation to do as he himself hoped to do: to get about the really important business, sooner or later, of producing extensive instrumental works in a modern style.

In about 1839 Schumann began to show signs of doubt that this would ever happen. In April of that year he observed that most of the sonata composers were neither the romantics nor the composers left over from the preceding generation, but young unknowns for whom the category was nothing but an exercise in form.[18] In July he remarked sadly on the backwardness of the few contemporary symphonies—almost all of them imitated the early style of Beethoven, or even that of Haydn and Mozart. Schumann mentioned one conspicuous exception—the *Symphonie fantastique* of Berlioz.[19] But it is perfectly clear that by this time Berlioz' orchestral works hardly exemplified what Schumann had in mind for a continuation of the

13. NZfM, *1* (1834), 114.
14. NZfM, *7* (1837), 200.
15. NZfM, *10* (1839), 74.
16. NZfM, *14* (1841), 181–82; *18* (1843), 13.
17. NZfM, *17* (1842), 175; *19* (1843), 17.
18. NZfM, *10* (1839), 134.
19. NZfM, *11* (1839), 1.

romantic tradition of Beethoven and Schubert. Already in June of
1838 Schumann saw that the string quartet, too, was not a very live
category; the only really competent composers writing quartets were
Mendelssohn and Onslow.[20] Two months later Schumann was excited
by the quartets he reviewed in manuscript of an unknown young composer, Herrmann Hirschbach.[21] But Hirschbach apparently produced
nothing more, and by the time his quartets were published in 1842,
Schumann's enthusiasm for them had cooled.[22]

Schumann began to see at the end of the 1830s that instrumental
music was not progressing, and was not likely to progress as he had
hoped. The traditional large forms of instrumental music were in
danger of extinction, and the romantic composers did not seem particularly interested in reviving them. Schumann himself had serious
difficulties in constructing large movements, and at the same time
he thought little was to be gained in a continued preoccupation with
short pieces for piano. By 1840 instrumental music had in Schumann's
opinion arrived at a kind of impasse. A change of direction in his
interests was only natural; in his careers both as composer and critic
he abruptly turned to vocal music.

There was another factor operative in Schumann the critic's shift of
interest. The NZfM had been founded largely to assail the Parisian
virtuosi's tyrannical rule over piano music, and Schumann's early
criticism was firmly committed to this cause. But by the end of the
1830s this battle was drawing to a close; the greatest vogue of the
virtuosi was fading, and the romantic composers were more and more
given a hearing. In the Franz review, Schumann describes this struggle
against the *Floskelwesen* in piano music very much in retrospect; it
was clearly over, he felt, and the initial goals of his own work as a
critic had been achieved. Thus Schumann's feeling about instrumental
music in 1840 was strangely divided. He saw a victory being won
against Philistinism and gross vulgarization; but this victory was a
hollow one in the face of his growing doubts, amounting at times to
disillusionment, about the direction instrumental music was now to
take. Both parts of this dichotomy are mentioned in the Franz review.
"The passage-work pieces," Schumann says, "gave way to more
thoughtful structures in which one could detect the influence of two

20. NZfM, 8 (1838), 194.
21. NZfM, 9 (1838), 51.
22. See NZfM, 16 (1842), 159.

masters in particular: Beethoven and Bach." But he says too, somewhat despondently, "And in truth, the lied is the only category, perhaps, in which there has been really significant progress since Beethoven." [23]

For anyone wishing to explain Schumann's conversion to vocal music in 1840, a bothersome obstacle is raised by his statement in a letter to Herrmann Hirschbach of June 1839: "all my life I have considered vocal composition inferior to instrumental music—I have never regarded it as a great art. But don't tell anyone about it!" [24] What is surprising about this statement is when Schumann said it. By the middle of 1839, shortly before he was to plunge into almost exclusive composition of lieder, his earlier ideas about the relative importance of instrumental and vocal music must surely have been changing—and his use of the present perfect tense (which in German often refers to completed actions) may reflect this. But even if the statement is taken as his current opinion, it is important to notice to whom the letter is addressed. Hirschbach was a contributor to the NZfM whose impatience with the present state of affairs in music and whose impetuous way of expressing himself were reminiscent of the early days of the journal. And shortly before, Schumann had first seen Hirschbach's quartets—music that had temporarily kindled in him a new excitement and optimism about the future of instrumental music.[25] Hirschbach's writing and music revived in Schumann a spark of his earlier sanguine expectations, and for a moment pushed aside his uncertainty about what an instrumental composer can possibly do after Beethoven. The letter to Hirschbach must be seen in this context.

HIRSCHBACH, SCHAPLER, AND THOMAS

Schumann's acquaintance with Herrmann Hirschbach began in June 1838 when he received from the mercurial young composer two essays for publication in the NZfM.[26] Schumann was immediately at-

---

23. NZfM, *19* (1843), 35.
24. *Briefe*, p. 158.
25. See *Briefe*, pp. 156 and 158, and NZfM, *9* (1838), 42, and 51–52.
26. These essays, entitled "Klaviersonate und Streichquartett" and "Beethoven's neunte Sinfonie" were published in the NZfM, *8* (1838), 205–06 and *9* (1838), 19–21, 27–28. A third article received from Hirschbach, a spirited and well-documented defense of Beethoven's ability to write counterpoint, was a rejoinder to an essay in the AmZ by K. B.

tracted to the Berliner's forthright manner, and though he appended
objecting footnotes to certain points in Hirschbach's articles, he plainly
thought highly of them. On June 13 Schumann agreed with Hirschbach that the real proving ground for a musician was in writing
music, not writing about it ("I too write words but reluctantly—I
much prefer sonatas and symphonies")[27] and asked Hirschbach to send
him any compositions he cared to part with. Hirschbach promptly
obliged with three string quartets, a string quintet, a sonata, and an
overture. This music was accompanied with a letter setting forth
Hirschbach's musical credo. The most valuable quality in modern
music, he said, was "the characteristic," and the special task of the
modern composer was to express "genuinely poetic states of the soul."[28]

Hirschbach's statements struck a responsive chord with Schumann,
and this, no doubt, had its effect upon his judgments of the young
composer's music. In the third of his *Quartett-Morgen* series, Schumann discussed new works by W. H. Veit, J. F. E. Sobolewski, and
Leopold Fuchs; he appended these remarks:

> Should I wish for the highest sort of music—as Bach and
> Beethoven have given in certain of their works—should I speak
> of rare states of the soul that the artist ought to reveal to me,
> should I demand that in each of his works he lead me one step
> further in spiritual riches of the art, should I demand, in a word,
> poetic depth and originality throughout—in details and in the
> whole—I would have a long search ahead of me. For none of
> these works, in fact hardly any music that has recently appeared,
> would satisfy me. But in the following *Quartett-Morgen* we must
> hear more about the music of a certain young man; this music, it
> seems to me, flows at times from the depths of real, live genius—
> though such a statement demands certain modifications. More
> about all of this in one of the following issues.[29]

About two weeks later, in the fourth *Quartett-Morgen*, Schumann
revealed that the music he was talking about was Hirschbach's. The

von Miltitz. Entitled "Ueber Beethoven als Kontrapunctist," Hirschbach's article was
rushed into print immediately, and appeared before the other two. NZfM, 8 (1838), 189–90.
In 1843 Hirschbach established his own journal, the *Musikalisches-kritisches Repertorium,*
in which he systematically denounced almost everything and everyone in contemporary
music. His criticism made enough enemies that he was finally forced to quit the field.

27. *Briefe*, p. 123.

28. Quoted in Pessenlehner, *Herrmann Hirschbach,* pp. 14–15.

29. NZfM, 9 (1838), 42. See Appendix I, 83.

players assembled for the occasion (for the *Quartett-Morgen* reviews, it will be remembered, Schumann arrranged private performances of chamber music at his home) performed the three quartets and the quintet—all unpublished—and Schumann's enthusiasm in the first half of his review seemed boundless:

> This much I know: his is the most significant endeavor, supported by the greatest ability, that I have seen for a long time among the younger talents. Words can hardly describe how his music is put together, and all the things that it expresses. His music is itself speech, such as the flowers speak to us, or as mysterious tales are related by the eyes, or as kindred spirits commune together from afar—the speech of the soul, profound, rich, genuine musical life.[30]

Seldom did Schumann strain his syntax this way in support of anybody's music. His impressions of Hirschbach's compositions, Schumann frankly admits, were conditioned by the "great similarity of his course as a composer to my own." [31] Hirschbach was doing exactly what Schumann himself more and more aspired to do in the late 1830s—to compose quartets, symphonies, and the like. Schumann did not feel he was prepared, as yet, to meet Beethoven on his own ground, and despite his initial raptures over Hirschbach's efforts, he did not think Hirschbach was either. The review continues:

> And now for the "but." Just as upon first observation of a picture by a young painter full of genius we are captivated by the dimensions of his composition (also in an external sense), and by the richness and realism of the colors so that, astonished, we overlook individual faults of draftsmanship, so too here. But upon a second listening some passages began to irritate me— passages that do not so much violate explicit rules of the craft, but sin against the sense of hearing itself, against the natural laws of harmony. I don't mean only parallel fifths and the like, but also certain bass progressions and modulations that sound amateurish to me.[32]

At least three of Hirschbach's four quartets, later published under the

30. NZfM, 9 (1838), 51. See Appendix I, 84.
31. Schumann mentioned this artistic kinship he felt with Hirschbach directly to the composer (*Briefe*, p. 125), and in a letter to Clara (*Jugendbriefe*, p. 288). But here he added, "Yet he is much more passionate and tragic than I."
32. NZfM, 9 (1838), 51–52. See Appendix I, 85.

title *Lebensbilder in einem Cyclus von Quartetten,* are in the standard
four-movement form (I have not seen the first quartet of this set).
But the movements themselves have strange shapes, with abrupt shifts
from one kind of material to another, and from one tonality to another. Schumann pointed to the late Beethoven quartets as models for
Hirschbach's work, and in many places the resemblance is unmistakable. But Hirschbach was not Beethoven, and his unorthodoxies, to
Schumann's ears, sometimes fell flat. Hirschbach's quartets, for all
their unevenness, are at their best convincing music; and they are at
their best when the gnarled late Beethovenian style is least in evidence,
as in the introduction to the last movement of the second quartet (see
Ex. 26).

Example 26. H. Hirschbach, Quartet no. 2, 4th movement

Schumann's early career as a critic had been spent in an expectant
attitude. He looked confidently, at first, for the further development
of romantic music, and for the arrival of some Messiah-like heir to
Beethoven's mantel. Both Chopin and Berlioz looked like promising
candidates, but both—especially Berlioz—proved somewhat disappointing. Just as disillusionment was setting in, there, suddenly, was

Hirschbach, and for a moment Schumann thought the savior of modern music had come after all. But in 1842, having incorporated some of the revisions Schumann recommended, Hirschbach published the first quartet of the cycle, and Schumann reviewed it in the NZfM; his feeling about this music was now distinctly more lukewarm:

> In its initial fresh attack, much of this is successful; but again and again faulty musicianship breaks through, and one gets the same sort of feeling as when he comes on a gross spelling error in an otherwise effectively written letter. One sees the same thing— only much oftener—in Berlioz' compositions.[33]

Schumann was disturbed by Hirschbach's technical flaws partly because they were perpetrated in the quartet—a distinctly "strict" genre in Schumann's time; in a review of a quartet by one Leopold Fuchs in 1838 he said, "the severity of the form [of the quartet in general] is itself its beauty." [34] This "severe form," like several of the traditional instrumental categories, seemed to Schumann on the brink of extinction. In 1842 the *Musikverein* of Mannheim offered a prize for the best string quartet submitted. A young composer from Magdeburg, Julius Schapler, was the winner; Schumann's review of Schapler's quartet was vaguely favorable but pessimistic:

> The idea of offering a prize for a quartet was a good one. For one thing, because the category is such a noble one, a high degree of cultivation among the contestants is presuppposed; furthermore, the quartet has come to a serious standstill. Who does not know the quartets of Haydn, Mozart and Beethoven, and who would wish to say anything against them? In fact it is the most telling testimony to the immortal freshness of their works that yet after a half-century they gladden the hearts of everyone; but it is no good sign that the later generation, after all this time, has not been able to produce anything comparable. Onslow alone met with success, and later Mendelssohn, whose aristocratic-poetic nature is particularly amenable to this genre.[35]

Because of this "standstill" in quartet writing, Schumann had occasion to review only fourteen quartets in his ten-year tenure as a critic. The composers represented in these reviews are about the same group as those who wrote sonatas: older men like Cherubini and

33. NZfM, *16* (1842), 159–60. See Appendix I, 86.
34. NZfM, *8* (1838), 182.
35. NZfM, *16* (1842), 142–43. See Appendix I, 87.

Spohr, and the more conservative (and insignificant) young composers, such as C. G. Reissiger, J. J. H. Verhulst, and Wilhelm Taubert.
Hirschbach, not at all conservative, was an exception. Schumann actually liked Schapler's[36] quartet about as well as any he reviewed:

> Unfortunately, I have not heard the quartet. It has been
> sounding inside my head, however, and I find no blemish in it.
> I would not care to point out any single movement as better than
> the others, as they are all interrelated. To describe its character in
> a few words: from an initial gloomy, elegiac mood it progresses to
> a humorous one, then to a serene seriousness and finally to bold,
> energetic activity.[37]

The last part of this quotation is obviously meant to be a description
of the successive movements of the quartet. Its first movement begins
with a sizable slow introduction; both this and the Allegro Vivace
that follows are subdued in dynamics. The following Scherzo and
Adagio account for the "humor" and "serene seriousness." The first
theme of the final movement, though largely pianissimo, is vigorous
rhythmically:

Example 27. J. Schapler, Prize Quartet, 4th movement

It seems to be this last movement that satisfied Schumann most; he
implies as much at the end of his review. Its animation and inventiveness distinguish it sharply from the predominately tame and back-
ward chamber music that so afflicted the 1830s and 1840s.

A more standard and humdrum chamber composition that Schumann reviewed was the early Trio op. 3 of Ambroise Thomas. The
trio was considered quite a different problem, really, than the quartet.

36. In the published score, the composer's name appears as "Schabler" (and is so cata-
logued in the one American library where I have been able to find the quartet, the Boston
Public Library). Schumann's review begins: "That's real German luck! What a royal mis-
fortune! A man writes a prize quartet, polishes it off, publishes the score, and there, right
in the title, in the winner's name—is a misprint." NZfM, *16* (1843), 142.

37. NZfM, *16* (1842), 143. See Appendix I, 88.

In the decade after Beethoven's death trios took a sharp turn toward the popular side: string parts often became rudimentary, and acted mostly as an accompaniment to the piano. In his very first review of a trio in the NZfM Schumann said what is needed to perform such a composition: "a fiery player at the piano, and two understanding friends who accompany softly." [38] Such an ensemble would do very nicely for Thomas' trio—and the pianist would not even have to be particularly fiery. Schumann calls the piece

> a salon-trio, which permits one to peer about through his lor-
> gnette without entirely losing the thread of the music. It is neither
> difficult nor easy, neither profound nor insipid, not classic, not
> romantic, but always well-sounding, and in places full of beauti-
> ful melody, for example in the mild principal theme of the first
> movement. In major, though, this melody loses much of its charm
> and even sounds vulgar—such a difference there often is between
> the major and minor third.[39]

That theme is a pleasant tune first stated as shown in Example 28.

Example 28. A. Thomas, Trio op. 3, 1st movement

38. NZfM, 5 (1836), 4.
39. NZfM, 5 (1836), 41. See Appendix I, 89.

In the recapitulation (measure 154) it appears in major, doubled by the cello (see Ex. 29).

Example 29. A. Thomas, Trio op. 3, 1st movement

All the movements of this trio, Schumann observes, are brief and compressed in form, in the first, so much so that "a genuine second theme never appears, but instead only a little melodic scale passage in the violin, which is then taken up by the cello." Here Schumann goes astray because, reviewing the work in parts, he miscounted measures. The "melodic scale passage," like much of the string music in this trio, is played by the violin and cello together (see Ex. 30).

Example 30. A. Thomas, Trio op. 3, 1st movement

Schumann finishes by warning the future composer of *Mignon* against excessive "sweetness and effeminateness"—an often-repeated refrain in Schumann's reviews of all the large instrumental categories. The bulk of the sonatas, chamber music, and music for orchestra Schumann criticized were wholly unaffected by the craggy melodic lines and violent rhythms of the later Beethoven sonata forms. Smooth melody, gentle rhythm (especially in compound meters), bland harmony, and brief, clear formal designs were very much the norm. Thomas' trio is a good example of that norm.

LACHNER AND RIETZ

A much more publicized composition contest than the Mannheim quartet competition was held in Vienna in 1836: the *Concerts spirituels* offered a prize of 50 gold ducats for the best symphony submitted. The winning composition by Franz Lachner (1803–90) was widely played and became the object of a good deal of heated debate in Germany and Austria. This symphony was coolly received in Leipzig, and Schumann, in his review of November 1836, agreed with the Gewandhaus audience that the piece was exceedingly dull. This review is cast as an answer to a spritely little essay by Schumann's friend Anton von Zuccamaglio which had appeared in the previous number of the NZfM.[40] Here Zuccamaglio (writing, as he sometimes did, under the pseudonym "Gottschalk Wedel") recounts awakening in a cold sweat from a dream in which he had sought to win the Viennese prize with a wild symphony in the style of Berlioz. What a relief, he said, that a sensible, solid German work had really won. In his review Schumann, though offering no particular defense of Berlioz, makes no bones about his displeasure with Lachner's enormously long (304 pages in the Haslinger score) and rather old-fashioned symphony:

> Were there but uncouth blunders, formal weaknesses, excesses, then there would be something to talk about and improve, and some reason for encouragement. Here, though, one can only say things like "it is tedious," or "it will pass," or sigh, or think about something else.[41]

Schumann does not agree with Zuccamaglio about the "Germanness" of Lachner's symphony:

> In a word, the symphony has no style; it is put together from German, Italian and French elements, something like the Romansh language. Lachner uses the German manner for his beginnings (i.e. canonic imitations), Italian style cantilena, and French transitions and closes. When this is done expertly, in rapid suc-

40. NZfM, 5 (1836), 147–48.
41. NZfM, 5 (1836), 151–52. See Appendix I, 90.

cession, as with Meyerbeer, one can take it with better humor; but when the listener is conscious of it to the point of boredom— this could be seen plainly in the faces of the Leipzig audience— only the most indulgent review could do other than dismiss it.[42]

Schumann always frowns on stylistic eclecticism, and whenever he comes across it, he is reminded of Meyerbeer. Another similarity to Meyerbeer's music he notes (as we have seen in the *Huguenots* review) is Lachner's oppressive use of "that well-known rhythm with an upbeat of three eighth notes," in which, he complains, the first and second movements move throughout. Here Schumann seems to have grown hypersensitive to a rhythmic figure that was, to be sure, badly overused; the three-note anacrusis is present in Lachner's first and second movements, but in a wide variety of guises. Example 31 shows the principal and subsidiary themes of the first movement and the principal theme of the second movement.

Example 31. F. Lachner, Prize Symphony op. 52

42. NZfM, 5 (1836), 151. See Appendix I, 91.

In view of Schumann's sensitivity to this rhythm it is surprising that he should use it pervasively and with no apparent embarrassment in the *Romanza* of his own Fourth Symphony. As in Lachner's Andante, the three-note upbeat—in a slower tempo—underlies the entire movement; in the middle section in D major, the horns play this figure relentlessly (in his rescoring of the symphony Mahler suppressed this horn part): 𝄴 ♫♫ | ♩. ♫♫ | ♩.

Symphonies like Lachner's only confirmed Schumann's suspicion that Beethoven had virtually exhausted the category. As early as 1835, in his review of Berlioz' *Symphonie fantastique*, he said,

> Mendelssohn, a productive, reflective, and great artist, must have realized that nothing more could be accomplished on this path [the symphony], and struck out on a new one (unless one would wish to consider something such as the first *Leonore* overture a precedent). With his concert-overtures, where he compressed the idea of the symphony into narrower confines, he has gained for himself the crown and scepter over all the instrumental composers of the day. It was to be feared that the name symphony, from this time on, belonged only to history.[43]

Of the two-dozen or so examples of the concert overture, the "successor to the symphony," Schumann reviewed, the majority have programmatic titles (such as Bennett's *The Naiads* and Julius Rietz' *Ouverture zu Hero und Leander*), and most of them were written by German composers. Those without programs, identified only by number and key, Schumann observed, were usually plagued with the same stylistic backwardness and mediocrity as the contemporary symphony. Johann Kalliwoda's overtures, for example, make several appearances in Schumann's criticism; he said they were all pleasant, simple, undistinguished—and exactly alike.[44]

Julius Rietz (1812–77), composer, conductor and cellist, student of Zelter and friend of Mendelssohn, produced a number of distinguished overtures, some with, and some without programmatic titles. In 1840, Rietz' Overture op. 7 was performed at two concerts which Schumann reviewed. Both reviews mention it very favorably; in the first one Schumann calls the overture "most significant . . . German,

43. NZfM, *3* (1835), 34. See Appendix I, 92.
44. NZfM, *1* (1834), 38.

artistic . . ." [45] But Schumann was even more impressed with Rietz's *Ouverture zu Hero und Leander* op. 11. On the strength of this composition, Schumann declared in 1843:

> In fact, a period that produces such works, and can display such excellent talents as Rietz, for example, need not so much blush before any great era of the past, as a few reactionaries would have us believe. And this period can look with confidence to an even more promising future.[46]

Schumann finds only one fault in this overture: "certain similarities to well-known compositions"—again Schumann's very active musical memory was producing sensations of *déjà entendu*.[47] But here, he says, similarities to the music of Mendelssohn and to Beethoven's *Coriolanus* Overture and Ninth Symphony are more stylistic than thematic. One passage he selects as "too Mendelssohnian" is the gentle theme in F major shown in Example 32.

Example 32. J. Rietz, Overture zu Hero und Leander

After crediting the overture with "mastery of form . . . inventiveness, significance and beauty of individual motives, and, overall, a noble bearing," Schumann admits to some embarrassment about not

45. NZfM, *12* (1840), 143.

46. NZfM, *18* (1843), 132. See Appendix I, 93.

47. In a review of 1837 Schumann found most of the music of Herz' Concerto op. 87 in assorted earlier compositions by Chopin, Moscheles, Kalkbrenner, Weber, and several others. NZfM, *6* (1837), 50.

being able to discern which episode of the Hero and Leander legend the composer had in mind. Was it the last, fatal night when both were drowned? Or was Rietz simply thinking of the lovers as they were when Leander happily swam the Hellespont for their nightly trysts? Schumann says he cannot really tell; but he is quite satisfied with the music for its own sake.

Rietz' composition shows real imagination and competence. Its form is the usual one for concert overtures of this period: a rather long adagio introduction is followed by a sonata-allegro form with a sparkling, fanfare-like coda. But the individual themes are uncommonly attractive; they avoid the featureless triadic patterns so pervasive in contemporary orchestral music, and there are satisfying individualistic twists in the harmony and instrumentation. More conservative and "German" than Berlioz' orchestral music, but showing more profile than much of Mendelssohn's, this overture is an example that at least approaches Schumann's ideal for orchestral composition in the romantic era.

CHAPTER 10

Ȝhe Ƀirtuosi

Some of Schumann's liveliest writing is his criticism of the Parisian piano virtuosi. In dealing with these men—on the whole villains who degraded the muse, he said, for applause and money—Schumann's humor ranges from wry amusement to towering rage. During his ten years with the NZfM he reviewed compositions by all the leading virtuosi: Kalkbrenner, Herz, Hünten, Döhler, Bertini, Thalberg, Liszt, and many others. These last two, he believed, were much better musicians than the rest. Among the others he did not care to draw any important distinctions; their style, he claimed, was uniform, routine, and cliché-ridden, their intentions were often of the worst, and their influence, especially in Germany, was disastrous.

Most of what the virtuosi composed and played, as we have seen, was based on preexistent music. This was true not only of the variations and fantasias, but also (with good historical precedent) of the capriccios and (with less historical precedent) of the rondos. Schumann grew up in a milieu in which arrangements, transcriptions, and variations comprised a large share of the standard musical fare, and he had little predisposition against such pieces per se. Bach, after all, had written them. His own first published work is a set of variations (not on a current tune, but on the pitch names A, B-flat, E, G, G), and he subsequently published a set of etudes on capriccios of Paganini as op. 3 and 10, and impromptus on a theme of Clara Wieck as op. 5. His first music review, an encomium to Chopin, is a critique of the Polish pianist's variations on "Là ci darem la mano" from *Don Giovanni*. The fault of the virtuosi's productions lay not so much with their type as with their style.

Of the various kinds of second-hand music the virtuosi cultivated, most popular were fantasias and variations on operatic arias. In his introduction to a series of reviews of such variations in 1836 Schumann almost explodes:

For surely in no genre of our art has more bungling mediocrity been perpetrated—and it is still going on. One could scarcely imagine such wretchedness springing up on every side, such vulgarity that no longer knows any shame. Before, at least, we had good, boring German themes. But now one has to swallow the most hackneyed Italian tunes in five or six successive states of watery decomposition. And the best are the ones that stop there. But just let them come from the provinces—the Strohmillers, Genserts, or whatever their names happen to be. Ten variations, with double reprises. And even that would be all right. But then the *minore* and the *finale* in 3/8 time—gad! One shouldn't waste his breath over it—snip, snap into the fire! We think too much of our readers and ourselves to present such rubbish (the fitting word for it) in individual reviews as other blissful journals do. Things that are spectacularly bad or authentically amateurish will sometimes be mentioned; but in this cross-section, except for this first series, only the better things that have appeared will be considered.[1]

In the following volume of the NZfM, Schumann comments on this kind of music somewhat more charitably. After listing an enormous number of sets of variations he is about to review, he begins:

None of the above works is immortal, though many of them are pretty enough. If one could only know how the respective composers themselves would evaluate these works. Should they think such things have lasting value, then one would have to try to disillusion them. If they should laughingly admit that these are but trivia over which few words need be wasted, then one would have to praise their modesty. For we cannot all be Bachs at every moment, however desirable that might be.[2]

Schumann was often uncertain, as these quotations show, about what sort of criteria he ought to apply to such music. Viewed as simple amusement, the common run of variations and fantasias seemed harmless enough; but considered as "real" music, and the contemporary contribution to the progress of an art that included the works of Bach, Beethoven, and Schubert, he thought them simply destestable.

1. NZfM, 5 (1836), 63. See Appendix I, 94.
2. NZfM, 6 (1837), 175. See Appendix I, 95.

What discouraged Schumann most of all was that this kind of music
for piano was cultivated almost to the exclusion of anything better.
It flooded the music markets, filled the concert programs, and was
enthusiastically promoted by almost all of the musical journals, while
the more serious piano music of Chopin, Hiller, and Schumann himself was hard to publish, and frequently dismissed by the public as
too difficult or bizarre.

However it is to be judged, Schumann thought, virtuoso piano
music hardly merited much of the critic's time. His reviews of this
music seldom indulge in any detail; he did not feel it was worth the
effort, and, moreover, the style was already thoroughly familiar. In
his review of a typical "combination piece"—one that includes both
a fantasia and a set of variations—by Theodore Döhler, Schumann
wrote,

> these are nothing but brilliant variations on a theme of Donizetti
> —and you know all about them in advance. So long as the com-
> poser and public only see these things for what they are, there is
> no harm done. When they are made out to be something impor-
> tant, however, they come into the range of our heavy cannon.
> Now it is absurd that the musical journals try to open the eyes
> of the world to what they call "agreeable" talents, such as Kalk-
> brenner, Bertini, etc. We can already see through glass; for this
> we need no boring interpreter.[3]

The piece Schumann is talking about is Döhler's *Fantasia and
Bravura Variations on a Theme of Donizetti* op. 17. He considers it
representative of its category, though a bit more interesting than the
usual piano variations:

> he appears to be a distinguished virtuoso, he presents some things
> that are new, and it always sounds good. He writes everything
> down industriously, has a good sense of rhythm, and his music is
> playable on the piano. All this is valuable.[4]

Schumann could assume that his readers were perfectly familiar with
this style of composition; but because the modern reader is not likely
to have any such acquaintance with it, let us examine this composition
—typical, in Schumann's opinion, but a cut above the average—in
some detail.

3. NZfM, 5 (1836), 80. See Appendix I, 96.
4. Ibid. See Appendix I, 97.

Döhler's Fantasia and Variations is based on two tunes from Donizetti's *Anna Bolena,* one for the fantasia and one for the variations. It
begins with a quick alternation of fast and slow passages (this is typical of such introductions) in which there is a tantalizing hint of both
of the melodies to come (see Ex. 33).

Example 33. Th. Döhler, Fantasia and Variations op. 17, Introduction

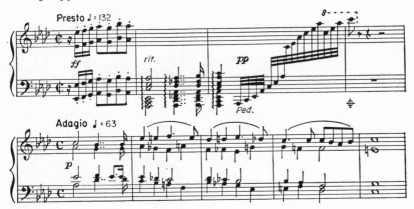

The second statement of the adagio dissolves into an ornamental
single-line passage in the right hand, which, as it approaches a cadence,
makes use of a figure that made Schumann cringe. (See Ex. 34; the
portion in brackets is the musical example Schumann gives in a footnote.)

Example 34. Th. Döhler, Fantasia and Variations op. 17, Introduction

He said,

There are two ornamental figures with which we hope composers will not enrage us again. They are printed below. They

have gradually become such clichés that one really can no longer bear to hear them. A curse on anyone who writes them once more. If someone wants us to suggest other decorations for cadential passages, we are ready to provide thousands.[5]

The other "decoration" Schumann pointed out (the brackets again indicate his own musical example) is shown in Example 35.

Example 35. Th. Döhler, Fantasia and Variations op. 17, Fantasia

After the second statement of the adagio finally ends, the principal tune of the fantasia is introduced in an arrangement of which Schumann approves: "I congratulate him for the passage for left hand alone on page two." The music he refers to, a low-lying melody with a triadic accompaniment in triplets beneath it, is shown in Example 36.

Example 36. Th. Döhler, Fantasia and Variations op. 17, Fantasia

This melody disintegrates into mellifluous scales and another single-line ornamental passage, which in turn leads into the second version of the principal theme of the fantasia, this time stated in full chords with a wide-ranging arpeggiated accompaniment. Schumann calls it "a really splendid roaring fortissimo with a genuinely pianistic accompaniment (see Ex. 37).

5. Ibid. See Appendix I, 98.

Example 37. Th. Döhler, Fantasia and Variations op. 17, Fantasia

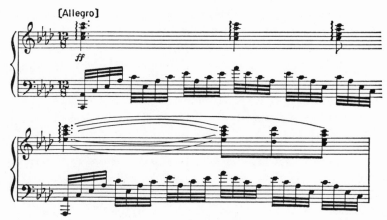

All this disappears in the usual way (Example 35 shows the end of it), and the fantasia is then concluded with an *animato* finale based on the variation theme to come.

Percy's aria *Nel veder la tua costanza* from the second act of *Anna Bolena* provides the lilting but mildly vulgar theme for these variations. Döhler arranges this tune into two large sections, each of them repeated, and he presents it rather simply except for some routine embellishments at cadential points. Example 38 shows how it begins.

Example 38. Th. Döhler, Fantasia and Variations op. 17,
Variation theme

The first variation features a figure in which the hands alternately play chords in the same register (see Ex. 39).

Example 39. Th. Döhler, Fantasia and Variations op. 17, Variation 1

This kind of figuration, familiar to present-day audiences from the twelfth variation of Mendelssohn's *Variations sérieuses,* makes a scintillating, rapid-fire effect; it was a regular part of the virtuosi's vocabulary.[6]

Schumann finds the third variation particularly interesting. It makes use of a pianistic device that all the virtuosi exploited sooner or later: a melody presented in a middle register of the piano—in this case in octaves—while arpeggios (and occasionally scales) are spun out above and below it (see Ex. 40).

Example 40. Th. Döhler, Fantasia and Variations op. 17, Variation 3

What is unusual about this variation is that the melody is in octaves instead of single tones; Schumann congratulates Döhler for maintaining the theme intact despite all the technical difficulties such an arrangement entails.

There follows an adagio movement (in lieu of the *minore* Schumann so despised) that treats the melody much more freely than the earlier variations, fragmenting it, dividing it between the hands, and some-

6. Werner (*Mendelssohn,* p. 364), mistakenly implies that this technique was new when Mendelssohn used it in 1841.

times losing it altogether. This variation, like the several sections of the fantasia, finally disintegrates into a series of arpeggios and scales. Next comes the *finale* (in 2/4 time, not the usual 3/8), a virtuoso tour de force that combines many of the standard techniques of this style: rapid staccato chords in the same register played by both hands, scale passages in octaves and in chords of the sixth, various kind of arpeggios, repeated notes, and tremolos. Initially the theme is preserved intact; but the following sections, like the latter part of the adagio movement, adopt the freedom of the opening fantasia: the theme is only intermittently suggested.

In pieces of this sort the composer and pianist luxuriate in the seemingly limitless possibilities of pedaling effects, rich sounds, and sheer power of the new piano. However he detested this style of music for its superficiality, Schumann—himself at one time an aspiring virtuoso—could not always successfully escape the spell of the roaring arpeggios and crackling octaves of the Parisian pianists. His review of Döhler's composition, though disapproving, betrays a kind of guilty fascination.

An orchestra participated in most of the concerts where the leading virtuosi performed, and many of them wrote their own concertos for these occasions. Of all the productions of the virtuosi Schumann liked their concertos least, because here, he felt, they were tampering with an important art form. In his review of Döhler's Concerto op. 7 he says,

> Anybody can write a jolly rondo and do it justice. But if one wants to woo a princess for his bride, it is presupposed that he must be of noble birth and disposition; or—to do away with the metaphors—if one works with so great an art form, before which even the best in the land are timid, he should know what he is doing.[7]

In his article "Das Clavier-Concert," written in 1839, Schumann evaluated the current condition of the piano concerto in general. The

---

7. NZfM, *4* (1836), 83. See Appendix I, 99. The motto immediately preceding this review is some lines from Goethe:

> Wohl unglückselig ist der Mann
> Der unterlässt das, was er kann,
> Und unterfängt sich, was er nicht versteht;
> Kein Wunder, dass er zu Grunde geht.

great strides made in piano construction and piano technique—and the
great egos of piano players—he concluded, had completely upset the
old relationship between solo instrument and orchestra in the concerto:

> This severing of the bond with the orchestra, as we have seen, was
> long in preparation. Modern pianistic art wants to challenge the
> symphony [orchestra], and rule supreme through its own re-
> sources; this may account for the recent dearth of piano con-
> certos, and of original compositions with [orchestral] accompani-
> ment in general. This journal, since its founding, has reviewed
> practically all the new piano concertos; in the past six years there
> have been only about sixteen or seventeen—a small number com-
> pared to former times . . . Surely it would be a loss, should the
> piano concerto with orchestra become entirely obsolete; but on
> the other hand, we can hardly contradict the pianists when they
> say, "We have no need of any assistance; our instrument can
> achieve a complete effect entirely by itself." And so we must
> confidently await the genius who will show us a brilliant new way
> of combining orchestra and piano, so that the autocrat at the
> keyboard may reveal the richness of his instrument and of his art,
> while the orchestra, more than a mere onlooker, with its many
> expressive capabilities adds to the artistic whole.[8]

In the virtuosi's concertos, the pianist played brilliant soloistic
music while the orchestra "looked on," contenting itself with but a
few brief tuttis. This lopsided domination of the piano is shown in the
way these pieces were published; the solo parts alone (with a few
small notes for the tuttis) were regularly issued for public consumption. Schumann, in his entertaining review of Kalkbrenner's Fourth
Concerto, speculated about how such pieces were put together:

> I am going to reprimand the composers of concert-concertos
> (no pleonasm intended) on two counts. First, the solos are all
> finished and ready to go before the tuttis—unconstitutionally
> enough, for after all the consent of the parliament, that is the
> orchestra, should be necessary before the piano undertakes a
> thing. And why not begin at the real beginning? Was our world
> created on the second day? . . . I'll wager that Herr Kalk-

8. NZfM, 10 (1839), 5. See Appendix I, 100.

brenner devised his introductory and internal tuttis later, and merely shoved them into place . . .[9]

Schumann's other complaint concerns a certain harmonic progression that all the concerto composers use, he says, when they don't know what else to do. He shows the progression this way:

$$7\flat \qquad 5$$
$$5 \qquad 3$$
$$\text{X Major to} \quad \text{X} + 1 \text{ Major}$$

In a footnote he gives an exaggeratedly elaborate explanation of what these figures mean ("X + 1" indicates a semitone above the original root), and adds facetiously, "if I am not mistaken, Gottfried Weber has advanced something similar in his *Theorie*." [10]

Another concerto in this style Schumann reviewed was the Second Concerto op. 74 of Henri Herz, the most inane, perhaps, of all the virtuosi. In his review Schumann hardly mentions the music except in a single sentence at the end of the article: "Herz's Second Concerto is in C minor, and is recommended to those who liked his first." [11] For the rest he discusses the place of virtuoso-composers like Herz in the contemporary musical scene; he concludes that they have—or ought to have—little to do with it. They are popular entertainers who (like Chaucer's physician) have a special love for gold; there is nothing particularly wrong about what they do, but it should not be confused with music.

Herz's concerto, a typical one, is nothing but a superficial adaptation of the most common virtuoso piano music for piano and orchestra. The orchestra plays a short "exposition" at the beginning of the first movement. But the material in the following brilliant piano solos, consisting in turn of arpeggios, trills, double thirds, octaves, and the like, resembles nothing in the orchestral introduction. Between these solos are interpolated short tuttis using material from the in-

9. NZfM, *4* (1836), 113. See Appendix I, 101.

10. Ibid. The figures, of course, symbolize a very common Neapolitan progression, shown in Example 41.

Example 41. Neapolitan progression

11. NZfM, *4* (1836), 111.

troduction. Thus from a purely formal standpoint the movement is more like the baroque concerto grosso than the concertos of Mozart and Beethoven. This form—but particularly this style—did not appeal to Schumann in the least.

In his eloquent diatribe about piano variations quoted above, Schumann said the worst of the composers were not the front-ranking virtuosi, but their imitators from the provinces—"the Strohmillers, or Genserts, or whatever their names happen to be" (apparently the provinces Schumann had in mind were German ones). While he never reviewed anything by anyone called Strohmiller or Gensert, Schumann encountered a perfect example of this type in a young piano composer named Rudolph Willmers. A student of Hummel, Willmers knew Schumann personally, and in 1839 submitted his Etudes op. 1 for review in the NZfM. Schumann's reaction was vaguely favorable, and he encouraged the young composer to try his hand at larger things, perhaps the orchestral forms.[12]

But in 1843, four subsequent works of Willmers came up for review in the NZfM, all of them for piano. Two are plain imitations of Parisian-type variations: a fantasia on a theme of F. Prume (op. 9), and a set of variations on a theme of Bellini (op. 10). These compositions enraged Schumann:

> From him we had certainly expected something different. For he has studied in a rigorous school, and, we are sure, knows the difference between Beethoven and Bellini. These things do not even show brilliant modern virtuosity as we find it with Liszt and Thalberg. No one can deny Liszt's genius for combining mechanical difficulties, for inventing really new instrumental effects, etc. Similarly, Thalberg has an undeniable salon-grace, and a sure ability to calculate effect so that he is bound to captivate and excite his listeners. To Herr Willmers' compositions there adheres a special insipidity and Philistinism . . . influenced by the manner of Liszt and Thalberg, they feature the same difficulties, but with none of their charm.[13]

Willmers' variations consist of an unrelieved parade of all the stock techniques: putting a melody in a middle register with brilliant arpeggios above and below, writing an octave melody in a soprano

12. NZfM, *11* (1839), 98.
13. NZfM, *18* (1843), 209. See Appendix I, 102.

range with arpeggios below, using rapid chromatic accompaniments in a middle register, and introducing flamboyant cadenzas between variations. These variations have only the most poverty-stricken harmonic framework, and, true to Schumann's generalization, both sets end with a *minore* and a *finale* in 3/8 meter.

THALBERG

As Schumann implied in the Willmers review above, he considered Liszt and Thalberg the best of the virtuosi. The elegant Thalberg, illegitimate son of Count Moritz von Dietrichstein and the Baroness von Wetzlar, student of Hummel and Sechter (though he told Fétis his only real piano teacher was the first bassoonist of the Vienna Imperial Opera), and Liszt's formidable rival in the later 1830s, made his first appearance in Schumann's criticism in 1835. In a thoroughly facetious review of Thalberg's *Grande fantasie et variations . . . sur des motifs de l'opera Norma de Bellini* op. 12, and Kalkbrenner's *Fantasie et variations . . . sur un thême de l'opera La straniera de Bellini* op. 123, the discussion of the music is repeatedly interrupted (always in mid-sentence) by the kind of insipid conversation such music is likely to accompany. But Schumann begins this review more earnestly:

> We group these compositions together with good reason. The single distinction between them lies in the additional "3" in the opus number. There are certain amiable characters whom the whole world has polished up until they are smooth and slippery, like ice. One learns flattery from being flattered; giver and receiver drink together the same draught of this sweet poison.[14]

Yet already at this time (June 1835) Schumann said there was something more worthwhile in the music of "the younger of these two" (Thalberg): "he speaks more profoundly than is permitted in higher circles." Thalberg's Fantasia and Variations is similar in most respects to Döhler's composition described above. But the Fantasia, consisting of alternating sections of "Allegro" and "Adagio con gran espressione," is much shorter than Döhler's and acts as an introduction. The theme with three variations and a finale that follow are also standard. The third variation, for example, has this very common

14. NZfM, 2 (1835), 178. See Appendix I, 103.

texture: the melody on top is accompanied by staccato notes in the bass, while in the middle register, divided between the hands, there is a chromatic figuration in fast sixteenth-note sextuplets. But what very likely caught Schumann's eye is the second variation; here the melody moves freely from one register to another and is completely reharmonized with strong added elements of chromaticism.

Again in 1836, in his review of Thalberg's Capriccio op. 15, and Nocturnes op. 16, Schumann detected some genuine virtues in this composer's music.[15] Shortly thereafter he pronounced Thalberg's *Variations on Two Russian Themes* op. 17 "the best and most successful composition I have yet seen from him," and honored it with the last place in the series he was reviewing. Schumann describes its general format:

> He selected two beautiful Russian themes; the first appears in the "Bildern aus Moskau" recently printed in this journal.[16] It is the plea of a child to its mother, and is full of genuinely touching expression. The second is the recent folk song, composed by Col. Alexis Lwoff,[17] that serves in Russia as a kind of "God Save the King." It is a virile song, and fiery though in a calm way. The practice of writing variations on two themes at once is not new, but it is now rarely seen. It is an admirable idea, at least when the themes bear some sort of relation to one another, as here— this is true not so much in an aesthetic sense, as in respect to their common national origin.[18]

For this observer, at least, it is not very clear what Schumann saw in Thalberg's Russian Variations that should make them preferable to all the others of this type. This set begins with a long introduction that acts exactly like the normal opening fantasia. Both of the principal themes show up in this introduction (always in minor, while the themes themselves are both major), though the first one predominates strongly. This melody is given twice over a simple

---

15. NZfM, *4* (1836), 167.

16. This song was not printed in the NZfM, as Schumann seems to suggest, but only described in the series "Bildern aus Moskau" (NZfM, *4*) by Anton von Zuccamaglio, here writing under the pseudonym "W. v. Wbrühl."

17. Alexis Fjodorowitsch Lwoff (or Lwow), 1798–1870, violinist and composer. There is an appreciative article on him in the NZfM, *12* (1840), 204.

18. NZfM, *5* (1836), 73. See Appendix I, 104.

accompaniment of broken triads; the first time, the accompaniment begins in advance, and itself contains the outline of the melody—this is a favorite device of Thalberg—as shown in Example 42.

Example 42. S. Thalberg, Variations op. 17, Introduction

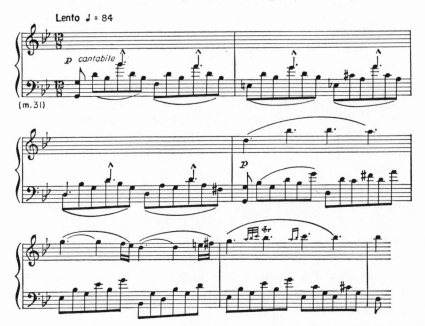

The sort of material shown in Example 43 is used to connect the various sections; already familiar to us from Döhler's variations, it is utterly commonplace in this style.

Example 43. S. Thalberg, Variations op. 17, Introduction

"The song of the child" (the first theme), Schumann declares, "emerges from behind the introduction charming and radiant, like the head of an angel." Example 44 shows the beginning of it.

Example 44. S. Thalberg, Variations op. 17, 1st theme

For most present-day listeners, probably, Thalberg's harmonization of this theme would not seem in the least "charming and radiant." What is particularly disturbing about it is the queasy augmented fifth chord (or V of II) that leads abruptly to the cadence on the supertonic. Schumann complains about certain harmonic progressions in this composition, but not about this one. Very possibly this harmony has come to sound saccharine only since Schumann's time from generations of use in bad popular music and third-rate Protestant hymns;[19] to him, apparently, it was not objectionable.

Schumann was quite satisfied, as well, with Thalberg's first two variations ("they could almost be called perfect"). These variations forgo the usual bravura passagework; their volume level is subdued, and the second has an interesting light filigree above the melody in a tenor range (see Ex. 46).

Example 46. S. Thalberg, Variations op. 17, Variation 2

19. How closely some revival hymns are related to this style can be seen in this refrain from "Living for Jesus" (Ex. 45):

Example 45. *Living for Jesus*, refrain

"To this intimate idyll," Schumann continues, "the brilliant folk song makes a strong contrast." Lwoff's "brilliant folk song" is presented in full chords (see Ex. 47).

Example 47. S. Thalberg, Variations op. 17, 2d theme

In his concluding fantasia-like section Thalberg reverts to the normal virtuoso style of writing: brilliant scales and thunderous octaves in both hands cover a great range of the keyboard.

More of Thalberg's music came up for review in 1841; this time Schumann explained more fully what he thought of the famous pianist:

> First of all, as everyone knows, he writes for himself and for his concerts. He wants to please the crowd with his glittering performances; the composition itself is a secondary concern. If in all this there were not a spark of something nobler here and there, and were there not, in individual passages, signs of a more industrious working-out, his compositions would simply have to be counted among the thousands of pieces of virtuoso hackwork that appear year in and year out, only to be forgotten immediately.[20]

Two of the compositions that prompted this mildly favorable notice were the Nocturne op. 35, no. 1, and the Scherzo op. 31. About the first of these Schumann wrote,

> The nocturne differs only slightly in tone and manner from the

20. NZfM, *15* (1841), 126. See Appendix I, 105.

well-known style (which has been somewhat modified by Chopin). The main melody is followed by a more animated middle section in minor (its tonic is a major third above the original key). Then the principal melody is repeated. This form is well balanced; it has already been used by Chopin.[21]

The effect of the novel key relationship Schumann notes in this piece is heightened by a facile enharmonic shift at the entrance of the middle section; F-sharp major is transformed to B-flat minor simply by dropping the F-sharp a semitone (see Ex. 48).

Example 48. S. Thalberg, Nocturne op. 35, no. 1

Thalberg's "worthier side," Schumann says, is particularly noticeable in the Scherzo in C-sharp minor.[22] Nevertheless, he continues,

> on account of the many good ideas it contains, we are doubly disappointed that no finished, well-rounded musical composition has resulted. The fault lies with the middle sections; they are weaker in invention, and they are not integrated successfully into the whole. Places such as that on p. 4, syst. 3, beginning with the last measure, this reviewer, at least, can only call unmusical. They are painstakingly wrung from the instrument; the soul has had no part in this.[23]

Thalberg's piece looks reasonably "well-rounded." Its form, ABACBA, resembles much less the traditional scherzo than it does the rondo. "B" behaves somewhat as a second theme in a sonata-allegro form; it appears first in the relative major and later in the tonic. The principal theme—apparently one of the "good ideas" Schumann mentions—begins as shown in Example 49.

21. NZfM, *15* (1841), 127. See Appendix I, 106.
22. Not A major, as Kreisig lists this piece in his catalogue (GSK, 2, 515).
23. NZfM, *15* (1841), 126–27. See Appendix I, 107.

Example 49. S. Thalberg, Scherzo op. 31

The passage Schumann brands as unmusical is the "C" theme: a somewhat vapid chromatic sequential figure (see Ex. 50).

Example 50. S. Thalberg, Scherzo op. 31

A favorite technique of Thalberg's was the kind of writing we saw in Döhler's Variations where a sonorous melody in a middle range is amplified by arpeggios above and below. (A familiar example of this device is in Liszt's *Liebestraum* no. 3.) Fétis, in fact, credits Thalberg with inventing this texture.[24] Schumann always associates it with Thalberg's music but says its origins are earlier; in his review of Thalberg's Etudes op. 26 he describes it:

> Many of our young fantasia and etude composers have become infatuated with a texture, commonly used earlier, that has now reappeared in conjunction with the rich new effects of the modern piano. One just gives a passably broad melody to some voice, and surrounds it with all sorts of arpeggios and artful figurations in the same harmony. This is perfectly all right if it is done interestingly and with originality; but one really ought to be able to come up with something else too.[25]

This texture amazed audiences not only with its luxuriant sound,

24. F.-J. Fétis, *Biographie universelle des musiciens*, 2d ed. (Paris, 1875), 8, 208. Fétis says the only possible precedent he could find for the technique was in the Adagio of Beethoven's Sonata op. 31, no. 2.

25. NZfM, 7 (1837), 47. See Appendix I, 108.

but also by creating an impression of (at least) three-handed playing. Joseph Mainzer, Paris correspondent for the NZfM, reported at the height of the Liszt-Thalberg rivalry,

> Anyone who is sitting where he can see Thalberg's fingers cannot help but be astonished; those who are not so lucky must believe that they are listening to a performance of an ordinary four-hand composition. Thalberg has contributed immeasurably to the advancement of technique, but he has done nothing for art.[26]

Schumann's writing about Thalberg is a monument to his integrity as a critic. There was no question but that Thalberg belonged to the "other side." He was a Parisian virtuoso—like all the others, Parisian by choice, not birth—and he composed glittering, often superficial music for the titillation of undiscriminating audiences. His influence, fully as much as anyone else's, helped form a public taste that made any kind of recognition difficult for composers like Schumann. Some of Schumann's reviews of Thalberg's music are unrelentingly severe. Nevertheless, when Thalberg wrote something of merit Schumann was ungrudging in his praise. At times, as in the case of the Russian Variations, he even seemed to lean over backwards to be fair. This composition has all the gaudy trappings of standard Parisian fare, but Schumann was willing to look beyond the shiny façade to find something he thought was worthwhile.

Liszt

In the Willmers review, as we have seen, Schumann mentioned Thalberg and Liszt in the same breath. He thought of these two as the best of the virtuosi, and there is no reason to suppose that he preferred Liszt's music to Thalberg's.[27] Schumann's basis for comparison of these composers could not include Liszt's most important music; the extended piano pieces, the orchestral works and concertos all came later. In fact during Schumann's years with the NZfM, Liszt's publications were decidedly slim; there are only two full-sized re-

---

26. NZfM, 6 (1837), 185. See Appendix I, 109.

27. Boetticher's claim that Schumann came to reject any "comparison between Liszt and the Jewish virtuoso" (Einführung, p. 263, n. 5) ignores the evidence.

views by Schumann of Liszt's music (of the Etudes op. 1 and their
first revision called *Grandes etudes,* and of the six Bravura-
Etudes after Paganini) plus the article on the *Symphonie fantastique*
in Liszt's piano transcription, and short notices of the *Valse di
bravura* op. 6 and three transcriptions of Swiss songs.

In 1839 Schumann wrote his first extended discussion of Liszt's
music, the Etudes op. 1 and *Grandes etudes;* this was the final
installment of a whole series of reviews of etudes by Willmers,
B. F. Philipp, J. Rosenhain, and Kalkbrenner. The op. 1 collection,
described in the score as a "travail de la jeunesse," was published by
Hofmeister of Leipzig, the other collection by the Viennese firm
Haslinger. Upon comparing these sets of etudes, Schumann noticed
that they were related:

> Upon closer examination, I discovered that most of the numbers
> of the latter collection [the Haslinger publication] are but re-
> workings of these early pieces which first appeared probably
> about 20 years ago in Lyon. On account of the obscurity of the
> publishing firm, they were quickly forgotten; and only now
> have they been sought out and reprinted by the German pub-
> lisher.[28]

These two collections, Schumann says, bear testimony to the pronounced changes in piano style that took place in the previous twenty
years, and they provide an interesting record of Liszt's own development as a composer. Schumann describes in some detail the revisions
the various etudes have undergone, and supplies musical examples of
the opening measures of several of them. All of the etudes of the
Haslinger collection except the numbers 6, 7, and 8, he reports, are
reworkings of the earlier compositions.

In his introduction to the first volume of the Liszt *Gesamtaus-
gabe,* Busoni somewhat irritably corrects several errors in Schumann's
review. The first publication of the op. 1 etudes had appeared eleven
years earlier in Marseille, not twenty years earlier in Lyon, as Schu-

---

28. NZfM, *11* (1839), 121. See Appendix I, 110. Two of the English translators of
Schumann's works have misunderstood this passage: Fanny Raymond Ritter, trans., *Music
and Musicians, 1,* 349; and Konrad Wolff, ed., Paul Rosenfeld, trans., *On Music and
Musicians,* p. 146. In the third translation, Henry Pleasants gets this part right, but with
no warning omits the entire second half of the review. H. Pleasants, trans., *The Musical
World of Robert Schumann,* pp. 154–55.

mann thought. And of the Haslinger collection, all except number 7 are arrangements of the earlier set (number 7 is an arrangement of the Impromptu op. 3).[29] Schumann was not always very accurate about things like publication dates, but it is surprising that he should miss the dependence of nos. 6 and 8 of the Haslinger collection upon the earlier set. At about this time (1839) Schumann, longing for more time to compose, began increasingly to chafe at his editorial duties; he simply did not study the music carefully enough.

But the real cause of Busoni's indignation must have been Schumann's more general—and, I believe, perceptive—statements about Liszt the composer:

> For protracted studies in composition he apparently did not have time; or perhaps, too, he was not able to find a suitable teacher. On account of this he studied all the more to be a virtuoso—as lively musical natures seem to prefer immediately expressive musical tones to dry paper work. If he attained unbelievable heights as a player, the composer was left behind. And this results, inevitably, in an imbalance that has had its effect even upon his most recent works. Other influences led the young artist in yet different directions. For one thing he wants to translate the ideas of French literary romanticism, among whose coryphaei he lives, into music; and fascinated by Paganini, who suddenly appeared on the scene, he has been moved to go even further with his instrument and strive for the most extreme effects. So we see him (for example in his *Apparitions*) indulging in murky fantasies or in an almost blasé indifference, while at other times he strives for reckless virtuosity, irreverent and half mad in its boldness.
>
> The sight of Chopin apparently first brought him to his senses. Chopin always has form; and under the marvelous structures of his music he always spins out a red thread of melody. But now it was too late for the towering virtuoso to regain what he lacked as a composer. Now dissatisfied, perhaps, with his own efforts, he began to seek refuge in other composers, in Beethoven and Franz Schubert, and to decorate their music with his own art . . . But if Liszt, with his eminently musical nature, had devoted to himself and to composition the time he has given to

29. Feruccio Busoni, "Vorbemerkungen" in *Franz Liszts musikalische Werke* (Leipzig, 1910), *1*, vii.

his instrument and to other masters, he would be, I believe, a significant composer. We can only speculate as to what can be expected of him.[30]

Schumann describes Liszt as a magical pianist and a prodigiously talented musician unable to find himself, as yet, as a composer. And in 1839 Schumann's opinion about the 28-year-old Liszt was eminently just.

When Schumann wrote this review in October 1839, his assessment of Liszt's playing was apparently based on the descriptions of others (including Clara); he had not yet heard the great pianist himself. The following month, when the two musicians met in Dresden, Schumann probably had his first opportunity to hear him. Four months later, on March 16, 1840, Schumann traveled to the capital city again, this time specifically to attend a Liszt concert. He accompanied the pianist back to Leipzig where between March 17 and 30 Liszt gave three public concerts and a private musical soiree at Mendelssohn's home.

At the end of this exhausting and exhilarating period Schumann wrote a long two-installment article on Liszt in the NZfM.[31] With cordial warmth he described the splendor and excitement of Liszt's concerts; he dwelt at length upon Liszt's inimitable stage manner and his famous lion-like visage (likening, somewhat incongruously, the lean Liszt to Napoleon); he heatedly took the pianist's part in an unsightly squabble that developed over a shortage of complimentary tickets. But in all this there is a curious reserve about the real issue— the music Liszt made. Though Liszt's playing, he said, was incomparable in "energy and boldness," Schumann showed unrestrained enthusiasm about only a few of all the things he heard in these two weeks, notably the *Concertstück* of Weber and an (unidentified) Chopin etude. The reason seems to be this: Schumann did not particularly care for most of the music Liszt performed. These programs, though diverse, were top-heavy with variations (including the famous *Hexameron*, with variations by Liszt, Thalberg, Herz, and Pixis) and arrangements. Schumann, as he says at the close of his article, longed for something different—more Chopin, for example.

In the final concert of March 30, a benefit for the Leipzig Institute

30. NZfM, *11* (1839), 121–22. See Appendix I, 111.
31. NZfM, *12* (1840), 102–03 and 118–20.

for Aged and Ill Musicians, Liszt offered one selection of which Schumann could hardly disapprove: ten numbers from the *Carnaval*. Liszt was one of Schumann's staunchest supporters; he played more of his music than anyone with the exception of Clara, and in 1837 he published a glowing account of Schumann's piano music—at a time when his works were scarcely known in Paris—in the *Revue et gazette musicale*.[32] Schumann was appreciative, and his personal relations with the virtuoso were always cordial; but his writing about Liszt—especially Liszt the composer—remained cautious.

When Schumann became a critic he was convinced that the piano virtuosi operating out of Paris were responsible for most of the musical ills of Europe. While his convictions in substance remained the same, the picture that emerges from his criticism, as we have seen, is not all black and white. It is easy to understand that he should find Liszt more acceptable than many of the other virtuosi. Liszt, after all, sometimes played Chopin, Schumann, and later, Beethoven in addition to his *Valse di bravura*, *Galop chromatique*, and variations on Meyerbeer. But Schumann relented in the case of Thalberg too, and on occasion, even Döhler. In his criticism of the virtuosi Schumann consciously avoided blanket condemnations; he considered each case individually on its merits. His scrupulousness has enhanced the value of his commentary on this music.

32. *Revue et gazette musicale, 4* (1837), 488–90. This volume of the *Revue* was unusually good to Schumann. On pp. 61–63 Berlioz thanks him for arranging the performance of his *Francs-Juges* overture in Leipzig (which Schumann had not done), and on p. 577 the editor gratefully acknowledges receipt of Schumann's letter protesting Rellstab's slighting remarks about the NZfM in an earlier issue.

CHAPTER 11

Ðe Romantics

SCHUBERT

Schumann's most important duty as a critic, he claimed, was "to promote those younger talents, the best of whom are called 'romantics'" [1] But as it turned out, the composer he promoted more vigorously and more consistently than any other was not a "younger talent" at all. In fact he had been dead for almost six years when the NZfM was founded. Schubert was in Schumann's eyes an undiluted romantic, a true heir of Beethoven, and a worthy paradigm for modern composers. And he figures prominently in Schumann's criticism because many of his works, especially the instrumental ones, scorned by publishers when he was alive, began to appear when Schumann was editor of the NZfM. Between 1835 and 1840 Schumann reviewed more than a dozen separate publications of Schubert's music; thus we have Schumann's commentary on nine piano sonatas (two of them for four hands), sets of waltzes and German dances, the late B-flat trio, the Impromptus op. 142, and the Great C-major Symphony (reviews of vocal music are limited to a few choral pieces, like "Mirjam's Siegessang").

In 1835 Schumann wrote his first review of Schubert's music: the three sonatas in A minor, D major, and G major (D. 845, 850, and 894), and the four-hand sonata in B flat (D. 617).[2] His opening statement reminds us how little Schubert was known in Germany, even in so important a musical center as Leipzig:

> Now we come to our favorites, the sonatas of Franz Schubert. Many know him only as a lieder composer, though most people, by far, hardly even know his name. We can make only certain

1. NZfM, *10* (1839), 1.
2. All of these works, as Schumann indicates, were first published between 1825 and 1827 by various Viennese firms. Schumann reviewed the Diabelli reprint of the A-minor and D-major sonatas and the four-hand sonata. The G-major "Sonata or Fantasia" he reviewed in the original Haslinger edition.

sketchy points here. It would require whole books to show in detail what works of pure genius his compositions are. Perhaps there will be time for this some day.[3]

Schumann promises only "certain sketchy points," and in this review he gives little more than that. His procedure is simply to pronounce all of this music "splendid" (*herrlich*) and then to say a few words about each composition. His favorite among them, "the most fulfilled in form and spirit," he says, is the G-major Sonata or Fantasia. And similar to it, he continues, is the A-minor sonata, whose first movement is "so still, so dreamlike as to move one, almost, to tears." The earlier four-hand sonata he calls one of the least original of Schubert's compositions, though even this, he writes, would be a laurel in the crown of any of a hundred lesser composers.

Schumann reacts to Schubert with rare sensitivity and unquestionable sincerity. But the strength of his reaction is in some ways a detriment to his criticism. Instead of pointing out what makes Schubert's style original and expressive, Schumann breaks into a pleasant—but not terribly informative—figurative description:

> He has tones for the finest feelings, ideas, even events and circumstances of life. Just as human passions and human striving have a thousand different forms, so diverse is Schubert's music. Whatever he sees with his eyes and touches with his hands is changed into music; from the stones he casts there spring, as with Deukalion and Pyrrha, living human figures.[4]

Toward the end of his essay Schumann posits an interesting comparison between the piano styles of Schubert and Beethoven:

> Particularly as a composer for piano, he has something more to offer than others, in certain ways, more even than Beethoven (however marvelously the latter, in his deafness, heard with his imagination). This superiority consists in his ability to write more idiomatically for the piano, i.e. everything sounds as if drawn from the very depths of the instrument, while with Beethoven we must borrow for tone color, first from the oboe, then the horn, etc.[5]

3. NZfM, 3 (1835), 208. See Appendix I, 112.
4. Ibid. See Appendix I, 113.
5. Ibid. See Appendix I, 114.

This is a reasonable observation. Schubert's music is perfectly suited to the light and sensitive Viennese piano which he (and Schumann) used, while Beethoven's explosive sforzati and orchestral effects, not always successful even on a modern piano, strain the capacities of an early nineteenth-century Broadwood or Erard, to say nothing of a Stein or a Streicher. While this is true of even Beethoven's early sonatas (think, for example, of op. 10, no. 1, in C minor), some of the late ones completely transcend the piano of Beethoven's time. And these were the sonatas that served particularly to fix Schumann's impressions of Beethoven's piano music; his favorite, in fact, was apparently the *Hammerklavier*.

Schumann's next important review of Schubert's music came about three years later;[6] this essay, entitled "Aus Franz Schuberts Nachlass," [7] discusses four works published posthumously by Diabelli: the four-hand Grand Duo or Sonata op. 140 (D. 812), and the collection called *Franz Schubert's allerletzte Composition. Drei grosse Sonaten für das Pianoforte* (the latter, including the sonatas D. 958, 959, and 960, was dedicated by the publishers to Schumann).[8] The eloquence and sensitivity of this tribute to Schubert assure it a place among Schumann's finest literary achievements.

This much is sure [he says], similar ages attract each other; a youthful spirit is always best understood by youth, and the forcefulness of manhood by the mature man. So Schubert will

6. In the meantime he wrote brief notices of the German dances op. 33 (D. 783), the Waltzes op. 9 (D. 365), and Trio in B flat (D. 898). NZfM, *4* (1836), 69–70 and *5* (1836), 208. The waltzes and German dances, featured at the end of a series of dance music by Kessler, Thalberg, Clara Wieck, and L. Meyer, are treated in a poetic review in which the *Davidsbündlerin* Zilia plays the music while other members of the half-imaginary band perform bizarre antics: Florestan stands on the table and orates, Serpentin (the name for Carl Banck) rides about on Walt's (Louis Rakemann's) shoulders, and Fritz Friedrich (Theodore Lyser in real life) casts shadows on the wall with his lantern. Finally Florestan, still on the table, talks about the waltzes, giving a short "poetic counterpart" for each.

The late B-flat trio is hastily discussed at the close of a long series of trio reviews. Schumann obviously did not take time to do this magnificent work justice. The difficulty in this case was not lack of a score; the Diabelli edition he reviewed—quite exceptionally for this period—included the three string parts in small notes above the staves of the piano part.

7. NZfM, *8* (1838), 177–79. A sequel in the NZfM, *13* (1840), 3, is a review of a few assorted choral works published by Diabelli. In the *Gesammelte Schriften* Schumann changed the title of the first installment to "Franz Schubert's letzte Compositionen," and omitted the second one.

8. It is indicative of Schumann's growing fame that on the title page of this publication his name appears in larger letters than Schubert's.

always be the favorite of young people. He gives what they desire: an overflowing heart, bold ideas, rash actions. He speaks of what they love best: romantic tales, knights, maidens, and adventures. And he adds wit and humor—but not so much as to disturb the gentleness of the mood. In this way he gives wings to the player's own imagination, as no other composer can but Beethoven. Because his idiosyncrasies are easily reproduced, one is always tempted to imitate him, to develop a thousand ideas he has only intimated. This is how he is, and this is why his effect will be lasting.[9]

One of the compositions reviewed here, the four-hand sonata, Schumann observed, did not at all show Schubert's usual idiomatic piano writing; though he had seen the autograph score,[10] clearly marked "sonata," Schumann could not discard the notion that Schubert had really intended the piece as a symphony. Others have agreed; in 1855 Joseph Joachim scored the work for orchestra and conducted a performance of it the following year in Hannover. Schumann and Joachim surely had a point: the ubiquitous tremolos, the repeated chords in the middle register (suggestive of brass parts), as well as an overall thickness of texture are not at all characteristic of Schubert's piano writing; the piece looks a good deal like the usual reduction of an orchestral score.

Schumann is hesitant, too, about accepting the three solo sonatas of Diabelli's publication as the final works of Schubert; they seem to him less advanced in style than the Trio in E flat (he was wrong in this case—the three sonatas all date from September 1828, and the trio from November 1827). He would have assigned these pieces to an earlier date, he says, because they differ from the other Schubert sonatas

in a much greater simplicity of invention, in a voluntary renunciation of the brilliant originality he otherwise demands of himself in such great measure, in a spinning out of certain common musical ideas, whereas he normally joins together period after period of new material.[11]

9. NZfM, 8 (1838), 177–78. See Appendix I, 115.

10. According to Kreisig the autograph at that time belonged to Clara (to whom this sonata was dedicated by Diabelli). GSK, 2, 415.

11. NZfM, 8 (1838), 178–79. See Appendix I, 116.

These sonatas do show a tighter construction and less prodigality of musical materials than was Schubert's habit. In the first movement of the B-flat Sonata, for example, the agile, graceful figure in eighth-note triplets (the last motive of the dominant area), is spun out at length through a variety of changes in tonality, and comes to dominate the movement. Schumann apparently thought this kind of procedure— reminiscent of Beethoven in its economy of means—indicative of an earlier stage in the composer's career.

On one other occasion Schumann expressed doubts about the titles under which Diabelli was printing Schubert's music. In December of 1838, at the end of a long series of reviews printed under the rubric "Phantasieen, Capricen, etc. für Pianoforte," he discussed the four Impromptus op. 142:

> Yet I hardly believe that Schubert really entitled these movements "Impromptus." The first is obviously the first movement of a sonata; it is so thoroughly developed and rounded out that there can scarcely be any doubt of it. I consider the second impromptu the second movement of the same sonata. In key and character it exactly fits with the first. What has happened to the final movements, and whether or not Schubert finished the sonata, his friends would surely know. One could possibly regard the fourth impromptu as the finale. Yet, though the key would tend to confirm this, the superficiality of its entire conception argues against it. These are of course presumptions which could be clarified only by an examination of the original manuscript.[12]

In the autograph these pieces are entitled "Impromptus"; Schubert intended them as a continuation (nos. 5–8) of the Impromptus op. 90. But, significantly, it was the publisher Haslinger, not Schubert, who gave this name to the first set. So while there is no external evidence that Schubert thought of op. 142 as a sonata, neither was it his idea, in the first place, to call these pieces "impromptus." And it must be remembered that at this time (December 1827) Schubert, as his agonizing correspondence with Schott and Probst shows, was desperate to publish his music. Anything called "sonata" would be virtually hopeless; even under the title "impromptus" this set of pieces was first accepted, and then rejected by Schott as "too difficult for

12. NZfM, 9 (1838), 193. See Appendix I, 117.

trifles." [13] I do not think Maurice Brown's peremptory dismissal of Schumann's supposition (unhesitatingly supported by Alfred Einstein[14]) that Schubert meant op. 142 as a sonata is justified.[15]

Schumann expressed a clear preference for the first two impromptus (or, as he thought, movements of a sonata):

> Few authors leave their seal so indelibly stamped on their works as he; every page of the first two impromptus whispers "Franz Schubert"—as we know him in his numberless moods, as he charms us, deceives us, and captivates us again, so we find him here. . . .
>
> As for the third impromptu, I would hardly have taken it for a work by Schubert, except, perhaps, as something from his boyhood. It consists of undistinguished variations on an undistinguished theme. It shows none of the invention or imagination Schubert exercises so masterfully elsewhere, even in other variations.[16]

The theme Schumann calls "undistinguished" was a favorite of Schubert's: he had already used it in his *Rosamunde* music and in his Quartet in A minor (D. 804). This innocent tune, with its rather artless variations, hardly comes up to the standard of the rest of op. 142, particularly of the equally simple but thoroughly disarming Impromptu in A flat. Einstein was "disappointed at Schumann's condemnation" of the movement. Perhaps, instead, we should be impressed by it. Schumann was Schubert's most outspoken champion; he was probably the only man alive who considered him a composer of unmistakable importance. And despite his declared partisanship, he could be very candid about individual things that disappointed him. Just as he saw some good in Thalberg, on occasion he saw some bad in Schubert. Such objectivity must have inspired confidence among his readers when he testified, a year and a half later, to the greatness of Schubert's C-major Symphony.

In his essay on the C-major Symphony Schumann is at his best. Without a trace of his earlier bravado he tells the fascinating story of discovering this work—of the visit to Schubert's and Beethoven's

---

13. O. E. Deutsch, *Schubert, a Documentary Biography,* trans. Eric Blom (London, 1946), p. 817.

14. A. Einstein, *Schubert, a Musical Portrait* (New York, 1951), pp. 283–84.

15. See M. Brown, *Schubert, A Critical Biography* (London, 1958), p. 269.

16. NZfM, 9 (1838), 193. See Appendix I, 118.

graves, of studying great stacks of manuscripts at the home of Ferdinand Schubert, and of selecting this one for performance and publication in Leipzig. He reflects with feeling on the beauties of Vienna and the effect they must have had on Schubert and his music. Because he always finds dissection of the best music distasteful, he hardly discusses details except to marvel at the gradual transition from the "splendid romantic introduction" [17] to the Allegro, and to point out a place in the second movement where a horn "calls from afar, coming as if from another world" (referring, undoubtedly, to the passage in measures 148–60 which leads back to the first theme).

Schumann saw in Schubert's symphony everything he hoped for in a major instrumental work: richness and variety of expression, novel, individual effects, but at the same time clarity of form and sure craftsmanship. It moved him to write animated and figurative prose reminiscent of his earlier style, but with more control and more coherence:

> To understand that in this symphony there is more than beautiful melody, more than mere pain or joy, such as has found expression in music a hundred times previously, to understand that it leads us into a region where we cannot remember having been before, for this, such a symphony must be heard. For here, besides masterful technique of musical composition, there is life in every fiber, color in the finest gradations, significance everywhere, sharply cut detail. And finally, over the whole there is poured out that romanticism we know to be characteristic of Franz Schubert. And these heavenly lengths, like a great novel in four volumes by one such as Jean Paul. . . .
>
> In the beginning, to be sure, some will be bewildered by the brilliance and novelty of instrumentation, by the length and

17. The opening of Schumann's own First Symphony seems to have been inspired by both the beginning of Schubert's symphony and the first measures of Chopin's Etude in A minor op. 25, no. 11 (See Ex. 51).

Example 51. (Schubert) Symphony in C, D. 944; (Chopin)
Etude op. 25, no. 11; (Schumann) Symphony no. 1

breadth of the form, by the enchanting fluctuation of feeling, and the wholly new world into which we are transported; so it always is with the first glimpse of the unfamiliar. But even then there ever remains a pleasurable feeling like that following an enchanted fairy tale; one senses that the composer was master of his story, and its connections, in time, will also be clear to you.[18]

This is somehow a melancholy picture: Schumann the revolutionary, the spokesman for the new era, finds ultimate satisfaction only in the music of a composer long since dead. Schubert was, in Schumann's eyes, the sole clear successor to Beethoven (though he survived him by only a year). His music reminded Schumann of his own youth, when he devoured all Schubert's available compositions, of his own early ambitions and optimism. In Schumann's writing about Schubert there are always overtones of misty-eyed nostalgia; he felt a stronger kinship with him than with any other composer.

CHOPIN

Schumann made his debut as a critic at the age of twenty-one with the essay (or, as we have seen, *half* an essay) on Chopin's *Là ci darem la mano* variations in the AmZ of December 7, 1831. This piece, the most purely Jean-Paulian thing Schumann published,[19] is cast as a narrative related in first person. The characters involved are the three principals of the *Davidsbund*, Florestan, Eusebius, and Raro, in addition to the ostensible narrator, Julius.[20] As in the later review

18. NZfM, *12* (1840), 82–83. See Appendix I, 119.

19. In the version of this essay in GS 1854 Schumann deleted some of his character description: "Florestan is, as you know, one of those peculiar musical individuals who seems to anticipate long in advance anything innovatory, new, or unusual. What is extraordinary seems so to him for but a moment; he grasps the unfamiliar in an instant. Eusebius, on the other hand, enthusiastic but composed, plucks his blossoms one at a time; he comprehends with more difficulty, but more surely; he is less often delighted with anything, but his satisfaction lasts longer. He studies more rigorously, and his piano playing is more intellectual, gentler, and mechanically more perfect than Florestan's." AmZ, *33* (1831), 805–06. See Appendix I, 120.

20. The signature of the article, originally "Julius," was changed by Fink to "K. Schumann" [sic]. Schumann apparently had in mind Julius Knorr, the editor-in-chief, initially, of the NZfM. Knorr had played the Chopin variations in a concert at the Gewandhaus the preceding October—the first public performance of Chopin's music by anyone other than the composer, according to Kreisig (GSK, 2, 365). Schumann's impressions of this music were formed much earlier; he had written the article by September 1831, and had himself played the variations shortly after they were published in the spring of 1830.

of the Schubert Waltzes and German Dances, Schumann portrays the members of the *Davidsbund* gathered about the piano while one of them, Eusebius in this case, plays the music in question. In all his reviews of this sort Schumann manages to weave into the story some description of the music; this time Florestan, dozing on Julius' sofa after the friends have dispersed, talks in his sleep about the individual variations and connects them with the episode in *Don Giovanni* between Zerlina and the Don:

> The Introduction, so complete in itself (do you remember Leporello's leaps in thirds?) seems to me least appropriate to the whole. But the theme (why did he write it in B flat?)—the variations, the last movement, and the adagio, that is really something—here genius shows in every measure. The dramatis personae, my dear Julius, are of course Don Giovanni, Zerlina, Leporello, and Masetto. Zerlina's answer in the theme comes out very amorously; the first variation could be called, perhaps, aristocratic and coquettish—the Spanish noble flirts amiably with the country girl. This is all perfectly clear in the second variation, which is much more intimate, comic, and quarrelsome, just as when two lovers chase each other about, laughing all the while.[21]

The meeting of the *Davidsbund* Schumann describes begins when Florestan, carrying Chopin's variations and wearing his "ironic smile," comes into the room and utters the phrase that has subsequently become famous: "Hats off, gentlemen—a genius." It is something of a tribute to Schumann's discernment that he should single out Chopin as the best of a horde of young pianist-composers seeking their fortunes in Paris. But it is astonishing that he should be able to make this judgment on the basis of the *Là ci darem* variations alone. Apart from its orchestral accompaniment and its rather novel last movement (marked *alla polacca*), this piece on the surface looks exactly like every other set of Parisian-style variations—though it was composed in 1827 before Chopin came to Paris. One feature that attracted Schumann, of course, was the theme taken from Mozart instead of Bellini or Donizetti. But there is more to it than that; Chopin's figurations deftly imply expressive chromatic harmonies, as in the second and third variations, and in the fourth, the common leaping virtuoso figu-

---

21. AmZ, *33* (1831), 807. See Appendix I, 121.

ration[22] includes something of Mozart's own orchestral transition between vocal phrases (see Ex. 52).

Example 52. F. Chopin, Variations on *Là ci darem*, 4th Variation

The difference between Chopin's variations and the common run of compositions of its kind is a subtle one; but Schumann saw it clearly.

Two and one half years after this review appeared the NZfM was launched and Schumann resumed his activities as a critic. At first there was a curious reserve about the "genius" Schumann had announced to the world in 1831. The NZfM of 1834 is almost totally silent about Chopin; an anonymous correspondence article from Paris mentions with no apparent enthusiasm the publication of his F-minor concerto ("the themes are not very distinguished—too Polish").[23] Schumann himself did not mention Chopin in the first volume of the journal, and in 1835 he made only passing references to him in some reviews of C. G. Müller, Hiller, and Loewe.[24] Finally in May of that year, when a rather substantial group of pieces by Chopin (the Nocturnes op. 15 and Scherzo op. 20) came up for review, Schumann almost ignored them. The *Davidsbündler,* he says, have promised a full account soon, but they cannot be hurried. In the meantime it can be noted, he continues, that "Chopin seems to have arrived, finally, at the point Schubert reached long before him; the latter did not have to overcome any tendencies toward virtuosity." [25]

Chopin's visit to Leipzig in October of 1835 was mentioned in two brief notices in the NZfM. It was then that Schumann heard him

22. Schumann used a version of this figuration in the "Paganini" movement of his *Carnaval.*

23. NZfM, *1* (1834), 16. This notice compares Chopin's unchanging style to that of Spohr, and concludes, "He sees many different things, but he always sees them with the same eyes." One of the aphorisms Schumann included in GS 1854 is a paraphrase of this statement. GSK, *1*, 23.

24. NZfM, 2 (1835), 43, 49, 57, and 127.

25. NZfM, 2 (1835), 155.

play for the first time (at Wieck's); and he reported, "Chopin was here, but only for a few hours which he spent in private circles. He plays just as he composes—uniquely." [26] It was not until April of the following year, two years after the founding of the NZfM, that Schumann printed a full review of Chopin's music; this essay is on the two piano concertos, the F-minor one just published, and the E-minor one reprinted by Kistner. Schumann's review is not particularly well organized. In the first section Florestan derides Rellstab and the criticism of Chopin in *Iris*:

> I might mention in passing that a famous petticoat paper, so I hear (for I do not read it, and flatter myself that in this respect I am like Beethoven—see Beethoven's *Studien* edited by Seyfried) shoots dagger-like glances at me from under its smiling mask, only because I once laughingly remarked to one of its writers, who had printed something about Chopin's *Don Giovanni* variations,[27] that he (the writer), like a bad verse, had a couple of feet too many, and someone ought to chop them off for him.[28]

Florestan then launches into a diatribe against all journals and all criticism ("What is a whole volume of a journal in the face of a Chopin concerto? What is the pedant's lunacy compared to poetic frenzy"?). Eusebius, in his calmer way, observes that the journal still owes Chopin some kind of notice, and explains its long silence:

> If we have not yet honored him in words—though he has already the highest honor in a thousand hearts—it may be, on one hand, because of diffidence about speaking of that which is closest to us, for fear of not finding the proper words, of failing to assess the object in its full height and depth. On the other hand, there is the intimate artistic kinship we feel with this composer. And finally, we have held our peace because Chopin seemed to be achieving in his latest compositions, if not a different manner, a higher one; we hoped to understand its direction more clearly and give an account of it to our friends everywhere.[29]

26. NZfM, *3* (1835), 112.
27. An unfavorable review of Chopin's variations had appeared in the *Iris* of November 5, 1830.
28. NZfM, *4* (1836), 137. See Appendix I, 122.
29. NZfM, *4* (1836), 138. See Appendix I, 123.

Schumann still pledges his fealty to Chopin in this essay, but he does it somewhat laboriously; the keen edge of his first excitement about Chopin seems to have been dulled. And any discussion of the ostensible subject of the review, Chopin's concertos, is strangely absent. If Schumann was not altogether satisfied with these compositions, the reason may lie close at hand: they belong to the virtuoso type where, as he said three years later, "the autocrat at the keyboard rules supreme," while "the orchestra only looks on." [30] And in that same article, "Das Klavier-Konzert," he maintained that no one, including Chopin, apparently, had yet found a way to reconcile the new piano style with the form of the concerto.

Between 1836 and 1842 Chopin published a great deal of piano music, and Schumann reviewed most of it in the NZfM.[31] All these reviews are favorable enough, but hardly any of them are ecstatic. Schumann always admired the drama and passion of Chopin's music, but gradually came to think his style was too much the same; it showed scant change from his earliest works. In 1838 (in a review of the Impromptu op. 29, the Mazurkas op. 30, and the Scherzo op. 31) he was inclined to justify this uniformity:

> Chopin can hardly write anything now but that we feel like calling out in the seventh or eighth measure, "It is by him!" His music has been called "mannered," and some say that he makes no progress. But one ought be more grateful. Is this not the same original power that was so marvelously dazzling in his early works, confusing you at first, but later thoroughly captivating you? And when he has given you a whole succession of the rarest creations, and you understand him more easily, do you suddenly demand something different? This is like chopping down your pomegranate tree because it produces, year after year, nothing but pomegranates.[32]

Schumann seems to be trying to persuade himself that this is true. Three years later his feelings are somewhat different (this is from a

30. NZfM, *10* (1839), 5.

31. There are reviews (given in chronological order) of the Trio op. 8 (published in 1833), Boleros op. 19, Waltzes op. 12, Polonaises op. 22, Etudes op. 25, Mazurkas op. 30, Impromptu op. 29, Scherzo op. 31, Preludes op. 28, Mazurkas op. 33, Waltzes op. 34, Sonata op. 35, Nocturnes op. 37, Ballade in F major op. 38, Waltzes op. 42, Concert Allegro op. 46, Nocturnes op. 48, Fantasia op. 49, and Tarantella op. 43.

32. NZfM, *9* (1838), 179. See Appendix I, 124.

review of the Nocturnes op. 37, the F-major Ballade,[33] and Waltzes op. 42):

> Now Chopin could publish everything anonymously; everyone would recognize him anyway. In this there is both praise and blame—praise for his talent, blame for his effort. For he surely still has within him his great initial powers which, whenever they show themselves, leave little doubt about his identity. And he also makes many new forms, both gentle and daring, that demand admiration. Always new and inventive in externals, in the shape of his compositions, in his special instrumental effects, yet he remains in essence the same. Because of this we fear he will never achieve a level higher than that he has already reached. And though this is quite enough to assure him a lasting place in the recent history of art, his effectiveness is limited to the narrow confines of piano music. With his abilities he could have achieved far more, influencing the progress of our art as a whole.[34]

Schumann had earlier expressed similar fears in his review of Chopin's Etudes op. 25. This article is really less about Chopin's music than it is about Chopin's playing of it. Schumann describes the composer's performance of the Etude in A flat (he had heard him play it the previous year in Leipzig):

> It would be a mistake to think that he let us hear each of the small notes distinctly; it was more like a wave of sound in A flat, heightened from time to time by the pedal. But in the midst of the harmony one could perceive the melody written in large notes. And once in the middle section a glorious tenor voice emerged clearly from the chords to join the principal melody.[35]

Despite his admiration for these etudes—though he considered them on the whole "less significant" than the op. 10 collection—and for Chopin's style of playing them, Schumann ends this review on a mildly sour (but familiar) note: "Unfortunately our friend is composing little now, and he neglects entirely any works of larger di-

---

33. This ballade is dedicated to Schumann. In this review he recalls having heard Chopin play it (no doubt in September 1836 during Chopin's second brief visit to Leipzig) in a version that ended in F major instead of A minor.

34. NZfM, *15* (1841), 141. See Appendix I, 125.

35. NZfM, *7* (1837), 199. See Appendix I, 126. The tenor voice is written in large notes in measures 17 ff.

mensions; perhaps the glitter and dissolution of Parisian life have something to do with this." [36]

Almost four years after he wrote this, Schumann had an opportunity to review a "work of larger dimensions" by Chopin: the Sonata in B-flat minor, op. 35. One might expect from Schumann a good deal more enthusiasm than he shows in this review. For here, finally, one of the most individualistic of the romantic composers, one who had cultivated his art in the small genres, applied his talents to the solid, traditional sonata. But Chopin's violent composition did not coincide very well, it seems, with Schumann's notion in 1841 of what a sonata should be like:

> To look at the first measures of the sonata last named,[37] and yet to have doubts about its authorship would be a disgrace for a good critic. For only Chopin begins thus, and only he ends thus: from dissonance, through dissonance, to dissonance. And yet there is a good deal of beauty in this piece. He calls it a "sonata." One might regard this as capricious, if not downright presumptuous, for he has simply tied together four of his most unruly children—perhaps to smuggle them under this name into places they could never otherwise have reached.[38]

The beauty Schumann found in this sonata was all in the first two movements. He remarks that in the midst of the "stormy, passionate" first movement there is a fine cantilena (he refers, surely, to the "second theme" in measures 41 ff. that recurs in the recapitulation), and he obviously prefers the cantilena to the storm and passion. This passage, he says, shows that Chopin's melodies are losing their strong Polish flavor, and turning more Italianate; except for one chord progression "after the close of the first melody of the second part," [39] he claims, this passage could almost have been written by Bellini. The chord progression he meant is shown in Example 53.

36. NZfM, 7 (1837), 200.
37. As usual, Schumann is discussing Chopin's music at the end of a whole series of reviews.
38. NZfM, *14* (1841), 39. See Appendix I, 127.
39. By "second part" Schumann means "second thematic area"—here in relative major. A standard terminology for the parts of sonata-allegro form had not yet come into being. A theoretical work most influential in establishing such a terminology was A. B. Marx's *Kompositionslehre,* which first appeared in 1847. Marx was probably the first theorist to describe the sonata-allegro unambiguously as consisting of three parts instead of two.

Example 53. F. Chopin, Sonata op. 35, 1st movement

The Funeral March, Schumann says, is "largely repulsive—in its place an adagio, perhaps in D flat, would have made an incomparably better effect."

And what we get in the last movement [he continues] under the title "Finale" is more like mockery than any kind of music. Yet one has to admit that even from this unmelodious and joyless movement there breathes on us a singular and terrifying spirit which pins down with mailed fist whatever would resist it. So we listen, uncomplaining, as if transfixed, to the end—but not to praise; for this is not music.[40]

Here Schumann returns the remark Chopin is supposed to have made to Schlesinger about Schumann's *Carnaval*: "it is not music at all." [41]

Chopin did not care for Schumann's music, nor did he ever show any appreciation for his criticism. About the latter he had almost nothing to say except for a derisive remark or two about the *Là ci darem* review in a letter of December 1831.[42] His opinion of Schumann's writing was dramatically clarified (or so it seemed) when some of the spurious Chopin–Delphina Potocka letters were made public in 1949. Substantial extracts from these letters (the erotic passages carefully omitted) appeared in a commemorative volume for Chopin

40. NZfM, *14* (1841), 40. See Appendix I, 128.

41. See Frederick Niecks, *Frederick Chopin as a Man and Musician*, 2, 113.

42. See Arthur Hedley, ed., *Selected Correspondence of Fryderyk Chopin* (London, Melbourne, Toronto, 1962), p. 99. These remarks may refer not to Schumann's, but Wieck's review of the piece.

brought out by the Kosciuszko Foundation; one includes some remarks about Schumann: "what he writes is fiddle-faddle, idle talk,
and nonsense, but no critique . . . After reading his critiques I feel
nauseated as though I had eaten a pot of honey . . . I even prefer
Rellstab, who is lashing me . . . For my Etudes he [Rellstab] will
gouge out my eyes." [43] Chopin did not write this—a certain pathetic
Mme. Czernicka did [44]—but he may well have harbored some such
sentiments. Chopin, fastidious and dapper, was probably embarrassed
by the bizarre trappings of this young German's first essay in creative
criticism, and there is no reason to think he ever felt any gratitude for
Schumann's—in 1839 Chopin still misspelled his name "Schuhmann"
—advocacy.

Schumann's writing on Chopin is perceptive. He always considered
him clearly the best of the Parisian pianist-composers, and he acknowl-

43. Bronislaw E. Sydow, trans., "Ipse Dixit, Chopin's Comments on Music, Musicians,
Music Critics, Himself, and his Works," in *Frederick Chopin, 1810–1849,* ed. Stephen P.
Mizwa (New York, 1949), pp. 53–54.

44. Hedley tells the story of this sensational fraud (including Mme. Czernicka's suicide
in celebration of the centennial of Chopin's death) in the Appendix of his 1962 edition
of the Chopin correspondence.

To be wise after the fact is always easy. Still it is astonishing that these letters should so
long have been taken at face value and allowed to bedevil a full decade of Chopin studies.
Even the short extract about Schumann and Rellstab looks bogus: it is chronologically all
askew. I do not know whether or not this part of Mme. Czernicka's typescript is dated. But
if Chopin was, as it says, expecting a review of his Etudes by Rellstab, the date would have
to be either late 1833 (op. 10) or 1837 (op. 25). But in 1837 Rellstab was not "lashing"
him, as is claimed (he reviewed nothing of Chopin's in that year), and in 1833 he could
not have been nauseated by Schumann's "critiques," since Schumann had published only
one and that was two years earlier.

The anonymous writer of the "Notes of the Day" in the *Monthly Musical Record, 80*
(1950), 1–2, cites this passage and eagerly agrees with "Chopin" that Schumann "was sometimes exceedingly silly . . . he certainly was not the 'great critic' he was once commonly
taken to be. He admittedly backed three notable winners—Chopin, Berlioz, and Brahms
(odd trinity!)—but if you bet as lavishly as Schumann did you can hardly fail to bring off a
few lucky hits."

Jean-Paulian pieces like the *Là ci darem* review may look a bit adolescent to the modern
observer; but, we must remember, they constitute only a tiny part of Schumann's writing,
the earliest part (Schumann wrote the Chopin essay when he was a rather immature
twenty-one). And even in his "silliest" essays he shows more understanding of the contemporary musical scene than any other critic of his time.

As to the "lucky hits," Mme. Czernicka's anonymous advocate forgets two other dark
horses Schumann supported: Bach and Schubert—and who are all these others he bet on?
However that may be, our assessment of his criticism ought not to depend only upon his
ability to predict the contents of twentieth-century concert programs.

edged the immediate and healthy influence he exerted on other piano composers, such as the young Adolph Henselt. He described him as a man who early in his career developed an individualistic, persuasively expressive—but limited—style, and then simply wrote in it for the rest of his life. At first he waited patiently for Chopin to expand and develop; but before very long he saw that this would never happen. For the rest of his tenure as a critic he remained appreciative, but clearly disappointed.

BERLIOZ

When he first came out in support of Chopin in 1831, Schumann was acting at least partly in reaction to a sour review of the *Là ci darem* variations by Rellstab. Three and one half years later he came to the defense of another Parisian composer who, he thought, had suffered injury at the hands of an established critic—Louis Hector Berlioz.

Schumann's interest in Berlioz was first aroused in February of 1835 when Heinrich Panofka, a music teacher of his acquaintance living in Paris, and a correspondent for the NZfM, sent him a long essay, "Ueber Berlioz und seine Compositionen"; Schumann printed it in two installments as lead articles in the NZfM of February 27 and March 3. This essay gives a capsule biography of Berlioz—considerably idealized—including the struggles with his family over a musical career, his life as a medical student ("often in the dissection room . . . the rhythm of the hammer and saw that were used to open skulls he accompanied with melodies from *Vestale* or *Cortez*"),[45] and his love for Harriet Smithson, now his wife. "To her," says Panofka, "we owe the origins of the *Symphonie fantastique.*" The second part of his article is a rapturous description of this symphony: the program, the passion—all, he says, autobiographical—the novelty of form and instrumentation.

This article made a real impression on Schumann, and much of his early sympathies with Berlioz can be traced to it. In his own review of the *Symphonie fantastique* he recalls Panofka's macabre talk about the Frenchman's medical training: "Berlioz could hardly feel more pained at dissecting the head of a handsome murderer than I feel at

45. NZfM, 2 (1835), 68.

dissecting his first movement." [46] And this article is the source, undoubtedly, of Schumann's notion that the program of the *Symphonie fantastique* is autobiographical.

About two months after Panofka's essay appeared, Fétis took note of Berlioz' growing fame (both as composer and journalist) and wrote an injurious article about him and his *Symphonie fantastique* in the *Revue musicale*. He had first encountered Berlioz, he said, many years earlier when the young composer was a student at the Conservatoire. Fétis, one of the examiners for a composition class, had shaken his head in despair at Berlioz' ignorance of counterpoint; but Berlioz had brazenly replied that an artist of genius had no need of counterpoint. A patient man, Fétis sat through several painful rehearsals and performances of Berlioz' music in succeeding years, and graciously said nothing against the brash young man's work. But "about eight years ago," he continued, he attended the première of the *Symphonie fantastique,* and this was too much:

> From this moment on my opinion of Berlioz was settled; I saw that he has no sense for melody, virtually no conception of rhythm, that his harmony consists, for the most part, of monstrous bunches of notes simply thrown together—and yet it was flat and monotonous. In a word, I found him utterly lacking in melodic and harmonic ideas, and predicted that his barbaric style would never improve. Yet I saw that he had a certain instinct for instrumentation.[47]

His curiosity pricked, Schumann wrote to Schlesinger for a score of the *Symphonie fantastique* and printed a brief comment in the NZfM about Fétis' "fulminating but entertaining article against Berlioz." [48] Shortly thereafter, in June of 1835, Schumann printed a German translation of Fétis' essay; in an editor's note he expressed his disagreement with it, and promised to print his own review of the *Symphonie fantastique*—he had in the meantime received the score from Schlesinger—as soon as possible.[49]

The first installment of Schumann's essay on the *Symphonie fantastique* appeared promptly as the lead article in the NZfM of July 3.

46. NZfM, *3* (1835), 37.
47. The volume of the *Revue musicale* for 1835 was not available to me. This section is quoted from the German translation printed in the NZfM, 2 (1835), 198.
48. NZfM, 2 (1835), 114.
49. NZfM, 2 (1835), 197.

This is the immoderate, impressionistic encomium (signed "Flore-stan") that Schumann later deleted from the *Gesammelte Schriften*. In the first paragraph, with a wild excess of metaphor, Schumann springs to Berlioz' defense:

> Not with savage cries, like our Old German forefathers, but, like the Spartans, let us go to battle to the accompaniment of merry flutes. He to whom these lines are dedicated needs no sword-bearer, to be sure; his destiny will be the reverse, it is to be hoped, of Homer's Hector; for he has finally conquered and pulled after him in chains the Troy of the old era—but if his art is the flaming sword, so may these words be the preserving shield.[50]

After a space of about a month the other five installments of the *Symphonie fantastique* review followed in quick succession. They are signed with Schumann's own name, and they could hardly be more unlike the opening section. To avoid confusion, he says, Schumann briskly presents an outline of the things he plans to discuss:

> I prefer to go through it . . . according to the four main points of view from which one can consider music, i.e. according to form (of the whole, of single movements, periods, and phrases), according to musical composition (harmony, melody, setting, elaboration, style), according to the special idea the composer in-tends to convey, and according to the spirit that rules over form, material, and idea alike.[51]

Then, following his outline more or less faithfully, he writes the long-est and one of the most impressive articles of his career. Schumann felt at least faintly embarrassed about the academicism of this essay —it is replete with footnotes and musical examples—but there was a good reason for it: the review was meant as a rebuttal to the scholarly Fétis, and Fétis, he felt, must be met on his own ground.

Almost every book on either Schumann or Berlioz mentions that this essay on the *Symphonie fantastique* is very long and very detailed. But this detail has been difficult to appreciate because Schumann used Schlesinger's first edition of Liszt's piano transcription, now extremely rare, and his countless references to the music are by page number.

50. NZfM, *3* (1835), 1. See Appendix I, 129.
51. NZfM, *3* (1835), 33. See Appendix I, 130.

A comparison of all of these references with the copy of Schlesinger's edition in the British Museum (accompanied by thoughts that no music critic before or since has ever asked so much of his reader) has convinced me of the extraordinary acuity of Schumann's analysis. While others (even Panofka) talked of the utter novelty of Berlioz' form, Schumann showed with indisputable evidence that as to form the *Symphonie fantastique* was reasonably orthodox. Even Berlioz' warmest friends, said Fétis, could not defend his weakness in the invention of melody. Schumann pointed out that the *Symphonie fantastique* is full of good melodies—though often with irregular periodization—but what Berlioz *does* lack, he said, is middle parts and bass lines. And he arrived at these eminently right conclusions from an examination of the piano transcription alone.

Schumann says the *Symphonie fantastique* is not particularly surprising in its sequence of movements or in its key schemes, especially if the last two movements are taken together. That leaves an Introduction–Allegro in C, a "Scherzo" (really a Waltz) in A, an Adagio in F, and a two-part Finale in G minor and C.[52] Choosing the first movement for a detailed formal analysis, Schumann describes the slow introduction as "two variations on a theme with free episodes." With the page-and-measure citations converted to measure numbers, his analysis is this:

Theme	mm. 1–16
Episode	mm. 17–27
Variation 1	mm. 28–39
Episode	mm. 40–49
Variation 2	mm. 50–58
Episode	mm. 59–71

With good reason he feels uncertain about "Variation 2"; the resemblance to the theme, he says, lies in the intervals—and dotted-note rhythm, he might have added—of the horn part.

The forty measures often taken as the *idée fixe* theme Schumann divides into three parts: measures 72–86, 86–103, and 103–111. He calls only the first of these segments the *idée fixe* proper (it is impossible to determine from the description in Berlioz' program how much

52. NZfM, 3 (1835), 34.

of this music the designation covers). The second segment, beginning
in measure 86, Schumann observes, is not merely a spinning out of
that which precedes; it is taken from the Introduction (see Ex. 54).

Example 54. H. Berlioz, *Symphonie fantastique*, 1st movement

Schumann proceeds: the remainder of the exposition (he does not use
the word, but calls it "first part") he divides into two sections, measures 111–49 and 150–67. This last he calls the "real second theme,"
but with the observation that it is "gently reminiscent of what has
preceded"—namely the beginning of the *idée fixe*. And so he continues
to the end of the movement, finding the form lucid and reasonable except for the irregular passage in the development section from measure 285 to the appearance of the second theme in measure 312. The
only questionable point in this analysis is the derivation of measures
331 ff. from the "third motive of the first theme" (i.e. measure 103).
It comes from measures 119 ff.—though this passage itself bears some
family resemblance to the "third motive." In a later reference to the
passage Schumann corrects himself.

Schumann begins the third installment of his review with a sum-
mary and rough diagram of what he has said so far, comparing the
form of Berlioz' first movement with the usual one[53] (see page 240).

All this has to do, as yet, only with form, and there remain several
other features of the symphony Schumann proposes to discuss. In this
third part of his review, again with Fétis' denigration of the symphony in mind, he plunges into a compact, painstaking defense—
bristling with citations of the score and musical examples—of Berlioz'
harmonic practice. His conclusion:

---

53. NZfM, *3* (1835), 37. The measure numbers given here are derived from Schumann's
preceding description of the movement.

FIRST THEME
G major

First theme
(C major) . . . (G major, E minor) . . . Transitional sections with second theme . . . Middle section — A minor (working of both themes) . . . Transitional sections with the second theme . . . (E minor, G major) . . . First theme (C major) . . . Closing (C major)

Introduction
(C major) [sic] [54]

[Measure 1 72 111, 150 240 313 412 493]

"We shall give the older form for comparison:"

First theme
C major . . . Second theme G major . . . First theme C major . . . Second theme C major

54. Though Schumann frequently refers to the C-minor tonality of the Introduction, this error crept somehow into the NZfM and has been reproduced without comment in all editions of the *Gesammelte Schriften*.

I should say that his harmonies, despite the manifold combinations he makes with only a minimum of material, are distinguished by a certain simplicity, or, in any case, a solidness and compression such as one finds—though in a more cultivated form —with Beethoven. Or does he, perhaps, deviate too far from the principal key? Just look at the first movement: first part,[55] clearly C minor. Then he reproduces the intervals of the first motive exactly in E flat.[56] After this he remains for a long time in A flat [mm. 46 ff.], and then moves easily to C major. The Allegro, as can be seen from my sketch in the last number, is constructed of the simplest C major, G major, and E minor. And so it goes throughout. The whole second movement is constructed of the penetrating, bright A-major sound, the third of F major with the closely related C and B-flat major, the fourth of G minor with B flat and E flat. Only in the final movement, despite a dominance of C, everything is run together, as befits infernal weddings.[57]

After this strong positive assertion, Schumann promptly points out scores of isolated passages he considers harmonically deficient: "insipid and vulgar" harmonies, unclear ones, places that "sound bad— are tortured, distorted." Here the lower half of the columns in the NZfM are completely filled by footnotes and musical examples showing the places he has in mind. There is a clear pattern in the things he finds objectionable. Berlioz' habit of using a sudden, crashing chord in a remote harmony—to become later a trademark of his orchestral writing—did not in the least appeal to Schumann (as in the fourth movement, measures 129–30). But the passages he criticizes most unrelentingly are those where Berlioz' part writing is thin or nonexistent, where the instruments simply slide up and down in parallel (and usually chromatic) motion.

In the Introduction, for example, he calls the harmonies of measures 21–22, shown in Example 55 (all examples given here are from Liszt's transcription), "insipid and vulgar." [58]

---

55. Schumann cites page and measure numbers; here, converted to measure numbers, it is 1–28.
56. Measure 29.
57. NZfM, 3 (1835), 42. See Appendix I, 131.
58. NZfM, 3 (1835), 42. All of Schumann's discussion of the harmony of Berlioz' symphony is compressed into this single page.

Example 55. H. Berlioz, *Symphonie fantastique,* 1st movement

The doubled—tripled in the orchestral score—melody line sinking chromatically with no bass support in measures 25–26, he says, is "faulty" (see Ex. 56), as is a similar progression in measures 108–09 of the first movement. (Ex. 57).

Example 56. H. Berlioz, *Symphonie fantastique,* 1st movement

Example 57. H. Berlioz, *Symphonie fantastique,* 1st movement

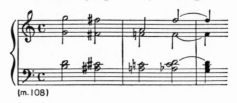

Schumann mentions the typically Berliozian parallel motion in measures 115–19 of the first movement twice: he describes it as "faulty,"
and later as "bad-sounding, distorted." He points disapprovingly to a
very similar place in the last movement as well (measures 408–10),
where the strings play the Witches' Dance theme in bald parallel octaves and thirds (see Ex. 58).

Example 58. H. Berlioz, *Symphonie fantastique,* 5th movement

And the six-three chords moving chromatically in measures 317–19
of the same movement, he says, are harmonically "unclear and vague"
(see Ex. 59).

Example 59. H. Berlioz, *Symphonie fantastique,* 5th movement

Schumann is not simply reprimanding Berlioz for harmonic unorthodoxies. Many passages fully as unorthodox as these, in fact, he
defends. The blatant juxtaposition of unrelated chords in the *Marche
au supplice* (measures 154–58), for example, does not offend him,
and even the "sixth chords, constantly rising and falling chromatically" (first movement, measures 200 ff.), he says, "amount to nothing in themselves, but must be uncommonly effective in this context."
Schumann is not acting like a composition teacher ferreting out mis-
takes in a student's work; his observations about Berlioz' harmony
are a candid and expert appraisal of artistic effect.

Deviating slightly from his proposed outline, Schumann next
plunges into an appreciative appraisal of what he calls "the artistic,
well-wrought detail" of the symphony.[59] This is for the most part a

59. NZfM, *3* (1835), ·3–44, 45–46.

description of Berlioz' varied treatment of certain musical materials. Schumann describes the different forms in which the *idée fixe* theme appears, for example, and, with Fétis' criticism still in mind, carefully points out any contrapuntal procedures he can find; his favorites are the quasi-fugal treatment of the second theme in measures 327 ff. of the first movement, and the contrapuntal writing in the main theme of the fourth movement.

Schumann returns to his original course with a discussion of Berlioz' melodies:

> If, as Herr Fétis maintains, not even Berlioz' warmest friends will defend him in regard to *melody*, then I must be one of his enemies. But this does not mean he writes Italian-style melodies, the kind you already know by heart before they ever begin.
>
> True, the oft-recurring principal melody of the symphony has something banal about it and Berlioz praises it rather too much in his program when he ascribes to it "a certain passionate character, but noble and timid." Yet it must be borne in mind that he did not mean this as an important idea, but rather a persistent, haunting theme that one cannot shake out of his head for days on end. It is a perfect expression of monotony and derangement.
>
> Likewise in that review [Fétis'], the principal melody of the second movement is called vulgar and trivial; but here Berlioz is leading us into a dance hall (something like Beethoven in the last movement of his A-major symphony)—nothing more and nothing less . . . And again with the first melody of the third movement, which Herr Fétis called, I think, morose and tasteless. One needs only to wander musingly in the Alps or anywhere among the shepherds, listening to their pipes and alpenhorns; this sounds exactly like that. . . .
>
> If Berlioz can be criticized for anything, it is for his neglect of middle voices. But his is a special case, such as I have seen in few other composers: his melodies are characterized by such an intensity, almost to the individual tone, that they, like many old folk songs, can hardly bear a harmonic accompaniment.[60]

Melody, Schumann is saying, is the dominant element in Berlioz' style, and he is certainly better at it than he is at harmony. His melodies, to be sure, are not very regular, and Schumann is perfectly content that

60. NZfM, *3* (1835), 46–47. See Appendix I, 132.

they should not be. And if they do not always satisfy certain abstract standards for "beautiful melody," Schumann says, it is because Berlioz had something else in mind; he wanted to remind his listeners of situations and events that are evocative of special emotions: the deranged melancholy of an artist, a ball (Schumann too was fascinated with balls), a walk in the Alps, witnessing an execution. Fétis misjudges Berlioz' melody, in Schumann's opinion, because he fails to understand the composer's intent. The point is not so much "Are these melodies beautiful?" but "Do they express what Berlioz meant to express?" In almost every case, Schumann feels, they do.

Despite his defense of Berlioz' realistic expression, Schumann likes best of all the parts that are most lyrical—and in a sense least programmatic. He is especially fond of the third movement, and the passages he commends in the first movement are all especially melodic: the opening theme of the Introduction, the section in measures 24 ff. (though he objected to the voice-leading in measures 25–26, shown in Example 56), and the espressivo oboe solo combined with the *idée fixe* theme in measures 360 ff. The grotesqueries of the last movement, for the most part, Schumann does not care for at all: "it whirls and tumbles about too chaotically; except for a few original places it is unlovely, shrill, repulsive." [61] Here Schumann shows again a rare ability to maintain his perspective in the thick of polemic writing. This review is in the main a rebuttal of Fétis' charges against Berlioz, but Schumann freely admits that at certain points he and Fétis agree.

Schumann's review of the *Symphonie fantastique* may well be the most detailed discussion of a piece of music ever written by a major composer. A bit embarrassed about all the "dissection," he explained (at the beginning of the third installment) that he wanted only to demonstrate the futility of analytic criticism for the reader unacquainted with the music, to point out a few details that may have been overlooked by the casual peruser of the score, and to enlighten those who knew the score but could not understand it—thinking, obviously, of Fétis. [62]

Many incidental factors surely helped ignite Schumann's sympathetic interest in this music—the story of Berlioz' early life artfully

61. NZfM, *3* (1835), 43.

62. NZfM, *3* (1835), 37. Schumann may also have known about Mendelssohn's opinion of the *Symphonie fantastique*. In a letter to Moscheles of April 1834, Mendelssohn called it a "deadly bore . . . what is vulgar, shameless, impudent, and inappropriate can sometimes be amusing, but this is only insipid and stale."

embroidered by Panofka, the use, in the title of the symphony, of one of Schumann's favorite words, *fantastique*, and the very fact that this was a *symphony* by a daring unknown composer of Schumann's generation. Still another incidental reason for Schumann's admiration was this: he was under a gross misapprehension about the date of composition. "At first," he said, "I thought Berlioz' symphony followed in the footsteps of Beethoven's Ninth . . . but it was already played at the Paris Conservatoire in 1820." [63] Knowing (from Panofka's article) the date of Berlioz' birth, Schumann saw the symphony as a work of astonishing power by a student in his teens. All these things help explain why Schumann took the symphony so seriously. But they probably had little effect on his favorable opinion of the music; the review shows, beyond a doubt, that he arrived at it empirically.

Schumann wrote only two other reviews, both of them rather short and casual, of Berlioz' music: the *Francs-Juges* Overture, reviewed in 1836, and the *Waverly* Overture, reviewed in 1839. While Liszt's masterful transcription of the *Symphonie fantastique*[64] had made a detailed assessment of the work possible, the piano reduction of the *Francs-Juges* Overture, Schumann complained, was pitifully inadequate, and there was little he could say about the music.[65] After this overture was played at one of the *Euterpe* concerts in Leipzig late in 1836 (the first performance of Berlioz' music in Germany) the composer thanked Schumann profusely in the *Revue et gazette musicale* for his part in the affair. Schumann reprinted the letter in the NZfM, disclaiming in a footnote, however, any credit—or responsibility.[66]

Shortly thereafter the *Francs-Juges* Overture was the object of a lively controversy in the pages of the NZfM. J. C. Lobe (1797–1881),

63. NZfM, 3 (1835), 34. The *Symphonie fantastique* was first performed at the Conservatoire on December 5, 1830. I have not been able to locate the source of Schumann's misinformation. Fétis mistakenly spoke of hearing the work performed "about eight years ago" (i.e. early in 1827), but Schumann is still wider of the mark.

64. This transcription is an impressive monument to Liszt's ability to make orchestral sounds at the piano. Figurations are subtly altered to reproduce not the notes, but the effect of a passage; judicious octave displacements of certain lines (as in the combination of the *Ronde du sabbat* and *Dies irae*) sometimes even clarify Berlioz' texture. Though Berlioz himself corrected proofs, the transcription was printed with one glaring error: measure 410 of the first movement is missing.

65. NZfM, 4 (1836), 101. Berlioz himself (with the help of several pianists, including Chopin) prepared the four-hand arrangement published by Richault. But the Hofmeister edition, which Schumann reviewed, had, according to Berlioz, been simplified and abridged. See C. Hopkinson, *A Bibliography of the Works of Hector Berlioz* (Edinburgh, 1951), p. 36.

66. *Revue et gazette musicale*, 4 (1837), 61–62, and NZfM, 6 (1837), 71–72.

living at this time in Weimar, contributed an ecstatic open letter to Berlioz ("Your overture to *Francs-Juges* is so profound, so true to nature, a creation that will ennoble mankind").[67] A brief notice by Schumann in the NZfM of October 20 explains that a rejoinder to Lobe by Anton von Zuccamaglio (writing under the pseudonym G. Wedel) cannot be printed because it is too long; in any case, the overture, says Schumann, "is not worth all this talk." [68] But the talk went on. Zuccamaglio persuaded Schumann to print a shortened version of his article; it appeared in three parts in December of 1837, followed by a few of Schumann's own comments. Lobe and Wedel were both wrong, he said, to get so excited about this piece, a first effort that even the composer would never consider a masterpiece. Schumann later acknowledged receiving a further disquisition on the subject from Lobe, but declined to print it.[69]

It was very much against his will that Schumann was drawn into the Zuccamaglio-Lobe controversy; after the *Symphonie fantastique* review he clearly preferred to be rather quiet about Berlioz. His reactions, as we have seen, to Zuccamaglio's attack on the Frenchman in the *Preissinfonie* article were pointedly noncommittal.[70] In 1838 he wrote a paragraph about Berlioz to himself in his diary, calling the *Francs-Juges* overture a "youthful piece full of errors begotten by the boldness of the work"; he remarked that Berlioz was still sometimes confused with Beriot—"they are about as similar as mock-turtle soup and lemonade." [71] In a withering review in the same year of some piano pieces by C. V. Alkan—Schumann would have been astonished at Mr. Raymond Löwenthal's efforts to resuscitate this composer—he remarked that Berlioz, at least, "despite all his aberrations, shows here and there a human heart." [72] Otherwise, during these years, while storms of controversy over Berlioz raged about him, Schumann held his peace.

67. NZfM, 6 (1837), 147.
68. NZfM, 7 (1837), 128. Schumann told Zuccamaglio in a letter of August 20 that he felt embarrassed about Lobe's immoderate essay, and had printed it with serious misgivings. But in the same letter he cautioned Zuccamaglio against forming his opinions without hearing the music performed. "You simply cannot imagine," he said, "how well he handles the orchestra." *Briefe*, p. 91.
69. NZfM, 8 (1838), 36. See Schumann's comments on Zuccamaglio's article in Appendix II, 11.
70. See above, p. 191.
71. Printed in GSK I, 30–31.
72. NZfM, 8 (1838), 169.

This reserve about Berlioz was broken in 1839 with a review, cordial but not entirely complimentary, of the *Waverly* Overture. This essay ends with the ringing declaration, "For all its youthful weaknesses, this work is in largeness of conception and individuality the best foreign instrumental music of recent times." [73] Yet the "youthful weaknesses" sorely disturbed Schumann: "He flashes like a lightning bolt, but leaves behind a sulphurous odor; he sets down exalted pronouncements and truths, only to indulge, immediately after, in the most childish drivel." That devastatingly frank (and just) assessment of Berlioz' work is accompanied with an observation whose pertinence is easy enough to see in retrospect; but it showed exceptional insight in 1839. Berlioz' music, he said, must be heard to be judged. Everything depends upon the sound of the orchestra; "ordinary, even trivial" musical material, he declared, with Berlioz' instrumentation can have a marvelous effect.

After the *Waverly* review Schumann again lapsed into near-silence about Berlioz. In the twelfth volume of the NZfM (1840) began a long series of reviews and reports by Berlioz translated from the *Journal des debats*,[74] and in the same volume there is a lengthy and excited article by Heller on the *Romeo and Juliet* symphony.[75] Yet in the essay on the Schubert C-major Symphony, also in that volume, Schumann remarks in passing that "Berlioz belongs to France, and is occasionally mentioned only as an interesting foreigner and wild man." [76] Berlioz was regarded in Germany mostly as a curiosity, and he offended the taste of many Germans, Schumann's, often, among them. But despite his mixed personal reaction to Berlioz' music, Schumann remained convinced of its historical importance. In his review of a season of Leipzig concerts in the spring of 1840, he commented:

> We were disappointed that Berlioz was totally missing from the repertory . . . He should not be omitted, for whatever one may think of him, ignoring him will never blot his work out of the history of music—any more than an event of world history can be suppressed by striking it out of the books. He must assume a prominent place in any evaluation of the course modern music has taken.[77]

73. NZfM, *10* (1839), 187.
74. Beginning in NZfM, *12* (1840), 59.
75. It is in five installments, NZfM, *12* (1840), 31–32, 34–36, 39–40, 51–52, and 56.
76. NZfM, *12* (1840), 82.
77. NZfM, *12* (1840), 152. See Appendix I, 133.

There was never any doubt in Schumann's mind but that Berlioz was an important composer. In the *Symphonie fantastique* review he resolutely set about showing that this was true, though already at this point he had certain clearly articulated criticisms to make of Berlioz' style. As time passed the things he objected to in Berlioz loomed larger in his thinking; this explains at least partly why, when Berlioz appeared in Leipzig in February of 1843 to conduct his own works, Schumann wrote not one word about it in the NZfM.[78] But a stiff rebuke for his "indifference" from Robert Griepenkerl, an ardent Berlioz enthusiast from Braunschweig, quickly aroused him from his silence. To Griepenkerl's feuilleton Schumann answered that the NZfM had championed Berlioz from the first, that recent works had not been reviewed because the scores were not printed, and that the Leipzig concerts included only old works, "already often discussed in the NZfM." But, he said, there were further grounds for his reticence:

At present, I confess, I should be harsher with much of his work [harsher, that is, than in the *Symphonie fantastique* review]. The years make one more severe, and the unlovely things I found in Berlioz' early music (and I think I pointed them out then) have become no more beautiful in the interim. But this I also said: there is a divine spark in this musician. I hoped that maturity would improve and purify it to produce a clear flame. Whether this has happened I cannot tell, for I know no mature works of Berlioz—none have been printed.[79]

If Schumann found Berlioz' music compelling, startling, and historically significant, but not much to his taste, he never questioned the Frenchman's motives as an artist. This is part of his answer to Zuccamaglio's attack on Berlioz:

people worship the Divinity in various ways, all different. If Berlioz still often slays people at the altar, or raves about like an

78. Hirschbach wrote a generally favorable (but unpleasantly chauvinistic) notice of Berlioz' German tour in the NZfM, *18* (1843), 55–56. A sneering, condescending report of Berlioz' Berlin concert written by one S.v.Alvensleben was printed, without comment, three months later. NZfM, *18* (1843), 125–26, 130.

79. NZfM, *18* (1843), 177–78. See Appendix I, 134. Schumann was generally right; in 1843 only about twelve opus numbers of Berlioz' work had appeared. Important works such as the *Romeo and Juliet Symphony* had been performed but not published—this composition first appeared in 1847, and even the orchestral score of the *Symphonie fantastique* was not printed until 1845.

Indian fakir, he is as sincere about it as someone like Haydn when he offers, with humble demeanor, a cherry blossom. On no one do we wish to impose our ideas by force.[80]

HILLER AND HELLER

Among Berlioz' intimate friends in Paris in the early 1830s was Ferdinand Hiller (1811–85), certainly one of the most versatile and cosmopolitan musicians of the century. Always in the right place at the right time, seemingly, as a youth of fifteen he visited Beethoven on his deathbed; he studied piano with Hummel and church music with Baini; he put on an Italian opera with Rossini's help at La Scala, associated with Chopin, Berlioz, and Liszt in Paris, with Mendelssohn and Schumann in Leipzig, and with Wagner in Dresden, and became the teacher, finally, of Max Bruch and Engelbert Humperdinck. A superlative pianist, he was the first to play the Emperor Concerto in Paris, and he later held important conducting posts in Frankfurt, Dresden, Düsseldorf, Paris and Cologne. He was an able composer, and achieved eminence as the director of a conservatory and a writer on musical subjects.

Schumann had not yet met Hiller in 1835 when he wrote a long and searching critique of the young pianist's Etudes op. 15. This review begins with the plain statement that Hiller, in Schumann's opinion, is one of the romantic composers:

> Franz Schubert, in his most individual way, developed a strain of Beethovenian romanticism (which one could call *provençal*) to the point of virtuosity. Upon this foundation has arisen, consciously or unconsciously, a new school, not yet fully developed and recognized . . . Ferdinand Hiller, one of its members, is among its most remarkable representatives.[81]

Once this is understood, Schumann gives vent to mixed feelings about this music: "He deceives you into thinking him a genius, but then admits in the next moment that he is an intolerable Philistine . . . What he has written is full of contradictions, so what I write must be too." [82]

This review, though hardly "full of contradictions," is bothersomely

80. NZfM, 5 (1836), 151. See Appendix I, 135.
81. NZfM, 2 (1835), 5. See Appendix I, 136.
82. Ibid.

discursive. Here, at the very beginning of his editorship of the NZfM, Schumann talks in fits and starts about basic problems of criticism (embracing, for the moment, the doctrine of creative criticism),[83] and frets about the special difficulties facing the music critic:

> I proceed with a deep sigh. In no other kind of criticism is it so difficult to prove one's point as in music. Science argues with mathematics; poetry has the decisive, golden word; other arts have nature herself as arbiter, for they borrow their forms from her. But music is the fair orphan whose father and mother no one can name.[84]

Mixed with such expansive observations is a scrupulous and painstaking assessment of Hiller's Etudes. They range, says Schumann, from some of the "best [piano music] since Beethoven's Sonata in F minor [op. 57] and certain pieces of Franz Schubert"[85] to things "I would not for anything have allowed to be printed."[86] This last he says about no. 19 of the set whose persistent parallel octaves he finds unforgivably offensive (see Ex. 60a). There is no saving this piece, he claims,

Example 60. F. Hiller, Etudes op. 15, no. 19

for any solutions for the left hand such as the one he suggests (Example 60b) would destroy the technical purpose of the etude—namely to make the left thumb play a continuous melody. Schumann gives several other examples of the bad writing that mars these etudes, for

83. This review includes his famous statement about creating the same effect in a critique as that left by the art work itself. See above, p. 72.
84. NZfM, 2 (1835), 42. See Appendix I, 137.
85. NZfM, 2 (1835), 43.
86. NZfM, 2 (1835), 55.

instance the "ghastly doubled thirds" in the second measure of no. 9 (see Ex. 61).[87]

Example 61. F. Hiller, Etudes op. 15, no. 9

Despite the unevenness of quality he points out, Schumann is enormously impressed with some of the etudes. The ones he calls "as good as anything since Beethoven and Schubert" are nos. 2, 17, 22, and 23; and when at the close of his review he recapitulates with a capsule characterization of each piece, these move him to shift from technical language to poetic description. For no. 2 he says, "Dream. Subterranean striving. The earth-spirits sing and hammer; fairies on diamond-like flowers curtsy to each other." And no. 17 is "apparently the most rewarding in the whole volume, if played *prestissimo*. Lookalikes, one-legged people, men without shadows, mirror images walk about in it." [88] This little Jean-Paulian fantasy is strongly reminiscent of the scene in *Flegeljahre* with which Schumann at one time associated his own *Papillons*. And there is, in fact, a startling similarity between this etude's main theme and that of *Papillon* no. 4. (See Ex. 62.)

Schumann expended intense effort on the Hiller review. Like the critique of the *Symphonie fantastique* of the same year, it is divided into separate discussions of three aspects of the music—this time "poetry of the work, its effect, spirit; theoretical considerations, relationship of melody to harmony, form and period structure; and technical value." Under the second heading Schumann carefully dissects the first etude and presents his results in a kind of table (his conclusion is that it is formally "disorderly"). Schumann was willing to invest this much time on a single article partly, perhaps, as the result of a miscalculation (this is also true to some extent of the Hummel op. 125 review): early in 1835, having decided to do all the reviews of

87. Schumann considers the first chord in measure 2 a dominant ninth in first inversion (with the root missing). He still remembered this doubled *G* a year later when he found a very similar construction in Hiller's Concerto op. 5. NZfM, *4* (1836), 84.

88. NZfM, *2* (1835), 57.

Example 62. F. Hiller, Etudes op. 15, no. 17, and
R. Schumann, *Papillons* no. 4

instrumental music himself, he simply was unaware as yet of the
work involved. Yet there can be no doubt but that he considered the
Hiller Etudes extraordinarily important. He saw that they were
among the first after Chopin's op. 10 to use really novel pianistic
figurations; and they were expressive music in the newest style.

Hiller's most famous work, in all likelihood, was his oratorio *Die
Zerstörung Jerusalems,* composed partly in Milan in 1839, finished in
Leipzig and first performed at the Gewandhaus in the spring of 1840.
Schumann wrote two reviews of this composition, one immediately
after the performance,[89] and the other when the score was published
the following January. The concert review is very short; Schumann
only expresses his satisfaction that Hiller has not been ruined by his
stay in Italy, and says he considers this oratorio a work of real value.

Schumann's review of the score of this composition is one of his
most detailed discussions of any vocal music. He muses, first, about
the course of recent church music and about Mendelssohn's revival of
older forms. In Beethoven's time, he says, church music was overrun
by sickly, saccharine sentimentality. It was cultivated by composers
who "wrote by the yard, today for the church, tomorrow for the dance
hall." He continues:

> Others such as Bernhard Klein, though better, were too ascetic to
> gain any real influence. Mendelssohn was the first among the
> North Germans to get back onto the right track, to reestablish

89. NZfM, *12* (1840), 120.

contact with Bach and Handel . . . the genuine heroes of the
faith in our art.[90]

Hiller's oratorio, he says, is part of this North-German tradition revived by Mendelssohn. Schumann then recounts the narrative of the
text,[91] describes the five principal characters and the distribution of
musical forces, and finally proceeds at a leisurely pace through the
entire oratorio, discussing the dramatic situations and Hiller's musical
realization of them.

In the concert review Schumann had said that Hiller's oratorio was
rather more modern in style than the prototype for all contemporary
oratorios, Mendelssohn's *St. Paul*. Now he singles out as particularly
progressive Jeremiah's lament (from prison) "Um Juda trag' ich
schweres Leid." There is nothing new about its anguished falling chromatic melody, but the constant dialogue of voice and winds is interesting and novel (see Ex. 63).

The following chorus, too, Schumann likes very much, especially its
"brilliant orchestral accompaniment." This chorus (number 35) is
not like the others in the oratorio. Almost all of them have a contrapuntal texture with pseudo-fugal entries in the voices, and the orchestral accompaniment usually is little more than a doubling of the
voice parts. But here the chorus is all homophonic; the voice parts
are doubled by the winds, while the violins play independent leaping
figures. The ending of this oratorio disappoints Schumann—particularly the setting of Jeremiah's final lines:

> Then follow perhaps the most important words of all in Jere-
> miah's speech, "Zur letzten Zeit wird Gottes Haus höher stehen
> denn alle Berge und erhaben über alle Hügel!" The composer has
> treated them much too superficially; for this he should have saved
> his finest, most productive hour.[92]

These words are set in recitative of the kind that carries most of the
narrative portions of the drama; the text is declaimed smoothly within
a small melodic range while the strings provide a "realized continuo"

---

90. NZfM, *14* (1841), 3. See Appendix I, 138.

91. The subject of the oratorio is the Babylonian conquest of Jerusalem. The libretto is
ostensibly by A. Steinheim; but in an *Erklärung* in the NZfM, *16* (1842), 84, Steinheim
said that because of extensive changes Hiller had made in the libretto, he no longer wanted
his name associated with it.

92. NZfM, *14* (1841), 4. See Appendix I, 139.

Example 63. F. Hiller, *Um Jada trag' ich* from
Die Zerstörung Jerusalems

accompaniment. In a later review of another dramatic work, Reissiger's opera *Adéle de Foix*, Schumann makes a very similar criticism; in a moment of strong emotional tension, he says, "a recitative-like delivery is simply not effective enough." [93] This generalization is somewhat surprising in view of what recitative style seems to have meant to early nineteenth-century composers. The ending of Schubert's *Erlkönig*, for example, and the late works of Beethoven (especially the Sonata op. 110) show how expressive it can be.

When Schumann called Hiller's oratorio "progressive," what he meant, surely, was "progressive for an oratorio." For oratorios in his time were anything but progressive. *Da capo* arias, clear-cut distinction between recitative and aria, fugal choruses, and the use of chorale tunes at points of dramatic importance were all standard (Hiller's oratorio has all of these things except the chorales). Schumann, though usually uncharitable toward the imitation of earlier styles, was willing to accept it here. In a review of Eduard Sobolewsky's *Der Erlöser*, he

93. NZíM, *17* (1842), 80.

specifically condoned the use in the oratorio of the old "learned" techniques:

> No one can quarrel with the use of the more elaborate forms in the church style. There are a great many of them here. Double canons, double fugues, and the like bear eloquent testimony in many places to this composer's industry and learning.[94]

Schumann saw the nineteenth-century oratorio as a deliberate resuscitation of an eighteenth-century genre; this was one place where he thought an imitation of eighteenth-century style was fitting.

Hiller quit Paris late in 1835; almost as if to replace him, Stephen Heller (1813–88) joined the company of romantic musicians in the French capital two years later. Schumann had made Heller's acquaintance in January of 1835 when the Hungarian-born pianist was living in Augsburg, and this marked the beginning of a long friendship by correspondence between the two musicians. Heller became an occasional correspondent for the NZfM, first from Augsburg (beginning in April, 1836), and later from Paris. At the same time Schumann began to review some of Heller's piano pieces. There were brief notices in 1836–37 of a set of variations on an aria from Hérold's *Zampa* and the Rondo Scherzo op. 8. In September of 1837 Schumann wrote something that was ostensibly a review of Heller's Impromptus op. 7. But really it was a kind of public recommendation of the composer; the impromptus are scarcely mentioned. Here Schumann emphatically includes Heller in the camp of the romantic composers, telling us, at the same time, something of what he means (or does not mean) by "romantic":

> I am sick and tired of the word "romantic," though I have not spoken it ten times in my entire life. And still, if I had to call our young seer anything, it would be that—and what a romantic he is! Of that vague, nihilistic negativism in which many look for romanticism, or of the crude, literal daubing that delights the French neoromantics, this composer, thank God, knows nothing. On the contrary, he is full of natural sentiment, and he expresses himself clearly and intelligently.[95]

This was written in September 1837; by this time Schumann al-

94. NZfM, *15* (1841), 2. See Appendix I, 140.
95. NZfM, *7* (1837), 70. See Appendix I, 141.

ready saw a real difference between the German and French romantic composers. The "crude, literal daubing" refers, of course, to programmatic effects—particularly, it seems, in the music of Berlioz, the foremost of the French "neoromantics." Heller, though he moved more or less permanently to Paris soon after this, never succumbed, Schumann thought, to the dangerous artistic vices of the city. His piano music continued to find a favorable reception with Schumann: the Sonata op. 9 (1839), the Etudes op. 16 (1841), the Scherzo op. 24 (1843), and even things like "Boleros on a theme from *La Juive* of Halévy" op. 32 (in this piece, Schumann said, Heller distinctly improved on Halévy).[96]

One cannot help thinking that Schumann's judgment about Heller's music was influenced by the younger musician's witty and astute commentary on the Parisian musical scene in various musical journals, the NZfM among them. The early compositions of Heller reviewed in the NZfM hardly amount to much. The Scherzo op. 24, for example, Schumann praised over-generously ("full of humor, and it has an artistic form; we feel from beginning to end that we are in the company of a most lively, agreeable spirit"[97]). Though it shows a certain facility, this piece is rather pedestrian, and certainly old-fashioned for 1843. Its texture is thin and its harmony bland; it sounds much more like Hummel or Weber than like Chopin or Liszt—or, for that matter, Schumann. Schumann may have felt some embarrassment in writing this review, for, as in the case of the Impromptus, he quite avoided discussing the music. Instead he got on to one of his favorite subjects and exhorted Heller to expand his field of activity and compose for orchestra. Heller, though he lived to be seventy-five, never followed Schumann's advice; his compositions are without exception for piano. Some of his later music has real merit, and Schumann's high estimate of Heller's abilities—an estimate made on the basis of slim evidence—has been largely justified.

SCHUNKE AND SCHUMANN

During the hectic preparations for launching the NZfM in late 1833–early 1834, Schumann's constant companion was the brilliant young pianist from Stuttgart, student of Reicha and Kalkbrenner, and

96. NZfM, *19* (1843), 90.
97. NZfM, *18* (1843), 13.

dedicatee of Schumann's Toccata, Ludwig Schunke. In his single year
in Leipzig Schunke performed at three Gewandhaus concerts, and before his death in December 1834 he had completed about fifteen compositions, all but one for solo piano.[98] Schumann reviewed a half-dozen
of his published compositions in 1835 and 1836: a sonata, two capriccios, two four-hand pieces for piano, and a set of variations on waltzes
of Schubert. First to appear was the review of Schunke's unfinished
Sonata in G minor op. 3 (a misprint in the NZfM designates the key
as C minor). Written five months after Schunke's death, this article
is charged with emotion. Schumann makes no pretense of objectivity,
and tells of his immediate friendship with the young pianist, of
Schunke's narrowly averted duel with a composer from Berlin (Otto
Nicolai), and, almost incidentally, of Schunke's playing of his own
sonata for the assembled *Davidsbündler.*

This narrative hovers precariously between straight reporting of
real events and an effusion of Schumann's imagination. Florestan, before this unconvinced that Schunke was anything more than a virtuoso, upon hearing the sonata pronounced, "You are a great artist, and
I consider this sonata your best work—especially as you play it your-
self." [99] Schumann closes with a highly personal recollection (this
section he later deleted from the *Gesammelte Schriften*):

> Later, at home, as I looked out once more at the hurrying
> blanket of clouds, an unknown but friendly sounding voice un-
> der the windows was calling, "Ludwig . . . Ludwig." It was
> probably a stranger who knew nothing of what had happened.
> But I quickly shut the window and plunged with closed eyes into
> the deep, deep night. Outside a light rain fell, as though weeping,
> from the sky.[100]

The only other sizable review of Schunke's music, the essay on the
Capriccios op. 9 and 10, is also more anecdotal than critical. Schumann recalls that Schunke was able to learn the Toccata Schumann
dedicated to him, amazingly, by studying it only away from the piano.
And he recounts having jokingly suggested that Schunke call his
Capriccio op. 10 "Beethoven, scène dramatique"—which is how it
appeared on a Gewandhaus concert program.[101]

98. Jansen gives a list of Schunke's compositions in *Die Davidsbündler,* pp. 137–38.
99. NZfM, 2 (1835), 146.
100. Ibid. See Appendix I, 142.
101. NZfM, 4 (1836), 182.

Most of Schunke's music was published in single editions by small local firms such as Wunder of Leipzig, and copies are now exceedingly scarce. But the Deutsche Staatsbibliothek in East Berlin fortunately has all the compositions Schumann reviewed. This music corroborates his lofty notions of his friend's promise as a composer ("Death's snuffing-out of the spark of genius could hardly be more untimely or more painful").[102] The sonata, though roughhewn, and in some places harmonically awkward, is a convincing piece; the beginning of its second movement is shown in Example 64.

Example 64. L. Schunke, Sonata op. 3, 2d movement

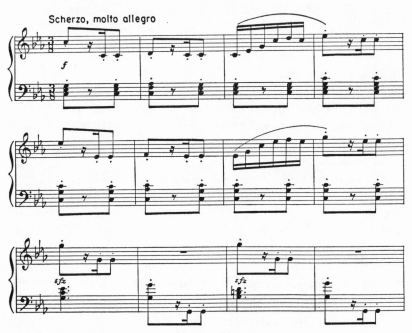

If this scherzo seems to have borrowed its opening motive from the scherzo of Beethoven's Ninth Symphony, this is only one of a host of such reminiscences. It was no accident either that the Capriccio op. 10 reminded Schumann of Beethoven; its principal theme, in its various forms, recalls the Sonatas op. 10, no. 1 (first movement), op. 27, no. 2 (last movement), and op. 53 (first movement). The opening of this theme in its second occurrence—raised, à la Beethoven, a semitone—is shown in Example 65.

102. NZfM, 2 (1835), 156.

Example 65. L. Schunke, Capriccio op. 10

On the basis of his surviving music we can scarcely consider Schunke
a significant composer who was somehow overlooked by posterity—
even Schumann would not claim that for him. But, like Burgmüller,
he could easily have become important; his supercharged, appassionato
rhythms and brusque modulations, modeled on Beethoven, and quite
unlike anything in the usual piano styles of the salon or parlor, showed
strong promise.

Whenever someone on the staff of the NZfM published any of his
music, Schumann had a delicate editorial decision to make. Could it
properly be reviewed in the NZfM? For occasional contributors like
Heller his answer was clearly "yes," but in the case of Schunke, one
of the journal's founders, he carefully held up any mention of his
music until after the composer's death. The most prolific composer on
the staff, of course, was Schumann himself, and his own music presented a special problem. Because of the feud with Fink, Schumann's
music was even deleted from the lists of new releases in the AmZ. And
if propriety demanded silence about his own work in the NZfM,
Schumann's music would be denied any notice in the Leipzig musical
journals. This difficulty was circumvented in various ways: sometimes
Schumann included his own pieces in lists of compositions that came
up for review without discussing them; twice he printed other people's critiques (both times favorable) of his music;[103] and once, with
no apologies to anyone, he wrote a full review of his own work.

103. There is a long review (by Moscheles?) of the F-sharp minor sonata in the NZfM,
5 (1836), 135–37; and in the NZfM, 6 (1837), 65, Schumann quotes from a letter of
Moscheles in praise of the Concert sans orchestre.

The article in question is on Schumann's *Etudes on Capriccios of Paganini* op. 10. This was Schumann's second group of etudes on these Paganini pieces (op. 1); he explains in his review how it differs from the earlier set (op. 3):

> In contrast to an earlier set of etudes after Paganini where I copied down the originals almost note for note (perhaps to their disadvantage) and merely filled them out harmonically, this time I freed myself from the pedantry of a literal transcription in the hope that the present set might give the impression of an autonomous piano composition, and that the violinistic origins might be forgotten without detriment to the poetic idea of the work.[104]

Schumann comments in some detail on individual pieces. In the second etude, he explains, he replaced Paganini's tremolo accompaniment because it would be "too tiresome for player and listener alike." This etude is modeled on Paganini's Capriccio no. 6. In Schumann's arrangement, a measured tremolo in sixty-fourth-note triplets has been replaced by repeated chords in sixteenth-note triplets. This change reduces to nothing the devilish technical difficulty of Paganini's capriccio, but the result is musically far more satisfying—as is amply demonstrated by the adjacent performances of the two pieces in the History of Music in Sound recordings (Volume 9).

The third etude, Schumann candidly admits, is "not rewarding enough in relation to its difficulty." [105] These are his remarks on the following piece:

> While I was working on no. 4, the funeral march from Beethoven's *Eroica* Symphony hovered before me. Perhaps the listener could hear this for himself. The chords on p. 11, syst. 6, m. 3 are in the original merely the runs in thirds of the upper voices. I knew of no other solution for making them presentable. The
> $$9\flat$$
> sudden transition from B to C, $6\sharp$ $7\natural$ cannot but have a strik-
> $$3\sharp \text{ to } 5\natural$$
> $$b \qquad g$$
> ing effect.[106]

---

104. NZfM, *4* (1836), 134. See Appendix I, 143.
105. NZfM, *4* (1836), 135.
106. Ibid. See Appendix I, 144.

This etude, the fourth, is based on the capriccio also fourth in Paganini's collection.[107] The "runs in thirds" of Paganini's composition (shown in Example 66a) Schumann renders as full chords with rapidly changing harmonies (Example 66b).

Example 66. N. Paganini, Capriccios op. 1, no. 4; R. Schumann, Etudes on Capriccios of Paganini op. 10, no. 4

The modulation for which Schumann congratulates himself occurs much later in the piece (measures 88–89). A striking harmonic turn at this point is his doing alone; Paganini had only an enharmonic change resulting in a diminished seventh chord. Schumann added the G in the bass to produce the dominant ninth, as shown in Example 67.

Example 67. R. Schumann, Etudes on Capriccios of Paganini op. 10, no. 4

Schumann's review performs exactly the same function as the extended preface to his op. 3 collection, and it is a welcome commentary on this music. He simply explains what he intended as a composer; he does not pretend to adjudicate as a critic.

107. The opening theme of this piece (especially in Schumann's arrangement) does bear a family resemblance to the first theme of Beethoven's funeral march.

MENDELSSOHN AND BRAHMS

Early in 1835, when the NZfM had just fallen entirely under Schumann's control, the directors of the Gewandhaus concerts were quietly negotiating to replace their rather undistinguished conductor, C. A. Pohlenz.[108] Because of persistent efforts by Leipzig's patrons of music, particularly Schumann's friends Carl and Henrietta Voigt, the replacement was none less than Felix Mendelssohn-Bartholdy. Mendelssohn, only twenty-six, was already one of Germany's most admired musicians, and Schumann (a nonentity by comparison) rejoiced with all Leipzig when Mendelssohn first appeared on the Gewandhaus stage in October to conduct his own Overture "Calm Sea and Prosperous Voyage," a scene from *Freischütz*, compositions of Spohr and Cherubini, and Beethoven's Fourth Symphony.[109] This marked the beginning of a steady improvement of the Gewandhaus orchestra and its repertory; under Mendelssohn's tutelage it was gradually transformed from a competent provincial orchestra to one of the finest ensembles on the continent—even so demanding a critic as Berlioz testified that this was true.

Schumann's report on this initial Gewandhaus concert is disguised in the first of the *Schwärmbriefe*—spritely products of his fancy in which Mendelssohn is promptly dubbed (hardly to his satisfaction, as we may imagine) "F. Meritis.[110] Schumann had written his first review of published music by Mendelssohn the previous June: a warmly appreciative little essay on the second set of *Lieder ohne Worte* (op. 30).[111] From this time until his retirement from the NZfM he wrote on enormous amounts of music by Mendelssohn, more, in fact, than by any other composer. The only possible conclusion to be drawn from all this writing is that Schumann admired Mendelssohn as a composer and considered him simply without peer as a general musician.

108. Christian August Pohlenz (1790–1843) was also organist at the Thomaskirche and director of the Leipzig Singakademie. Until this time at the Gewandhaus, a baton-wielding conductor was used only for performances involving chorus and orchestra; at purely orchestral concerts the concertmaster was in charge.
109. See Werner, *Mendelssohn*, p. 263.
110. NZfM, 3 (1835), 126–27.
111. NZfM, 2 (1835), 202.

This point must be made very clear. For in both his books on Schumann, Boetticher, interested in making Schumann out to be anti-Semitic, has deliberately distorted his opinions about Mendelssohn.[112] Boetticher's arguments are too patently specious to deserve serious refutation. He simply gathers together from Schumann's diaries a few suggestions of personal friction between the two composers (Werner has shown how carefully Boetticher has doctored some of his quotations from these sources)[113] and some of Schumann's more lukewarm comments; he concludes, despite overwhelmingly plain evidence to the contrary, that Schumann despised both Mendelssohn and his music. The reason, of course, was Mendelssohn's "racial deficiency." Boetticher explains, for example: "Schumann recognized Mendelssohn's inability, because of his race, to penetrate into the mythical world of ancient drama and Nordic poetry."[114] Conclusions like this are manufactured out of whole cloth; Schumann said nothing of the sort.

Schumann's commentary on Mendelssohn's music embraces everything except lieder and organ music: overtures, concertos, chamber music, one symphony (op. 56, "The Scotch"), and reams of piano music. The *Lieder ohne Worte* op. 30 Schumann reviewed in 1835 was the second of seven collections Mendelssohn published under that title.[115] Schumann described the style of these pieces as improvisations with a distinct melody and accompaniment—rather like an impromptu song with the words crossed out.[116] Always impatient with composers

112. See especially *Einführung*, pp. 255–62, and *Schriften*, pp. 106–15 (these two passages are substantially the same). Boetticher does similar violence to Schumann's opinions about many Jewish musicians: Moscheles, Hirschbach, Thalberg, and others. Several times in the course of his two books he cites Schumann's question to Clara: "Is Heller Jewish? I don't believe it. He seems to me to be so lazy." To this last sentence Boetticher adds an "aber" to give it the proper anti-Semitic coloring. See *Einführung*, p. 186, and *Schriften*, pp. 233–34 and 256.

There is no evidence of anti-Semitism in Schumann's criticism. The only statement he made about Jewish musicians in general, so far as I know, occurs in a review of etudes by Jacob Rosenhain. After admonishing Rosenhain to eschew the eclecticism of his coreligionist Meyerbeer, Schumann explains to his readers, "Our young composer also belongs to this talented, perceptive people that has exerted such a significant influence in the progress of recent music." NZfM, *11* (1839), 113–14.

113. Werner, *Mendelssohn*, p. 265.

114. Boetticher, ed., *Schriften*, p. 108.

115. Many composers borrowed this name from Mendelssohn; Schumann reviewed *Lieder ohne Worte* by A. Dreyschock, C. A. Strube, J. Schaeffer, and Eduard Marxsen (Brahms' teacher in Hamburg).

116. NZfM, 2 (1835), 202.

who wrote comfortably in an unchanging style, Schumann looked carefully for signs of development in succeeding volumes of *Lieder ohne Worte*—and thought he found them. In his review of the op. 38 set (1837), he noted that the last number was not a "solo song," but a "duet." [117] And the third piece of the following collection (op. 53), he said, showed a clear four-part texture. Thus even in these, his most unpretentious compositions, Schumann reported, "Mendelssohn has progressed . . . from the simple song through the duet to polyphonic and choral types." [118]

In 1843 Schumann observed that Mendelssohn had now written about every kind of music there is except opera; the occasion for this observation was the publication of his first "real" symphony, the "Scotch"—Schumann was inclined not to count the very early C-minor symphony and the Symphony-Cantata *Lobesang*. In his review of this symphony Schumann made an unfortunate mistake: he took it for the "Italian" Symphony (not published until after Mendelssohn's death). Mendelssohn had done preparatory work on both symphonies many years earlier—on one in Italy and the other in Scotland. When the Symphony in A minor was published as op. 56 by Breitkopf und Härtel, Schumann was informed "at third hand," he reported, that it was the one begun years before in Rome. So this symphony, the impressionable Schumann declares, "places us under Italian skies."

Wrong as he is about geography (the sound of bagpipes made him think not of heather, but only of a *Volkston*), Schumann has some perceptive things to say about the music. He points out that the symphony owes less to Beethoven than to the Schubert symphony Mendelssohn had premiered not long before:

> As with Schubert's symphony, it is its characteristic, enchanting colors that will win Mendelssohn's composition a special place in the symphonic repertory. It does not offer the usual instrumental pathos and massive size—nothing here looks like an extension of Beethoven. It resembles much more closely, in its general character, Schubert's symphony . . . It must be said that the more recent of the two [i.e. of Schubert's and Mendelssohn's symphonies] has a more gracious, well-bred air, and is the more

117. NZfM, 7 (1837), 58.
118. NZfM, *15* (1841), 142.

readily accessible. But Schubert's symphony has other excellences; it shows, particularly, a richer inventiveness.[119]

Schumann recognized that this composition, like Schubert's symphony, owes its effect to the special character of its themes and to novel instrumentation (the heavy, dark scoring in the first movement, the indefatigable clarinets in the second) rather than to any serious working out of musical material. The Scotch Symphony, dedicated to Queen Victoria, is clearly a generation removed from Beethoven.

When Schumann called Meyerbeer's *Les Huguenots* and Mendelssohn's *St. Paul* "the two most important compositions of these times" [120] he did not mean that they were the best in recent music. Of course he thought nothing of the sort of *Les Huguenots;* nor, as a careful reading of his article shows, did he really think this of *St. Paul.* He simply referred to the fact that these were the most performed and most discussed major works of the time. The huge success of *Les Huguenots* at Paris was probably equaled by the popularity of *St. Paul* in cities and towns throughout Germany. The journals from the late 1830s are filled with reports of performances of Mendelssohn's oratorio and with lively discussions of it. *St. Paul* was unquestionably the most decisive single factor in Mendelssohn's burgeoning fame in this period.

In this essay on *Les Huguenots* and *St. Paul,* his first full-scale review of dramatic music, Schumann showers Mendelssohn with compliments:

> besides the inner meaning, the pure Christian spirit that we have already pointed out, let all observe the musical mastery and fittingness of the work, such elegant song throughout, such marriage of word and tone, such musical speech—so that we perceive all in lifelike depth, such effective grouping of characters, and grace breathed as it were over the whole, such freshness, such unquenchable color in the instrumentation, not to mention the thoroughly cultivated style, the easy mastery of all the styles of musical setting—with this, I should think, one ought to be satisfied.[121]

Despite all this, Schumann showed that he, for one, was not entirely

119. NZfM, *18* (1843), 155. See Appendix I, 145.
120. NZfM, *7* (1837), 73.
121. NZfM, *7* (1837), 75. See Appendix I, 146.

satisfied. He pointed out several dramatic flaws in the work, especially that the climax comes in Part I, much to the detriment of Part II, and that Stephen, ostensibly a secondary character, overshadows Paul himself. And however masterful the music, Schumann said, Mendelssohn seemed to cultivate deliberately a style that would be "transparent and popular"—in the long run a bad policy. But he hastened to add that *St. Paul* was a youthful work; perhaps some day Mendelssohn would write a mature one,[122] and "until then let us be satisfied with what we have, enjoy it, and learn from it."

As this review shows, any criticisms Schumann had to make of Mendelssohn's music were put very gently. This was not only because the two composers were friends (Schumann was always more friendly to Mendelssohn than the other way around), but also because Schumann was awe-struck by Mendelssohn's facility as a musician—"the finest living musician in the world" he said in 1842[123]—and thoroughly approved of what he was doing for music in Leipzig. If somewhat extraneous considerations like these often led Schumann to err on the side of too much generosity to Mendelssohn's music, he showed his usual acuity of judgment when Mendelssohn produced something really first-rate. Such a work is the D-minor Trio, op. 49; with almost prophetic insight Schumann wrote of it:

> This is the master-trio of the present, just as in their times were the trios of Beethoven in B flat and D,[124] and that of Schubert in E flat.[125] It is a beautiful composition that years from now will delight our grandchildren and great-grandchildren.[126]

In pieces like this, Schumann felt, Mendelssohn redeemed the times:

> He is the Mozart of the nineteenth century, the most brilliant musician, the one who sees most clearly through the contradictions of this period, and for the first time reconciles them. And he will not be the last of such artists. After Mozart came Beethoven; this new Mozart will also be followed by a Beethoven—perhaps he is already born.[127]

122. In a footnote in the GS Schumann called attention to *Elijah*—Mendelssohn had fulfilled his expectations.
123. *Briefe,* p. 213.
124. Op. 97 and 70.
125. D. 929.
126. NZfM, *13* (1840), 198. See Appendix I, 147
127. Ibid. See Appendix I, 148.

Ten years after he had given up the NZfM, about to lose his job as music director at Düsseldorf, and heading inexorably toward personal ruin, Schumann recognized this new Beethoven, this musical messiah in a young composer from Hamburg, Johannes Brahms. Brahms' first compositions moved Schumann to reestablish contact with an earlier period in his life. Recalling his former expectations, and suddenly seeing the possibility of their fulfillment, he wrote one last essay for the NZfM. In *Neue Bahnen* he described Brahms with perfect confidence as the composer "called to give ideal form to the highest expression of his times, one who does not present us the gradual unfolding of mastery, but springs forth fully equipped, like Minerva from the head of Zeus." [128]

In this last essay, as in his first one (the Chopin review of 1831), Schumann points to a young unknown as the most important composer in sight. From our vantage point it is not hard to understand his admiration for Brahms; for his work seems to fulfill perfectly Schumann's lifelong ideal of expressive, romantic sounds in a context of traditional procedures and forms. Had he lived to witness the Wagner–Brahms dichotomy there can be no question about what Schumann's position would have been. He knew *Tannhäuser* (his reactions were mixed), and he at least knew *about* the *Flying Dutchman* and *Lohengrin*. Yet, in a footnote to the Brahms essay, he gives a list of promising composers that includes Joachim, Gade, Franz, Heller, and even F. E. Wilsing, but not Wagner. Brahms, he says, is the best of them all. Here again, as with Chopin, Schumann could see the superiority of Brahms' music at a glance; for when he wrote the essay Brahms had yet to publish his first composition.

IN RETROSPECT

Schumann's story, both as composer and critic, is a melancholy one. Equipped with the greatest musical talent of his generation and with literary abilities of almost a similar magnitude, he set about his double career with keen ambition and optimism. He felt almost a moral responsibility to artistic culture as a whole, and he hoped from the outset to serve expansive ends: the future of German musical style, the continuance of important musical forms, the nurture of better musical taste. But the expectations he expressed as a critic were again and again

128. NZfM, *39* (1853), 185.

dashed to the ground, and as a composer he never could rid himself of
the notion that the things he did best—the short movements, for example, of *Carnaval* and *Kreislerianna,* and the lieder—were but
"Kleinigkeiten." It was hard for Schumann to accept the bitter
reality that most composers did not care to follow in Beethoven's
footsteps, and that those who did were not able to. His own symphonies, for all their merits, illustrate this, and, had he lived to see Brahms'
maturity, it would not have escaped him that Brahms at his most
Beethovenian (in his development sections for example) is least successful.

Troubled by a growing lack of confidence in his own powers, by
nagging personal difficulties, and by the progressive mental disorder
that finally overcame him, Schumann still struggled persistently to
realize his initial goals as a critic. The resulting body of criticism, like
his *oeuvre* as a composer, is a mixed bag, but it is without question the
most important corpus of writings about music from the earlier part
of the nineteenth century.

In his introduction to a recent anthology of poetry, W. H. Auden
says, "chances are, that in the course of his lifetime, the major poet
will write more bad poems than the minor." [129] This probably goes for
critics too. Schumann was, by any accounting, a major critic; and still
he wrote a good many bad reviews. At his worst he could be tiresomely
vague and sentimental. And his judgment of a man's work was sometimes too much swayed by his impressions of the man—where he lived,
how he looked, what he said. This led him astray in his writing about
Hirschbach and, to a lesser degree, Heller. At times Schumann was not
at all interested in writing criticism; but the music was there to be
reviewed and the journal had to go on. As a result, he occasionally substituted a facile pen for careful study, and his conclusions seem, in a
few cases, ill considered. In his review of Field's Seventh Concerto, for
example, he simply recorded his immediate enthusiasm for the work,
as we have seen, without bothering to reflect on what was so good
about it.

But at his best Schumann hardly has a rival among music critics of
his century or any other. He understood the greatest of his contemporaries, Schubert, Chopin, and Berlioz, with a clarity for which it is
hard to find a parallel. Schumann was always in splendid form when

129. W. H. Auden, ed., *Nineteenth-Century British Minor Poets* (New York, 1966), p.
15.

embroiled in controversy; and each of these three composers became a special cause that stimulated his best effort. On the work of the minor composers of his time, too, he commented with rare perception. People like Moscheles, Klein, Loewe, and Hiller have at best a fuzzy profile in our view of musical history; a careful reading of Schumann draws them much more sharply into focus. No other contemporary observer had so much of value to say about recent changes in piano style, about the development of the lied, about the precarious status of large instrumental forms in the earlier nineteenth century. This is true first of all because no one else of Schumann's caliber was regularly writing music criticism.

Schumann's musical horizons were admittedly somewhat limited. He was never cosmopolitan like Mendelssohn, Liszt, Hiller, or Chopin. Except for his brief stay in Vienna and his final move to Düsseldorf, he spent his entire life in the area of his birth—the same corner of Germany in which Bach had moved about. His writings reflect, in a way, a local point of view: an interest in German traditions and the future of German music. Schumann had little to say about Italian opera, and his unfavorable impressions of the musical scene in Paris were acquired second-hand. But preoccupied as he was with German music, in his criticism Schumann consciously resisted the impulse to be chauvinistic. This must be clear from his ungrudging support (at least initially) of Chopin, Berlioz, Bennett, and Gade.

In the portrait of German musical culture in the 1830s and 1840s Schumann draws for us, only one figure of real importance is missing: Schumann himself. In reading his criticism one tends to forget that the writer was a composer too—every bit as serious about it, surely, as Berlioz, Liszt, or Wagner. Such forgetfulness is never possible in reading the prose works of these last three. Schumann's writings on music have a quality Kant (and many others) have said is essential for making any aesthetic judgment: disinterest.[130] What he said about people like Mendelssohn, his fellow Leipziger who seemed to eclipse him so thoroughly, bore no tinge of jealousy; and his generosity toward aspiring musicians—his own competitors—was always spontaneous and sincere. Looking back in later years at his work for the NZfM, Schumann called it "the best thing in my life."

130. Only in the review of the *Marienlieder* of Carl Banck (his former colleague and sometime rival for Clara) and possibly in the critique of A. B. Marx's *Moses* did Schumann slip from his usual objectivity.

ORIGINAL TEXTS OF QUOTATIONS

1. GS 1854, *1*, iii: Zu Ende des Jahres 1833 fand sich in Leipzig, all-
abendlich und wie zufällig, eine Anzahl meist jüngerer Musiker zusammen, znächst zu geselliger Versammlung, nicht minder aber auch zum
Austausch der Gedanken über die Kunst, die ihnen Speise und Trank
des Lebens war,—die Musik. Man kann nicht sagen, dass die damaligen
musikalischen Zustände Deutschlands sehr erfreulich waren. Auf der
Bühne herrschte noch Rossini, auf den Klavieren fast ausschliesslich
Herz und Hünten. Und doch waren nur erst wenige Jahre verflossen,
dass Beethoven, C. M. von Weber und Franz Schubert unter uns lebten.
Zwar Mendelssohns Stern war im Aufsteigen und verlauteten von
einem Polen Chopin wunderbare Dinge,—aber eine nachhaltigere
Wirkung äusserten diese erst später. Da fuhr denn eines Tages der
Gedanke durch die jungen Brauseköpfe: lasst uns nicht müssig zuse-
hen, greift an, dass es besser werde, greift an, dass die Poesie der Kunst
wieder zu Ehren komme. So entstanden die ersten Blätter einer neuen
Zeitschrift für Musik. Aber nicht lange währte die Freude festen
Zusammenhaltens dieses Vereins junger Kräfte. Der Tod forderte ein
Opfer in einem der teuersten Genossen, Ludwig Schunke. Von den
andern trennten sich einige zeitweise ganz von Leipzig. Das Unternehmen stand auf dem Punkt, sich aufzulösen. Da entschloss sich
einer von ihnen, gerade der musikalische Phantast der Gesellschaft,
der sein bisheriges Leben mehr am Klavier verträumt hatte als unter
Büchern, die Leitung der Redaktion in die Hand zu nehmen, und
führte sie gegen zehn Jahre lang bis zum Jahre 1844.

2. NZfM, *1* (1834), 297: Ich sehe mich genöthigt, den geehrten
Herren Mitarbeitern und den Beförderern dieser Zeitschrift bekannt zu
machen, dass von dieser Nummer an mit der Redaction eine Verän-
derung eintreten musste. Ein Theil der bisherigen Herren Herausgeber
ist freiwillig, ein anderer durch Umstände von mir dazu veranlasst,
von den Redactions-Functionen zurückgetreten; trotz dieser Verän-
derung aber ist die Fortführung der "neuen musikalischen Zeitschrift"

in sicheren und erfahrenen Händen geblieben, so dass dieses in reger Kunstliebe begonnene Institut mit voller Kraft fortgeführt werden wird. Somit wird der Fortgang desselben durchaus nicht gestört und daher auch im nächsten Jahre regelmässig wöchentlich, wie bisher, zwei Nummern erscheinen.

3. NZfM, *10* (1839), 1: Aber wie oft, wo die Menschen noch so fest zusammenhalten und unzertrennlich scheinen, trennt sie auf einmal das plötzlich hervortretende Schicksal. Selbst der Tod forderte ein Opfer; in Ludwig Schunke starb uns einer der theuersten und feurigsten Genossen. Andere Umstände machten die ersten Bande noch lockerer. Das schöne Gebäude schwankte. Die Redaction kam damals in die Hände eines einzigen, er gesteht es, gegen seinen Lebensplan, der auf Ausbildung eigener Kunstfertigkeit ausging. Aber die Verhältnisse drängten, die Existenz der Zeitschrift stand auf dem Spiele.

4. *Revue et gazette musicale*, 1838, p. 151: Voilà le concert le plus cher de l'anée: personne, depuis Paganini, n'avait osé mettre l'exhibition de son talent à un taux aussi élevé que le jeune et célèbre S. Thalberg. Loin de nous la pensée de lui en faire un reproche! au contraire, nous signalons le fait comme honorable et significative: de toutes les formules d'éloge, nous choisissons la moins banale, la moins équivoque, et nous disons que, bien qu'on payât 20 francs pour entendre le grand pianiste, la foule se pressait, s'entassait dans les salons d'Erard: vous comprenez quelle sorte de foule, la fine fleur, le premier choix, l'aristocratie du dilettantisme! Il y a vraiment plaisir à grossir le chiffre des impôts artistiques avec des gens qui les acquittent si facilement et de si bonne grâce!

5. *Revue et gazette musicale*, 1836, p. 104: "Le public appréciera facilement les motifs qui ont engagé M. Henry Herz à tenter cette *falsification* en mettant sur le titre en gros caractères les *Huguenots* et le nom de M. *Meyerbeer*."

6. NZfM, *1* (1834), 1–2: Diese Zeitschrift liefert:
Theoretische und historische Aufsätze, kunstästhetische, grammatische, pädagogische, biographische, akustische u.a. Nekrologe, Beiträge zur Bildungsgeschichte berühmter Künstler, Berichte über neue Erfindungen oder Verbesserungen, Beurtheilungen ausgezeichneter Virtuosenleistungen, Operndarstellungen; unter der Aufschrift: *Zeitgenossen*, Skizzen mehr oder weniger berühmter Künstler, unter der Rubrik: *Journalschau*, Nachrichten über das Wirken anderer

kritischer Blätter, Bemerkungen über Recensionen in ihnen, Zusammenstellung verschiedener Beurtheilungen über dieselbe Sache, eigne Resultate darüber, auch Antikritiken der Künstler selbst, sodann Auszüge aus ausländischen, Interessantes aus älteren musikalischen Zeitungen.

Belletristisches, kürzere musikalische Erzählungen, Phantasiestücke, Scenen aus dem Leben, Humoristisches, Gedichte, die sich vorzugsweise zur Composition eignen.

Kritiken über Geisteserzeugnisse der Gegenwart mit vorzüglicher Berücksichtigung der Compositionen für das Pianoforte. Auf frühere schätzbare, übergangene oder vergessene Werke wird aufmerksam gemacht, wie auch auf eingesandte Manuscripte talentvoller unbekannter Componisten, die Aufmunterung verdienen. Zu derselben Gattung gehörigen Compositionen werden öfter zusammengestellt, gegen einander verglichen, besonders interessante doppelt beurtheilt. Zur Beurtheilung eingesandte Werke werden durch eine vorläufige Anzeige bekannt gemacht; doch bestimmt nicht das Alter der Einsendung die frühere Besprechung, sondern die Vorzüglichkeit der Leistung.

Miscellen, kurzes Musikbezügliches, Anekdotisches, Kunstbemerkung, literarische Notizen, Musikalisches aus Goethe, Jean Paul, Heinse, Hoffmann, Novalis, Rochlitz u. A. m.

Correspondenzartikel nur dann, wenn sie eigentliches Musikleben abschildern. Wir stehen in Verbindung mit Paris, London, Wien, Berlin, Petersburg, Neapel, Frankfurt, Hamburg, Riga, München, Dresden, Stuttgart, Cassel u. a.—Referirende Artikel fallen in die folgende Abtheilung.

Chronik, Musikaufführungen, Concertanzeigen, Reisen, Aufenthalt der Künstler, Beförderungen, Vorfälle im Leben. Es wird keine Mühe gescheuet, diese Chronik vollständig zu machen, um die Namen der Künstler so oft, wie möglich, in Erinnerung zu bringen.

Noch machen wir vorläufig bekannt, dass, wenn sich die Zeitschrift bald einer allgemeinen Theilnahme erfreuen sollte, der Verleger sich erboten hat, einen Preis auf die beste eingesandte Composition, für's erste auf die vorzüglichste Pianofortesonate, zu setzen, worüber das Nähere seiner Zeit berichtet wird.

Ueber die Stellung, die diese neue Zeitschrift unter den schon erscheinenden einzunehmen gedenkt, werden sich diese ersten Blätter thatsächlich am deutlichsten aussprechen.

Wer den Künstler erforschen will, besuche ihn in seiner Werkstatt. Es schien nothwendig, auch ihm ein Organ zu verschaffen, das ihn anregte, ausser durch seinen directen Einfluss, noch durch Wort und Schrift zu wirken, einen öffentlichen Ort, in dem er das Beste von dem, was er selbst gesehen im eigenen Auge, selbst erfahren im eigenen Geist, niederlegen, eben eine Zeitschrift, in der er sich gegen einseitige oder unwahre Kritik vertheidigen könne, so weit sich das mit Gerechtigkeit und Unparteilichkeit überhaupt verträgt.

Wie sollten die Herausgeber die Vorzüge der bestehenden, höchst achtbaren Organe, die sich ausschliesslich mit musikalischer Literatur beschäftigen, nicht anerkennen wollen. Weit entfernt, die etwaigen Mängel der Unbekanntschaft mit den Forderungen, die jetzt der Künstler an den Kritiker machen darf, oder einem abnehmenden Kunstenthusiasmus zuzuschreiben, finden sie es auf der einen Seite unmöglich, dass das Gebiet der Musik, welches quantitativ sich so ausgedehnt, von einem Einzelnen bis in's Einzelne durchdrungen werden könne, auf der andern natürlich, dass beim Zusammenwirken Mehrer, von welchen sich im Verlauf der Zeit Viele ausscheiden, an deren Stelle Andersgesinnte eintreten, der erste Plan vergessen wird, bis er endlich im Lockern und Allgemeinen vergeht.

Künstler sind wir denn und Kunstfreunde, jüngere, wie ältere, die wir durch jahrelanges Beisammenleben mit einander vertraut und im Wesentlichen derselben Ansicht zugethan, uns zur Herausgabe dieser Blätter verbunden. Ganz durchdrungen von der Bedeutung unsers Vorhabens legen wir mit Freude und Eifer Hand an das neue Werk, ja mit dem Stolz der Hoffnung, dass es als im reinen Sinn und im Interesse der Kunst von Männern begonnen, deren Lebensberuf sie ist, günstig aufgenommen werde. Alle aber, die es wohl meinen mit der schönen Kunst der Phantasie, bitten wir, das junge Unternehmen mit Rath und That wohlwollend zu fördern und zu schützen.—

Die Herausgeber

7. NZfM, 1 (1834), 183: Aus dem Allen erhellt, dass die Kritik dieses Blatts das Zugeständniss des Geistreichen, Genialen, so wie den offnen Kampf gegen das Mittelmässige, Talentlose mit gleicher Vorsicht umgeht. Ihre Tendenz ist die höchste Toleranz, gleichweit entfernt vom Lob der Begeisterung und vom Tadel der Verwerfung; ihr Wahlspruch: leben und leben lassen.

8. NZfM, 1 (1834), 231: Nun erlaube uns Hr. Fétis eine Frage. Steht die Musik in Frankreich wirklich auf der hohen Stufe, dass eine

Kritik des Neuen, Guten wie Schlechten gar nicht nöthig ist? Der Schlechtunterrichtete müsste das glauben, wenn er im ganzen Halbjahrgang der *Revue* blos vier Sachen recensirt findet.

9. NZfM, *1* (1834), 193: Wie? Rellstab machte es zu arg?—Soll denn diese verdammte, deutsche Höflichkeit Jahrhunderte fortdauern? Während die literarischen Parteien sich offen gegenüber stehen und befehden, herrscht in der Kunstkritik ein Achselzucken, ein Zurückhalten, das weder begriffen, noch genug getadelt werden kann. Warum die Talentlosen nicht geradezu zurückweisen? Warum die Flachen und Halbgesunden nicht aus den Schranken werfen sammt den Anmassenden? Warum nicht Warnungstafeln vor Werken, die da aufhören, wo die Kritik anfängt? Warum schreiben die Autoren nicht eine eigne Zeitung gegen die Kritiker und fordern sie auf, gröber zu sein gegen die Werke?

10. *Iris im Gebiete der Tonkunst,* *5* (1834), 91: Wir haben oft geklagt, dass die jungen Componisten der neueren Zeit keine eigentlichen Lehrer der Compositionen hätten, kaum einen des Generalbasses, und sie daher ohne Führung und Studium wild darauf los componirten. Wir dachten was schon daraus für ein Unheil entstünde. Allein es kommt noch ganz anders. Jetzt haben sie nicht nur keine Unterweisung im Guten, sondern förmliche Unterweisung im Schlechten und aus der Verkehrtheit wird ein Studium gemacht. Offenbar haben Chopins neueste Compositionen diesem jüngern Talent zum Vor- oder Irrbilde gedient. . . .

Also dahin geht die Tendenz, etwas zu erzielen was auf dem Instrument unerhört ist, sei es noch so trivial und verbraucht im musikalischen Gedanken. Leider sehen wir, dass sich eine ganze Schule für Irrungen bildet, wie wir jüngst an Chopin, dann an Schumann, und andern, und jetzt auch an diesem jungen Componisten wahrnehmen konnten.

11. NZfM, *8* (1838), 28: Und darauf stützt Hr. Rellstab eine so verletzende Aeusserung, und das gagen ein mit Opfern erhaltenes Institut, das seine ganze Ehre gerade in seine bewiesene Unparteilichkeit, seine treu bewahrte Künstlergesinnung setzt, und gegen Künstler, die für die Verläugnung ihrer Interessen, ihre Liebe zur Sache nicht einmal die Genugthuung hatten, ihre Leistungen besprochen zu haben, ja freiwillig darauf verzichteten! Entscheide denn hier das Publicum!

12. AmZ, *34* (1832), 1–3: Es gibt zwei Arten Componisten, die

sich einander gegenüber stehen. Die Ersten sind die Modemänner, die da fragen: "Gefällt euch das Polonaischen?" und die anderen stehen da wie gerüstete Leute und wollen solid seyn. Der ersten sind viele, der anderen wenige. Die ersten treiben auf voller, breiter Strasse: die anderen suchen die enge Pforte. Die ersten klopft das Gedränge freundlich auf die Schulter und die anderen lässt man laufen. Beides ist natürlich, kann nicht anders seyn und ist nie anders gewesen . . . Es geschiet also beyden Künstlergattungen nicht das kleinste Unrecht.

13. AmZ, 34 (1832), 580: Bey Erwähnung wahrhaft schöner Pianoforte-Compositionen können wir nicht umhin, zugleich des in sehr schöner Ausgabe erschienenen Rondo's zu gedenken. Es ist klein, es zählt 9 Seiten: aber es ist schön. Es hat äusserst Nettes und stark Pikantes. Es sieht sich an, als spiele es sich leicht: es ist auch nicht eigentlich schwer: allein das Staccato! die Schattirungen! sie erfordern doch ihre Spieler! Dann erhält es aber auch Werth und wird für gesellige Zirkel sich ganz besonders angenehm machen.

14. NZfM, 4 (1836), 208–9: Ueber das erste Rondo würde man sich im Hausbackenthum der mus. Kritik so ausdrücken: "Das nicht leichte Rondo geht aus As-dur und ist über ein Thema des vielbeliebten, vielschreibenden Auber gearbeitet. Wenn nun dem (muthmasslich noch jungen) Componisten eine Kenntniss moderner, brillanter Passagen nicht abzusprechen ist, so u.s.f.—Das Werkchen wird sich bei einer gewissen Classe von Pftespielern Freunde erwerben u.s.w.— Die Druckfehler sind nicht bedeutend." Gestehe ich nur, dass mir viele schlechte Rezensionen vorgekommen sind,—eine talentlose Ohnmacht aber, eine trostlosere Nullität, eine gar nicht zu sagende Schlechtigkeit einer Composition noch nie. Hiergegen verschwindet Alles, was je in kurzen Anzeigen angezeigt worden ist, ja aller anspielende Witz auf Säge, Zimmermannsarbeit und derg. Zwischen zwei Bretern eingeklemmt, steht man am Ende der Welt und kann weder vor noch zurück. Zum Fenster hinaus!

15. AmZ, 33 (1831), 805: Wir geben hier einmal über ein Werk zwey Beurtheilungen; die erste von einem jungen Manne, einem Zöglinge der Neusten Zeit, der sich genannt hat; die andere von einem angesehenen und würdigen Repräsentanten der ältern Schule, der sich nicht genannt hat: allein, wir versichern und haben es kaum nöthig, von einem durchaus tüchtigen, vollgeübt und umsichtig kenntnissreichen.

16. AmZ, *34* (1832), 339: Eines ungereimten Vorfalls wegen, den wir aus Schonung gegen den Urheber unberührt lassen wollen, sehen wir uns genöthigt, nochmals zu erinnern: Keine Recension kann angenommen werden, die nicht im Voraus dem Verfasser von der Redaction zugestanden worden ist. Unordnungen und Misshelligkeiten unnützer Art gingen ja sonst in's Weite. Erfahrene wissen das, billig Denkende nehmen gern Rücksicht, und die Uebrigen werden sich und uns nicht umsonst bemühen wollen.

17. AmZ, *36* (1834), 180: Bündler rechts, Bündler links; Figaro hier, Figaro da! Da hätten wir dennoch einen Vorschlag zur Güte, den wir lieber gleich mit abdrucken liessen, zu Gunsten aller der Seelen, unglücklicher Weise in diesen Blättern nicht genug gelobt worden sind, nämlich nach ihrer eigenen hochweisen Taxe ihres ausserordentlichen Weltwerthes, der nicht leicht mit Worten aller Sprachen gehörig anzudeuten, wie viel weniger auszusprechen ist. Zur rechten Zeit wird sich schon ein Plätzchen und ein aufrichtiges Wort dafür finden.

18. AmZ, *42* (1840), 298: Die Karnevalszenen von R. Schumann machten ungeachtet des vortrefflichen Spiels des Herrn Liszt nicht die Wirkung, die man von ihnen erwartet hatte; es lag dies wohl mit an der grossen Länge, und es wäre gewiss vortheilhafter gewesen, eine beschränktere Auswahl dieser Szenen zu treffen, statt so viele derselben (10) auf einmal und unmittelbar hinter einander folgend vorzutragen.

19. NZfM, *16* (1842) 8: Hr. Dr. Fink, der sonst immer leise auftritt, nimmt einen ziemlich polternden Abschied von der Redaction der Allgem. mus. Zeitung. Man lese ihn. Er spricht auch von Feinden, die er sich "verdient," und zielt deutlich auf diese Blätter. Er irrt. Wir haben uns nie viel um ihn gekümmert und werden's auch künftig nicht.

20. AmZ, *1* (1798), Intelligenz-Blatt no. 1:
a) Es werden nur die wichtigsten und vortrefflichsten musikalischen Produkte auführlich durchgegangen; wobey gezeigt wird, nicht nur dass sie vortrefflich sind, sondern auch warum sie es sind.
b) Nicht schlechte, aber doch auch nicht ausgezeichnete gute Kompositionen werden kurz angezeigt, ihr Eigenthümliches angegeben, und ihr Publikum bestimmt: damit die Liebhaber nicht, wie so

oft, genöthigt sind Musikalien zu kaufen, die wenn sie auch an sich gut, doch für sie nicht sind.

c) Unbeträchtliche und schlechte Kompositionen werden blos im Intelligenz-Blatte, als existirend, angezeigt.

21. NZfM, 6 (1837), 6: der Grundsatz Anderer, nur das anzuzeigen, was eingesandt wird, durchaus nicht der unsrige ist, wir uns im Gegentheil das Bemerkenswertheste, was der Hofmeister'sche Monatsbericht angiebt, anzeichnen und zu verschaffen suchen. Sodann tritt aber durch eine solche Zusammenstellung das Werthvollere schärfer hervor und erhält das grössere räumliche Verhältniss, das ihm vor dem minder Guten gebührt.

22. NZfM, 18 (1843), 27: War es doch in seinem Hause, wo die Namen Mozart, Haydn, Beethoven zu den täglich mit Begeisterung genannten gehörten, in seinem Hause, wo die sonst in kleinen Städten gar nicht zu hörenden selteneren Werke dieser Meister, vorzugsweise Quartette, mir zuerst bekannt wurden, wo ich oft selbst am Clavier mitwirken durfte.

23. NZfM, 1 (1834), 152: Da wir leider mit den Gründen unsrer Verschleierung noch zurückhalten müssen, so ersuchen wir Herrn Schumann (sollte dieser einer verehrlichen Redaction bekannt sein) uns in Fällen mit seinem Namen vertreten zu wollen.

-Die Davidsbündler

Ich thu's mit Freuden.

-R. Schumann

24. NZfM, 1 (1834), 73–75; Der erfahrene reflectirende Meister schreibt andere Studien als der junge, phantasirende. Jener kennt die Kräfte, die er zu bilden hat, Anfang und Ende ihrer Mittel und Zwecke, zieht sich seine Kreise und überschreitet die Linie nicht. Dieser setzt Stück auf Stück, wirft Felsen über Felsen, bis er selbst nur mit Lebensgefahr über den Herkulesbau kommen kann. . . .

Bei der Blitzesschnelle der Entwicklung der Musik zur höhern poetischen Freiheit, wie keine andere Kunst ein Beispiel aufstellen kann, muss es wohl vorkommen, dass selbst das Bessere selten länger als vielleicht ein Jahrzehend im Munde der Mitwelt lebt. Dass viele der jungen Geister so undankbar vergessen und nicht bedenken, wie sie nur eine Höhe anbauen, zu der sie gar nicht den Grund gelegt, ist eine Erfahrung der Intoleranz, die jede Epoche der jüngeren gemacht hat und künftig machen wird. . . .

Schönes Eusebiusgemüth, Du machst mich wahrhaftig zum Lachen. Und wenn Ihr alle Eure Uhrenzeiger zurückstellt, die Sonne wird nach wie vor aufgehen.

So verdammt hoch ich Deine Gesinnung schätze, jeder Erscheinung ihre Stelle anzuweisen, so halt' ich Dich doch für einen verkappten Romantiker—nur noch mit etlicher Namensscheu, welche die Zeit wegspülen wird.

Wahrlich, Bester, ging's nach dem Sinn Gewisser, so kämen wir ja bald an jene goldnen Zeiten, wo's Ohrfeigen gab, wenn man den Daumen auf eine Obertaste setzte.

Auf die Falschheit einzelner Deiner Schwärmereien lass' ich mich gar nicht ein, sondern gehe geradezu auf's Werk selbst los.

Methode, Schulmanier bringen wohl rascher vorwärts, aber einseitig, kleinlich. Ach! wie versündigt Ihr Euch, Lehrer! Mit Eurem Logierwesen zieht Ihr die Knospen gewaltsam aus der Scheide! Wie Falkeniere rupft Ihr Euren Schülern die Federn aus, damit sie nicht zu hoch fliegen—Wegweiser solltet Ihr sein, die Ihr die Strasse wohl anzeigen, aber nicht überall selbst mitlaufen sollt! (Ich kann vor Gedanken gar nicht auf die eigentlichen kommen.) . . .

Wer dürfte läugnen, dass die meisten dieser Studien musterhaft angelegt und vollendet wären, dass in jeder eine reine Gesinnung ausgeprägt ist, dass endlich alle in jener Meisterbehaglichkeit entsprungen sind, welche eine lange, weiseverlebte Zeit gibt?—Aber das, wodurch wir die Jugend anreizen, dass sie über die Schönheit des Werkes die Mühsamkeit es sich eigen zu machen, vergesse, fehlt durchgängig—*das Neue der Phantasie*. . . . so nenn' ich die Phantasie, die Seherin mit dem verbundenen Auge, der nichts verschlossen ist und die in ihren Irrthümern oft am reizendsten erscheint.—Was sagt Ihr aber, Meister?

Jünglinge, Ihr irrt beide—nur Du schöner, Eusebius! Ein würdiger Name hat den einen befangen, den andern trotzig gemacht. Was steht doch im westöstlichen Divan?

> Als wenn das auf Namen ruhte,
> Was sich schweigend nur gestaltet—[sic]
> Lieb' ich doch das schöne Gute,
> Wie es sich aus Gott gestaltet.

25. NZfM, 3 (1835), 152: Lachen (so fing Florestan an und zugleich den Anfang der A-Dur-Symphonie) lachen musst' ich über

einen dürren Actuarius, der in ihr eine Gigantenschlacht fand, im
letzten Satze deren effective Vernichtung, am Allegretto aber leise
vorbei schlich, weil es nicht passte in die Idee . . . Am meisten jedoch
zuckt es mir in den Fingerspitzen, wenn Einige behaupten, Beethoven
habe sich in seinen Symphonieen stets den grössten Sentiments hingegeben, den höchsten Gedanken über Gott, Unsterblichkeit und Ster-
nenlauf, während der genialische Mensch allerdings mit der Blü-
thenkrone nach dem Himmel zeigt, die Wurzeln jedoch in seiner
geliebten Erde ausbreitet. Um auf die Symphonie zu kommen, so ist
die Idee gar nicht von mir, sondern von Jemandem in einem alten
Hefte der Cäcilia (aus vielleicht zu grosser Delicatesse gegen Beethoven, die zu ersparen gewesen) in einen feinen gräflichen Saal oder so
etwas versetzt. . . . es ist die lustigste Hochzeit, die Braut aber ein
himmlisch Kind mit einer Rose im Haar, aber nur mit einer. Ich
müsste mich irren, wenn nicht in der Einleitung die Gäste zusammen
kämen, sich sehr begrüssten mit Rückenkommas, sehr irren, wenn
nicht lustige Flöten daran erinnerten, dass im ganzen Dorfe voll
Maienbäumen mit zitterndem Blicke wie zu fragen schiene: "weisst du
auch, dass wir uns trennen müssen?" und wie ihr dann Rosa ganz
überwältigt in die Arme stürzt, mit der andern Hand die des
Jünglinges nachziehend . . . Nun wird's aber sehr still im Dorfe
draussen (Florestan kam hier in das Allegretto und brach hier und da
Stücke heraus), nur ein Schmetterling fliegt einmal durch oder eine
Kirschenblüthe fällt herunter. . . . Die Orgel fängt an; die Sonne
steht hoch, einzelne langschiefe Strahlen spielen mit Stäubchen durch
die Kirche, die Glocken läuten sehr—Kirchgänger stellen sich nach und
nach ein—Stüle werden auf- und zugeklappt—einzelne Bauern
sehen sehr scharf in's Gesangbuch, andre an die Emporkirchen hin-
auf—der Zug rückt näher—Chorknaben mit brennenden Kerzen
und Weihkessel voran, dann Freunde, die sich oft umsehen nach dem
Paare, das der Priester begleitet, die Eltern, Freundinnen und hin-
terher die ganze Dorfjugend. Wie sich nun Alles ordnet and der
Priester an's [sic] Altar steigt und jetzt zur Braut und jetzt zum
Glücklichsten redet und wie er ihnen vorspricht von den heiligen
Pflichten des Bundes und dessen Zwecken und wie die ihr Glück finden
möchten in herzinniger Eintracht und Liebe, und wie er sie dann fragt
nach dem "Ja," das so viel nimmt für ewige Zeiten und sie es aus-
spricht fest und lang—lasst es mich nicht fortmalen das Bild und thut's

im Finale nach eurer Weise . . . brach Florestan ab und riss in den Schluss des Allegrettos und das klang, als würfe der Küster die Thüre zu, dass es durch die ganze Kirche schallte.

26. NZfM, *1* (1834) 151: Warum rümpft ihr bei Aphoristischem so vornehm die Nase, lange Philister!—bei Gott, ist denn die Welt eine Fläche? und sind nicht Alpen darauf, Ströme und verschiedene Menschen? und ist denn das Leben ein System? und ist es nicht aus einzelnen halb zerrissenen Blättern zusammengeheftet, voll von weissen Censurlücken des Schicksals? Ich behaupte das letztere—ja es dürfte gar nicht ohne Interesse sein, das Leben in der Kunst so abzuschatten, wie es liebt und lebt, wie ja schon ähnlich Platner und Jacobi ganz philosophische Systeme gaben.

27. NZfM, *2* (1835), 42: Man hat den Herausgebern dieser Blätter den Vorwurf gemacht, dass sie die poetische Seite der Musik zum Schaden der wissenschaftlichen bearbeiten und ausbauen, dass sie junge Phantasten wären, die nicht einmal wüssten, dass man von äthiopischer und andrer Musik im Grund nicht viel wisse u. dgl. Dieser Tadel enthält eben das, wodurch wir unser Blatt von andern unterschieden wissen möchten. Wir wollen weiter nicht untersuchen, in wie fern durch die eine oder die andre Art die Kunst schneller gefördert werde, aber allerdings gestehen, dass wir die für die höchste Kritik halten, die durch sich selbst einen Eindruck hinterlässt, dem gleich, den das anregende Original hervorbringt. . . . In diesem Sinn könnte Jean Paul zum Verständniss einer Beethoven'schen Symphonie oder Phantasie durch ein poetisches Gegenstück möglich mehr beitragen (selbst ohne nur von der Phantasie oder Symphonie zu reden), als die Dutzend Kunstrichtler, die Leitern an den Koloss legen und ihn gut nach Ellen messen.

28. NZfM, *10* (1839), 187: Ein Leichtes wär' es mir die Ouverture zu schildern, sei's auf poetische Weise durch Abdruck der Bilder, die sie in mir mannichfaltig angeregt, sei's durch Zergliederung des Mechanismus im Werke. Beide Arten, Musik zu verdeutlichen, haben etwas, die erste wenigstens den Mangel an Trockenheit für sich, in die die Zweite wohl oder übel fällt.

29. *Damenkonversationslexikon,* 1, 149: Allemande, ursprünglich ein fröhlicher Tanz, aus Schwaben stammend, der nun ziemlich verschwunden ist. In früher Zeit theilte eine besondere Gattung

von kürzeren Musikstücken diesen Namen. An ihre Stelle, wie an die der Giguen, Sarabanden und anderen, sind jetzt die Scherzi, Capricci, Bagatelles, u.a., getreten.

30. NZfM, 6, (1837), 40: In der Zeit, wo sich alle Blicke auf einen der grössten Schöpfer aller Zeiten, J. Seb. Bach, mit verdoppelter Schärfe richten, mag es sich wohl schicken, auch auf dessen Zeitgenossen aufmerksam zu machen. Kann sich freilich, was Orgel- und Claviercomposition anlangt, Niemand seines Jahrhunderts mit ihm messen, ja will mir Alles andere, gegen seine ausgebildeten Riesengestalten gehalten, wie noch in der Kindheit begriffen erscheinen, so bieten einzelne Stimmen jener Zeit ihrer Gemütlichkeit wegen noch Interessantes genug dar, als dass man sie ganz überhören dürfte.

31. NZfM, 10 (1839), 153: Scarlatti hat viel Ausgezeichnetes, was ihn vor seinen Zeitgenossen kenntlich macht. Die so zu sagen geharnischte Ordnung Bach'schen Ideenganges ist in ihm nicht zu finden; er ist bei weitem gehaltloser, flüchtiger, rhapsodischer; man hat zu thun, ihm immer zu folgen, so schnell verwebt und löst er die Fäden; sein Styl ist im Verhältniss seiner Zeit kurz, gefällig und, pikant . . . so wollen wir uns nur gestehen, das uns auch vieles daran nicht mehr behagen kann, und nicht mehr behagen soll. Wie könnte sich ein solches Tonstück mit dem eines unserer besseren Componisten nur messen können . . . Nun gar im Vergleich zu Bach! Es ist, wie ein geistreicher Componist schon bei einer Vergleichung zwischen Emanuel und Sebastian Bach sagte: "als wenn ein Zwerg unter die Riesen käme."

32. NZfM, 8, (1838), 22: Czerny's Verdienst besteht also in einem Vorwort, in der Angabe des Fingersatzes, der Tempobezeichnung nach Mälz [sic], und Andeutungen über Charakter und Vortrag. Ersteres ist etwas kurz ausgefallen und flüchtig niedergeschrieben. An dies Werk aller Clavierwerke liessen sich wohl allerhand reiche Gedanken knüpfen . . . Die meisten der Bachschen Fugen sind aber Charakterstücke höchster Art, zum Theil wahrhaft poetische Gebilde, deren jedes seinen eigenen Ausdruck, seine besonderen Lichter und Schatten verlangt.

33. *Damenkonversationslexikon, 1*, 400: Wie gross und reich stach sein inneres Leben gegen das äussere ab! Nicht allein Fleiss war es, der ihn hinaushob über alle Schwierigkeiten der Musikalischen Kombinationen, sondern angestammtes Genie des Scharfsinnes. Was wir

Nachkömmlinge für Wunderbares in der Verflechtung der Töne gefunden zu haben meinen, liegt schon in ihm angesponnen und oft ausgewickelt. Zu dieser vollkommenen Beherrschung des Physischen kommt nun auch der Gedanke, der Geist, der seinen Werken innewohnt. Dieser war durch und durch Mann. Daher finden wir in ihm nichts Halbes, sondern alles ganz, für ewige Zeiten geschrieben.

34. NZfM, 6 (1837), 40: Die neuen Ausrufer alter Musik versehen es meistens darin, dass sie gerade das vorsuchen, worin unsre Vordern allerdings stark waren, was aber auch oft mit jedem andern Namen, als mit dem der "Musik" belegt werden muss, d.h. in allen Compositions-Gattungen, die in die Fuge und den Canon gehören, und schaden sich und der guten Sache, wenn sie die innigeren, phantastischeren, und musikalischeren Erzeugnisse jener Zeit als unbedeutender hintansetzen.

35. NZfM, 7 (1837), 120: Aber auch der alten Zeit soll gedacht werden. Namentlich liegt uns an Verbreitung vieler noch ungedruckter Compositionen von J. S. Bach, deren sich bereits einige der herrlichsten in unserm Besitz befinden.

36. NZfM, 1 (1834), 73: Ruhe, Grazie, Idealität, Objectivität, die Träger der antiken Kunstwerke, sind die der Mozart'schen Schule. Wie der menschliche Grieche seinen donnernden Jupiter noch mit heiterm Gesicht zeichnete, so hält Mozart seine Blitze.

37. NZfM, 2 (1835), 5: Einen Zug der Beethoven'schen Romantik, den man den provencalischen nennen könnte, bildete Franz Schubert im eigensten Geist zur Virtuosität aus. Auf dieser Basis stützt sich, ob bewusst oder unbewusst, eine neue noch nicht völlig entwickelte und anerkannte Schule.

38. NZfM, 7 (1837), 70: Nimmt man von der Musik einen romantischen und classischen Charakter an, so war Prinz Louis der Romantiker der classischen Periode, während Henselt der Classiker einer romantischen Zeit ist.

39. NZfM, 19 (1843), 34–35: Man weiss, dass in den Jahren 1830–34 sich eine Reaction gegen den herrschenden Geschmack erhob. Der Kampf war im Grunde nicht schwer; er war gegen das Floskelwesen, das sich, Ausnahmen wie Weber, Löwe u. A. zugegeben, fast in allen Gattungen, am meisten in der Claviermusik zeigte.

40. NZfM, 2 (1835), 3: Unsere Gesinnung war vorweg festgestellt.

Sie ist einfach, und diese: die alte Zeit und ihre Werke anzuerkennen,
darauf aufmerksam zu machen, wie nur an so reinem Quelle neue
Kunst-schönheiten gekräftigt werden können—sodann, die letzte Ver-
gangenheit als eine unkünstlerische zu bekämpfen, für die nur das
Hochgesteigerte des Mechanischen einigen Ersatz gewährt habe—
endlich eine junge, dichterische Zukunft vorzubereiten, beschleunigen zu helfen.

41. NZfM, *10* (1839), 131–32: Wo stecken die Teufelsromantiker?
Der alte gute M. D. Mosevius in Breslau erklärt sich plötzlich als
ihren entschiedensten Gegner; auch die Allg. musik. Zeitung wittert
deren immer. Wo stecken sie aber nur? Sind es vielleicht Mendelssohn,
Chopin, Bennett, Hiller, Henselt, Taubert? Was haben die alten Herren gegen diese einzuwenden? Gelten ihnen Wanhal, Pleyel, oder Herz
und Hünten mehr? Hat man aber jene und andere nicht gemeint, so
drücke man sich doch deutlicher aus . . . Man höre doch auf, alles
durcheinander zu mengen, und wegen dessen, was in den Compositionen der deutsch-französischen Schule, wie in Berlioz, Liszt etc.
tadelnswerth erscheinen mag, das Streben der jüngern deutschen Componisten zu verdächtigen. Behagt euch aber auch dieses nicht, so gebt
uns doch selbst Werke, ihr alten Herren—Werke, Werke!

42. AmZ, *37* (1835), 100: Die sogenannte *romantische* Schule, die
man auch die *phantastische* von ihren Anhängern benannt findet, hat
eine Schwester erhalten. Italienische Blätter nennen jetzt die Rossini'sche Schule die romantische im Gegensatze der klassischen oder
altitalienischen. Ob wohl die neuesten Romantiker Teutschlands und
vornehmlich Frankreichs die italienische Namensschwester anerkennen
werden?

43. NZfM, *10* (1839), 187: Dazu nun schrieb Berlioz eine Musik.
Man wird fragen, zu welchem Capitel, welcher Scene, weshalb, zu
welchem Zweck? Denn Kritiker wollen immer gern wissen, was ihnen
die Componisten selbst nicht sagen können, und Kritiker verstehen
oft kaum den zehnten Theil von dem was sie besprechen.

44. NZfM, *2* (1835), 65: Beethoven hat gar wohl die Gefahr
gekannt, die er bei der Pastoral-Symphonie lief. In den paar Worten,
"mehr Ausdruck der Empfindung als Malerei," die er ihr voransetzte,
liegt eine ganze Aesthetik für Componisten und es ist sehr lächerlich,
wenn ihn Maler auf Portraits an einem Bache sitzen, den Kopf in die
Hand drücken und das Plätschern belauschen lassen.

45. NZfM, 3 (1835), 50: Man irrt sich gewiss, wenn man glaubt, die Componisten legten sich Feder und Papier in der elenden Absicht zurecht, dies oder jenes auszudrücken, zu schildern, zu malen.

46. NZfM, 18 (1843), 140: Gewiss sie irren, wenn sie glauben, ein Componist, der nach einer Idee arbeite, setze sich hin wie ein Prediger am Sonnabend-Nachmittag und schematisire sein Thema nach den gewöhnlichen drei Theilen, und arbeite es überhaupt gehörig aus; gewiss, sie irren.

47. NZfM, 8 (1838), 201: Man hat diese Ueberschriften über Musikstücke, die sich in neuerer Zeit wieder vielfach zeigen, hier und da getadelt, und gesagt "eine gute Musik bedürfe solcher Fingerzeige nicht." Gewiss nicht: aber sie büsst dadurch eben so wenig etwas von ihrem Werth ein, und der Componist beugt dadurch offenbarem Vergreifen des Charakters am sichersten vor.

48. NZfM, 1 (1834), 10: die weniger gebildeten Menschen im Ganzen geneigt, aus der Musik ohne Text nur Schmerz oder nur Freude, oder (was mitten inne liegt) Wehmuth herauszuhören, die feineren Schattirungen der Leidenschaft aber, als in jenem den Zorn, die Reue, in dieser das Gemächliche, das Wohlbehagen etc. zu finden nicht im Stande sind, daher ihnen auch das Verständniss von Meistern, wie Beethoven, Franz Schubert, die jeden Lebenszustand in die Tonsprache übersetzen konnten, so schwer wird.

49. NZfM, 12 (1840), 82: Ich will nicht versuchen, der Symphonie eine Folie zugeben, die verschiedenen Lebensalter wählen zu verschieden in ihren Text- und Bilderunterlagen, und der 18-jährige Jüngling hört oft eine Weltbegebenheit aus einer Musik heraus, wo der Mann nur ein Landesereignis sieht, während der Musiker weder an das Eine, noch an das Andere gedacht hat.

50. NZfM, 3 (1835), 50: Jedenfalls hätten die fünf Hauptüberschriften genügt; die genaueren Umstände, die allerdings der Person des Componisten halber, der die Symphonie selbst durchlebt, interessiren müssen, würden sich schon durch mündliche Tradition fortgepflanzt haben.

51. NZfM, 11 (1840), 186: Denn so fein wühlt die Phantasie des Musikers, dass einmal die Spur verloren oder von der Zeit zugeschüttet, sie später nur durch glücklichen Zufall in seltenem Augenblick wieder aufgefunden wird; darum wird auch ein unterbrochenes,

bei Seite gelegtes Werk nur selten ein fertiges; lieber fange der Componist ein neues an, entschlag sich der Stimmung ganz.

52. NZfM, 3 (1835), 158: Beethoven singt in seiner Pastoralsymphonie so leichte Themas, wie sie irgend ein kindlicher Sinn erfinden kann; sicher aber schrieb er nicht alles auf, was ihm die erste Begeisterung eingab, sondern wählte unter Vielem.

53. NZfM, 4 (1834), 71–72: Ueberall aber wünschten wir noch mehr Sichtung, Wahl und Verfeinerung. Der erste Entwurf des Ganzen bleibt allerdings immer der glücklichste; wodurch sich aber das Talent Achtung und seinem Werke Dauer verschaffen kann, das Detail, muss oft gemodelt und durchfeilt werden, damit das Interesse, was die Conception des grossen Ganzen nicht gibt, dadurch wach gehalten werde. Dahin rechnen wir Eleganz der Passagen, Reiz des Accompagnments zu Gesangstellen, Colorit in den Mittelstimmen, Ausarbeitung und Verarbeitung der Themen, Gegeneinanderstellung und Verbindung verschiedener Gedanken.

54. NZfM, 10 (1839), 74: Soll der Künstler erst Alles an sich selbst durchmachen und versuchen, und kommt er nicht schneller zum Ziel, wenn er das vorhandene Beste studirt, nachbildet, bis er sich Form und Geist unterthan gemacht? Aber auch die Meister der Gegenwart muss er kennen, vom ersten bis zum letzten, also auch z. B. Strauss, als in seiner Weise einen höchsten Ausdruck seiner Zeit.

55. NZfM, 1 (1834), 22: Exercicen, Studien für das Pianoforte, deren es seit des grossen Meisters Bach Compositionen in dieser Art unzählige gibt, üben einen ungleich grössern Einfluss auf die Behandlung des Instruments aus, als alle anderen Musikstücke . . . Mit Vergnügen zeigen wir an, dass ein geschätzter Mitarbeiter im Sammeln von Materialien zu einer "verständigen Uebersicht und Kritik aller seit J. S. Bach erschienenen Clavier- und Pianoforte-Studien" begriffen ist.

56. NZfM, 4 (1836), 16: Im weitesten Sinne ist jedes Musikstück eine Etude und das leichteste oft die schwerste. Im engen müssen wir aber an eine Studie die Forderung stellen, dass sie etwas Besonderes bezwecke, eine Fertigkeit fördere, zur Besiegung einer einzelnen Schwierigkeit führe, liege diese in der Technik, Rhythmik, im Ausdruck, Vortrage u.s.w.; finden sich untermischte Schwierigkeiten, so gehört sie dem Genre der Caprice an.

57. NZfM, 8 (1838), 170: Merkwürdig an ihnen erscheint das Auflehnen gegen die enge Form, daher sie sich oft in das Gebiet der phantastischeren Caprice verlieren und nur missmuthig wieder in das Gleis einlenken. Etwas Aehnliches bemerkten wir schon bei dem früheren Hefte; doch geschah es dort nicht mit Aufopferung der schönen Form, die wir einmal von der Etude fordern müssen, und auch nicht mit Hintenansetzung eines klar ausgeprägten mechanischen Zweckes, wie wir ebenfalls von dieser Compositionsgattung verlangen dürfen.

58. NZfM, 4 (1836), 45: Wie viel Clementi und Cramer aus ihm schöpften, wird Niemand in Abrede stellen. Von da bis Moscheles trat eine Pause ein. Vielleicht dass es der Einfluss Beethovens war, der allem Mechanischen feind, mehr zum reinpoetischen Schaffen aufforderte. In Moscheles und noch in höherem Grad in Chopin waltet daher neben dem technischen Interesse auch das phantastische. Hinter diesen Fünf, die am grössten hervorragen, stehen am originellsten L. Berger und C. Weyse. Ries und Hummel haben ihren eigentlichen Styl klarer in freien Compositionen niedergelegt, als gerade in Etuden. Als solid und tüchtig müssen Grund und Kessler genannt werden, auch A. Schmitt, dessen liebliche Klarheit jungen Herzen wohltun muss. Kalkbrenner, Czerny und Herz lieferten keine Riesenwerke, aber Schätzenswerthes wegen ihrer Instrumentkenntniss. Potter und Hiller dürfen ihres romantischen Geistes wegen nicht übergangen werden, auch die zarte Szymanowska nicht und der liebenswürdige C. Mayer. Bertini täuscht, aber anmuthig. Wer Schwierigstes will, findet sie in den Paganini-Etuden des Unterzeichneten.

59. NZfM, 4 (1836), 25: In der ersten ist eine Figur durchgeführt, die Finger der rechten Hand, namentlich die schwächern zu stärken. Ein Zug, der dem Componisten beinahe Manier geworden, zeichnet diese Etude wie ziemlich alle andern aus, dass nämlich nach dem Ende hin gewöhnlich ein neuer melodischer Gedanke auftritt, wodurch die eigentliche Uebung wie etwas zurückgedrängt scheint, ohne jedoch ganz still zu stehen; es gefällt uns diese Weise ausnehmend.

60. NZfM, 4 (1836), 25: Sanft und eben, ohne besondere Auszeichnung. Das Pedal heben wir erst zu Ende des Tactes auf, da die Vorhalte durch die vielen Hauptaccordnoten doch im Augenblicke zum Schweigen gebracht werden. In Bachs Exercices Heft 1, Nr. 2 steht eine ganz ähnliche Etude.

61. NZfM, *11* (1839), 186: Hut ab vor dem ersten Satz; er gilt mir die ganze Sonate; in ihm ist Weihe, Schwung und Phantasie; die andern stehen zurück. Es gibt eine ähnlich geformte Sonate von Beethoven, eine der wundervollsten, wo dem kühn leidenschaftlichen ersten Satz (in E-moll) ein einfacher arioser (in E-dur) nachfolgt und damit schliesst.

62. NZfM, *11* (1839), 186–87: Wollt' ich grübeln, so wäre es gegen die Melodie des übrigens äusserst belebend eintretenden Zwei-vierteltactes, wo ich im 3ten Tact statt des b der syncopirten Melodie lieber das fliessende a wünschte; mein a gefällt mir weit besser, so geringfügig die Aenderung scheint.

63. NZfM, *10* (1839), 134: Es ist lange her, dass wir über die Leistungen im Sonatenfach geschwiegen. Von ausserordentlichen haben wir auch heute nicht zu berichten. Immerhin erfreut es, im bunten Gewirr der Mode- und Zerrbilder auch einmal einigen jener ehrenvesten Gesichte zu begegnen wie sie, sonst an der Tagesordnung, jetzt zu den Ausnahmen gehören. Sonderbar, dass es, einmal, meist Unbekanntere sind, die Sonaten schreiben: sodann, dass gerade die älteren, noch unter uns lebenden Componisten, die in der Sonatenblüthezeit aufgewachsen, und von denen als die bedeutendsten freilich nur Cramer und dann Moscheles zu nennen wären, diese Gattung am wenigsten gepflegt. Was die Ersteren, meist junge Künstler, zum Schreiben anregt, ist leicht zu errathen; es gibt keine würdigere Form, durch die sie sich bei der höheren Kritik einführen und gefällig machen könnten; die meisten Sonaten dieser Art sind daher auch nur als eine Art Specimina, als Formstudien zu betrachten; aus innerem starken Drang werden sie schwerlich geboren. Schreiben aber die älteren Componisten keine mehr, so müssen sie ebenfalls ihre Gründe dazu haben, die zu errathen wir Jedem überlassen.

Auf Mozart'schem Weg war es namentlich Hummel, der rüstig fortbaute, und dessen Fis-Moll-Sonate allein seinen Namen überleben würde; auf Beethoven'schem aber vor allen Franz Schubert, der neues Terrain suchte und gewann. Ries arbeitete zu schnell. Berger gab einzelnes Vorzügliche, ohne durchzudringen, ebenso Onslow; am feurigsten und schnellsten wirkte C. M. von Weber, der sich eigenen Styl gegründet; namentlich auf ihn bauen mehre der Jüngeren weiter. So stand es vor zehn Jahren um die Sonate, so steht es noch jetzt. Einzelne schöne Erscheinungen dieser Gattung werden sicherlich hier und da zum Vorschein kommen und sind es schon; im Uebrigen aber scheint es, hat die Form ihren Lebenskreis durchlaufen.

64. NZfM, *14* (1841), 53: im Uebrigen bleibt er der Meister, wie wir ihn lange kennen und lieben; ja es hebt gerade die ungewohnte Form seine Eigenthümlichkeit noch schreiender hervor, wie denn etwa ein irgend von der Natur ausgezeichneter sich nirgends leichter verräth, als wenn er sich maskirt. So ging Napoleon einstmals auf einen Maskenball, und kaum war er einige Augenblicke da, als er schon— die Arme ineinanderschlug. Wie ein Lauffeuer ging es durch den Saal: "der Kaiser." Aehnlich konnte man bei der Symphonie in jedem Winkel des Saales den Laut "Spohr" und wieder "Spohr" hören.

65. NZfM, *10* (1839), 6: Einen besondern Dank votiren wir neueren Concertschreibern, dass sie uns zum Schluss nicht mehr mit Trillern, namentlich mit Octavspringen langweilen. Die alte Cadenz, in die die alten Virtuosen an Bravour einpackten was irgend möglich, beruht auf einem weit tüchtigeren Gedanken und wäre vielleicht noch jetzt mit Glück zu benutzen. Sollte nicht auch das Scherzo, wie es uns von der Symphonie und Sonate her geläufig, mit Wirkung im Concert anzubringen sein? Es müsste einen artigen Kampf mit den einzelnen Stimmen des Orchesters geben, die Form des ganzen Concerts aber eine kleine Aenderung erleiden. Mendelssohn dürfte es vor Allen gelingen.

66. NZfM, *10* (1839), 6: In Moscheles haben wir das seltenere Beispiel eines Musikers, der, obschon in älteren Jahren und noch jetzt unablässig mit dem Studium alter Meister beschäftigt, auch den Gang der neueren Erscheinungen beobachtet und von ihren Fortschritten benutzt hat. Wie er nun jene Einflüsse mit der ihm angeboren Eigenthümlichkeit beherrscht, so entsteht aus solcher Mischung von Altem, Neuem und Eigenem ein Werk, eben wie es das neuste Concert ist, klar und scharf in den Formen, im Charakter dem Romantischen sich nähernd, und wiederum originell, wie man den Componisten kennt.

67. NZfM, *4* (1836), 122: Die beste Recension wäre, der Zeitschrift 10,000 Exemplare für ihre Leser beizulegen und freilich eine theure. Denn ich bin ganz voll von ihm und weiss wenig vernünftiges darüber zu sagen als unendliches Lob. Und wenn Goethe meint: "wer lobe, stellte sich gleich," so soll auch er Recht haben wie immer—und ich will mir von jenem Künstler gerne Augen und Hände binden

lassen und damit nichts ausdrücken, als dass er mich ganz gefangen und dass ich ihm blind folge. . . . .

Ja freilich ist Alles *bon* und zum Küssen und namentlich du, ganzer letzter Satz in deiner göttlichen Langweiligkeit, deinem Liebreiz, deiner Tölpelhaftigkeit, deiner Seelenschönheit, zum Küssen vom Kopf bis auf die Zehe.

68. NZfM, 7 (1837), 73: Ist mir's doch heute wie einem jungen muthigen Krieger, der zum erstenmal sein Schwert zieht in einer grossen Sache! Als ob dies kleine Leipzig, wo einige Weltfragen schon zur Sprache gekommen, auch musikalische schlichten sollte, traf es sich, dass hier, wahrscheinlich zum erstenmal in der Welt neben einander, die zwei wichtigsten Compositionen der Zeit zur Aufführung kamen—die *Hugenotten* von Meyerbeer und der *Paulus* von Mendelssohn. Wo hier anfangen, wo aufhören! Von einer Nebenbuhlerschaft, einer Bevorzugung des Einen vor dem Andern kann hier keine Rede sein. Der Leser weiss zu gut, welchem Streben sich diese Blätter geweiht, zu gut, dass, wenn von Mendelssohn die Rede ist, keine von Meyerbeer sein kann, so schnurstracks laufen ihre Wege auseinander, zu gut, dass, um eine Charakteristik Beider zu erhalten, man nur dem Einen beizulegen braucht, was der Andere nicht hat, —das Talent ausgenommen, was Beiden gemeinschaftlich. Oft möchte man sich an die Stirn greifen, zu fühlen, ob da oben Alles noch im gehörigen Stande, wenn man Meyerbeers Erfolge im gesunden musikalischen Deutschland erwägt, und wie sonst ehrenwerthe Leute, Musiker selbst, die übrigens auch den stilleren Siegen Mendelssohn's mit Freude zusehen, von seiner Musik sagen, sie wär' etwas.

69. NZfM, 7 (1837), 73–74: sein theuerstes Lied auf den Bretern abgeschrieen zu hören, empört es, das blutigste Drama seiner Religionsgeschichte zu einer Jahrmarktsfarce heruntergezogen zu sehen, Geld und Geschrei damit zu erheben, empört die Oper von der Ouverture an mit ihrer lächerlich-gemeinen Heiligkeit bis zum Schluss, nach dem wir ehestens lebendig verbrannt werden sollen. Was bleibt nach den Hugenotten übrig, als dass man geradezu auf der Bühne Verbrecher hinrichtet und leichte Dirnen zur Schau ausstellt.

70. NZfM, 7 (1837), 74: Meyerbeer's äusserlichste Tendenz, höchste Nicht-Originalität und Styllosigkeit sind so bekannt, wie sein Talent, geschickt zu appretiren, glänzend zu machen, dramatisch zu behandeln, zu instrumentiren, wie er auch einen grossen Reichthum

an Formen hat. Mit leichter Mühe kann man Rossini, Mozart, Herold, Weber, Bellini, sogar Spohr, kurz die gesammte Musik nachweisen. Was ihm aber durchaus angehört, ist jener berühmte, fatal neckernde, unanständige Rhythmus, der fast in allen Themen der Oper durchgeht; ich hatte schon angefangen, die Seiten aufzuzeichnen, wo er vorkömmt (S. 6, 17, 59, 68, 77, 100, 117), ward's aber zuletzt überdrüssig.

71. NZfM, 5 (1836), 151: So bewegt sich der erste und zweite Satz durchgehends in dem bekannten mit drei Achteln Auftact anfangenden Rhythmus, dem freilich (wie man sich vielleicht aus einer Bemerkung im Triocyklus dieses Bandes entsinnen wird) schon viele Componisten als Opfer zugefallen sind.

72. NZfM, 17 (1842), 9: Ueberhaupt ist schon die Fähigkeit des Künstlers, den Sinn eines Gedichtes zu fassen, es zu beherrschen, der Rede werth in einer Zeit, wo im Liederwesen so viel höchst Mittelmässiges erscheint, wo die meisten selbst beliebteren Componisten ihre Gedichte gar nicht durchgelesen zu haben scheinen, in solch' verkehrtem Verhältniss steht ihre Musik oft zum Gedicht, und meistens taugt jene auch an sich nur wenig.

73. NZfM, 5 (1836), 143: Wie viel musikalische Elemente die Handlung übrigens in sich begreift, sieht Jeder; ein übermüthiger Herrscher und ein gedrücktes Volk, ein grosser König und eine schöne Jüdin, der Schmerz der Mutter und die Aufopferung für ihr Volk: Gegensätze, wie sie die Musik wiederzugeben und wie sie, ihrem Charakter nach, Niemand besser als gerade Löwe zu einem Gemälde vereinen vermag.

74. NZfM, 5 (1836), 143: Im vierten Liede Freude Esthers an ihren Zwillingstöchtern, die man ihr gelassen, mit eigenthümlicher Begleitung. Meldung vom Tode ihres Sohnes "Gott Abrahams, du hast gegeben, was du genommen hast, ist dein." Prächtige Accorde, die sich in ein Glockengeläute verlieren. Der Marschall sagt den Tod des Königs an. Sie wird fortgewiesen "Kommt Kinder, kommt zu unserm Volke, die Jüdengasse nimmt uns auf." Der Rückblick auf den Anfang des Ganzen hebt sich in der Musik zart hervor.

75. NZfM, 5 (1836), 144: Wenn Loewe fast jedes Wort des Gedichtes charakteristisch ausmalt in der Musik, so zeichnet B. Klein seinem Gegenstand, gleich viel welcher es sei, nur in den nöthigsten Umrissen hin, in einer Einfachheit, die oft unglaublich wirkt, oft

aber auch beengend und quälend. Einfachheit macht das Kunstwerk noch nicht und kann unter Umständen eben so tadelnswerth sein, als das Entgegengesetzte, Ueberladung; der gesunde Meister aber nutzt alle Mittel mit Wahl zur rechten Zeit.

76. NZfM, 5 (1836), 144: So mag der Gott und die Bajadere, dieses schön-menschlichste aller Gedichte, was dessen ruhige, grossartige Stellen betrifft, kaum würdiger aufgefasst werden, als es B. Klein gelungen ist. Wo die Dichtung aber sinnlicher, malerischer, indischer wird, bleibt die Musik meistens zu ungefällig zurück. . . . Denke man sich nur an manchen Stellen die bedeutenden Worte weg und man findet oft fast nichts als allgemeine Harmonieen, gewöhnliche Rhythmen und Melodieen.

77. NZfM, 18 (1843), 120: die sich namentlich auch die Fortschritte des einstweilen weiter ausgebildeten Begleitungsinstruments, des Claviers, zu Nutze machte. Der Componist nennt seine Lieder auch Lieder mit Pianoforte, und es ist dies nicht zu übersehen. Die Singstimme allein kann allerdings nicht alles wirken, nicht alles wiedergeben; neben dem Ausdrucke des Ganzen sollen auch die feineren Züge des Gedichts hervortreten, und so ist's recht, wenn darunter nicht der Gesang leidet. Darauf hat nun freilich auch dieser junge Componist zu achten. Seine Lieder erscheinen häufig als selbstständige Instrumentalstücke, die oft kaum des Gesanges zu bedürfen scheinen, um eine vollständige Wirkung zu machen; . . . der Gesang in ihnen erscheint daher oft wie ein leises Hinlispeln der Worte, und der Hauptausdruck liegt meistens in der Begleitung.

78. NZfM, 11 (1839), 71: Alles finden wir hier, was wir von einem Lied fördern dürfen: poetische Auffassung, belebtes Detail, glückliches Verhältniss des Gesanges zum Instrument . . . Am wenigsten kann ich mich indess mit dem Goethe'schen Gedicht einverstanden erklären; die Figur, wiewohl sie sich durch den Harfenspieler deuten liesse, scheint mir zu äusserlich, zu zufällig, und das zarte Leben des Gedichtes zu übertönen. Bei Franz Schubert erschien dies Festhalten einer Figur das ganze Lied hindurch als etwas neues; junge Liedercomponisten sind vor der Manier sehr zu warnen.

79. NZfM, 16 (1842), 207: Noch haben die Lieder fast durchgängig das Besondere, dass die Clavierbegleitung meist mit der Melodie zusammengeht, so dass jene auch ohne Gesang selbstständig bestehen könnte. Es ist dies gerade kein Vorzug einer Liedercomposition und

namentlich für den Sänger beengend; wir begegnen ähnlichem aber bei allen jungen Componisten, die sich vorzugsweise früher mit Instrumentalcomposition beschäftigten.

80. NZfM, *13* (1840), 118: Auch den hartherzigsten Kritiker wandelt einmal die Lust zu loben an. "Was hilft es—sagte ich mir—leidliche Anfänger in der Gesangscomposition passabel aufzumuntern, oder mittelmässigen Schreiern die Kehle verstopfen zu wollen. Lieber setz' ich mir einen ganzen Stoss neuer Lieder her, und ruhe nicht eher, als ich einige gute gefunden, um einmal nach Herzenslust nichts als loben zu können."

81. NZfM, *13* (1840), 118: Das Gedicht mit seinen kleinsten Zügen im feineren musikalischen Stoffe nachzuwirken, gilt ihm das höchste, wie es allen gelten sollte. Nur selten, das ihm ein Zug entgeht, oder dass er ihm, wo er ihn gefasst, missglückt.

82. NZfM, *19* (1843), 34–35: Ueber die Lieder von R. Franz liesse sich viel sagen; sie sind keine vereinzelte Erscheinung und stehen im engen Zusammenhange mit der ganzen Entwickelung unserer Kunst in den letzten zehn Jahren. Man weiss, dass in den Jahren 1830–34 sich eine Reaction gegen den herrschenden Geschmack erhob. Der Kampf war im Grunde nicht schwer; er war einer gegen das Floskelwesen, das sich, Ausnahmen wie Weber, Löwe u. A. zugegeben, fast in allen Gattungen, am meisten in der Claviermusik zeigte. Von der Claviermusik ging auch der erste Angriff aus; an die Stelle der Passagenstücke traten gedankenvollere Gebilde, und namentlich zweier Meister Einfluss machte sich in ihnen bemerklich, der Beethoven's und Bach's. Die Anzahl der Jünger wuchs; das neue Leben drang auch in andere Fächer. Für das Lied hatte schon Franz Schubert vorgearbeitet, aber mehr in Beethoven'scher Weise, dagegen in den Leistungen der Norddeutschen die Wirkung Bach'schen Geistes sich kund gab. Die Entwicklung zu beschleunigen, entfaltete sich auch eine neue deutsche Dichterschule: Rückert und Eichendorff, obwohl schon früher blühend, wurden den Musikern vertrauter, am meisten Uhland und Heine componirt. So entstand jene kunstvollere und tiefsinnigere Art des Liedes, von der natürlich die Früheren nichts wissen konnten, denn es war nur der neue Dichtergeist, der sich in der Musik wiederspiegelte. Die Lieder von R. Franz gehören durchaus dieser edlen neuen Gattung an. . . . Vergleicht man z.B. an den vorliegenden Liedern den Fleiss der Auffassung, der den Gedanken des Gedichtes

bis auf das Wort wiedergeben möchte, mit der Nachlässigkeit der älteren Behandlung, wo das Gedicht nur eben so nebenher lief, den ganzen harmonischen Ausbau dort mit den schlotternden Begleitungsformeln, wie sie die frühere Zeit nicht loswerden konnte, so kann nur Bornirtheit das Gegentheil sehen. Mit dem Vorigen ist schon das Charakteristische der Lieder von R. Franz ausgesprochen; er will mehr als wohl- oder übelklingende Musik, er will uns das Gedicht in seiner leibhaftigen Tiefe wiedergeben.

83. NZfM, 9 (1838), 42: Denk' ich nun freilich an die höchste Art der Musik, wie sie uns Bach und Beethoven in einzelnen Schöpfungen gegeben, sprech' ich von seltenen Seelenzuständen, die mir der Künstler offenbaren soll, verlang' ich, dass er mich mit jedem seiner Werke einen Schritt weiter führe im Geisterreich der Kunst, verlang' ich mit einem Wort poetische Tiefe und Neuheit überall, im Einzelnen wie im Ganzen: so müsste ich lange suchen, und auch keines der erwähnten, der meisten erscheinenden Werke genügten mir. Da hörten wir in den folgenden Quartett-Morgen Mehres von der Musik eines jungen Mannes, von der mir schien, sie käme zuweilen aus lebendiger Geniustiefe; doch fordert dieser Ausspruch mannichfache Einschränkung, wovon wie über die ganze Erscheinung in einem der nächsten Blätter.

84. NZfM, 9 (1838), 51: So viel weiss ich aber, dass es das bedeutendste, von den grössten Kräften unterstützte Streben, das ich unter jüngeren Talenten seit lange angetroffen. Die Worte suchen's vergeblich, wie seine Musik gestaltet ist, was Alles sie schildert; seine Musik ist selbst Sprache, wie etwa die Blumen zu uns sprechen, wie sich Augen die geheimnissvollsten Mährchen erzählen, wie verwandte Geister über Flächen Landes mit einander verkehren können; Seelensprache, innerlichstes, reichstes, wahrstes Musikleben.

85. NZfM, 9 (1838), 51–52: Und jetzt kommt mein "Aber". Wie bei erster Betrachtung uns oft Bilder junger genievoller Maler durch die Grossheit der Composition (auch im Aeusserlichen), durch Reichthum und Wahrheit der Farben etc. völlig einnehmen, dass wir nur staunen und das einzelne Falsche, Verzeichnete etc. übersehen, so auch hier. Bei'm zweitenmal Anhören fingen mich schon einzelne Stellen zu quälen an, Stellen, in denen, ich will nicht sagen, gegen die ersten Regeln der Schule, sondern geradezu gegen das Gehör, gegen die

natürlichen Gesetze der Harmoniefolgen gesündigt war. Dahin zähle ich nicht sowohl Quinten etc., als gewisse Ausgänge des Basses, Ausweichungen, wie wir sie oft von Weniggeübten anhören müssen.

86. NZfM, *16* (1842), 159–60: Im ersten frischen Anlauf gelingt auch Vieles; hin und wieder bricht aber die lückenhafte Bildung als Musiker hindurch, und man hat dann ungefähr das Gefühl wie nach einem orthographischen Schnitzer in einem sonst geistreich geschriebenen Briefe. Aehnlichem, und nur noch öfter, begegnet man in Berlioz'-schen Compositionen.

87. NZfM, *16* (1842), 142–43: Schon der Gedanke der Preisausschreiber gerade auf ein Quartett, war gut. Einmal, da die Gattung an sich eine so edle ist, eine höhere Bildung der Kämpfenden vorausgesetzt, dann, da in ihr ein bedenklicher Stillstand eingetreten war. Haydn's, Mozart's, Beethoven's Quartette, wer kennte sie nicht, wer dürfte einen Stein auf sie werfen? Ist es gewiss das sprechendste Zeugniss der unzerstörbaren Lebensfrische ihrer Schöpfungen, dass sie noch nach einem halben Jahrhundert aller Herzen erfreuen, so doch gewiss kein gutes für die spätere Künstlergeneration, dass sie in so langem Zeitraume nichts jenen Vergleichbares zu schaffen vermochte. Onslow allein fand Anklang, und später Mendelssohn, dessen aristokratisch-poetischem Charakter diese Gattung auch besonders zusagen muss.

88. NZfM, *16* (1842), 143: Gehört habe ich leider das Quartett nicht. Es hat mir aber innerlich wiedergeklungen, ich wüsste keine dunkle Stelle. Einen der Sätze besonders vorziehen möchte ich nicht; sie stehen auch in einem inneren Zusammenhange. Den Charakter in kurzen Worten zu bezeichnen: eine anfangs trübe elegische Stimmung steigert sich durch Humor und ruhigeren betrachtenden Ernst zu kühner energischer Thatenlust.

89. NZfM 5 (1836), 41: ein Salontrio, bei dem man schon einmal lorgnettiren kann, ohne deshalb den Musikfaden gänzlich zu verlieren; weder schwer, noch leicht, weder tief, noch seicht, nicht classisch, nicht romantisch, aber immer wohlklingend und im Einzelnen sogar voll schöner Melodie, z. B. im weichen Hauptgesange des ersten Satzes, der aber im Dur viel von seinem Reiz verliert, ja sogar gewöhnlich klingt,—so viel macht oft die kleine und grosse Terz.

90. NZfM, 5 (1836), 151–52: Gäbe es grobe Schnitzer, Formen-

schwächen, Extravaganzen, so liesse sich darüber sprechen, bessern, aufmuntern; hier aber kann man nichts sagen als etwa "es ist langweilig," oder "recht gut," oder seufzen, oder an etwas Anderes denken.

91. NZfM, 5 (1836), 151: Mit klarerem Worte, die Symphonie ist styllos, aus Deutsch, Italiänisch und Französisch zusammengesetzt, der romanischen Sprache vergleichbar. Von deutscher Weise benutzt Lachner zu den Anfängen, zu canonischen Nachahmungen, von italiänischer zur Cantilene, von französischer zu den Verbindungssätzen und Schlüssen. Wo dies mit so viel Geist, oft Schlag auf Schlag, wie bei Meyerbeer, compilirt ist, mag man es bei milder Stimmung noch anhören; wo man sich dies aber bis zur Langeweile bewusst wird, wie es auf dem Gesicht des Leipziger Publicums zu lesen war, so kann nur die nachsichtsvollste Kritik nicht geradezu verwerfen.

92. NZfM, 3 (1835), 34: Mendelssohn, ein productiv wie reflectiv gleich grosser Künstler, möchte einsehen, dass auf diesem Wege nichts zu gewinnen sei und schlug einen neuen ein, wollte man nicht etwa ihn von der ersten Ouverture zur Leonore vorgebrochen nennen. Mit seinen Concertouverturen, in welchen er die Idee der Symphonie in einen kleinern Kreis zusammendrängte, errang er sich Kron' und Scepter über die Instrumentalkomponisten des Tages. Es stand zu fürchten, der Name der Symphonie gehöre von nun an nur noch der Geschichte an.

93. NZfM, 18 (1843), 132: In der That, eine Zeit, die solche Werke hervorbringt, solche tüchtige Talente aufzuweisen hat, wie Rietz u. A., braucht vor einer entschwundenen grossen Periode nicht zu sehr zu erröthen, wie einige Zurückgebliebene uns so gern einreden möchten, und darf auch mit Zuversicht auf eine noch ergiebigere Zukunft hoffen.

94. NZfM, 5 (1836), 63: Denn gewiss ist in keinem Genre unsrer Kunst mehr Stümperhaftes zu Tag gefördert worden—und wird es auch noch. Von der Armseligkeit, wie sie hier aus dem Grunde blüht, von dieser Gemeinheit, die sich gar nicht mehr schämt, hat man kaum einen Begriff. Sonst gab's doch wenigstens gute langweilige deutsche Thema's, jetzt muss man aber die abgedroschensten italiänischen in fünf bis sechs wässerigen Zersetzungen nach einander hinterschlucken. Und die Besten sind noch die, die's dabei bewenden lassen. Kommen sie nun aber aus der Provinz, die Strohmillers, die Genserts und wie sie heissen! Zehn Variationen, doppelte Reprisen. Und auch das ginge

noch. Aber dann das Minore und das Finale im 3/8tel Tact—hu! Kein Wort sollte man verlieren und Ritz Ratz in den Ofen! Solchen mittelmässigen Schofel (das treffende Wort) in einzelnen Anzeigen, wie andere selige Zeitungen, unsern Lesern vorzustellen, halten wir sie und uns für zu gut. Ausgezeichnet-Schlechtes, Echt-Schülerhaftes soll indess manchmal erwähnt werden; im Durchschnitt wird aber, bis auf diesen ersten Gang, in späteren nur der besseren Erscheinungen gedacht.

95. NZfM, 6 (1837), 175: Unsterblich ist keines der obigen Werke, hübsch manches. Es käme nur darauf an zu wissen, was die resp. Componisten selbst über ihre Werke urtheilten. Hielten sie solche für ewig, so müsste man sie von ihrer Idee abzubringen suchen: gäben sie aber lachend zu, dass es ja Kleinigkeiten, über die nicht viel Worte zu verlieren, so müsste man ihre Bescheidenheit loben; denn Bach's können wir nicht in jeder Stunde sein, obwohl solches wünschenswerth.

96. NZfM, 5 (1836), 80: indessen sind es eben brillante Variationen über ein Thema von Donizetti und man weiss Alles im Voraus. Sobald nur der Componist und das Publicum solche Dinge für das erklären, was sie sind, so lässt man es passiren. Sobald es sich aber etwa breit machen will, so soll sich dem kanonenschwer entgegengestellt werden. Nichtsnützig ist es nun gar, wenn selbst musikalische Zeitungen über solche, wie sie nennen, "freundliche" Talente, als Kalkbrenner, Bertini etc., der Welt die Augen öffnen wollen. Durch Glas lässt sich schon sehen; da brauchen wir keinen langweiligen Erklärer.

97. NZfM, 5 (1836), 80: er scheint ein bedeutender Virtuos, bringt manches Neue und stets Gutklingendes, notirt alles sehr fleissig, hat rhythmischen Sinn, schreibt im Verhältniss zur claviergemässen Schwierigkeit dankbar. Dies ist alles schätzenswerth.

98. NZfM, 5 (1836), 80: Aber mit zwei Verzierungen möchten uns die Componisten nicht mehr wüthend machen: sie stehen unten in der Anmerkung und sind nach und nach so zu Gemeinheiten worden, dass man's wirklich nicht mehr hören kann. Todfeindschaft Allen, die sie noch einmal drucken lassen. Wünscht man von uns andere Zierrathen an Cadenzstellen, so stehen wir mit Tausenden bereit.

99. NZfM, 4 (1836), 83: Denn schreibt jemand ein lustiges Rondo, so thut er Recht daran. Bewirbt sich aber jemand um eine Fürsten-

braut, so wird vorausgesetzt, dass er edler Geburt und Gesinnung sei; oder, ohne überflüssig Bildern zu wollen, arbeitet jemand in einer so grossen Kunstform, vor welcher die Besten des Landes mit Bescheidenheit und Scheu treten, so muss er das wissen.

100. NZfM, *10* (1839), *5*: Diese Trennung von dem Orchester sehen wir schon seit länger vorbereitet: Der Symphonie zum Trotz will das neuere Clavierspiel nur durch seine eigenen Mittel herrschen und hierin mag der Grund zu suchen sein, warum die letzte Zeit so wenig Clavierconcerte, überhaupt wenig Original–Compositionen mit Begleitung hervorgebracht. Die Zeitschrift hat seit ihrem Entstehen ziemlich von allen Clavierconcerten berichtet; es mögen auf die vergangenen sechs Jahre kaum 16 bis 17 kommen, eine kleine Zahl im Vergleich zu früher . . . Sicherlich müsste man es einen Verlust heissen, käme das Clavierconcert mit Orchester ganz ausser Brauch; anderseits können wir den Clavierspielern kaum widersprechen, wenn sie sagen "Wir haben Anderer Beihülfe nicht nöthig; unser Instrument wirkt allein am vollständigsten." Und so müssen wir getrost den Genius abwarten, der uns in neuer glänzender Weise zeigt, wie das Orchester mit dem Clavier zu verbinden sei, dass der am Clavier herrschende den Reichthum seines Instruments und seiner Kunst entfalten könne, während dass das Orchester dabei mehr als das blosse Zusehen habe und mit seinen mannichfaltigen Charakteren die Scene kunstvoller durchwebe.

101. NZfM, *4* (1836), *113*: Zweierlei rüge ich besonders an Concert-concertcomponisten (kein Pleonasmus), erstens, dass sie die Solis eher fertig machen und haben als die Tuttis, unconstitutionell genug, da doch das Orchester die Kammern vertritt, ohne deren Zustimmung das Clavier nichts unternehmen darf. Und warum nicht beim ordentlichen Anfang anfangen? Ist denn unsre Welt am zweiten Tage erschaffen worden? . . . Es gilt aber eine Wette, dass Hr. Kalkbrenner seine Einleitungs- und Mitteltuttis später erfunden und eingeschoben habe.

102. NZfM, *18* (1843), *209*: Gerade von ihm, der eine strenge Schule durchgemacht, von dem wir wissen, dass er gar wohl Beethoven von Bellini zu unterscheiden weiss, erwarteten wir etwas ganz anderes. Ja, es tritt uns in diesen Sachen das moderne Virtuosenthum nicht einmal in ihren glänzenden Seiten entgegen, wie sie Liszt und Thal-

berg vertreten werden, von denen dem ersteren Niemand Genialität
in Combination mechanischer Schwierigkeiten, Erfindung wirklich
neuer Instrumentaleffekte etc. absprechen kann, eben so wenig wie
dem andern eine Salongrazie, eine Berechnung und Kenntniss des
Effectes etc., dass er überall einnehmen und enthusiasmiren muss. Den
Compositionen des Hrn. Willmers klebt eine ganz eigne Trockenheit
und Philisterhaftigkeit an . . . die sich nun eben in Liszt-Thalberg'-
scher Manier bewegt, dieselben Schwierigkeiten ohne deren Reize
bringt.

103. NZfM, 2 (1835), 178: Mit gutem Grund stellen wir obige
Compositionen zusammen. Der einzige Unterschied liegt in der 3
mehr bei der Opuszahl. Es sind liebenswürdige Charactere, welche die
grosse Welt glatt und blank wie Eis geschliffen. Man lernt schmeicheln,
indem einem geschmeichelt wird: Geber und Empfänger trinken in
gleichen Zügen vom süssen Gift.

104. NZfM, 5 (1836), 73: Zwei schöne russische Themas nahm er
sich: das erste steht in den vor Kurzem in diesen Blättern abgedruck-
ten "Bildern aus Moskau"—die Bitte eines Kindes an die Mutter, voll
wahrhaft rührenden Ausdrucks. Das andere ist das neue Volkslied,
vom Oberst Alexis von Lwoff componirt und im ganzen russischen
Reich statt des *God save the king* eingeführt, ein männlicher, ruhig
feuriger Gesang. Der Gedanke, zwei Themas auf einmal zu verändern,
ist nicht neu, doch selten gebraucht und gewiss lobenswerth, zumal
wenn sie in irgend einer Beziehung zu einander stehen, wie hier,—
wenn letzteres auch weniger im ästhetischen Sinn, als ihres gleichen
nationalen Ursprunges halber.

105. NZfM, 15 (1841), 126: Zunächst, wie man weiss, schreibt er
für sich und seine Concerte; er will zuerst gefallen, glänzen, die Composition ist Nebensache. Blitzte nicht hier und da zuweilen ein edlerer
Strahl hervor, und sähe man in einzelnen Partieen nicht einen sorg-
licheren Fleiss in der Ausarbeitung, seine Compositionen wären ohne
weiteres den tausend andern Virtuosenmachwerken beizuzählen, wie
sie jahraus jahrein zum Vorschein kommen, um bald wieder zu ver-
schwinden.

106. NZfM, 15 (1841), 127: Das *Notturno* weicht in Ton und
Haltung von der bekannten, durch Chopin etwas modificirten Weise,
nur wenig ab. Der Hauptcantilene folgt ein bewegter Mittelsatz in der

Molltonart der grossen Terz und dieser wiederum die erste Cantilena.
Die Form hat ein glückliches Verhältniss, ist auch schon von Chopin
gebraucht.

107. NZfM, 15 (1841), 126–27: und es dauert uns der manchen
guten Gedanken wegen, die es enthält, doppelt, das kein vollkommen
abgerundetes Musikstück daraus geworden. Die Mängel liegen in den
Mittelpartieen, die auch in der Erfindung schwächer, sich nicht geschickt genug in das Ganze einfügen. Stellen wie auf S. 4, Syst. 3,
vom letzten Tact an kann Ref. wenigstens nicht anders als mit "musik-
los" bezeichnen; sie sind mit Mühe dem Instrument abgerungen, die
Seele hat keinen Antheil daran.

108. NZfM, 7 (1837), 47: Viele unserer jungen Phantasien- und
Etudencomponisten haben sich in eine Satzform verliebt, die, früher
schon häufig benutzt, durch die reichen Mittel, die man von Neuem
im Clavier entdeckt, in verschiedenen Arten wieder zum Vorschein
gekommen ist. Man theilt nämlich irgend einer Stimme eine leidlich
breite Melodie zu und umschreibt diese durch allerhand Harpeggien,
und künstliche Figurationen der ihr angehörigen Accorde. Macht man
dies einmal neu und interessant, so mag es gelten; dann aber sollte man
auch auf Anderes sinnen.

109. NZfM, 6 (1837), 185: Wer so sitzt, dass er auf die Finger
Thalbergs sehen kann, muss unwiderstehlich zum Erstaunen hinge-
rissen werden; wer nicht so glücklich ist, glaubt höchstens eine
gewöhnliche vierhändige Composition ausführen zu hören. Für den
Mechanismus hat Thalberg unendlich viel, nichts aber für die Kunst
gethan.

110. NZfM, 11 (1839), 121: Bei genauerer Durchsicht ergibt sich
denn, dass die meisten Stücke der letzteren nur Umarbeitungen jenes
Jugendwerkes sind, das schon vor vielen, vielleicht 20 Jahren in Lyon
erschienen, der unbekannten Verlagsfirma wegen bald verschollen,
jetzt vom deutschen Verleger wieder vorgesucht und neu gedruckt
worden ist.

111. NZfM, 11 (1839), 121–22: Zu anhaltenden Studien in der
Composition scheint er keine Ruhe, vielleicht auch keinen ihm ge-
wachsenen Meister gefunden zu haben; desto mehr studirte er als
Virtuos, wie denn lebhafte musikalische Naturen den schnellberedten
Ton dem trocknen Arbeiten auf dem Papier vorziehen. Brachte er es
nun als Spieler auf eine erstaunliche Höhe, so war doch der Componist

zurückgeblieben, und hier wird immer ein Missverhältniss entstehen, was sich auffallend auch bis in seine letzten Werke fortgerächt hat. Andere Erscheinungen stachelten den jungen Künstler noch auf andere Weise. Ausserdem dass er von den Ideen der Romantik der französischen Literatur, unter deren Koryphäen er lebte, in die Musik übertragen wollte, ward er durch den plötzlich kommenden Paganini gereizt, auf seinem Instrument noch weiter zu gehen und das Aeusserste zu versuchen. So sehen wir ihn (z. B. in seinen *Apparitions*) in den trübsten Phantasieen herumgrübeln und bis zur Blasirtheit indifferent, während er sich andersseits wieder in den ausgelassensten Virtuosenkünsten erging, spottend und bis zur halben Tollheit verwegen. Der Anblick Chopin's, scheint es, brachte ihn zuerst wieder zur Besinnung. Chopin hat doch Formen; unter den wunderlichen Gebilden seiner Musik zieht sich doch immer der rosige Faden einer Melodie fort. Nun aber war es wohl zu spät für den ausserordentlichen Virtuosen, was er als Componist versäumt nachzuholen. Sich vielleicht selbst nicht mehr als solcher genügend, fing er an sich zu andern Componisten zu flüchten, sie mit seiner Kunst zu verschönen, zu Beethoven und Franz Schubert. . . . Dass Liszt aber bei seiner eminenten musikalischen Natur, wenn er dieselbe Zeit, die er dem Instrument und andern Meistern, so der Composition und sich selbst gewidmet hätte, auch höchst bedeutender Componist geworden wäre, glaub' ich gewiss. Was wir von ihm noch zu erwarten haben, lässt sich nur muthmassen.

112. NZfM, 3 (1835), 208: Wir kommen zu unsern Lieblingen, den Sonaten von Franz Schubert, den Viele nur als Liedercomponisten, bei Weitem die Meisten kaum dem Namen nach kennen. Nur Fingerzeige können wir hier geben. Wollten wir im Einzelnen beweisen, für wie reine Geniuswerke wir seine Compositionen erklären müssen, so gehört das mehr in Bücher, für die vielleicht noch einmal Zeit wird.

113. NZfM, 3 (1835), 208: Er hat Töne für die feinsten Empfindungen, Gedanken, ja Begebenheiten und Lebenszustände. So tausendgestaltig sich des Menschen Dichten und Trachten bricht, so vielfach die Schubertsche Musik. Was er anschaut mit dem Auge, berührt mit der Hand, verwandelt sich zu Musik; aus Steinen, die er hinwirft, springen, wie bei Deukalion und Pyrrha lebende Menschengestalten.

114. NZfM, 3 (1835), 208: Namentlich hat er als Componist für das Clavier vor Andern, im Einzelnen selbst vor Beethoven etwas voraus (so bewundernswürdig fein dieser übrigens in seiner Taubheit

mit der Phantasie hörte),—darin nämlich, dass er Claviergemässer zu
instrumentiren weiss, das heisst, das Alles klingt, so recht vom Grunde,
aus der Tiefe des Claviers heraus, während wir z. B. bei Beethoven zur
Farbe des Tones erst vom Horn, der Hoboe u.s.w. borgen müssen.

115. NZfM, 8 (1838), 177–78: So viel ist gewiss, dass sich gleiche
Alter immer anziehen, dass die jugendliche Begeisterung auch am
meisten von der Jugend verstanden wird, wie die Kraft des männ-
lichen Meisters vom Mann. Schubert wird so immer der Liebling der
ersteren bleiben; er zeigt, was sie will, ein überströmend Herz, kühne
Gedanken, rasche That; erzählt ihr, was sie am meisten liebt, von
romantischen Geschichten, Rittern, Mädchen und Abenteuern; auch
Witz und Humor mischt er bei, aber nicht so viel, dass dadurch die
weichere Grundstimmung getrübt würde. Dabei beflügelt er des Spie-
lers eigene Phantasie, wie ausser Beethoven kein anderer Componist;
das Leicht-Nachahmliche mancher seiner Eigenheiten verlockt wohl
auch zur Nachahmung; tausend Gedanken will man ausführen, die
er nur leichthin angedeutet; so ist es, so wird er noch lange wirken.

116. NZfM, 8 (1838), 178–79: durch eine viel grössere Einfalt
der Erfindung, durch ein freiwilliges Resigniren auf glänzende Neuheit, wo er sich sonst so hohe Ansprüche stellt, durch Ausspinnung von
gewissen allgemeinen musikalischen Gedanken, anstatt er sonst Periode
auf Periode neue Fäden verknüpft.

117. NZfM, 9 (1838), 193: Doch glaub ich kaum, dass Schubert
diese Sätze wirklich "Impromptus" überschrieben; der erste ist so
offenbar der erste Satz einer Sonate, so vollkommen ausgeführt und
abgeschlossen, dass gar kein Zweifel aufkommen kann. Das zweite
Impromptu halte ich für den zweiten Satz derselben Sonate; in Tonart
und Charakter schliesst es sich dem ersten knapp an. Wo die Schluss-
sätze hingekommen, ob Schubert die Sonate vollendet, oder nicht,
müssten seine Freunde wissen; man könnte vielleicht das vierte Impromptu als das Finale betrachten, doch spricht, wenn auch die Tonart
dafür, die Flüchtigkeit in der ganzen Anlage beinahe dagegen. Es sind
dies also Vermuthungen, die nur eine Einsicht in die Originalmanu-
scripte aufklären könnte.

118. NZfM, 9 (1838), 193: nur wenigen Werken ist das Siegel
ihres Verfassers so klar aufgedrückt, als den seinigen. So flüstert es
denn in den zwei ersten Impromptus auf allen Seiten, "Franz Schubert"

wie wir ihn kennen in seiner unerschöpflichen Laune, wie er uns reizt, und täuscht und wieder fesselt, finden wir ihn wieder. . . .

Was das dritte Impromptu anlangt, so hätte ich es kaum für eine Schubert'sche Arbeit, höchstens für eine aus seiner Knabenzeit gehalten; es sind wenig oder gar nicht ausgezeichnete Variationen über ein ähnliches Thema. Erfindung und Phantasie fehlen ihnen gänzlich, worin sich Schubert gerade auch im Variationsgenre an andern Orten so schöpferisch gezeigt.

119. NZfM, 12 (1840), 82–83: dass in dieser Symphonie mehr als blosser schöner Gesang, mehr als blosses Leid und Freud, wie es die Musik schon hundertfältig ausgesprochen, verborgen liegt, ja dass sie uns in eine Region führt, wo wir vorher gewesen zu sein uns nirgends erinnern können, dies zuzugeben, höre man solche Symphonie. Hier ist, ausser meisterlicher musikalischer Technik der Composition, noch Leben in allen Fasern, Colorit bis in die feinste Abstufung, Bedeutung überall, schärfster Ausdruck des Einzelnen, und über das Ganze endlich eine Romantik ausgegossen, wie man sie schon anderswoher an Franz Schubert kennt. Und diese himmlische Länge der Symphonie, wie ein dicker Roman in vier Bänden etwa von Jean Paul . . . Im Anfange wohl wird das Glänzende, Neue der Instrumentation, die Weite und Breite der Form, der reizende Wechsel des Gefühllebens, die ganze neue Welt, in die wir versetzt werden, den und jenen verwirren, wie ja jeder erste Anblick von Ungewohntem; aber auch dann bleibt noch immer das holde Gefühl etwa wie nach einem vorübergegangenen Märchen- und Zauberspiel; man fühlt überall, der Componist war seiner Geschichte Meister und der Zusammenhang wird dir mit der Zeit wohl auch klar werden.

120. AmZ, 33 (1831), 805–06: Florestan ist, wie Du weisst, einer von den seltenen Musikmenschen, die alles Zukünftige, Neue, Ausserordentliche schon wie lange vorher geahnt haben; das Seltsame ist ihnen im andern Augenblicke nicht seltsam mehr; das Ungewöhnliche wird im Moment ihr Eigenthum. Eusebius hingegen, so schwärmerisch als gelassen, zieht Blüthe nach Blüthe aus; er fasst schwerer, aber sicherer an, geniesst seltener, aber langsamer und länger; dann ist auch sein Studium strenger und sein Vortrag im Klavierspiele besonnener, aber auch zarter und mechanisch vollendeter, als der Florestans.

121. AmZ, 33 (1831), 807: die Einleitung, so abgeschlossen sie in

sich ist—(kannst Du Dich auf Leporello's Terzensprünge besinnen?—) scheint mir am wenigsten in das Ganze einzuklappen; aber das Thema—(warum hat er's aber aus B geschrieben?)—die Variationen, der Schlussatz und das Adagio, das ist freylich etwas und zu viel—da guckt der Genius aus jedem Tacte. Natürlich, lieber Julius, sind Don Juan, Zerline, Leporello und Masetto die redenden Charactere (die Tutti nicht mitgerechnet)—Zerlinen's Antwort im Thema ist verliebt genug bezeichnet, die erste Variation wäre vielleicht etwas vornehm und kokett zu nennen—der spanische Grande schäkert darin sehr liebenswürdig mit der Bauernjungfer.

122. NZfM, *4* (1836), 137: Sollte ich vielleicht hier beiläufig einer berühmten Pantoffel-Zeitung erwähnen, die uns zuweilen, wie wir hören (denn wir lesen sie nicht und schmeicheln uns hierin einige wenige Aehnlichkeit mit Beethoven zu besitzen [s. B's Studien, v. Seyfried herausgeg.]), die uns also zuweilen unter der Maske anlächeln soll mit sanftestem Dolchauge und nur deshalb, weil ich einmal zu einem ihrer Mitarbeiter, der etwas über Chopins Don-Juan-Variationen geschrieben, lachend gemeint: er, der Mitarbeiter, habe wie ein schlechter Vers, ein Paar Füsse zu viel, die man ihm gelegentlich abzuschneiden beabsichtigte!

123. NZfM, *4* (1836), 138: Denn wenn eine Verherrlichung durch Worte (die schönste ist ihm schon in tausend Herzen zu Theil worden) bis jetzt ausgeblieben, so suche ich den Grund einestheils in der Aengstlichkeit, die Einem bei einem Gegenstande befällt, über den man am öftersten und liebsten mit seinem Sinnen verweilt, dass man nämlich der Würde des Vorwurfs nicht angemessen genug sprechen, ihn in seiner Tiefe und Höhe nicht allseitig ergreifen könnte,—anderntheils in den innern Kunstbeziehungen, in denen wir zu diesem Componisten zu stehen bekennen; endlich aber unterblieb sie auch, weil Chopin in seinen letzten Compositionen nicht einen andern, aber einen höhern Weg einzuschlagen scheint, über dessen Richtung und muthmassliches Ziel wir erst noch klarer zu werden hofften, auswärtigen geliebten Verbündeten davon Rechenschaft abzulegen.

124. NZfM, *9* (1838), 178: Chopin kann schon gar nichts mehr schreiben, wo man nicht im 7ten, 8ten Tacte ausrufen müsste: "das ist von ihm!" Man hat das Manier genannt und gesagt, er schreite nicht vorwärts. Aber man sollte dankbarer sein. Ist es denn nicht dieselbe originelle Kraft, die euch schon aus seinen ersten Werken so wunder-

bar entgegenleuchtet, im ersten Augenblick euch verwirrt gemacht, später euch entzückt hat? und wenn er euch eine Reihe der seltensten Schöpfungen gegeben, und ihr ihn leichter versteht, verlangt ihr ihn auf einmal anders? Das hiesse einen Granatenbaum umhacken, weil er immer Granaten, euch jährlich dieselben Früchte wiederbringt.

125. NZfM, 15 (1841), 141: Chopin könnte jetzt alles ohne seinen Namen herausgeben, man würde ihn doch gleich erkennen. Darin liegt Lob und Tadel zugleich, jenes für sein Talent, dieser für sein Streben. Denn sicherlich wohnt ihm jene bedeutende Originalkraft inne, die, sobald sie sich zeigt, keinen Zweifel über den Namen des Meisters zulässt; dabei bringt er auch eine Fülle neuer Formen, die in ihrer Zartheit und Kühnheit zugleich Bewunderung verdienen. Neu und erfinderisch immer im Aeusserlichen, in der Gestaltung seiner Tonstücke, in besonderen Instrumenteffecten, bleibt er sich aber im Innerlichen gleich, dass wir fürchten, er bringe es nicht höher, als er es bis jetzt gebracht. Und ist dies hoch genug, seinen Namen den unvergänglichen in der neueren Kunstgeschichte anzureihen, so beschränkt sich seine Wirksamkeit doch nur auf den kleinern Kreis der Claviermusik, und er hätte mit seinen Kräften doch noch viel Höheres erreichen und Einfluss auf die Fortbildung unserer Kunst im Allgemeinen gewinnen müssen.

126. NZfM, 7 (1837), 199: Man irrt aber, wenn man meint, er hätte da jede der kleinen Noten deutlich hören lassen; es war mehr ein Wogen des As-Dur-Accordes, vom Pedal hier und da von Neuem in die Höhe gehoben; aber durch die Harmonieen hindurch vernahm man in grossen Tönen Melodie, eine wundersame und nur in der Mitte trat einmal neben jenem Hauptgesang auch eine Tenorstimme aus den Accorden deutlicher hervor.

127. NZfM, 14 (1841), 39: Die ersten Tacte der zuletzt genannten Sonate sich ansehen und noch zweifeln zu können, von wem sie sei, wäre eines guten Kennerauges wenig würdig. So fängt nur Chopin an und so schliesst nur er: mit Dissonanzen durch Dissonanzen in Dissonanzen. Und doch wie viel Schönes birgt auch dieses Stück. Dass er es "Sonate" nannte, möchte man eher eine Caprice heissen, wenn nicht einen Uebermuth, dass er gerade vier seiner tollsten Kinder zusammenkoppelte, sie unter diesem Namen vielleicht an Orte einzuschwärzen, wohin sie sonst nicht gedrungen wären.

128. NZfM, 14 (1841), 40: Denn was wir im Schlutzsatze [sic]

unter der Aufschrift "Finale" erhalten, gleicht eher einem Spott, als irgend Musik. Und doch gestehe man es sich, auch aus diesem melodie- und freudelosen Satze weht uns ein eigener grausiger Geist an, der, was sich gegen ihn auflehnen möchte, mit überlegener Faust nieder- hält, dass wir wie gebannt und ohne zu murren bis zum Schlusse zuhorchen—aber auch ohne zu loben: denn Musik ist das nicht.

129. NZfM, 3 (1835), 1: Nicht mit wüstem Geschrei, wie unsre altdeutschen Vorfahren, lasst uns in die Schlacht ziehen, sondern wie die Spartaner unter lustigen Flöten. Zwar braucht der, dem diese Zeilen gewidmet sind, keinen Schildträger und wird hoffentlich das Widerspiel des homerischen Hector, der das zerstörte Troja der alten Zeit endlich siegend hinter sich herzieht als Gefangene,—aber wenn seine Kunst das flammende Schwert ist, so sei dies Wort die verwahrende Scheide.

130. NZfM, 3 (1835), 33: daher ich es vorziehe, sie in einzelnen Theilen, so oft auch einer von dem andern zur Erklärung borgen muss, durchzugehen, nämlich nach den vier Gesichtspuncten, unter denen man ein Musikwerk betrachten kann, d.i. je nach der Form (des Ganzen, der einzelnen Theile, der Periode, der Phrase), je nach der musikalischen Composition (Harmonie, Melodie, Satz, Arbeit, Styl), nach der besondern Idee, die der Künstler darstellen wollte, und nach dem Geiste, der über Form, Stoff und Idee waltet.

131. NZfM, 3 (1835), 42: ich möchte sogar behaupten, seine Harmonie zeichne sich trotz der mannichfaltigen Combinationen, die er mit wenigem Material herstellt, durch eine gewisse Simplicität, jedenfalls aber durch eine Kernhaftigkeit und Gedrungenheit aus, wie man sie, freilich durchgebildeter, bei Beethoven antrifft. Oder entfernt er sich vielleicht zu sehr von der Haupttonart? Nehme man gleich die erste Abtheilung: erster Catz lauter C-Moll: hierauf bringt er diesel- ben Intervalle des ersten Gedankens ganz treu im Es-Dur: dann ruht er lange auf As und kömmt leicht nach C-Dur. Wie das Allegro aus den einfachsten C-Dur, G-Dur und E-Moll gebaut, kann man in dem Umrisse nachsehen, den ich in der letzten Nummer zeigte. Und so ist's durchweg. Durch die ganze zweite Abtheilung klingt das helle A-Dur scharf durch, in der dritten das idyllische F-Dur mit dem ver- schwisterten C- und B-Dur, in der vierten G-Moll mit B- und Es-Dur; nur in der letzten geht es trotz des vorherrschenden C-Princips bunt durcheinander, wie es infernalischen Hochzeiten zukömmt.

132. NZfM, 3 (1835), 46–47: Wenn Herr Fetis behauptet, dass selbst die wärmsten Freunde Berliozs ihn im Betreff der Melodie nicht in Schutz zu nehmen wagten, so gehöre ich zu Berliozs Feinden: nur denke man dabei nicht an italiänische, die man schon auswendig kann, ehe sie anfängt.

Es ist wahr, die mehrfach erwähnte Hauptmelodie der ganzen Symphonie hat etwas plattes und Berlioz lobt sie fast zu sehr, wenn er ihr im Programm einen "vornehm-schüchternen Charakter" beilegt (*un certain caractère passioné, mais noble et timide*); aber man bedenke, dass er ja gar keinen grossen Gedanken hinstellen wollte, sondern eben eine festhängende quälende Idee in der Art, wie man sie oft tagelang nicht aus dem Kopfe bringt; das Eintönige, Irrsinnige kann aber gar nicht besser getroffen werden. Eben so heisst es in jener Recension, dass die Hauptmelodie zur zweiten Abtheilung gemein und trivial sei; aber Berlioz will uns ja eben, (etwa wie Beethoven im letzten Satze der A-Dur-Symphonie), in einen Tanzsaal führen, nichts mehr und nichts weniger. . . .

Wollte man Berlioz einen Vorwurf machen, so wär' es der der vernachlässigten Mittelstimmen; dem stellt sich aber ein besonderer Umstand entgegen, wie ich es bei wenigen anderen Componisten bemerkt habe. Seine Melodieen zeichnen sich nämlich durch eine solche Intensität fast jedes einzelnen Tones aus, dass sie, wie viele alte Volkslieder, oft gar keine harmonische Begleitung vertragen.

133. NZfM, 12 (1840), 152: Gänzlich vermissen wir auf dem Repertoir noch Berlioz. . . . Fehlen aber sollte er nicht länger, der, wie er auch sein möge, durch Uebergehen der Geschichte der Musik eben so wenig vergessen gemacht werden wird, wie durch blosses Ueberschlagen ein Factum der Weltgeschichte, und zur Beurtheilung des Entwickelungsganges der neueren Musik doch immer von Bedeutung ist.

134. NZfM, 18 (1843), 177–78: Gegen manches, ich gesteh' es, würde ich freilich jetzt weit verdammender auftreten; die Jahre machen strenger, und Unschönes, wie ich es wohl in den Jugendarbeiten Berlioz's gefunden und, glaub' ich, auch nachgewiesen, wirb [sic] mit der Zeit nicht schöner. Doch auch hab' ich gesagt, es ruht ein göttlicher Funken in diesem Musiker, und gewünscht, das reifere Alter möge ihn läutern und verherrlichen zur reinsten Flamme. Ob dies in Erfüllung gegangen, weiss ich nicht; denn ich kenne von den Arbeiten

aus Berlioz's reiferem Mannesalter nichts, und es ist noch nichts davon
erschienen.

135. NZfM, 5 (1836), 151: die Völker beten die Gottheit verschieden, ja jeder Mensch sie anders an. Berlioz, wenn er noch oft Menschen
schlachtet am Altar oder sich toll gebehrdet wie ein indischer Fakir,
meint es eben so aufrichtig, als etwa Haydn, wenn er eine Kirsch-
blüthe darbringt mit demuthigem Blick. Gewaltsam wollen wir aber
Niemandem unsern Glauben aufdringen.

136. NZfM, 2 (1835), 5: Einen Zug der Beethoven'schen Romantik, den man den provençalischen nennen könnte, bildete Franz Schubert im eigensten Geist zur Virtuosität aus. Auf dieser Basis stützt
sich, ob bewusst oder unbewusst, eine neue noch nicht völlig entwik-
kelte und anerkannte Schule. . . .
    Ferdinand Hiller gehört zu ihren Jüngern, zu ihren merkwürdig-
sten Einzelheiten.

137. NZfM, 2 (1835), 42: Mit einem tiefen Seufzer fahre ich fort
—keiner andern Kritik wird das Beweisen so schwer, als der musikalischen. Die Wissenschaft schlägt mit der Mathematik, der Dichtkunst
gehört das entschiedene, goldene Wort, andre Künste haben sich die
Natur, von der sie die Formen geliehen, zur Schiedsrichterin gestellt,
—aber die Musik ist die schöne Waise, deren Vater und Mutter Keiner
nennen kann.

138. NZfM, 14 (1841), 3: Andere, immerhin aber bessere, wie B.
Klein, verfuhren wieder zu trappistisch, als dass sie Einfluss gewinnen
konnten. Mendelssohn aber hat unter den Norddeutschen zuerst
wieder auf die wahre Spur hingelenkt, auf Händel und Bach . . . auf
die wahren Glaubenshelden unserer Kunst.

139. NZfM, 14 (1841), 4: Es folgen die vielleicht bedeutendsten
Worte des Ganzen aus Jeremias Munde: "Zur letzten Zeit wird Gottes
Haus höher stehen denn alle Berge und erhaben über alle Hügel!"—
doch hat sie der Componist zu leicht behandelt, die er sich gerade für
seine glücklichste, kräftigste Stunde hätte aufbewahren müssen.

140. NZfM, 15 (1841), 2: "Dass aber kunstvollere Formen überhaupt im kirchlichen Styl angewandt werden, kann nur Zustimmung
erhalten. Wir finden davon eine Menge. Doppelcanons, Doppelfugen
u.s.w. geben vom Fleiss und der Bildung des Componisten an vielen
Stellen ein rühmliches Zeugniss."

141. NZfM, 7 (1837), 70: Ich bin des Wortes "Romantiker" vom Herzen überdrüssig, obwohl ich es nicht zehnmal in meinem Leben ausgesprochen habe; und doch—wollte ich unsern jungen Seher kurz tituliren, so hiess ich ihn einen und welchen! Von jenem vagen, nihilistischen Unwesen aber, wohinter Manche die Romantik suchen, eben so wie von jenem groben hinklecksenden Materialismus, worin sich die französischen Neuromantiker gefallen, weiss unser Componist, dem Himmel sei Dank, nichts; im Gegentheil empfindet er meist natürlich, drückt er sich klug und deutlich aus.

142. NZfM, 2 (1835), 146: Und als ich zu Hause noch einmal den eilig ziehenden Wolken nachsah, rief unter den Fenstern eine fremde, aber wohlthuende Stimme: Ludwig——Ludwig——. Es mochte ein Fremder sein, der nichts wusste von dem was geschehen. Ich aber drückte schnell das Fenster zu und das Auge in tiefe, tiefe Nacht. Draussen fiel ein leiser Regen vom Himmel, als wenn er sich recht ausweinen wollte.

143. NZfM, 4 (1836), 134: Anders aber, als bei der Herausgabe eines früheren Heftes von Studien nach Paganini, wo ich das Original, vielleicht zu dessen Nachtheil, ziemlich Note um Note copirte und nur harmonisch ausbaute, machte ich mich diesmal von der Pedanterie einer wörtlich treuen Uebertragung los und möchte, dass die vorliegende den Eindruck einer selbstständigen Claviercomposition gäbe, welche den Violinursprung vergessen lasse, ohne dass dadurch das Werk an poetischer Idee eingebüsst habe.

144. NZfM, 4 (1836), 135: Bei der Ausführung von Nro. 4 schwebte mir der Todtenmarsch aus der heroischen Symphonie von Beethoven vor. Man würde es vielleicht selbst finden.—Die Accorde S. 11, Syst. 6, T. 3 sind im Original nur die Terzenläufe der obern Stimmen; ich wusste keine andere Rettung, sie geniessbar zu machen.— Der plötzliche Uebergang von H nach C   9♭ kann eine frap-

$$6\# \qquad 7\natural$$
$$3\# \text{ nach } 5\natural$$
$$h \qquad g$$

pante Wirkung nicht verfehlen.

145. NZfM, 18 (1843), 155: Das besondere reizende Colorit ist es denn auch, was, wie der Franz Schubert'schen Symphonie, so der Mendelssohn'schen eine besondere Stelle in der Symphonieliteratur

sichert. Das herkömmliche Instrumentalpathos, die gewohnte massenhafte Breite trifft man in ihr nicht, nichts was etwa wie ein Ueberbieten Beethoven's aussähe, sie nähert sich vielmehr, und hauptsächlich im Character, jener Schubert'schen . . . Darin liegt zugleich ausgesprochen, dass der jüngeren ein anmuthig gesitteterer Charakter innewohnt und dass er uns weniger fremdartig anspricht, indess wir freilich der Schubert'schen wieder andere Vorzüge, namentlich den reicherer Erfindungskraft zusprechen müssen.

146. NZfM, 7 (1837), 75: ausser den innern Kern, den reinen christlichen Sinn, wie wir schon vorhin andeuteten, betrachte man all das Musikalisch-Meisterlich-Getroffene, diesen höchst edlen Gesang durchgängig, diese Vermählung des Wortes mit dem Ton, der Sprache mit der Musik, dass wir Alles in leibhaftiger Tiefe erblicken, die reizende Gruppirung der Personen, die Anmuth, die über das Ganze wie hingehaucht ist, diese Frische, dieses unauslöschliche Colorit in der Instrumentation, des vollkommen ausgebildeten Styles, des meisterlichen Spielens mit allen Formen der Setzkunst nicht zu gedenken —man sollte damit zufrieden sein, meine ich.

147. NZfM, 13 (1840), 198: Es ist das Meistertrio der Gegenwart, wie es ihrer Zeit die von Beethoven in B und D, das von Franz Schubert in Es waren; eine gar schöne Composition, die nach Jahren noch Enkel und Urenkel erfreuen wird.

148. NZfM, 13 (1840), 198: Er ist der Mozart des 19ten Jahrhunderts, der hellste Musiker, der die Widersprüche der Zeit am klarsten durchschaut, und zuerst versöhnt. Und er wird auch nicht der letzte Künstler sein. Nach Mozart kam ein Beethoven; dem neuen Mozart wird ein neuer Beethoven folgen, ja er ist vielleicht schon geboren.

Schumann's Contributions to the NZfM Not Included in Kreisig's Edition of the *Gesammelte Schriften**

1. NZfM, *1* (1834), 193–94, 198–99: Journalschau. (Fortsetzung.) III. Iris. (Redacteur: Ludwig Rellstab. Verleger: Trautwein in Berlin.) (Januar bis Juli.)

Im ehrendsten Sinn könnte man den Titel gleich für den Träger wie für die Last nehmen, theils für den Regenbogen selbst, theils für die Göttin, die auf ihm vom Himmel gleitet. Dort könnte man ihn als siebenfarbigen Halbkreis des Friedens deuten, hier wäre es die Himmlische, die Kunde bringt von ihren Ebenbürtigen. Die indische Sage geht noch weiter und lässt alle Götter auf dieser ätherischen Hängebrücke zur Erde herabsteigen. Es klänge nach Schmeichelei (wenn sie auch Recensenten Recensenten gegenüber mehr ausüben, als gegen Autoren), wollte man vom Vorliegenden das Letzte behaupten. Aber einzelne kommen in Augenblicken herab, nicht allein welche von Fleisch und Gestalt, sondern von Geist und Gedanken, dazu noch griechische, leise verhüllte.

Unstreitig würde Vieles von neueren Musikern, selbst von denen, die wir nicht einmal Meister nennen wollen, jetzt anders und besser gemacht werden, als von alten. . . . Jeder Schritt in der Zeit vorwärts ist auch einer vorwärts in der Sache und das Rückschreiten des Gebankens [sic] ist ein eben so scheinbares, als vorübergehendes Hinabsteigen in eine Schlucht, wenn man einen Gipfel erklimmen will, uns nur scheinbar weiter von der Höhe entfernt.

In einem andern Gleichniss . . . Darum zersplittre der Componist sich nicht so sehr an Kleinigkeiten, sondern wende sich mit Ernst auf grössere Leistungen; nur dann üben sich die Anlagen

---

* Brief editorial notes and the like are not included. Footnotes in Schumann's text have been numbered for the sake of convenience. [L.B.P.]

und bilden sich heraus; Felsen muss man wälzen wie Sisyphus, um zu kräftigen Muskeln zu kommen; an kleinen Kieseln ermüdet man sich und wächst nicht in der eignen Kraft.

In dieser Art findet sich noch Vieles, natürlich mehr Augenblickliches, Kategorisches, Unentwickeltes, wie es der kleinere Kreis nicht anders zuliess.

Aber auch Kobalde rutschen vom Bogen herunter und aufhuckende Graumännchen.

Die Pariser sehen Mozart und Rossini für gleiche Waare an und bedauern uns deutsche Esel oder Bären, die wir den Unterschied finden.

Den Gesangscomponisten sagt er Folgendes:

O Componisten, werdet doch erst Dichter, erst Menschen! lernt ein Gedicht nur ein wenig fühlen, lesen, vortragen, ehe ihr daran denkt, es durch die Musik in eine neue Kunstsphäre zu erheben.

Ueber Czerny:

Was für eine treffliche Hausfrau wäre er geworden, da er sich so meisterhaft darauf versteht, die Ueberbleibsel eines Gerichts aufzustutzen und sie in einer neuen Form auf die Tafel zu bringen.

Bei Gelegenheit von Begräbnissliedern finden wir:

Wir wollen es zum Besten Aller wünschen, dass die Lieder des Verfassers so wenig wie möglich Gelegenheit zur Anwendung finden mögen; denn Leben und Selbstsingen ist wahrlich besser, als Sterben und besungen werden.

Die Organisten ermahnt er:

Wenn Ihr doch statt eurer gemeiniglich etwas grausamen eigenen Phantasieen Nachspiele von Rink etc. geben wolltet, so würden die Kirchgänger nicht so eilig aus der Kirche drängen, ein Erfolg, den man nicht genug schätzen könnte, da leider die meisten bisher lieber gehen als kommen.

Wir beschliessen diese spasshafte Gattung mit einer Art classischen Recension über Lieder von Kupsch, welche lautet:

Der Componist hat diese Liederchen dem Dichtergreis Tiedge zu seinem 81. Jahr zum Geburtstag geschenkt; jetzt schenkt er sie der Welt. Das zweite hätte unterbleiben können. Vielleicht unser Urtheil auch; aber es steht nun einmal da und wir wollen es nicht ausstreichen, aber auch nicht verlängern.

Man könnte die Regenbogenvergleiche noch weiter treiben, etwa entschuldigend: "hat doch der Astronom Frauenhofer in den reinen Irisfarben dunkelschwarze Streifen entdeckt, und Du wolltest zürnen, wenn einmal eine schöne Seele irrt," oder tadelnd: "diese Iris ist allerdings ein Regenbogen, der, wie der idealische Mensch, mit dem Fuss an der Erde haftet, während das Haupt die Wolken berührt, er ist aber einfarbig," oder auf die Zeit angewandt: "der unbewölkte Himmel malt keinen, wohl aber der dunkle—desto fester tritt er dann hervor." Und dergleichen liesse sich viel sagen, wäre man nicht vom Ernst einer Journalschau lebhaft durchdrungen.

Rellstab selbst war es, (haben wir gehört), der sich einmal mündlich gegen einen Freund über die jetzige Zeit und die Kunstmenschen in ihr geäussert: einen Hasen können sie todtschiessen, einen Löwen aber nicht erwürgen. Dieser Timonsgedanke, ob schon er packt, schneidet denn auch überall durch.

Wir haben oft geklagt, dass die jungen Componisten der neuern Zeit keine eigentlichen Lehrer der Compositionen hätten, kaum einen des Generalbasses. . . .

Er geht aber im Tadel noch weiter:

Also dahin geht die Tendenz, etwas zu erzielen, was auf dem Instrument unerhört ist, sei es noch so trivial und verbraucht in musikalischen Gedanken. Leider sehen wir, dass sich eine ganze Schule für Irrungen bildet, wie wir längst an Chopin, dann an Schumann und jetzt auch an diesem Componisten (Kessler[1]) wahrnehmen konnten—

namentlich, wo er bei Gelegenheit der Chopin'schen Etuden schreibt:

Sowie Chopin ein Wunderwerk, etwa einen neuen Don Juan oder Fidelio, oder eine *Sinfonia eroica* oder eine Beethoven'sche Sonata in Cis moll liefert, so wollen wir ihn bewundern, dass uns

1. Siehe dagegen unser Urtheil Nr. 29.

die Sprache zum Ausdruck unserer Gefühle fehlt. So lange er aber solche Missgeburten ausheckt, wie obige Etuden, die ich allen meinen Freunden und zumal den Clavierspielern zur wahren Belustigung gezeigt, so lange wollen wir über diese eben so lachen, wie über seinen Brief [2]. . . . .

Wir glauben und hoffen nicht, dass Rellstab's Kraftmass als Virtuos ihn in seinem Urtheil bestimme. Er selbst wird nicht von Schiller verlangen, dass er seinen hundertstimmigen Wallenstein ungeschrieben lassen soll, weil ihn Winkeltruppen nicht aufführen können, oder einen Reisenden, der vielleicht nach Griechenland wandert, glauben machen wollen, er sei auf einem falschen Weg, weil er (R.) nach dem Norden zu will—verschiedene Kräfte verlangen verschiedene Nahrung und wir gehen eben nicht denselben Weg. Es scheint uns aber hier der Ort, obwohl dem Versprechen der Einleitungsworte der Journalschau entgegen, nach dem wir die einzelnen Organe durch sich selbst sprechen lassen wollten, unsere Meinung über diesen Gegenstand auszusprechen. Sie geht dahin.

Rellstab hat das Verdienst, der erste zu sein, der ohne Rücksicht, mit Ausdauer, daher mit Glück die Richtung unterbrochen hat, welche die Deutschen den Italiänern und Franzosen nachzugehen anfingen. Damit zugleich that er einen Angriff gegen die verkühlte kritische Sprachweise, gegen den Geist der Unentschiedenheit, der sich den Schein von Unparteilichkeit gab, um seine Charakterlosigkeit zu verbergen. Sonderbar kam es jedoch, dass, während er dem Feind auf den Fersen nachfolgte, mit allen Waffen des Witzes und Spottes, (das Engelsschwert ist noch einem Kunstgenie aufgehoben) im Rücken ein neuer aufstand, von dem er selbst zugibt, dass er vornehmerer Abkunft sei. Hätte er sich mit dem letzten vereint, so war jener ohne Weiteres verloren. So aber kam er dem edlern Gegner, der noch dazu jugendlich, zukunftsvoll, also mächtiger dasteht, keine Spanne entgegen, ja er blieb mit einem Starrsinn auf seiner Stelle, dass dieser ihn nun weniger beachtete, während er sonst einen wohlwollenden Vorwurf des Excentrischen und Extremen dankbar aufgenommen und benutzt hätte. Erst in der jüngsten Zeit scheinen sich beide Parteien anzu-

2. Es war ein Drohbrief, den Ch. an R. geschrieben haben sollte. Ob R. recht gethan, den Brief in der Iris abdrucken zu lassen, entscheiden wir nicht. Doch schien die Mystification zu deutlich. Ch. erklärte auch später, "dass er nie Veranlassung gefunden, ihm (R.) zu schreiben."

nähern; wenigstens erkannte die eine das neue Fürstenthum *de facto* an, was die andere schon *de jure* zu besitzen glaubt.

Damals eiferten wir gegen die Verkehrtheit des betretenen Wegs überhaupt und fühlten den Beruf, die Welt darauf aufmerksam zu machen; da seitdem diese Richtung eine allgemeine wird, so dass wir sie, wenn freilich nicht *de jure* doch *de facto* anerkennen müssen, so bleibt dieser Kampf ein vergeblicher.

Wie dem auch sei, möge durch diesen Gegendruck die neue Blüthe länger zurückgehalten worden, oder die künftige Frucht eine wirklich giftige sein, so bleibt an sich die Gesinnung dieser Götterbotin eine edle, ihres Ursprungs würdige und wenn auch die Ehrfurcht vor zwei Künstlern, Bernhard Klein und Ludwig Berger, die Schuld tragen sollte, dass Rellstab die späteren Zeitgenossen zurückmessen wollte, so bleibt es immer anzuerkennen, dass diese Geister, die vielleicht sonst, wenn nicht untergegangen, doch übersehen worden wären, von ihm verherrlicht worden sind, wie es [sic] in solchem Mass verdienen.

Wir gehen zum Text zurück. Man kann von einer Einmannszeitung nicht verlangen, dass überall, über jedes einzelne Instrument, bedeutende Sachkenntnis entwickelt werde; der Redacteur ist bescheiden genug, zu gestehen, dass er Bass so wenig könne, als Horn. In solchen Fällen wird nur auf die Existenz der Werke aufmerksam gemacht. Am liebsten hält er sich bei dem Gesang auf, dann aber mit so viel Ueberlegenheit im Urtheil, dass man den im Kritiker concentrirten Musiker und Dichter mit Freuden vertraut. Man sehe die Recensionen über Lieder von C. Banck[3], die er

in vielfacher Beziehung merkwürdig und jedenfalls eine erfreuliche Erscheinung der Kunst

nennt. Dann über das Miserere von Hasse, eine voll-lobende über Kurschmann, halblobende über Reissiger[4], Stegmayer, Hiller[5] u.s.w.

Im Ganzen möchte sich das Lob zum Tadel wie etwa eins zu fünf verhalten. Niemandem ist das Lob vollkommener Anerkennung ertheilt. Ein Accessit haben die oben erwähnten Lieder von Kurschmann und die Hebridenouverture von Mendelssohn erhalten. Völlig

3. S. auch allgem, musik. Zeitung Nr. 16.
4. Uebereinstimmend mit unserm Urtheil in Nr. 21.
5. S. dagegen Nr. 20 unsrer Zeitschrift.

verworfen sind die Motetten von Marx, theilweise, wie man schon oben gesehen, die ganze sogenannte "romantische" Schule, so sehr wir diesen Namen als unterscheidend, nicht als bezeichnend billigen.—Ueber Weber und Herold kann kaum besser gesprochen werden.—

Wir schliessen diese Bemerkungen mit Dank gegen einen ächten Künstler; er ist Ludwig Rellstab selbst. Der ältere Streiter hat uns jüngere Kunstkämpen unaufgefordert mit solcher Theilnahme der Welt als turnierfähige Jünglinge vorgestellt, dass wir die Schwerter um so schärfer schliffen, einzuhauen in alles Kranke, Unkünstlerische und Hässliche. Und wenn wir auch hier und da Anderes schützten und angriffen, so erinnere er sich der Worte, die er uns vor kurzem selbst schrieb: "Es gäbe grosses Unglück, wenn wir stets dieselbe Ansicht theilten, da selbst das Vielseitigste noch einseitig ist gegen die tausendseitige Welt in der Menschenbrust."   2.

2. NZfM, I (1834), 210–11: Journalschau. (Fortsetzung.) IV. Allgemeiner musikalischer Anzeiger. (Redacteur: J. F. Castelli. Verleger: Haslinger in Wien. Wöchentlich ein Viertelbogen. Preis für den Jahrgang 2 Thlr.) (Sechster Jahrgang. Januar bis September.)

Der Inhalt erfüllt das Versprechen des Titels. Das beigefügte "allgemeine" kann man im Sinn erklären, dass sich die Tendenz als eine wohlwollende, friedfertige zeigt, die keine gewisse Partei in Schutz nimmt oder gar vertritt. Denkt man es sich in der Bedeutung, als werde Alles in die Musik Einschlagende behandelt, so trifft das nicht, da sich das Blatt nur mit Kritik und Chronik der Gegenwart befasst oder (wie die Iris scheidet und reimt) mit Anzeige der Ereignisse und Erzeugnisse. Die unterlaufenden musikalischen "Bären" kommen nicht in Betracht und sind auch öfter Lämmer in Bärenhäuten. Erst in einer neuern Nummer vom Juli werden auch anderweitig interessirende Artikel versprochen.

Gelehrte musikalische Abhandlungen werden und können es freilich nicht sein, diese überlassen wir ausgedehntern Journalen, aber so Sächelchen, die zum musikalisch-literarischen Desert dienen, Bonbons, eingemachte Früchte picante bittere Mandeln und derlei kleines Zeugs, bald verschluckt und bald verdaut, wollen wir manchmal biethen etc.

Aus dem Angeführten kann man auf die Tonart schliessen, in der das Ganze gehalten. Sie ist durchweg naiv, bescheiden, so nach Art der "Dorfzeitung." Zu Zeiten guckt aber auch eine Faust heraus, der man es ansieht, dass sie derber anfassen könnte, wenn sie sonst wollte.

Die hämische Schicksalsgöttin erhört nicht einmal die einzige winzige Bitte, doch wenigstens zu mindern die unerträgliche Last von Schofel aller Art, die also unbarmherzig Jahr aus Jahr ein auf unsere Augen und Ohren losstürmt, mit cannibalischer Lust, dass wir oft gern tauschen möchten mit den Negersclaven auf Jamaica oder mit den Deportirten in Cayenne, deren Loos gegen unseres gestellt, noch das behaglichste *dolce far niente* des Schlaraffenlands heissen kann etc.

Die Kritik scheint im Durchschnitt in schätzbaren Händen zu sein, glauben wir auch nicht, das sich 101 kritische Finger zusammengeschlossen haben zum Bund, wie die unterschriebenen Zahlen, die bis 101 reichen, vermuthen lassen können. So wäre es z. B. wunderbar, wenn die Trias 7. 12. 46. sich auf einmal in die oft vorkommende Redeblume "dieses Stück möge Anwerth finden" verliebt hätte. Doch sind das Kleinigkeiten, die allenfalls die Aufmerksamkeit beweisen sollen, mit der man gelesen, durchgegangen.—Die Form der Darstellung bleibt sich immer gleich. Gemeinplätze, wie bei Gelegenheit der Hummel'schen Etuden "von Hummel lässt sich nur Treffliches erwarten" finden sich zu häufig vor.—

Mit wenigen Ausnahmen stützt sich das Urtheil auch auf eine ehrenwerthe, namentlich die sogenannte classische Schule hochhaltende Gesinnung.

Für diejenigen, die schwerer zu befriedigen sind und noch an gewissen altfränkischen Begriffen von Mozart'scher und Beethoven'scher Classicität hängen, hat Herz ohnedies nicht geschrieben.

In den frühern Jahrgängen wird nur wenig Haslinger'scher Verlag besprochen, wenigstens nicht öfter, als dass dadurch Anderes beeinträchtigt worden wäre. Und das war erfreulich. Jetzt kommt der Name dieser Verlagshandlung öfter vor, so gut er auch klingt—und namentlich räumt man Strauss, den kein Buchstabe um eine Linie berühmter machen kann, da er in Füssen und Herzen lebt, zu viel Platz. Auch dass das Unternehmen einer Herausgabe der *oeuvres complets* des Herz, des "Allbeliebten," ein "verdienstliches" genannt wird, hätte (leider ohne Schaden für Herz) wegbleiben können.

Von der poetischen Richtung mancher jungen Componisten scheinen die Wiener noch wenig zu ahnen. Man soll sich sogar verschworen haben und die jungen Stürmer förmlich unterdrücken wollen.   22.

3. NZfM, *1* (1834), 226–27; Journalschau. (Fortsetzung.) V. Allgemeiner musikalischer Anzeiger. (Redacteur und Verleger: A. Fischer in Frankfurt. Wöchentlich ein Viertelbogen. Pr. 1 Fl. 48 Kr.) (Januar bis Mai.)

Eigentlich ist dieses Blatt ein Phönix. Es nur nämlich vor Jahren zu Asche geworden, aus der es im letzten Januar von Neuem emporgestiegen. Aber, Wiener Anzeiger, du bist mir in deiner schlichten Weise um vieles lieber, als der Frankfurter mit seiner matten Klarheit, mit seinem Haschen nach Epitheten, die alle daneben schiessen und mit seinem Holz-Arm, der nach dem Land der Schönheit hinstarrt, fast übermüthig, wie das berühmte Thor, auf dem stand: "hier führt der Weg nach Byzanz." Wollte man die ganze Zeitschrift abschreiben, so wäre das leicht bewiesen. Dies geht natürlich nicht.

Einem schreibenden Musiker (denn diesen vermuthen wir hinter dem Dirigenten) verzeiht man wohl ein schiefes Wort, hat nur die Sache ihre Richtigkeit; aber das Urtheil ist hier offenbar zum Theil so verkehrt, dass das einzelne zufällig Getroffene gar nicht dagegen anzuschlagen ist. So heisst es über die Etuden von Hummel:

> Vorliegende Etuden dürften wohl von einer gelehrten Kritik nicht ganz unangetastet bleiben, aber Hummel hat in jeder einzelnen Etude ein lebendiges Bild des Schönen gegeben etc.

Ueber Etuden von Grund:

> Der eigentliche Etudenzweck, nämlich Bildung und Vollendung des Mechanismus, wird durch die musikalisch-poetische Tendenz gedeckt.

Ueber ein Concert von Deszczynski:

> Wiewohl der Componist dieses Concerts sehr einladend auf den Titel schrieb: *"non difficile,"* so möchte Referent doch der Ansicht sein, dass hier weit und breit kein Mangel an Schwierigkeiten ist.

Ueber Compositionen von Panny:

> Der Componist ist anderwärts durch seine genialen Compositionen längst bekannt.

Ueber ein Rondeau von Hermann:

> Vorliegendes Werk ist in dem sogenannten genialen Styl geschrieben, und ist eigentlich keine eigenthümliche Claviercomposition.

Dies ist Alles nicht wahr, Anzeiger! Du irrst wahrhaftig!—Ueber die musikalischen Pfennigmagazine kann er ordentlich in Zorn gerathen, lobt aber dabei die Wiener Tonblumen von Czerny:

> Eine aus der, durch die Pfennigmagazine in Deutschland alle Schranken der Mässigung und Achtung für die edle Kunst durchbrechenden musikalischen Ueberschwemmung lieblich-auftauchende Erscheinung bildet obgenanntes Werk, das wir abermals der kunst- und erfindungsreichen Musikhandlung Wiens verdanken. . . .

Von Wahrheiten ziehen wir noch folgende aus:

> Eine Hauptregel in Sachen der Kunst ist ja diese, das Schöne nur in seiner Quelle aufzusuchen; möge jeder Freund der Kunst diese Regel beherzigen und verfolgen!

Sodann:

> Nur die Vollendung darf das Ziel des ausübenden Künstlers sein, nicht die Gefallsucht im Gebiet der Fertigkeit."

Endlich:

> Möchte doch immer der Componist eines Werks bedenken, dass es sich um die grosse Aufgabe, der Kunst zu genügen, handelt, und jedes scheinbare Modegewand derselben vor dem Glanz eines ächten Kunstwerks verschwinden muss.

Wie lahm!—So geht's durch sämmtliche 18 Nummern, die wir kennen.

Und somit empfehlen wir diesen Anzeiger keineswegs, der übrigens seit Monat Mai nichts mehr von sich hören lasst. Sollte er untergegangen sein, so weinet nicht um ihn, Grazien! denn es starb kein Adonis. 22.

4. NZfM, 2 (1835), 109–10: Beispiel krankhafter Thätigkeit des Gehörorgans.

Unter ähnlicher Ueberschrift lasen wir vor kurzem in den Piererschen medicinischen Annalen einen Bericht des Dr. Greiner, den wir hier im Auszug mittheilen, zugleich mit dem Wunsch, dass der Himmel vor dieser neuen Art von Musik Jeden bewahren möge.

Eine alte 72jährige, beinahe ganz taube Frau, bekam im März v. J. besondre Gesichts- und Gehörserscheinungen. Die Töne bildeten sich nach und nach zu ordentlichen Gesängen. Die Wohnung der Frau liegt so, dass von derselben die Strasse aufwärts etwa 200 Schritte zum Markte und doppelt soviel unterwärts bis zum Thore gerechnet werden können. Nun hörte sie erst vom Markte her, dann von dem Thore, also weit entfernt, einen deutlichen Gesang, erst nur von einer Stimme, gleich dem Gesang des Nachtwächters, in der Folge vermehrten sich die Stimmen, unter denen sie jedoch deutlich die höhere Discant- und die tiefere Bassstimme unterscheiden konnte. Die höhere Stimme war ihr durch ihre Schärfe, Höhe und langes Aushalten besonders unangenehm. Die Gesänge selbst bestanden nicht etwa in einem bestimmten Ertönen, sondern in deutlich abgesungenen Worten, aber in bunter Abwechselung von Gesangbuchsliedern mit lustigen, besonders in älterer Zeit gangbaren Liedern. Allmälig kam die ganze singende Gesellschaft näher, bis vor die Hausthüre, wo nun mitunter Stunden lang ganze Lieder, welche die Kranke wörtlich im Gesangbuche nachlesen konnte, oder auch auswendig wusste, abgesungen wurden, doch mit der Abwechselung, dass es ihr zuweilen so klang, als wenn der ganze Trupp mit einem Geräusch und Lärmen, als wenn viele Menschen und Pferde tappelnd fortliefen, sich eilig entfernte. Doch nicht lange dauerte es, und Alle waren wieder vor der Hausthüre und fingen ihre Gesänge von neuem an. Dabei blieb es noch nicht. Nach wieder mehren Tagen zankten sich viele Menschen mit heftigem verworrenen Geschrei unten im Hause, so dass die Kranke im Anfange, ehe sie noch wusste, dass es Täuschung war, einige Mal aus ihrer Stube an die Treppe lief, um zu hören, was es unten gäbe. Endlich kam dies Gelärme noch näher, denn wenn sie in der Stube sass, so war es, als wenn vor der Stubenthüre grosser Zank entstände, welcher gewöhnlich mit Poltern, Kratzen und Scharren verbunden war und in welchem das laute Schelten der Köchin über die Katze, durch das wiederholte Geschrei: Katz, Katz, Katz u. s. w. sich besonders bemerklich machte. Leider vermehrte sich die Plage der armen Kranken aber noch immer. Wenn sie in der nebenan befindlichen Schlafkammer auf dem Bette lag, war die Stube voll Zank und Streit, mit demselben Kratzen und Gelärme auf den Dielen und demselben unaufhörlichen Geschrei:

Katz, Katz! Sass sie auf dem Sopha in der Stube, so stellte sich wenigstens das Kratzen und Scharren hinter ihrem Rücken, oder unter dem Sopha, oder an einer Seite ein. Dabei aber hatte das Singchor seine Thätigkeit nicht eingestellt, sondern es ertönte dazwischen bald vor der Hausthüre, bald auf dem Markte, auch, wenn sich etwas mehr Ruhe einstellte, vor dem Thore. Der Schlaf war dabei nicht ganz gestört, doch kürzer als sonst und sogleich mit dem Erwachen, oft schon früh um 4 Uhr, stellten sich auch die Lärm- oder Gesangscenen wieder ein. Nachdem das Uebel bis zu der beschriebenen Form seine höchste Stufe erreicht hatte, schien es allmälig wieder abnehmen zu wollen. Das Lärmen, Zanken und Poltern und anderes Geräusch nahm ab und kam seltener; das Singen beschränkte sich auf grössere Entfernung und fing meistens vor dem Thore an, von wo es allmälig bis vor das Haus näher rückte und nach einiger Zeit wieder abzog. In der Stärke und Art des Singens blieb es übrigens noch immer sich gleich, besonders in der widerlichen Höhe und dem langen Ziehen einzelner Stimmen und dem Wechsel der Lieder. Auch hierin aber zeigte sich etwa in der Mitte Aprils die erste Spur der Besserung dadurch, dass die Kranke mehr Macht des Willens über den Gesang bekam, was sie zufällig gewahr wurde. Da nämlich einmal der Gesang auf dem Markte wohl über eine Stunde lang gedauert und nur sogenannte weltliche Lieder vorgebracht hatte, wobei besonders die hohe und gellende Stimme sich auszeichnete und einen Refrain so unaufhörlich wiederholte, dass die Kranke in ihrer Ungeduld in den lebhaften Wunsch ausbrach, "wenn ihr doch nur statt des dummen Zeuges wenigstens ein gutes Lied sänget," so änderte sich augenblicklich Text und Melodie, und anstatt, dass bisher unzählige Male ertönt hatte: "ich liebe dich, ich liebe dich, ich liebe dich von Herzen," erscholl nun der Choral: "wer nur den lieben Gott lässt walten" und führte das ganze Lied völlig durch. Die Kranke war erfreut hierdurch und meistens gelang es in der Folge ihrer Willenskraft, sich, wenn das anhaltende Singen lustiger Lieder ihr endlich zuwider wurde, ein geistlich ihr bekanntes Lied zu bestellen.

Nach und nach verlor sich der Gesang mehr oder weniger, obgleich die Frau noch nicht völlig geheilt ist. Merkwürdig war aber, dass ihr Gehör während jener Gesangperiode merklich verbessert und leiser war, dann aber, als das Singen nachliess, die Schwerhörigkeit wieder in demselben, ja in einem Ohr in noch höhern Grade sich einstellte, wie sie vor dieser Periode war. 22.

5. NZfM, 2 (1835), 110: Franz Schuberts nachgelassene grössere Werke betreffend.

Wir beeilen uns, folgende Notiz zur Kenntnis unsrer Leser zu bringen und sie um Verbreitung dieser Nachricht, wie um Verwendung für die Sache selbst angelegentlichst zu ersuchen.

Franz Schubert, der zu früh verblichene geniale Tonsetzer, der seelenvolle Liedercomponist, hat mehre Tonwerke hinterlassen, welche sich in seines Bruders Händen befinden und welche derselbe, theils um der Welt diese Werke nicht vorzuenthalten, theils auch, um das geistige Erbe seines Bruders zu seinem eigenen Besten nach dem Wunsche des Verstorbenen zu verwenden, Bühnendirectionen und Musikern gegen billiges Honorar zur Aufführung überlassen will. Diese Werke sind I. Opern: des Teufels Lustschloss in 2 Acten (1814 vollendet)—Fernando in 1 Act (1815)—die Freunde von Salamanca in 2 Acten von Mayrhofer (1815)—der vierjährige Posten in 1 Act (1815)—die Bürgschaft in 3 Acten (1816)—die Zwillingsbrüder in 1 Act—die Zauberharfe, Melodrama in 3 Acten (1820)—häuslicher Krieg in 1 Act von Castelli (1823)—Fierabras in 3 Acten von Schober (1823). II. Symphonieen in D (1813), in D (1815), in B (1815), in C-Moll (1816), in B (1816), in C-Dur (1818), in C-Moll (seine letzte). III. Messen. In F für 4 Singstimmen und grosses Orchester (1814)— In G für 4 Singstimmen und kleines Orchester (1815)—in B für Singstimmen und mittleres Orchester—in As und in Es, beide für 4 Singstimmen und grosses Orchester (1822 und 1828). Wer hiervon etwas zu erhalten wünscht, beliebe sich schriftlich an Hrn. Ferdinand Schubert, Lehrer an der R. R. Normal-Hauptschule in Wien zu wenden.

6. NZfM, 2 (1835), 197: Fetis über Hector Berlioz und dessen Symphonie: *Grande Symphonie fantastique. Oeuv. 4. Partition de Piano par Fr. Liszt.—20 Frcs.—Paris, M. Schlesinger.*

Vorbemerkung der Redaction. Wir machten schon früher auf das Urtheil in der von Fetis redigirten *revue musicale* aufmerksam, damals, ohne die Symphonie, noch überhaupt etwas von den Compositionen des Berlioz zu kennen. Die über dasselbe Werk geschriebenen Briefe von Heinrich Panofka schienen uns mit dem geringschätzenden Ton der Fetisschen Recension in so interessantem Widerspruche zu stehen, dass wir flugs nach Paris um die Symphonie selbst schrieben. Seit einigen Wochen befindet sie sich in unsern Händen. Mit Entsetzen sahen und spielten wir. Nach und nach stellte sich unser Urtheil fest und dem des Hr. Fetis im Durchschnitt so hart gegenüber, dass wir, theils um die Aufmerksamkeit der Deutschen doppelt auf diesen geistreichen Republicaner zu ziehen, theils um Manchem Gelegenheit zu eigenem Vergleichen zu verschaffen, die Fetissche Recension kurz und frei übersetzt unsern Lesern vorzulegen beschlossen. Unser Urtheil folgt so bald wie möglich nach. Bis dahin würden wir denen, die sich für Ausserordentliches interessiren, angelegentlich Empfehlen, sich mit der Symphonie selbst bekannt machen zu wollen.

7. NZfM, 3 (1835), 80: Notiz.

Wir hatten vor Kurzem Gelegenheit, die drei königl. hannöverschen Kammermusiker Schmittbach und Rose (Vater und Sohn) in einem Concerte zu hören. Ersterer steht in Leipzig noch in so gutem Andenken, dass es zu bemerken genügt, wie sich Ton, Fertigkeit und Vortrag seines Spieles in grossem Grade vervollkommt haben und er den besten lebenden Fagottspielern beizuzählen ist. Auch die Composition war mehr als gewöhnliche Virtuosenbravade; namentlich scheint die Einführung des Recitativs in Fagottsätzen an der rechten Stelle. Die Hr. Rose, Künstler auf der Oboe, spielten zusammen wie Vater und Sohn. Der Ton des letztern schien sogar noch weicher und angenehmer, woran wohl Schuld war, dass er sich in dem der Oboe eigenen Mezzosopranumfange aufhielt, während der Vater mehr in den höheren schneidenden Tönen spielte. An gut componirten Oboeduetten fehlt es. Der Beifall in der Provinzialstadt, wo wir diese Künstler hörten, war ihren Leistungen angemessen. 12.

8. NZfM, 3 (1835), 119–20: Monstrum.

Unter dem Titel: "Geschichte der Musik aller Nationen. Nach Staffort und Fetis. Mit Benutzung der besten deutschen Hülfsmittel von mehren Musikfreunden. Mit 12 Abbildungen und 11 Notentafeln. Weimar 1835." ward uns vor Kurzem ein Buch zum Recensiren zugeschickt. Wir schlugen auf und fanden:

S. 252. Bellini ist ein junger Componist, dessen Ruf sich erst zu begründen beginnt. . . .

In Leipzig ist Otto Claudius ein guter dramatischer Componist; seine beste Oper ist Aladin oder die wunderbare Lampe.

S. 293. Oft hat man im Auslande ganze deutsche Musikerfamilien gesehen, deren Talente Bewunderung erregten, z. B. die Familie Rainier, die 1827 nach England ging, die Familie Herrmann in München, von der zwei Brüder auf Violine und Violoncell sich auszeichnen. Auch machen sich hier und da sehr junge Menschen durch Talent und

Virtuosität bemerklich, die zu schönen Erwartungen berechtigen, wie z. B. die Gebrüder Eichhorn als Violinisten. Ihre Volkslieder singen die Deutschen mit auffallendem Talent, wie schon früher Madame de Stael in ihrem Werk über Deutschland bemerkt hat.

Das Publicum wird demnach wohlthun, wenn es uns nachahmt, die wir vor den Augen Mehrerer das Buch feierlich zerrissen und hinter den Ofen werfen [sic].   12.

9. NZfM, 4 (1836), 48–49: Ehrenzeugniss.

Wie gern willfahr' ich dem Wunsche des Herrn Wilmers aus Copenhagen, ein paar Worte über seinen vierzehnjährigen Sohn Rudolph aus den Büchern der Davidsbündler abzuschreiben.

"—Bei weitem erstaunlicher als im Vortrage der Compositionen, die er bei Hummel einstudirt, trat sein musikalisches Talent im freien Phantasiren hervor. Euseb gab ihm das Hornthema aus dem ersten Satz der C-Moll-Symphonie. Erst stutzte der Knabe und tappte, da er nicht wusste, ob es nach B oder Es gehört, so liebenswürdig verlegen in den Harmonieen herum, dass es eine Freude war. Nach und nach aber erschloss sich ihm die Bedeutung der vier Töne und nun strömten ordentlich Blumen, Blitze und Perlen unter seinen Fingern hervor, so dass wir einen Jüngling zu hören meinten. Auf den gebt Acht, sagte Meister Raro nach dem Schluss, der wird Euch einmal etwas erzählen."

So steht im 20sten Buch der Davidsbündler.   Florestan.

10. NZfM, 7 (1837), 196: Der Gedanke, mit unserer Zeitschrift ein musikalisches Journal, das in vierteljährlichen Beigaben ausgesuchter Compositionen besteht, in's Leben treten zu lassen, hat einen guten Anklang gefunden, und es befindet sich bereits Treffliches in unsern Händen. Die erste dieser Beilagen wird im nächsten Januar ausgegeben und enthält Gesang- und Pianoforte-Compositionen von A. Henselt, F. Mendelssohn-Bartholdy, J. Moscheles und L. Spohr; Dank diesen verehrten Künstlern, dass sie sich unserer Idee so wohlwollend gezeigt und mit Einigem ihres Besten beigesteuert. Wie nun diese Beigaben den Sinn für edlere und tiefere Musik überall noch mehr verbreiten helfen möchten, so sollen sie, wie schon früher ausgesprochen wurde, auch zur Ausstellung von Compositionen unbekannterer Künstler da sein. Zu diesem Zweck haben wir denn eine der nächsten bestimmt, und ersuchen demnach Alle, uns noch einzuschicken, was für eine solche Sammlung passend scheint, namentlich Lieder, mehrstimmige auch, kürzere Compositionen jeder Art für Clavier,

Orgel etc. Ueber die Einsendungen, ob sie sich zur Aufnahme eignen oder nicht, wird die Zeitschrift regelmässig berichten.

Leipzig, am 12. December 1837. Die Redaction.

11. NZfM, 7 (1837), 199: Nachwort.

Wo hier anfangen, wo aufhören; Auf der einen Seite ein excentrischer Lobredner, auf der andern ein gepanzerter Ankläger, der Gegenstand der Schilderhebung ein dem Componisten vielleicht selbst schon entfremdetes Werk!—Wir glauben, alle drei müssen Zugeständnisse machen: Lobe, dass er die einzelnen Schwächen, die ihm bei ruhigem Blut nicht entgehen konnten, verschwiegen habe—Wedel, dass er, ohne die Partitur und ohne das Werk von einem grossen Orchester in Vollkommenheit gehört zu haben, sich nicht wohl zutrauen dürfe, einen Eindruck des Ganzen zu besitzen—Berlioz endlich, dass er selbst recht gut wisse, kein Meisterstück, das sich eben mit Beethoven'schem messen könne, geliefert zu haben. So hätten wir es denn mit dem Werk eines achtzehnjährigen Franzosen zu thun, der wenn auch etwas weniger Genie hat, als der Eine, doch auch mehr Schöpferkraft, als der Andere will. Eine genauere Auseinanderlegung der Gründe verlangte einen abermals so grossen Artikel. Besser man spiele die Ouverture aller Orten, am besten endlich, man mache, anstatt sich über die Jugendarbeit eines wenn auch ungebildeten, immerhin merkwürdigen Talentes zu erhitzen, schönere und die schönsten; und damit sei Eins dem Andern empfohlen! Die Redaction.

12. NZfM, 8 (1838), 28: Erklärung.

Hr. L. Rellstab in Berlin hat in Nr. 50 der *Gazette musicale de Paris* einen Bericht über den Zustand der Musik in Deutschland drucken lassen, in dem er auch unsere Zeitschrift erwähnt, ihr manches Gute nachrühmt, zuletzt aber mit der Bemerkung schliesst, "dass sich ihre Mitarbeiter leider gar zu oft unter einander selbst lobten." Dies veranlasst uns zu folgender Erklärung.

Feste Mitarbeiter am kritischen Theil des Blattes waren seit Begründung der Zeitschrift bis jetzt nur die H. H. Ludwig Schunke (vor drei Jahren gestorben), C. Banck, C. F. Becker, Osw. Lorenz und der die Redaction Unterzeichnende, der zugleich Alles, was mit der Bezeichnung "Davidsbündler" versehen, mit seinem Namen vertritt, wie er schon vor vielen Jahren (Bd I. S. 152) erklärt hat. Von L. Schunke's Compositionen wurden nur einige nach seinem Tode mit der Anerkennung angezeigt, die dieser treffliche Künstler verdiente; von C. Banck, der an die zwanzig Hefte weit und breit gesungener

Lieder componirt, etwa zwei oder drei in scherzhafter Weise von ihm
selbst; von C. F. Becker, der Manches zu Tage gefördert, eine einzige
seiner Ausgaben von Tonstücken älterer Componisten; von Osw. Lorenz, einem talentvollen Liedercomponisten, nichts; von Compositionen der Davidsbündler eine Sonate, über die Hr. Professor Moscheles
in London einen Aufsatz lieferte, für welchen ihm die musikalische
Welt eher zu Dank verpflichtet ist,—und scherzweise und vorüberge-
hend einige kleinere Stücke. Und dies in sieben Bänden und unter 1800
besprochenen Werken! Und darauf stützt Hr. Rellstab eine so verletzende Aeusserung, und das gegen ein mit Opfern erhaltenes Institut,
das seine ganze Ehre gerade in seine bewiesene Unparteilichkeit, seine
treu bewahrte Künstlergesinnung setzt, und gegen Künstler, die für
die Verläugnung ihrer Interessen, ihre Liebe zur Sache nicht einmal
die Genugthuung hatten, ihre Leistungen besprochen zu sehen, ja
freiwillig darauf verzichten!

Entscheide denn hier das Publicum! Hr. Rellstab sehe aber ein, dass
er sich leeren Einbildungen hingegeben, sich einer Unwahrheit schul-
dig gemacht habe; im andern Falle würde er uns künftighin zu einer
Art der Vertheidigung zwingen, dass er es unterlassen dürfte, sich an
unbescholtene Künstler noch einmal zu vergreifen.— Die Redaction:
R. Schumann.

13. NZfM, 8 (1838), 180: Wie wir beinahe vorausgesehen, so hat
die in Nr. 34 der Zeitschr. im Artikel "Liszt in Wien" enthaltene
Parallele Widerspruch gefunden. Hr. Baron von Lannoy hat in Nr.
95 der Wiener Theaterzeitung dagegen geschrieben. Wir lieben den
offenen Angriff, aber auch dann dürften keine Reden wie "erbärm-
liche Anmassung" u. dgl. vorkommen, am wenigsten aus dem Munde
eines Edelmannes. Was den Inhalt der Parallele selbst anbetrifft, so
geben wir die Gewagtheit solcher Vergleichungen zu. Dass sie aber
nichts weniger als eine Herabsetzung Liszt's beabsichtigte, von dessen
hohem Talente im Vorhergehenden mit der aufrichtigsten Bewunderung gesprochen war, wie dass sie überhaupt nicht aus irgend einer
Persönlichkeit, und nur aus der guten einfachen Absicht des Schreibers
hervorgegangen, der nämlich, sich und Andere über manche Eigenthümlichkeit jener vier Künstler in möglichster Kürze aufzuklären,
können wir auf's Wort versichern. Wozu also solche Schimpfreden!
Käme es aber darauf an, neue Fragen zu stellen, wie deren Hr. v. Lannoy eine Menge gethan, so wollten wir wohl welche finden, über die
auch Hr. v. L. nachzusinnen haben sollte.

Anlangend endlich Hrn. v. L's Verwunderung über die Bemerkung der Redaction, worin Henselt als Componist den Anderen vorangestellt wurde, so müssen wir es dem Publicum überlassen, wem es mehr Glauben schenkt, Hrn. v. L. oder uns, im Uebrigen auf unsern Ausspruch beharren. Die Gründe: warum? finden sich in den acht Bänden unserer Zeitschrift an verschiedenen Stellen. Ob die Henselt'schen Etuden mehr oder weniger bekannt seien, thut nichts zur Sache; man muss die Augen auch ohnedies offen haben. Die Redaction.

14. NZfM, *8* (1838), 187–88: Biographische Notizen über Ludwig van Beethoven von *Dr.* F. G. Wegeler und Ferdinand Ries. [Coblenz, bei Bädecker.]

Unter obigem Titel wird uns so eben ein 164 Seiten starkes Bändchen zugestellt, von dem wir unsere Leser schnell in Kenntniss setzen müssen. Es enthält die interessantesten, meist neue Beiträge zu Beethoven's Lebensgeschichte. Der Erstere der Herausgeber, Königl. Preuss. Geheime und Regierungs-Medicinal-Rath, Ritter mehrer Orden etc., in Coblenz lebend, war, wie sich aus dem Bändchen ergiebt, Beethoven's genauster Jugendfreund. Gerade über die früheren Jahre seines Lebens mangelte es an bestimmten Nachrichten; was man hier erfährt, kann als authentisch betrachtet werden. Wir möchten den ganzen Abschnitt abschreiben, beschränken uns aber auf kurze Angabe des Inhalts.

Zuerst sind über Beethoven's Herkunft und Familie die genausten Notizen beigebracht; eben so über Jahr und Tag, selbst über das Haus, wo er in Bonn geboren, dass kein Zweifel mehr aufkommen kann. Die Erfindung, dass B. ein Sohn Friedrich's II., wird als abgeschmackt zurückgewiesen, wie die Hypothese[6] eines englischen Autors im englischen Musikjournal *"Harmonicon"* v. Novemb., 1823. Hierauf folgt ein Abschnitt über B's Erziehung und erste Bildung. In Bonn war es nämlich das von Breuning'sche Haus, wo B. täglich aus- und einging; auch Wegeler, der sich später der Tochter des Hauses, Elenore vermählte. Stephan v. Breuning, Sohn vom Haus, bekannt als einer der von B. ernannten Testamentsexecutoren, der kurz nach B. starb, wird hier ebenfalls eingeführt. B's erste Lehrer; frühzeitiges Hervorbrechen seines mächtigen Talentes. Sein Beschützer, Graf Waldstein,

---

6. Wir setzen sie ihrer Naivität halber her: *"That Beethoven is a wonderful man, there can be no doubt; but if this prince were really his Father, he is the greatest prodigy the world ever saw, or most likely will ever see again; for as Frederich II. died in 1740, the period of Mad. Beethoven's gestation must in such a case have been exactly thirty years."*

der ihm zur Reise nach Wien verhilft. B's Bekanntschaft mit B. Romberg und Haydn in den Jahren 1786 und 87, ebenso mit Sterkel. Seine ersten Compositionen; namentlich wird eine Cantate erwähnt, die verloren gegangen scheint; ebenso ein Ritterballet, von dem sich der Clavierauszug noch im Besitz des Musikhändler Dunst in Frankfurt befinden müsse. Seine Abneigung gegen Unterrichtgeben und Spielen in Gesellschaften. Endlich B's Reise nach Wien, wo ihn Wegeler 1794 wiederfindet und bis 96 in täglichem Verkehr mit ihm bleibt.

Hierauf folgen Briefe von Beethoven an Wegeler aus den Jahren 1800 bis 1817, von denen nur der erste bekannt ist, ebenso Briefe an Elenore v. Breuning, später verehelichte Wegeler, aus dem Jahre 1793, zuletzt ein Brief von Stephan v. Breuning über die erste Aufführung des Fidelio, alle mit sehr interessanten Anmerkungen vom Herausgeber begleitet.

Ungleich wichtiger für den Musiker sind die Beiträge der zweiten Abtheilung von Ferdinand Ries. Aeusserst bescheiden entschuldigt sich Ries, dass man ihm, der kein Schriftsteller wäre, die Einfachheit seines Styles, wie den Mangel an Ordnung nachsehen möge. Was er liefert, ist ebenfalls fast durchgängig neu. In kleinen Abschnitten erfährt man über den schönen Grund, warum sich B. Ries'sens annahm [bekanntlich wollte er nur diesen und den Erzherzog Rudolph als seine Schüler genannt wissen]. Merkwürdige Notiz über die Entstehung der Sinfonia eroica. wie über mehre Compositionen; kleinere Anekdoten; über B's Verhältniss zu Steibelt, Haydn, Albrechtsberger, Salieri, Fürst Lobkowitz, Clementi, Himmel [sic], Prinz Louis, Erzherzog Rudolph. über die Art seines Unterrichts, [wobei auffällt, dass er noch 1823 bei gänzlicher Taubheit dem Erzherzog Rudolph oft täglich drei Stunden gab]; über den Anfang seiner Schwerhörigkeit, die sich, nach den Nachrichten von Wegeler, schon 1800 zeigte; sein auffahrendes Wesen, sein Misstrauen, schnelles Vergeben, grosse Gutmüthigkeit; über sein ausserordentliches freies Phantasiren, wie Bemerkungen über vieles Andere, mit deren Aufzählung wir der Freude des Lesers nicht weiter vorgreifen wollen.

Ein Schattenriss B's, als sechszehnjähriger Jüngling, und drei Facsimile's aus verschiedenen Lebensaltern sind ausserdem beigelegt, wie auch Textunterlagen von Wegeler zu einigen B'schen Compositionen.—

Das Buch wird viel gelesen werden, wie es dies verdient. Dass es mannichfache Gedanken anregt, erhebende wie auch betrübende, kann man versichert sein. Die Aufschlüsse über B's Ehrgeiz und Neigung zur Aristokratie, wie über seine Herzensangelegenheiten gehören zu den dankenswerthesten. Ueber Einiges sind wir im Dunkel. Beethoven spricht S. 142 in einem Brief von 1816 von einem Concert in F-Moll, ebenso S. 147 mehrmals von einem Quintett. Wir wissen nicht, was für Compositionen damit gemeint sein mögen. Sodann, könnte man nicht erfahren, wo sich B's jüngster Bruder, der nach Hrn. Dr. Wegeler's Vermuthung noch am Leben sein könnte und jetzt 62 Jahre alt wäre, im Augenblick aufhielte? Von den Lebenden wäre es namentlich Bernhard Romberg, der gewiss noch Manches über B. weiss. Hr. MD. Schindler in Aachen lässt leider noch immer warten.

Die Redaction.

15. NZfM, 10 (1839), 37: Reliquien von Franz Schubert.

Die nachfolgenden Briefe und Gedichte verdanke ich der Gefälligkeit des Hrn. Ferdinand Schubert, des Bruders des Verstorbenen. Es ist noch nichts derartiges von Schubert veröffentlicht, und auch wirklich nur wenig vorhanden, dies Wenige aber so charakteristisch in seiner Derbheit, wie in seiner Innigkeit, mit der er namentlich Naturschönheiten zu schildern versucht, dass die Mittheilung dem Leser eine willkommene sein wird. Von meiner Befürchtung, dass die Gedichte vielleicht nur von ihm abgeschrieben wären, wurde ich nach einmaligem Durchlesen befreit. Einmal beweisen es die Handschriften, die alle Zeichen von Originalergüssen an sich haben, dann die Gedichte selbst, die wenn auch einen dichterischen Geist, doch eine nur wenig geübte Hand verrathen, zuletzt die in ihnen vorherrschende Gemüthsstimmung, wie sie Näherstehende oft an Schubert bemerkt. Der "Traum" lässt tiefere Deutung zu; sie sei Theilnehmenden überlassen.

Wien, d. 8. Januar 1838.   R.S.

16. NZfM, 10 (1839), 84: Wien, den 26sten Februar. Lindpaintner's Genueserin ist bis jetzt viermal und mit grossem Beifall im Kärnthnerthortheater gegeben worden. Man nennt das hier eine deutsche Musik; sie ist es aber im Grunde nicht, sondern, wie Alles von Lindpaintner, einnehmend im ersten Augenblick, klar und leicht verknüpft, und namentlich in der Instrumentirung klangvoll und glänzend. Dabei herrscht der deutsche gesunde Sinn im Ganzen allerdings vor, weshalb wir auch gern in die dem Componisten (der die drei ersten Aufführungen selbst dirigirte, und zwar wie ein Meister) höchst ehrenvolle Anerkennnng [sic] einstimmen, die ihm vom Publicum an allen drei Abenden zu Theil geworden, und die Oper allen

deutschen Bühnen zur Aufführung empfehlen. Der Text ist freilich sehr gewöhnlich; Neuheit, oder gar Poesie in der Idee fehlen ihm gänzlich. Und was konnte doch aus der glücklich gewählten Localität (Venedig) gemacht werden; sie ist aber rein zufällig, und das Stück könnte eben so˙ gut in Braunschweig oder Algier spielen bei passend verwechselter Costumirung. Die schöne scenische Ausstattung (Marcusplatz, Marcuskirche) wird ebenfalls der Oper eine längere Theilnahme sichern. Als vorzüglichstes Musikstück galt mir die erste Arie des Hrn. Schober (er gab einen Bösewicht, dessen Name mir entfallen), die aber am Publicum ganz spurlos vorüberging. Der zweite Act enthält ebenfalls viel gute Musik, erinnert aber durchaus an die Kerkerscene im Fidelio. Eine ausführlichere Besprechung der ganzen Oper behalte ich mir bis auf mehrmaliges Anhören vor. Sie erscheint übrigens ehestens bei Tob. Haslinger im Clavierauszug. Frl. Lutzer, die HH. Staudigt und Schober hatten die wichtigsten Rollen und sangen wie immer höchst ausgezeichnet.—Im Kärnthnerthortheater gastirt, ausser Frl. Sabine Heinefetter auch Mad. Clara Stökl-Heinefetter und trat zuerst als Elvira im Don Juan auf.—Von älteren Opern hat man Spontini's wenig bekannten "Milton" wieder hervorgesucht, von neueren die Jüdin von Halevy. Auch dir [sic] Hugenotten von Meyerbeer werden mit verändertem Text nächstens in Scene gehen.—Von fremden Virtuosen waren es in der letzten Zeit der Violoncellist Menter aus München, ein ganzer Künstler von Aussen wie Innen, und der junge Nicolaus Schäfer aus Petersburg, dieser wirklich geistvolle Knabe, die Aufsehen machten; die Concerte waren indess wenig besucht.—Von Einheimischen gaben der Archivar der Gesellschaft der Musikfreunde Glöggl und Professor Jansa ihre jährlichen Abendunterhaltungen.—Hr. Vesque v. Püttlingen, der Componist der Turandot, arbeitet an einer neuen Oper, deren Sujet die Jungfrau von Orleans sein soll.—Zur Feier der Anwesenheit des Grossfürsten Thronfolger von Russland ist in nächster Woche Hof-Concert.—

17. NZfM, _10_ (1839), 132: [Berichtigung, Mozart's Originalpartitur das Requiem betreffend.]

Genaueren Untersuchungen zu Folge ist durch den Fund der Handschrift, von der in Nr. 3 aus Wien gesprochen wurde, die Echtheit des Requiem von Mozart noch lange nicht bewiesen. Der Einsender berichtete nur, was er von Mozart's Sohn und von dem als erprobten Handschriftenkenner bekannten Hrn. A. Fuchs darüber erfahren hatte. Süssmayr's Handschrift soll nämlich mit der Mozart's so viel

Aehnlichkeit haben, dass sie sich oft kaum unterscheiden lassen, und so mögen denn wieder allerhand Zweifel entstanden sein. Ehren wir denn, da die Sache schwerlich jemals zur Aufklärung kommen wird, den Schöpfer des Werkes, wenigstens seiner einzelnen Theile, und kümmern uns nicht um den Namen. Das Nähere über den neulichen Fund findet man übrigens in einer vor kurzem in Wien erschienenen Brochüre des Hrn. Hofrath v. Mosel.—Die in demselben Bericht (in Nr. 3) angeführten angeblich Mozart'schen Quartette haben sich ebenfalls als völlig unecht dargethan.—

18. NZfM, *10* (1839), 200: Mozart's Grab ist bekanntlich nicht aufzufinden. Als er beerdigt wurde, war eine stürmische Nacht, und es soll nur ein einziger alter Mann den Sarg begleitet haben. Eben so wenig weiss man Gluck's Grabstätte. Beethoven jedoch hat einen Denkstein erhalten. Es steht nichts darauf als *"BEETHOVEN."* Der Gedanke war gut, hätte nicht der Verfertiger des Denksteins einige Spannen darunter auch seinen Namen angebracht. Franz Schubert liegt nur einen Schritt davon. Auch Haydn's Ueberreste weiss man; sie ruhen, wenn ich nicht irre, auf einer Besitzung des Fürsten Esterhazy, der den Leichnam lange nach seiner Bestattung auf einem Gottesacker, unweit Wien, ausgraben liess. Bei der Ausgrabung vermisste man aber, wie man sagt,—den Schädel. Es war nicht zu entdecken, wo er hingekommen. Endlich vor einigen Jahren starb einer der ältesten Freunde von Haydn, in dessen Nachlass sich auch ein wohlbewahrter Schädel findet, der nach einer schriftlich hinterlassenen Anzeige des Verstorbenen der Haydn's ist. Der Erblasser hatte ihn der Gesellschaft der Musikfreunde testamentarisch überlassen, der Fürst Esterhazy ihn aber als sein Eigenthum reclamirt. So erzählt man wenigstens in Wien.—

19. NZfM, *12* (1840), 132: Im Feuilleton der "Jahrbücher des deutschen Nationalvereins" wird der Unterzeichnete als Verfasser einer vier Zeilen langen Definition des Wortes "Cantate" citirt, die er niemals gegeben zu haben sich erinnert. Wohl möglich, dass die Redaction des Damenconversationslexikons, der ich vor beinahe 10 Jahren einige kleinere biographische Artikel in den Buchstaben B and C lieferte, jener Definition, die übrigens dem Zwecke jenes Lexikons vollkommen entspricht, die Anfangsbuchstaben meines Namens untersetzte. Die Sache ist so unbedeutend, dass ich sie nicht anführen würde, wenn sie nicht abermals bewiese, zu welchen trivialen Mitteln Hr. Dr. Schilling seine Zuflucht nimmt, mit Männern anzubinden, die

nichts mit ihm zu schaffen haben wollen. Was die im nämlichen Feuilleton enthaltene Bemerkung betrifft, dass ich in dieser meiner eigenen
Zeitschrift nicht selten ein "genialer" und ähnlicher Mann genannt
werde, so hat Hr. Dr. Schilling die Zeitschrift mit seinem "Univer-
sallexikon" verwechselt, in dem neben andern Unrichtigkeiten auch
die obige steht. Man sieht abermals, wie Hr. Dr. Schilling mit Männern
anzubinden Lust hat, die nichts mit ihm zu thun haben wollen.   R.S.

20. NZfM, *13* (1840), 48: Leipzig, den 29. Juli.—Den 6ten August Abends 6 Uhr wird Hr. MD. Dr. Mendelssohn-Bartholdy in der
Thomaskirche ein Orgelconcert geben. Die Einnahme ist zu einem
Denkstein für Johann Sebastian Bach bestimmt, der ihm in der Nähe
seiner ehemaligen Wohnung gesetzt werden soll. Ein alter Wunsch,
gewiss Unzähliger, geht somit in Erfüllung, und wir wissen unsere
Freude über diesen Zug schönkünstlerischer Pietät kaum in Worten
auszudrücken. Wo sich aber ein solcher Künstler an die Spitze stellt,
sollten da nicht viele folgen, sollte der Gedanke nicht auch in der
Ferne anklingen? Könnte aus dem Denkstein nicht ein Denkmal werden? Ihm, dem Einzigen, Ewigen ein Monument zu setzen, das sich
würdig an die zu Ehren Mozart's und Beethoven's anreihete, dazu
wäre die Zeit da, dazu sollten sich die Hände aller Künstler und Kunstfreunde verbinden, dies würde unserm Zeitalter als ein Beweis seines
aufgeklärten Kunstsinns in der Zukunft angerechnet werden. Ueber
den Erfolg des ersten Anfangs hoffen wir bald etwas mitzutheilen;
möchten diese einfachen Worte dazu beitragen, dass wir es auch bald
über andere könnten.—   12.

21. NZfM, *14* (1841), 86: Die Plagiate des Dr. Schilling in Stuttgart betreffend.

Zur Würdigung eines Aufsatzes des Dr. G. Schilling in Stuttgart:
"die neue Zeitschrift für Musik und ich" werden Alle, die nur den
G. Schilling'schen Aufsatz kennen, ersucht, die Warnung des Hrn.
Hofrath Hand in Jena in Nr. 48 des 40sten Jahrgangs der Allg. Mus.
Zeitung, die Bekanntmachung des Hrn. Buchhändler Metzler in Stuttgart, die Warnung des Hrn. Buchhändler Köhler in Stuttgart in Nr.
7 der diesjährigen Buchhändlerbörsenblätter, die Recensionen des Hrn.
Organist C. F. Becker hier in Bd. 13. Nr. 40, die der Chiffre 4 in Bd.
14 Nr. 3 unserer Zeitschrift, wie die in den NNr. 195 u. 196 des vorigen Jahrgangs der Jenaischen Literaturzeitung gleichfalls nachzulesen,
um dadurch zu einem Urtheil über den genannten Mann zu gelangen,
wie auch darüber, ob hier nicht eine Pflicht gegen das Publicum vorlag,

auf das marktschreierische Treiben dieses Pfuschers aufmerksam zu machen, und ob man anständiger Weise sich mit einem solchen überhaupt einlassen dürfe. Wir antworten daher auf den sonstigen Inhalt jenes Aufsatzes nichts, verweisen nur auf die Sache, und warten getrost auf das "strafende Gericht," das Hr. Schilling zu seiner Vertheidigung anrufen will. Schliesslich auch noch die Versicherung, dass Hr. Prof. A. B. Marx in Berlin der Kritik des Schilling'schen sogenannten "Polyphonomos" völlig fremd ist, und dass wir gehörigen Ortes den Verfasser nennen werden, der in so gründlicher Weise jenen dünkelhaften und unwissenden Plagiator entlarvt hat.

Leipzig, im März 1841.

Die Redaction der Neuen Zeitschrift für Musik.

22. NZfM, *14* (1841), 138: Leipzig d. 23sten. Das gestrige Concert für die Armen im Saale des Gewandhauses wurde namentlich durch zwei neue Compositionen von Julius Rietz in Düsseldorf interessant: eine Ouverture zu "Hero und Leander," und einen "altdeutschen Schlachtgesang" für unisonen Chor mit Orchester, beide noch Manuscript; die Ouverture ist bedeutend, in einem höchst edeln Charakter geschrieben, überhaupt eine früher gehörte desselben Componisten in jedem Betracht überwiegend, namentlich auch was das Colorit der Instrumentation anlangt. Im "Schlachtgesang," so eigenthümlich kraftvoll er ist, hat der Componist, wie uns scheint, im Streben nach einer schönen Kunstform den rechten Wirkungspunct verfehlt. Vielleicht dass sich das Stück zu noch mehr concentrischer Kraft durch eine kleine Aenderung unwandeln lässt. Ausserdem traten im Concert Frl. Schloss auf in einer Romanze aus Tell von Rossini und zwei Liedern von F. Schubert und R. Schumann, und Hr. Pohlend, vormaliges Mitglied der Dresdner Capelle in einer Phantasie von Ernst und einem Rondo von Lipinski, beide mit Beifall. Den Schluss machte Beethoven's C-Moll-Symphonie.—   13.

23. NZfM, *20* (1844), 11: Wir stimmen dem Verf. nicht in Allem bei, z. B. nicht in dem, was er über das Verhältniss zwischen Form und Idee sagte; haben auch gar nicht so viel Formlosigkeit in Berlioz'scher Musik finden können, eher umgekehrt zu oft Form ohne Inhalt. Desto mehr pflichten wir ihm bei, dass es ein schlimmes Zeichen für einen beginnenden Componisten sei, wenn er nicht vor Allem blos Musik machen, sondern Allerhand durch die Musik darstellen will, wenn er die Musik nur als Dienerin oder Dollmetscherin gebrauchen will.—   d. R.

Bibliography

Abert, Hermann J., *Robert Schumann*, Berlin, Schlesische Verlagsanstalt, 1920.

Abraham, Gerald, "Modern Research on Schumann," *Proceedings of the Royal Musical Association*, 75 (1949), 65–75.

———, ed., *Schumann, a Symposium*, London, Oxford University Press, 1952.

Allgemeine musikalische Zeitung, ed. F. Rochlitz (1798–1819), G. W. Fink (1827–41), C. F. Becker (1842), Moritz Hauptmann (1843), J. C. Lobe (1846–48), Leipzig, Breitkopf und Härtel, 1798–1848.

Allgemeiner musikalischer Anzeiger, ed. J. F. Castelli, Wien, Haslinger, 1829–41.

Athenaeum, ed. A. W. Schlegel and F. Schlegel, 1798–1800, Facsim, Stuttgart, Cotta, 1960.

Auden, W. H, ed., *Nineteenth-Century British Minor Poets*, New York, Delacorte Press, 1966.

Babbitt, Irving, *Rousseau and Romanticism*, Cleveland and New York, The World Publishing Co, 1962.

Baldensperger, Fernand, " 'Romantique' et ses analogues et ses équivalents: tableau synoptique de 1650 à 1810," *Harvard Studies and Notes in Philology and Literature*, 19 (1937), 13–105.

Bate, Walter J, *From Classic to Romantic, Premises of Taste in Eighteenth-century England*, Cambridge, Mass., Harvard University Press, 1946.

Becker, Carl Ferdinand, *Systematisch-chronologische Darstellung der musikalischen Literatur*, Leipzig, R. Friese, 1836.

———, *Die Tonkünstler des neunzehnten Jahrunderts*, Leipzig, Kossling, 1849.

Becker [Constantine], Julius, *Der Neuromantiker*, Leipzig, J. J. Weber, 1840.

Bigenwald, Martha, *Die Anfänge der Leipziger Allgemeinen musikalischen Zeitung*, Diss. Freiburg, 1938.

Bobeth, Johannes, *Die Zeitschriften der Romantik*, Leipzig, Haessel Verlag, 1911.

Boetticher, Wolfgang, "Neue Materialien zu Robert Schumanns Wiener Bekanntenkreis," *Studien zur Musikwissenschaft*, 25 (1962), 39–55.

———, "Robert Schumann an seine königliche Majestät," *Die Musik*, 33 (1940) i, 58–65.

————, *Robert Schumann, Einführung in Persönlichkeit und Werk,* Berlin, Bernhard Hahnfeld, 1941.

————, "Robert Schumann in seinen Beziehungen zu Johannes Brahms," *Die Musik,* 29 (1837), ii, 548–54.

————, ed., *Robert Schumann in seinen Schriften und Briefen,* Berlin, Bernhard Hahnfeld, 1942.

Bosanquet, Bernard, *A History of Aesthetic,* New York, Meridian Books, 1957.

Boucourechliev, André, *Schumann,* trans. A. Boyars, New York, Grove Press, 1959.

Bray, René, *Chronologie du romantisme (1804–1830),* Paris, Boivin, 1932.

Brocklehurst, J. Brian, "The Studies of J. B. Cramer and his Predecessors," *Music and Letters,* 39 (1958), 256–61.

Brown, Maurice J. E., *Schubert, a Critical Biography,* London, Macmillan, 1958.

Caecilia, ed. Gottfried Weber, Mainz, Schott, 1824–39.

Cannon, Beekman C., *Johann Mattheson, Spectator in Music,* New Haven, Yale University Press, 1947.

Chantavoine, Jean, *L'Ère romantique: le romantisme dans la musique européenne,* Paris, A. Michel, 1955.

Chopin, Frederick, *Selected Correspondence of Fryderyk Chopin,* London and Toronto, Heinemann, 1962.

Critica musica, ed. Johann Mattheson, Hamburg, 1722–25.

Critischer Musikus, ed. J. A. Scheibe, Leipzig, Breitkopf, 1745.

Dadelsen, Georg von, "Robert Schumann und die Musik Bachs," *Archiv für Musikwissenschaft,* 14 (1957), 46–59.

Dahms, Walter, *Schumann,* Stuttgart, Deutsche Verlags-Anstalt, 1925.

Damenkonversationslexikon, ed. H. Herlsssohn, Leipzig, 1833–34.

Deutsch, Otto Erich, *Schubert, A Documentary Biography,* trans. Eric Blom, London, J. M. Dent and Sons, 1946.

————, *Schubert, Thematic Catalog of All his Works,* London, J. M. Dent and Sons, 1951.

Dieters, Hermann, Review of Robert Schumann, *Gesammelte Schriften,* iv. Auflage, ed. G. Jansen, *Vierteljahrschrift für Musikwissenschaft,* 9 (1893), 355–63.

Dolinski, K., *Die Anfänge der musikalischen Fachpresse in Deutschland,* Berlin, Hermann Schmidt, 1940.

Dörffel, Alfred, *Geschichte der Gewandhausconcerte zu Leipzig,* Leipzig, 1884.

Ehinger, Hans, *Friedrich Rochlitz als Musikschriftsteller,* Leipzig, Breitkopf und Härtel, 1929.

Ehmann, Wilhelm, "Der Thibaut-Behaghel-Kreis. Ein Beitrag zur Geschichte der musikalischen Restauration im 19. Jahrhundert," *Archiv für Musikforschung, 4* (1939), 21–67.

Einstein, Alfred, *Music in the Romantic Era,* New York, W. W. Norton, 1947.

——, *Schubert, A Musical Portrait,* New York, Oxford University Press, 1951.

Erler, Hermann, "Ein ungedruckter Canon für vier Männerstimmen und sechs ungedruckte musikalische Haus- und Lebensregeln Robert Schumanns," *Die Musik,* 5 (1906), iv, 107–09.

Faller, Max, *Johann Friedrich Reichardt und die Anfänge der musikalischen Journalistik,* Kassel, Bärenreiter, 1929.

Feldmann, Fritz, "Zur Frage des 'Liederjahres' bei Robert Schumann," *Archiv für Musikwissenschaft,* 9 (1952), 246–69.

Fétis, F.-J., *Biographie universelle des musiciens et bibliographie générale de la musique,* 2d ed., Paris, 1875–83.

Flechsig, Emil, "Erinnerungen an Robert Schumann," *Neue Zeitschrift für Musik, 117* (1956), 392–96.

Freystätter, W., *Die musikalischen Zeitschriften seit ihrer Entstehung bis zur Gegenwart,* München, Theodor Riedel, 1884.

Geiringer, Karl, "Ein unbekanntes Klavierwerk von Robert Schumann," *Die Musik, 25* (1933), ii, 721–26.

Granzow, Gerhard, "Florestan und Eusebius. Zur Psychologie Robert Schumanns," *Die Musik, 20* (1928), ii, 660–63.

Harrison, Frank Ll., Mantle Hood, and Claude V. Palisca, *Musicology,* Englewood Cliffs, N. J., Prentice-Hall, 1963.

Haym, R., *Die romantische Schule,* Berlin, R. Gaertner, 1870.

Hegel, G. W. F., *Selections,* ed. J. Loewenberg, New York, Charles Scribner's Sons, 1957.

Heinichen, Johann David, *Der General-bass in der Composition,* Dresden, 1728.

Hempel, Gunter, "Leipzig," *Die Musik in Geschichte und Gegenwart, 8,* 540–69.

Herder, Johann Gottfried von, *Kritische Wälder, 3, 4* in *Sämmtliche Werke,* ed. B. Suphan, Berlin, Weidmann, 1877–1913.

Hernreid, R., "Four Unpublished Compositions by Robert Schumann," *Musical Quarterly, 28* (1942), 50–62.

Hofmeister, Adolph, ed., *C. F. Whistling's Handbuch der musikalischen Literatur,* 3d ed., Leipzig, Hofmeister, 1844.

Homeyer, H., *Grundbegriffe der Musikanschauung Robert Schumanns,* Diss. Münster, 1956.

Hopkinson, Cecil, *A Bibliography of the Musical and Literary Works of Hec-*

tor Berlioz, 1803–1869, Edinburgh, Edinburgh Bibliographical Society, 1951.

Iris im Gebiete der Tonkunst, ed. H. F. Ludwig Rellstab, Berlin, Trautwein, 1830–41.

Jansen, F. Gustav, "Aus Robert Schumanns Schulzeit," *Die Musik,* 5 (1906), iv, 83–99.

———. *Die Davidsbündler, Aus Robert Schumanns Sturm- und Drang-periode,* Leipzig, Breitkopf und Härtel, 1883.

———. "Ein unbekannter Brief von Robert Schumann," *Die Musik,* 5 (1906), iv, 110–12.

Kamieński, Lucian, *Die Oratorien von Johann Adolf Hasse,* Leipzig, Breitkopf und Härtel, 1912.

Kant, Immanuel, *Critique of Judgment,* trans. J. H. Bernard, New York, Hafner, 1951.

Kerst, Friedrich, "Carl Maria von Weber als Schriftsteller," *Die Musik,* 5 (1906), iii, 324–30.

Kimmich, Anne, *Kritische Auseinandersetzungen mit dem Begriff "Neuro-mantik" in der Literaturgeschichtsschreibung,* Diss. Tübingen, 1936.

Kirchner, Joachim, *Das deutsche Zeitschriftenwesen, seine Geschichte und seine Probleme,* 2d ed., Wiesbaden, O. Harrassowitz, 1958–62.

———, *Die Grundlagen des deutschen Zeitschriftenwesens,* Leipzig, Karl W. Hiersemann, 1928–31.

Koch, Heinrich Christoph, *Versuch einer Anleitung zur Composition,* Leipzig, A. F. Böhme, 1782–93.

Kretzschmar, H., "Robert Schumann als Aesthetiker," *Jahrbuch der Musik-bibliothek Peters,* 13 (1906), 49–73.

Kristeller, Paul O., "The Modern System of the Fine Arts: A Study in the History of Aesthetics," *Journal of the History of Ideas,* 12 (1951), 496–527.

Kritische Briefe über die Tonkunst, ed. F. W. Marpurg, Berlin, 1759–63.

Krome, F., *Die Anfänge des musikalischen Journalismus in Deutschland,* Leipzig, Pöschel und Trepte, 1896.

Langer, Susanne K., *Philosophy in a New Key. A Study in the Symbolism of Reason, Rite, and Art,* New York, The New American Library, 1959.

Leichentritt, Hugo, "Schumann als Schriftsteller," *Signale für die musika-lische Welt,* 68 (1910), xxiii, 912–15.

Lippman, Edward A., "Schumann," *Die Musik in Geschichte und Gegenwart,* 12, 272–325.

———, "Theory and Practice in Schumann's Aesthetics," *Journal of the American Musicological Society,* 17 (1964), 310–45.

Liszt, Franz, *Gesammelte Schriften,* ed. L. Ramann, Leipzig, Breitkopf und Härtel, 1880–83.

Loesser, Arthur, *Men, Women, and Pianos, A Social History*, New York, Simon and Schuster, 1954.

Loewenberg, A., *Annals of Opera*, 2d ed. Geneva, Societas bibliographica, 1955.

Lovejoy, Arthur O., *Essays in the History of Ideas*, Baltimore, Johns Hopkins University Press, 1948.

Marpurg, F. W., *Historisch-kritische Beiträge zur Aufnahme der Musik*, Berlin, F. W. Birnstiel, 1759–63.

Martin, U., "Ein unbekanntes Schumann-Autograph," *Musikforschung*, 12 (1959), 405–15.

Mendelssohn, Felix, *Letters*, ed. G. Seldon-Goth, New York, Pantheon, 1945.

Meyer, Leonard, Review of Donald N. Ferguson, *Music as Metaphor, Journal of the American Musicological Society*, 15 (1962), 234–36.

Mizler, Lorenz, *Neu-eröffnete musikalische Bibliothek*, Leipzig, 1739–54.

Mizwa, Stephen P., ed., *Frederick Chopin, 1810–1849*, New York, Macmillan, 1949.

Möbius, P. J., *Über R. Schumanns Krankheit*, Halle, 1906.

Moser, H. J., and E. Rebling, eds., *Robert Schumann, aus Anlass seines 100. Todestages*, Leipzig, Breitkopf und Härtel, 1956.

Müller, Wilhelm Christian, *Aesthetisch-historische Einleitung in die Wissenschaft der Tonkunst*, Leipzig, Breitkopf und Härtel, 1830.

Musical World, The, London, J. A. Novello, 1836–50.

Nägeli, Hans Georg, *Der Streit zwischen der alten und der neuen Musik*, Breslau, Förster, 1826.

Neue Leipziger Zeitschrift für Musik, ed. Julius Knorr, Leipzig, C. F. H. Hartmann, 1834.

Neue Zeitschrift für Musik, ed. Robert Schumann (1835–44),Oswald Lorenz (1844), Franz Brendel (1845–68). Leipzig, J. A. Barth, 1835–37, R. Friese, 1837–51.

Niecks, Frederick, *Frederick Chopin, as a Man and Musician*, 3d ed., London, Novello and Company, c. 1902.

———, *Robert Schumann*, ed. C. Niecks, London, J. M. Dent and Sons, 1925.

Noren-Herzberg, G., "Robert Schumann als Musikschriftsteller," *Die Musik*, 5 (1906), iv, 100–06.

Pessenlehner, Robert, *Hermann Hirschbach, der Kritiker und Künstler*, Düren-Rhld., 1932.

Phöbus. Ein Journal für die Kunst, ed. Heinrich v. Kleist and Adam H. Müller, Dresden, C. G. Gärtner, 1808.

Preussner, Eberhard, *Die bürgerliche Musikkultur, ein Beitrag zur deutschen Musikgeschichte des 18. Jahrhunderts*, Hamburg, Hanseat, 1935.

Proelss, Johannes, *Das junge Deutschland*, Stuttgart, Cotta, 1892.

Redlich, Hans, "Schumann Discoveries," *Monthly Musical Record,* 80 (1950), 143–47, 182–84, 261–65; 81 (1951), 14–16.

Rehberg, Paula and Walter, *Robert Schumann, sein Leben und Werk,* Zürich and Stuttgart, Artemis Verlag, 1954.

Revue et Gazette musicale de Paris, Paris, Schlesinger, 1835–80.

Revue musicale, ed. J. F. Fétis, Paris, 1827–35.

Richter, Jean Paul Friedrich, *Vorschule der Aesthetik, Sämmtliche Werke, 18, 19,* Berlin, G. Reimer, 1826–38.

Schenk, Erich, "Robert Schumann und Peter Lindpaintner in Wien," *Festschrift für Joseph Schmidt-Görg,* ed. D. Weise, Bonn, Beethovenhaus, 1957, pp. 267–82.

Schering, Arnold, "Aus der Geschichte der musikalischen Kritik in Deutschland," *Jahrbuch der Musikbibliothek Peters, 35* (1928), 9–23.

——, "Kritik des romantischen Musikbegriffs," *Jahrbuch der Musikbibliothek Peters, 44* (1937), 9–28.

——, "Künstler, Kenner, und Liebhaber der Musik im Zeitalter Haydns und Goethes," *Jahrbuch der Musikbibliothek Peters, 38* (1931), 9–23.

Schilling, Gustav, ed., *Encyclopädie der gesammten musikalischen Wissenschaften oder Universal-Lexikon der Tonkunst,* Stuttgart, Franz Heinrich Köhler, 1840–42.

Schmieder, Wolfgang, *Thematisch-systematisches Verzeichniss der musikalischen Werke von Johann Sebastian Bach,* Leipzig, Breitkopf und Härtel, 1950.

Schmitz, Arnold, "Die aesthetischen Anschauungen Robert Schumanns in ihren Beziehungen zur romantischen Literatur," *Zeitschrift für Musikwissenschaft, 3* (1920), 111–18.

——, "Anfänge der Aesthetik Robert Schumanns," *Zeitschrift für Musikwissenschaft, 2* (1920), 535–39.

Schnapp, Friedrich, *Heinrich Heine und Robert Schumann,* Hamburg and Berlin, Hoffmann und Campe, c. 1924.

Schneider, Max, "Verzeichnis der bis zum Jahre 1851 gedruckten (und geschrieben in Handel gewesenen) Werke von Johann Sebastian Bach," *Bach-Jahrbuch,* 1906, pp. 84–113.

Schubart, Christian Daniel, *Ideen zu einer Aesthetik der Tonkunst,* Wein, J. V. Degen, 1806.

Schuberth, J., *Thematisches Verzeichniss sämmtlicher im Druck erschienenen Werke Robert Schumanns,* 4th ed., Leipzig and New York, J. Schuberth, 1868.

Schünemann, G., "Jean Pauls Gedanken zur Musik," *Zeitschrift für Musikwissenschaft, 16* (1934), 385–404, 459–81.

Schumann, Eugenie, *Robert Schumann, ein Lebensbild meines Vaters,* Leipzig, Koehler und Amelang, 1931.

Schumann, Robert, *Early Letters*, trans. May Herbert, London, George Bell and Sons, 1888.

——, *Gesammelte Schriften über Musik und Musiker*, Leipzig, Georg Wigand, 1854.

——, *Gesammelte Schriften über Musik und Musiker*, ed. F. Gustav Jansen, Leipzig, Breitkopf und Härtel, 1891.

——, *Gesammelte Schriften über Musik und Musiker*, ed. M. Kreisig, Leipzig, Breitkopf und Härtel, 1914.

——, *Jugendbriefe von Robert Schumann*, Leipzig, Breitkopf und Härtel, 1885.

——, *Music and Musicians, Essays and Criticisms*. trans. Fanny Raymond Ritter, London, William Reeves, n.d.

——, *The Musical World of Robert Schumann. A Selection from Schumann's Own Writings*, ed. Henry Pleasants, New York, St. Martin's Press, 1965.

——, *On Music and Musicians*, trans. Paul Rosenfeld, ed. Konrad Wolff, New York, Pantheon, 1946.

——, *Robert Schumanns Briefe, neue Folge*, ed. F. Gustav Jansen, Leipzig, Breitkopf und Härtel, 1904.

Silz, Walter, *Early German Romanticism, Its Founders and Heinrich von Kleist*, Cambridge, Mass., Harvard University Press, 1929.

Spitta, Philipp, "Ueber Robert Schumanns Schriften," *Musikgeschichtliche Aufsätze*, Berlin, Paetel, 1894, pp. 383–401.

Stege, Fritz, *Bilder aus deutscher Musikkritik*, Regensburg, Bosse, 1936.

Stravinsky, Igor, *An Autobiography*, New York, W. W. Norton, 1962.

——, *Poetics of Music in the Form of Six Lessons*, New York, Vintage Books, 1956.

Strunk, Oliver, ed., *Source Readings in Music History*, New York, W. W. Norton, 1950.

Sulzer, J. G., ed., *Allgemeine Theorie der schönen Kunste*, Biel, Heilmann, 1777.

Thibaut, A. F. J., *Ueber Reinheit der Tonkunst*, Heidelberg, J. C. B. Mohr, 1825, 2d ed., 1826.

Tiersot, Julien, "Schumann et Berlioz," *Revue musicale*, 16 (1935), 409–22.

Ullmann, Richard, and Helene Gotthard, *Geschichte des Begriffes "Romantisch" in Deutschland*, Berlin, Emil Ebering, 1927.

Van der Straeten, E., "Mendelssohns und Schumanns Beziehung zu J. H. Lübeck und Johann J. H. Verhulst," *Die Musik*, 3 (1903), i, 8–20, 94–102.

Wackenroder, W. H., *Werke und Briefe*, ed. Friedrich von der Leyen, Jena, Eugen Diederichs, 1910.

Wasielewski, W. von, *Life of Robert Schumann*, trans, A. L. Alger, Boston, Oliver Ditson, 1871.

Wehl, Feodor, *Das junge Deutschland*, Hamburg, J. F. Richter, 1886.

Wellek, René, *A History of Modern Criticism: 1750–1950, 1, 2*, New Haven, Yale University Press, 1955.

————, *Concepts of Criticism*, ed. Stephen G. Nichols, Jr., New Haven, Yale University Press, 1963.

————, "Periods and Movements in Literary History," *English Institutes Annual*, 1940, pp. 73–93.

Werner, Eric, *Mendelssohn, A New Image of the Composer and his Age*, trans. Dika Newlin, New York, The Free Press of Glencoe, 1963.

Wieck, Maria, *Aus dem Kreise Wieck-Schumann*, Dresden und Leipzig, E. Pierson, 1912.

Wöchentliche Nachrichten und Anmerkungen die Musik betreffend. Ed. J. A. Hiller, Leipzig, 1766–70.

Wolff, V. E., *Lieder Robert Schumanns in ersten und späteren Fassungen*, Berlin, 1913.

Wörner, Karl H., *Robert Schumann*, Zürich, Atlantis, 1949.

Wustmann, Gustav, "Zur Entstehungsgeschichte der Schumannischen Zeitschrift für Musik," *Zeitschrift der Internationalen Musikgesellschaft*, 8 (1907), 396–403.

Zoff, Otto, *Great Composers through the Eyes of their Contemporaries*, New York, E. P. Dutton, 1951.

Index

079773